Come from Afar

A Novel by

Gayla Reid

The publisher gratefully acknowledges the support of the Canada Council for the Arts and the Ontario Arts Council for its publishing program. We acknowledge the financial support of the Government of Canada through the Canada Book Fund (CBF) for our publishing activities, and the Government of Ontario through the Ontario Media Development Corporation, an agency of the Ontario Ministry of Culture, and the Ontario Book Publishing Tax Credit Program.

LIBRARY AND ARCHIVES CANADA CATALOGUING IN PUBLICATION

Reid, Gayla
Come from afar / Gayla Reid.

ISBN 978-1-77086-044-5

1. Title.

PS8585.E5C65 2011   C813 .54   C2011-904031-X

Cover art and design: Angel Guerra/Archetype
Interior text design: Tannice Goddard, Soul Oasis Networking
Printer: Friesens

Printed and bound in Canada.

This book is printed on 100% post-consumer waste recycled paper.

CORMORANT BOOKS INC.
215 Spadina Avenue, Studio 230, Toronto, Ontario, Canada M5T 2C7
www.cormorantbooks.com

For F.B.D.

*T*his is the story my mother carried with her in the streets throughout the years of my childhood. Neighbours would notice her
around midnight when they were acting as their cat's servant, or early
in the morning, when they opened the door to pick up the bottle of milk
on the steps.

On her walks my mother strode rapidly, full of purpose, alert, speaking
to the sky: one of those restless walkers gripped in solitary conversation.
"Incision knife, tissue knife, one straight scissors, one curved scissors, one
suture scissors, mousetooth forceps, six small curved clamps, six straight
clamps ... "

My mother was known in the suburb as that barmy Mrs. Tillman,
war widow — by which it was assumed she had lost a husband in the
Second World War. That other war, the one before, the fascist rehearsal,
had receded so quickly it could have been ancient Troy for all anyone
cared.

As for me, I belonged to the backyard, to the tough yellow grass, to
the rainbow flash of parrots, and to the harbour at the bottom of the

I

hill. I spent the summer holidays fishing from the pier with bits of string, getting sunburned at the baths. Climbing onto the high diving board with its soaked matting, showing off, doing scissors.

At times my mother would respond to coaxing and follow me home from her epic walks. She'd sit with me out in the garden. "They want so little," she'd say. "Food for their children. Bit of a cuddle, bit of a laugh. Water for their crops." She'd reach over, touch my hair, tuck an errant strand behind an ear as if I were a toddler.

"But the shooting never stops."

Although I was by then an adolescent, I did not shrink away. She would call me her little one, admire my mouth, the bones of my face, the palms of my hands, and whisper — for me alone — how like him I was becoming. I gleamed with power.

At other times when I begged her to come home, she would look me over quickly. Feel my forehead. "Perfect," she'd say, in a dismissive, slightly angry voice. Then move swiftly, around the corner, away.

My mother didn't believe in gods but she did believe in the ghosts of memory. And when after many years I came to write her story down, I found that we speak in one voice, my mother and I.

Part One

Tuesday, February 21, 1939

I claim to know what's up — a tryout, a rehearsal. But the child keeps coming. A home birth: nothing unusual about that. The home isn't mine. Nor does it belong to the man who stands, courteous but restless, beside the recently cleaned-up bed.

At this moment we are focused not on the crib but on the brown Bakelite radio on the bedside table. I sit in the golden syrup of the lamplight, limp in my bed-jacket, and we listen to the BBC's crackling words. When the news is finished we remain in silence.

You might mistake this for a tranquil domestic scene. But we are both foreigners, and there is in the room the utterly dead smell of defeat.

Catalonia has fallen. Spain has become a cemetery, a cradle of blood. In Barcelona, Franco's forces fill the streets with their vulgar prancing. Do they really think they can control Catalonia? For how long?

I say something to the man about going north, about the refuge of pale lochs and purple mountains, salmon in deep pools. He gives me a withering look and walks stiffly to the window. Not a single glance in the direction of the crib. For him, the infant is less than a weed and he, for one, has no interest in gardening.

I go by the name of Mrs. Tillman, an Anglicization of Thaelmann, which raised no eyebrows amongst the sleepy British clerks who surveyed and stamped my documents in the final months of 1938.

"You should catch the boat," the man is saying. "Go back to Australia." He pronounces the word carefully because it is so unfamiliar in his mouth. He is German; he is not my husband in any sense other than the fictional legal one. And while I can return to my home, he cannot.

"Go as soon as a berth can be arranged."

"I've just had one," I say, with a weak laugh.

He does not smile.

I have every intention of returning to Australia, but not yet. We'll stay here until word arrives. In the confusion, in the rush to the border, it is natural that news becomes tangled, delayed.

The German has walked over to the window and is looking out. The days are growing longer and in the early evening, a few birds have begun to sing. For a moment I consider getting out of bed and attempting to walk to the window, to stand beside him and stare at the driveway and beyond, to the beech wood.

A few days before this (forever ago, before you came) I stood at the window and watched a taxi draw up. The man whose house this is climbed slowly out. His name is Alec and once I was in love with him. Alec's back has healed but he is not yet limber. He didn't glance up — why should he? His body had to concentrate on the effort of pushing himself up and out of the taxi.

It was strange to look down at him with a professional, dispassionate eye: a wounded man was at last returning home after months in hospital. A generous man, one who was willing to give me shelter. No longer a man who made my lips tremble. Not that.

You begin to whimper. Promise me, the whimper demands. Promise me I am the apple of your eye. My heart, your orchard.

I reach into the crib, scoop you up.

I think I may have stuffed up on your name. I've called you Dolores.

"It will be the best for the child, Clarice," the man at the window is saying in his precise, foreign voice. He's using my formal first name to bolster his tone, in which there is the beginning of an order. Not that he has any rights in this matter, none at all.

You burrow in.

Monday, February 27, 1939

The letter, when it comes, is slender. Posted in France but written in Spain. Sitting on the hall table when I emerge for the day, shortly before eleven.

It isn't his handwriting.

Something official, on letterhead.

To hold the stranger's letter in my hands is to feel darkness, spreading.

In his final days in Spain, the League of Nations official had personally visited the Mac-Paps at Cassà de la Selva, where they were waiting for the Canadian government to stop dithering, for some arrangements to be made. The Americans were gone; the British were gone; so many of the others were gone, back home or into exile.

The official had Douglas Ross, Mac-Pap written on a list. He'd made enquires, having been besieged back in Ripoll by me, a pregnant woman who'd stood before him, shaking, shawl awry, like a stock character in a play. He was accustomed to being harangued, but not by women. Round I was, and immensely embarrassed, but desperation made me demanding.

On a fine windy afternoon in January, for something to do, the Mac-Paps had walked down to the port, with its shallow beach.

In response to the official's questions, one of the men had approached him.

A mortar attack.

HERE IS THE GULLY. Above it, a hill shaped like a pear. Rock walls, slippery stones, a donkey. A thin trail. The sudden sickly sweet smell in the limestone crags of the Sierra de Cavalls.

After dark, Ross was taking up water. Water disinfected with iodine, mixed with cognac.

He was lying over a rock, mouth open to the sky. Hands black with blood.

In the mortar attack, the donkey must have slipped, fallen upon him. Over they went, man and animal, down the barranco, the gully.

What was the countryside like? Like an accordion: hill, valley, hill. Sage, stones, sage. Limestone rock that crumbles, friable.

The official regretted to have such news.

I READ THE LETTER, lines of ink neat on the page.

On the far side of the river, Ross is moving along the ridge with supplies. The donkey falls upon him, they tumble together down the gully.

It doesn't happen like that, I know. Not the quiet folding, silent from the distance of Cassà de la Selva.

Fear is running over the donkey and down its back. The donkey's breathing breaks. Muscles tighten. It lifts its head, pins its ears. Shudders; starts. Its head is snaking; it is falling.

Try not to see anything else. Stay with the donkey. The donkey is what's falling. The donkey is down there, at the bottom of the barranco.

I read the letter again.

A mortar flare is like an exploding flower pot. Ross told me that once, and I'd seen a bright geranium flame.

I fold the letter; put it back in its envelope. Alec and everyone else in this house know that a letter has arrived. They've seen it on the hall table, waiting for me.

I will have to tell them something.

"There is no news."

The Mac-Paps cooling their heels at Cassà de la Selva were no help at all. "That League fellow was able to find out absolutely nothing."

When your father comes, I'll hold you up, say something lame to hide the turmoil, give him time. Fait accompli. See how totally accompli, I'll boast, how finely formed: fat cheeks pumping away, the head a whole round world (careful, be careful). Fingers furling and unfurling, surprising in their infant strength.

Ross will arrive in a taxi from the station. The way Alec came, easing himself out of the car with such difficulty, the way I came at last year's end. For Alec it was a homecoming; for months he'd been lying on his stomach in a London hospital. Before that he was in Spain with the rest of us.

Ross and I will be able to make our plans for Australia. Where we'll find the money, who knows? We're going, it's already agreed. Agreed, not planned.

Of course I've written to Aid for Spain asking them to find out what they can. No baptismal cup for you, and certainly no silver spoon. An inauspicious year to be born: 1939. It feels like everyone is waiting, all over the world.

Do not think about Barcelona and the fall of Catalonia; do not think of the delays that are preventing your father from reaching us. The French government has recognized Franco; the border has reopened and many thousands are trying to cross over, fleeing.

Pray to all the gods ever concocted that you will come into your own. But the omens are good; they must be, for you arrived in my arms so complete, so robust. Nobody could say I was prepared for you; you are one tough little flower.

Your cradle is a sturdy rectangular affair but it rocks. See, I put my foot on this little slab of wood, and there you go. You like that, don't you? Not in the treetop, but at the top of this house.

I've been making enquiries. Ross may still be in Spain or he may be in France. It is difficult to get news out of Spain these days.

When the bough breaks the cradle will fall.

I shut my eyes and feel his hands. At the back of my neck, the warmth of his breath. And everywhere, his tongue.

YOU WILL NOT SLEEP; you're awake, wide awake. Listening for whatever I might have on offer.

Your first fragment, a beginning:

On New Year's night there is a blizzard. Out in this blizzard, two people are making their separate ways up a mountain in Spain. It has taken them all of their lives to reach this point. From opposite sides of the world, these two have travelled across oceans and are struggling up that mountain to meet each other — but they don't know that. They're thinking about how cold their feet are.

Footprints in the snow: two sets, far apart.

The snowfall lessens. Snow drifts soft as a shawl, settles in their eyelashes.

Up the mountain they go, carrying the stories they will tell you.

With your father not yet here with us, your first story will be mine. What did the man say, watch and pray? I don't know much about praying but I do know about watching. And I'm learning about hope, how it must be approached obliquely.

My way of waiting for Ross will be this tale for you. Quiet and slow like your cradle rocking, but just as insistent, ceaseless. More of a Scheherazade for myself than a proper lullaby.

A word of caution here: the woman I am is not the mother you see.

One

A CHILD WITHOUT A mother, my first home was Cliffend. A ghost town on the edge of the tablelands in northern New South Wales, Australia. Once it was a river of gold.

A high, brick chimney reached into an empty, dry sky. Air hung thick between the narrow gorge walls; the sun burned with it. In the cleared patches around old mine shafts, the bush had grown back. I breathed in the silence, a great deep draught. I lay on the ground and pushed myself to the edge of an old mine shaft, stared into the earth, cool and dark and quiet.

Reported back to Father.

"Plenty of lost dreams in the earth," said Father. "Can you feel them, Clancy?"

I inspected the crumbling remains of the furnace and battery. Trees had covered the bare slopes; grasses sprouted on raw mounds of tailings. You could no longer tell where the town stopped and the bush took over.

WITH FATHER, I WALKED down green gullies where creeks fell away over the lip of the gorge. Stepped on tangles of logs, sat on small mountains of moss and watched the bellbirds eating the blossoms. A world of staghorn ferns, liana vines, and mine shafts, abandoned.

A bird cried out with a loud whip crack, "e-chong, e-chong." His mate answered with "we chew, we chew, we chew."

Down the gorge, I found leeches, with parts of their bodies flowing into one another.

"Look," I showed Father. "No heads, no tails."

"Gambler's nightmare," he said.

At the creek, our silence was for the bird, stately and motionless in the black pool. Its neck, suddenly, darted. Dark purple plumes flashed into green.

Father and I camped out. From the tent, we could see the lamps of fungi on the moist old logs, on the trunks of trees. The pale glows had names, Father said. *Luciferin* and *luciferase*. They meant light. Different kinds of light in darkness.

In the morning Father started the fire and jumped to warm up, pretending to be a boxer skipping rope. "I feel in fine fettle," he said. "How about you, Clancy girl, are you in fine fettle?"

We sat by the fire, Father and I, and sipped sweet tea from chipped enamel mugs.

IN CLIFFEND THERE WERE few streets that still had people in them. My father had once run the local newspaper, the *Cliffend Examiner*. When the gold was exhausted and the town collapsed, he became the barber. The real barber had walked out on the lot; it was not unusual. Left his gear: his razors, his mugs, his towels and combs, and chair. The chair made up Father's mind about the future.

By the time I was born, the town was on the road to nowhere, wild country on the edge of gorges that slide down narrow valleys to the coast. The brawling had all but petered out because the pub was gone. The churches had called it a day — except for the Catholics, who doggedly kept at it, the priest arriving on Sunday, on horse-back. The newspaper that had been my father's living folded.

Mutatis mutandis, Father said, and forgot to explain what it meant.

WE LIVED IN THE old barber's shop where my father provided amateur but adequate shaves.

Father sat in the comfy barber's chair, reading his books in the morning, then again in the afternoon. If he had customers, it was usually for a shave. As he shaved the man, my father recited the poetry everybody loved, working his way up to my favourite, "Clancy of the Overflow."

> *I had written him a letter which I had, for want of better*
> *Knowledge, sent to where I met him down the Lachlan,*
> *years ago.*

Most of the time nobody came. I'd take a turn in the chair and my father would pretend to shave me. He talked to me about his books.

The Lachlan was a river and that other Clancy in the poem was a drover. Clancy saw the vision splendid of the sunlit plains extended. And at night the wondrous glory of the everlasting stars.

We had rooms behind the shop. The milk jug cover was crocheted, its edges decorated with bright green beads. My mother made that.

In the photograph on the wall my father is a young man wearing longish trousers. He has on strange little black running shoes rather like ballet slippers. *New South Wales Junior Track Championships*, the picture says, with my father's signature on the right hand side: *Charlie Cox.* And at the bottom, *Solomon's Studios, 1901.*

Father cut me toast soldiers. We sat out on the front verandah — we ate exactly where we pleased — because a house was lumbering by. When this place died, the people who could afford to do so put their houses on long bullock-drawn drays and took them west to the nearest town, one the railway had not passed by.

Now the houses were bought and moved by strangers. I liked the bullocks. Their slow procession of dust.

CLIFFEND SAT ON A secret river of gold. The gold had been in the earth for centuries, hidden since the end of the Paleozoic. *Paleozoic.* A strange word, to turn in the mouth like toffee. Molten basalt flowed over the granite. The old watercourses were sealed, left intact, folded into silence. Birds flashed, feet padded, fires were lit, leaves crumbled in crevices, and nothing was disturbed.

But when the earth was exposed, gold.

Gold brought stores, a school, even a skating rink. Thirteen pubs, six churches, four thousand people, mine shafts down to 1700 feet. To tell the story, the *Cliffend Examiner*, where Father was both editor and compositor. In the comp room, the letter "g" was worn flat as a creek pebble.

Many of the diggers, Father said, were educated men. One day they decided. Just like that. (Father clicked his fingers together.) Stopped the plough, jumped ship, closed shop, deserted the classroom. In timber slab huts and tents, they lived on dreams.

WHEN FATHER HAD ONE of his turns he went into the bush, alone.

I could see this coming. He'd be up all night, pacing, busy writing leaders for the defunct *Cliffend Examiner*.

Then he'd be gone, and our neighbour, Eti, would take me in to his sisters, the Misses Cox.

My aunts lived in the nearest town, Armidale. That's where the bullocks carted the houses to. The sisters owned land west of the town, in sparse, open country. But they didn't live out there. They lived in town and the property was run by an overseer.

I decided I wouldn't mind being an overseer myself, or maybe a drover. I could see the vision splendid of the tablelands extended.

On the piano in the lounge room were pictures of the soldiers they'd meant to marry. Both men looked so mild it was no wonder they got themselves killed in Mesopotamia. The sisters kept to the house and the small garden, reluctant to let the pictures on the piano out of their sight.

For the first few weeks there was much tut-tutting about the state of my clothes. I'd have orders to wear shoes even on hot days. After new dresses had been chosen from the catalogue, after my hair had been pushed and pulled at, the aunts would go back to who they were before I arrived and disrupted their world.

I was left to myself, to walk out to the edge of town to investigate the paddocks. I knew I must wait until Father was well enough to take me home to Cliffend.

When at last he came, we waved at the aunts, clutching cuttings we promised to plant.

Father winked. "We'll give these to Eti next door," he told me. "We won't have to lift so much as a green thumb, let alone a finger."

My father returned to his barber's chair, to his reading. He kept his small library on a shelf in the shop: Palgrave's *Golden Treasury*, Henry Lawson, Banjo Paterson, Dickens, Ibsen, Wordsworth's *Preludes*. The teacher visited the barber's shop for the chat, for the books.

THE LONG ARM OF the New South Wales Education Department did not reach as far as Cliffend. Mr. MacDonald, failed miner, failed pacifist, may have been forced back into teaching but pursued his own unique curriculum. In the classroom, he stared at the map on the wall, brimming with Empire red, as if it were something he could barely remember.

He roused himself, turned.

"You have been instructed all of your lives to believe it is your patriotic duty to go to war and to have yourselves slaughtered at their command. Is that right?"

"Yes, sir." Having been taught only by Mr. MacDonald, we knew the correct answer.

"But in the history of the world no war by any nation has ever been declared by the people. Do you find that strange?"

Outside the schoolroom, cockatoos screamed in the pepper tree, and beyond, the hills were filled with purple-blue haze from a small bushfire down one of the gorges. A ribbon of smoke drifted in the air, the first true smell of summer.

Yes, we found it strange.

Having hit his stride, the Scot moved on to his favourite topic: Keir Hardie, member of the British Parliament, founder of the Labour Party. That was how you spelled it in Britain. Here it was Labor. Mr. MacDonald said.

"This should be of interest to you for a few seconds," he announced, with one of his bitter but harmless laughs. We relaxed.

The lesson flowed along its predictable channel.

"Where was James Keir Hardie born?"

"In Scotland, sir."

"At what age did Keir Hardie have to work, and what work did he have to do?"

"At the age of seven he went to work as a delivery boy for a baker, sir."

"For how long?"

"Twelve-and-a-half hard hours a day, sir."

"What happened when his younger brother was dying, and Keir Hardie had to spend most of the night looking after him?"

"He was late for work, sir."

"What did his employer do when he was late?"

"Sacked him, sir."

"And how old was he when he started to work down the coal mine?"

"Eleven, sir."

"So he didn't have time to learn to read, did he?"

"No, sir."

"No, he had to learn to read from his mother, when he returned home from the mine. But you have learned to read, haven't you?"

"Yes, sir."

"And what did Keir Hardie die of?"

"A broken heart, sir."

"When and why was his heart broken?"

"In 1915, sir. Because of the outbreak of war, sir."

"And how many men of the British Army alone died in one single day at the Battle of the Somme?"

"Twenty thousand, sir."

Eti the belgian, the bloke next door, was a Johnny-come-lately. Eti made baked custards with caramel in the bottom. (Back home Eti had been a baker, among many other things.) Eti gardened, turned seeds into flowers, showed me plants that looked like weeds but could be eaten. In his backyard he kept chooks — White Leghorns like lady bowlers and handsome Rhode Island Reds. Eti also owned two cows, which every morning he took down to the paddock behind the cemetery. In the evening they could be trusted to find their own way home, stepping carefully between the graves. Eti treated them pretty much as pets. He'd run his hands over each in turn, scratching in their favourite places. When agitated, Eti would throw his arms around one of the cows, sink his face into her back, and groan. The cow would turn her neck, let her tongue come out, warm and grassy.

We were on the verandah and we'd finished our breakfast of toast soldiers. I was crowning Father with a newsprint crown, crafted from a yellowing page of the *Cliffend Examiner*. He bowed his head to accept. He lingered on the verandah to take part in my small absolute rule, unable to turn away from what comforted him.

It was common knowledge around Cliffend that Father had been wooed back to life by my younger self, teetering on pudgy legs.

This fact gave me the impossible belief that broken things can be put right.

ON THE LOUNGE ROOM wall, the single wedding photograph, the grave image: the two of them breathless and solemn in their clothes.

My mother was a bush nurse who travelled by horse and buggy to farms deep in the hills. We had a snapshot of her with Blackie, her sturdy mutt, sleek on a rich diet of afterbirth. His eyes on the bucket, Blackie waited until they had reached home. Blackie knew how to behave.

The aunts revealed the news about my mother, dispensed in tight whispers. She gave her life. If it's a toss-up, baby or mother, baby trumps mother. *She gave her life.* These words were spoken to me, a girl on the verandah of my aunts' home in Armidale, on a Sunday afternoon during a season of drought with the sky hard as blue stone. No greater love than this, she laid down her life for her child. And I could tell what the aunts were thinking: fool.

So you will understand why I was apprehensive when you began to arrive. But you bolted on out, the midwife having to be quick-smart about catching you, and me crying out for your father in a voice to fill a cricket ground. Trust him to possess exactly the right name for the breathing required: *Ross, Ross, Ross.*

I DIGRESS. BACK TO Cliffend, and Father. One night when the settlement became a village, Father was there to record the event. A formal claim to property, with miners pegging out blocks. "Most took possession of their current holdings, but a few of the more adventurous seized the post office and the Wesleyan church, and even Wade's pigsty, where, though the enemy effected a lodgement in some of the outbuildings, the principal sty remained in the hands of its defenders."

On winter evenings, Father would read me such paragraphs from old copies of the paper. The barber's house creaked in the cold. In the fireplace, a log collapsed into scarlet embers.

When I walked to the outhouse my shoes crunched in the frost.

MY FATHER TOLD ME about my mother, what she was capable of.

On a freezing August night, Father said, on a night much like this one, my mother was attending a birth on one of the remote farms.

The baby came out. A dreadful silence filled the room. Not a sound. Stillborn.

Did my mother droop and murmur sympathies? No. Right away she ran to the kitchen, snatched up the bucket by the door, hurried out into the night, and filled the bucket with water from the tank. Returning to the bedroom, my mother seized the lifeless little one and plunged it into the freezing water.

Had she gone completely mad?

One moment passed. Another. Then tiny cries.

"Your mother brought the baby back to life. She had the gift."

Mother's name was Hope. Hope: the sound your voice makes when it echoes down an empty mine shaft.

"St. Augustine wrote that hope had two beautiful daughters: anger and courage," Father said. I was an only child.

OUT IN THE BUSH were blackfellers, especially in the autumn and then again in spring. Moving in groups, down to the coast to escape the frost, back to the tops for summer. Sometimes a mob travelling through would make camp behind one of the empty houses, light a fire in the backyard, and sit around yarning. One day the women would be coming to the house for flour and sugar, asking for the missus, only our house didn't have a missus. Next day, they'd be gone.

Also out in the bush were miners who lived, Father said, on the smell of an oil rag. They panned in the creeks, trapped rabbits, and helped themselves to sheep on the big station. Unwashed, unshaven, in worn, collarless shirts and fusty trousers, they occasionally left their shacks or humpies and came out of the bush, heading for the general store. In one trouser pocket, wrapped in a dirty hankie, paltry flecks of gold.

The store — there was only one — had weights to measure small amounts of gold. Once every two months an assayer came, to buy. The man who ran the store took care of the details. Kept what Father called meticulous accounts.

Miners who sneaked into town with a lamb could depend on Eti cooking it up for them if he hadn't got the hump. If he'd got the hump he'd scowl and wouldn't call back to you over the fence.

When the fancy took him, Eti whipped up delicate pastries for sale. Strangers were amazed to find such goods on offer in the Cliffend General Store. But strangers were few, especially after the hotel burned down.

Father could cook, too. Toast, chops, and plum duff. Duff, Father said, means pudding, and plum doesn't mean plum.

He showed me how to make it. "Three good handfuls of raisins," he said, getting out the pudding bowl. "Same goes for currants." Father's hands were big. The currants and raisins formed a steep hill in the blue bowl. "Now, flour and sugar." I was allowed to sieve the flour. A cloud of white covered the hill in the bowl, drifted up into the kitchen. "Now you stick a bit of mutton fat in the middle," he said, taking over.

Father tied it all up tight in the sleeve of an old shirt, twirled a bit of string around it, and put it in boiling water. When you fished it out it was steaming. Father mixed a bit of arrowroot, hot water, sugar, and vanilla. Best sauce in the world, Father said, and it was.

All of the houses had gardens, including the ones that weren't lived in anymore. Spuds, pumpkin, bit of rhubarb. Fruit trees, too: quince, plums, and apricots. You could live quite well in Cliffend. You could take the vegetables and fruit, you could trap rabbits. We did.

Although the hotel had burned down, it was possible to get drunk in Cliffend on bottles of grog from the general store. A miner would buy the cheap plonk then sit on the verandah of one of the deserted houses, drinking, alone. I watched and learned.

"It's more than just thirst," Father explained.

After a certain point a lone drunk would begin to talk. Stumbling but driven, insistent. Words spilled out of him, gathering strength. The solitary drunk would yell at himself and yell back, a dialogue of reproach and longing. In the end he broke down or passed out. If he was lying in the grass, Father said, if the man's boots were sticking out of the vegetable patch, I should come and tell him. In winter a man could freeze to death in the frost. If he was safe on a verandah, or had found the shelter of an old washhouse, I was not to interfere. Sooner or later, one of his mates would come and take him away in a wheelbarrow.

There were other children, but they didn't live in Cliffend. They lived on the surrounding farms; their parents worked for the landed gentry on the big sheep station. The Wrights were the gentry. The two families who had kids in the school were the Hardys and the Faints. "Like *Pilgrim's Progress*," Father said.

The Faint boys had honey mixed with cocoa in their sandwiches. The Hardys, being the poorer, had bread and dripping. I ran home for lunch. A meat pie, a baked apple. Often Eti made it, to share with Father and me.

FATHER TOOK ME TO the coast.

He packed hard-boiled eggs, with pepper and salt wrapped in twists of white paper. We moved down the gullies on a rough red mountain road. Above us, huge stands of cedar.

We started off in a horse carriage. For part of the way, the steepest part, we had to travel by bullock dray. The bullocks, named for the generals of the Great War, stood in the shallow blackcreek pools. The bullocky was tetchy; the bullocks, sweet and patient. Placidly, they came to the call of their names and lined up, in order, waiting for the yoke.

The journey didn't end until we had made our way down the rutty track to the cottage. Once a week, the mailman arrived on horseback with mail and papers and loaves of bread.

When you re-enter a house, Father said, you become the person you were when you lived there before.

I awoke to little wattle birds yelling *get up, get up*. My father's bathing togs were already on the verandah railing. He was back from a dip in the surf and cooking porridge for breakfast.

As my father took me to the beach, I will take you. We'll go together. Your father and I, my father and you: the four of us, three generations. Feel the sand whitesoft on the soles of your feet. See the seagulls on little red legs. They run from the wave, run back as soon as the wave recedes, pecking fast-fast-fast. Pelicans slide along, bills resting on their chests, fat old businessmen after dinner, eyes on their own reflection.

My father will put down among the sea grass and we'll sit in the boat, feeling the slight strain against the anchor, the drift of the tide. My father with his pipe in his mouth, your father at the other end of the dingy, their lines waiting to draw up snapper. I'll be holding you; you'll be so very safe.

Look down there, look. Just below the clear surface a carpet shark is moving, quiet and lazy as water.

When I was a child I journeyed to the beach with Father for Christmas, for the heat of plum pudding and chook with gravy, at my aunt's place. She was my mother's sister. Her tribe lived in an unpainted shack by the saltwater creek. The shack smelled of fish fried in bacon fat. The front room had a fly-spattered "Monarch of the Glen" on the back wall, a piano, and literally nothing else. My aunt had been *dragged down* by her gambling husband. Mr. MacDonald the teacher claimed marriage was an institution devoted to the preservation of property but in my aunt's shack this did not appear to be the case.

At the copper under the lemon tree in the backyard, my aunt was poking at some sheets with a defeated air. Her husband was away again on the boat. I knew better than to pipe up, *What boat?*

A westerly had smoothed the ocean. I rowed out with Father. Listened to the solid sound of wooden oars moving in oarlocks. Looked back at the chalk-white paperbarks and the flat sandstone rocks. Behind the green-grey of the she-oaks, I could pick out the bright green of the banana tree by the tank stand, and my father's towel on the verandah.

On the beach, birds were going after soldier crabs.

In winter you could see schools of mullet, their noses into the current. Now, in summer, we had to make do with a few whiting.

The little fish slithered in the bucket. *She gave her life.*

The doctor pulled me from my mother's body while it was still warm. Father, incredulous, plunged into what was called deep mourning. At that time it was acceptable to be in mourning for years, decades, forever.

ON NEW YEAR'S EVE Father and I heard human voices snatched out of the air.

One of the cousins had hitched up an antenna on a clothes prop and the Sydney post office clock boomed into our ears, with each of us taking turns. After the excitement of the crystal set there were songs around the piano: Irish songs, then "Yes Sir, That's My Baby," and dancing.

My father had brought a big bag of lollies, and my aunt made a jam sponge for supper. I was wearing a new dress with a sash of green satin.

Father and I walked home by the gleam of the paperbarks. Father stood at the edge of the ocean, quickly took off his best clothes. In his underpants, he streamed into the surf, dived neatly into the dark cream rollers.

"Ah," Father cried, running at last out of the waves, "the investiture of night." Above us, the arc of the Milky Way, with Orion upside down and the Hyades a diamond bracelet.

I watched Father shake his head like a wet dog. I had to step back to avoid getting salt stains on my dress.

"What's next," Father shouted, "what's next?"

I WAS FOURTEEN AND they said I was a strong rower, for a girl. As soon as the tail end of the cyclone had left us, I took the boat out in the river at slack tide. I wasn't going fishing — things were still too stirred up for that — just out for a poke around the island.

For days, the huge breakers had come so fast and thick they'd whipped the sea to peaks of froth, completely covering the sea bird island. The island sat at the mouth of the river, where rich brown silt and salt water mixed.

Sea birds were resting on the main beach, subdued, too exhausted or too wary to re-establish themselves on their island. Parts of battered pandanus palm lay on the beach, looking brown and very tired. The retreating ocean had left lines of foam, streaks of dirty curd. The sand dunes ran with tiny, bustling creeks of bark-brown water that had escaped the river, unable to wait.

By the island, a boy I'd never seen before hauled himself into the boat. A boy with tremendous black hair, tightly curled, springy even when wet. A broad, handsome high forehead. He lifted himself easily by his arms, knowing how to do this and not upset the small rowboat. He sat against the stern, wet and daring, his white teeth grinning. The muscles visible in his neck. More muscles ran down into his chest, assured, tight. Those muscles gathered around his belly, swept into the abdomen. He sat erect, like a dancer, with the unimaginable parts of his body riding under the close, damp cotton of his pants. He had no swimming trunks; he would not think of such things.

Thin fine legs, so thin you could see the ribbons of tendons where they joined to bolster and decorate the bones.

I guessed he was a boy from one of the shacks farther up the river, in backwaters clogged with blue water hyacinth.

He sat in the boat with his mild manner and the splendid arrogance of his body, a mixture of resentment and pride.

See, his body said. *See*.

Without a word, the boy balanced himself lightly on his arms and with one economical move dived back in, surfacing with a twist of his head, again showing his white teeth. Then he lifted his chin, and as if by some prior agreement with himself, turned his back and disappeared into the water.

All I could see were the ripples where he had once been.

That's when I knew what my life might be, what I might become.

Two

England, 1930–1931

I BECAME A NURSE and I took the ship to Britain. At the time, both were considered accomplishments.

After a dreary stint in London, my luck turned and I obtained a position here in the countryside. Alec met me at the station. It was my first season in the northern hemisphere and the English spring came in with such a long, green slowness.

In the fields in front of this house there's a beech wood I've pointed out to you. When I first came I walked in it every day — walking was expected, and I was pleased about that. Alec accompanied me, with the spaniels, Jitters and Custard. At that time of year the brown beech leaves were sodden but a grassy dyke runs through the wood, providing higher ground. We strolled along the dyke, with the spaniels making urgent forays into the damp undergrowth on either side.

I'd been hired to nurse Alec's mother in her final illness. She died in this room, in the bed you were born in. What I remember most about her dying is the lengthening of the days.

Alec was the first man to hold you in his arms, to comfort you. It should have been your father, but it was Alec.

I am getting ahead of myself.

At the station I'd been anticipating a car but he arrived with horse and buggy. The motor was on the blink, Alec said, and his pony was quite the best little fellow in the world. Did I mind?

Nurses did not mind.

Jitters and Custard climbed in between us, keeping warm and enjoying themselves.

"Tea at the end of the road," Alec promised.

I sat up in the chill and wondered if he called this thing a buggy. Probably not. The English had so many different words. We trotted past drenched fields with bits of sky in them, and the pony's rump was silky from recent rain.

Alec was telling me he'd done his medical training at Guy's.

"Like Keats," I said. "John Keats."

"I hope not," he said, and put on a mock coughing fit.

"But I'm going to Cardiff for my residency, so you never know," he added.

What was taking him to Wales? I wondered, but did not ask.

"Around the next bend," he said, with happy disapproval, "you'll catch your first glimpse of the sore thumb."

The house did indeed stick out, a confused Victorian pile of red-brick, with a shot gravel drive and, at the side, tidy flowerbeds. "My father," Alec announced, "was a scion of the *rentier* class." Gesturing at the house he said, "For this, families in Carlisle lived on bread and dripping."

It was a declaration, inviting contradiction. But not from me. The indignant tone would be meant for his father.

"You'll find the place full of disgusting things in glass domes with *Great Exhibition* on the side. All exceptionally dead."

"At least that's something to be thankful for."

He looked at me with faintly more interest.

We were approaching the driveway. "The sandstone dressing around the doors is passable," he said. "I suspect they repented at the last minute."

My first glimpse of your birthplace was not accompanied by any sense of premonition. I felt nothing more than mild anxiety, afraid of making a fool of myself, of putting a foot wrong.

We entered by the back way. Down a cluttered passage with a rail of large hooks that held a scythe, old buckets, and rope. Below, on the stone floor, stacks of dusty black enamel tins. Alec kicked at the tins, which were covered with binder twine. "Father's nest-and-egg collection."

I KNEW WELL ENOUGH by then that everyone in the whole nation of Great Britain was slotted by birth and accent, like some arcane alphabet. There was another alphabet entirely for colonials, which started after the English had reached "Z" with their own people. But even from the beginning it didn't feel like that with Alec.

His sister was in the kitchen. "I'm told you're just the ticket," she said. She was wearing a green overcoat indoors.

The kitchen had a wood stove and tall dressers that disappeared into the gloom. His sister was banging about at the stove, frying bacon and preparing to add the eggs. Bet she nipped into the hall for one of her father's collection, said a silly voice in my head. But the eggs, none too clean, were clearly fresh, probably from chooks in their own yard. Coming around the back way I'd noticed a hen house, gone quiet for the night.

His sister lit a cigarette and waved out the match. "I've put you in the attic room." She led the way. At the door she turned, thrust out her hand. "No formalities here," she declared, "call me Helen and we'll get along famously."

Helen was extremely thin, with a pointed chin and sharp nose, brown hair pulled sternly back. When Helen sat down her hips and thighs appeared to vanish and it looked as if there were just an empty skirt, arranged as over a doll. In the family Helen was understood to be attractive, with a lithe body and great natural energy. Alec took this for granted, and, as far as I could tell, so did Helen. Soon I too saw her as handsome. I admired how she hopped on her bike, switched on the torch, and effortlessly rode back up the steep hill to the school where she was mistress of both history and games.

That first night Helen took me upstairs to my room at the top of the house, with its fine view of the beech wood, then down one flight to the bedroom of their dying mother, whom I had been summoned to nurse.

The old lady was a small sleeping lump under an eiderdown. Chairs were arranged around the bed. The chair closest to the bed belonged to the eldest son, Rolly, who had not come home from the Great War.

"Don't move that chair, whatever you do," instructed Helen. "And mind the green light."

I looked inquiring.

"The green light above the chair," she explained patiently, "is Rolly's spirit." Brother and sister spoke in a matter-of-fact manner about the green light but the old lady was the only one who claimed to see it.

At dinner Helen did most of the talking, with Alec directing her from topic to topic. As an only child, I watched this with interest. They were treating me exceptionally well. Usually in England, as soon as I opened my mouth, I could feel the air go flat. A nurse is little more than a servant, especially a nurse from the colonies.

"Our eldest brother Rolly," said Helen, "was killed towards the end of the war, on the Italian front."

Childe Roland to the dark tower came. Probably not much older than a child.

"We have another brother," added Helen. "Marcus." Helen smiled with small, secretive lips. "Marcus was in the war, too."

Every day they spoke of those two elder brothers — the ones who had been in the war. I realized it must be difficult to be the children who came after.

But they had their own interests, contemporary ones. In the uproar that accompanied the general strike in the mid-twenties, Alec had taken a trip to Wales and had seen how miners lived.

"Alec's idea of a good time," said Helen, "is chalking bolshie slogans on pavements in the city."

"Not *bolshie*, please," replied Alec, taking pretend offence. He fed Jitters some bacon.

"Alec," said Helen, "laps up the meetings." I imagined rooms somewhere in London, Chelsea maybe, with dense blue smoke curling from men's pipes.

"I do not," he said indignantly. "I do not *lap up* the meetings."

"Yes you do, you do," she said, adopting a silly high voice, the one she used for the dogs. "He does, doesn't he boys?" she said, addressing Jitters and Custard directly.

The dogs looked up at her, hoping this would lead somewhere.

"The boys know better," Alec said, putting his plate on the floor, which both dogs began to lick, pushing it nosily around under the table.

"I grew up in an old mining town," I said, and was surprised at myself. (When I was sent to stay with my father's aunts, I discovered that the place I came from was shabby, that Father's friends were weirdos, possibly even crims, and that the rellies down the coast were no-hopers, and the less said about any of this, the better.)

I wished I hadn't spoken.

Alec and Helen stopped pursuing their exchange and turned to me, faces bright.

"Well, it wasn't really a mining town. It was a ghost town. The gold had gone." I stopped. But they were waiting.

"There were still some miners, though. Panning for gold."

"Tell us," commanded Alec, energized by the prospect.

Perhaps it would be all right. Perhaps this pair was so very peculiar that it wouldn't matter.

"They came in threes," I explained. "One would sink the hole, one would barrow the washdirt, and one would rock the cradle."

"We three kings of Orient are," said Helen, in a friendly way.

"One day they just decided." (Father's words.) "Stopped the plough, jumped ship, closed the shop."

"What were conditions like, down in the mine?" Alec asked eagerly. He has a round face, brown eyes, and at that time wore round brown-rimmed glasses that made him appear terribly serious and soft all at once.

"The mining was over," I said. "Just a few people panning in the creek at the bottom of the gorge."

Alec stood up, pushed back his chair from the dining table. "Ladies and dogs, shall we adjourn to the morning room?" They called it that, even though they used it at all hours. "Clancy here can tell us more about her mining town."

"There isn't much more to say about it," I ventured, when we settled in and Helen brought cups and a teapot on a tray.

Alec lit his pipe. Helen, having poured the tea, produced her cigarette case while I fished in my pocket for a roll-your-own.

"People will tell you that it's insignificant," declared Helen. "But it's *your life.*"

Father, the teacher Mr. MacDonald, and Eti the Belgian in Cliffend, so far away. My *life.*

I wished the pair of them weren't so enthusiastic about this. What would they want from me next?

"The place where I grew up is called Cliffend."

It came bubbling up. I told them about my father sitting in the barber's chair, reading his beloved books.

"Your father became a barber?" asked Alec, as if this were a source of special delight. "Did he barber himself?"

"Don't go on," said Helen. For a moment I thought she was telling me to stop, but she was addressing her brother.

"Of course he did," I replied. "From time to time."

I told them that the owner of the mine had gone broke. As a child I'd come across him panning at the bottom of the gorge. I'd sit beside him as he tossed the pan, lazily, in the clear light. The Helena seam, he'd called it, after his wife. In the old days, when he was the boss and able to name things.

I'd believed Helena to be the most sophisticated name imaginable.

"The capitalist owner, down on his knees panning for gold," marvelled Alec. "Now that's the New World for you."

"The Helena seam," Helen giggled.

By the end of the evening I had the unnerving feeling that whatever I said, I could do no wrong.

It was a relief to go back to the old lady. To be alone, to be myself. To talk to Father in my mind.

What time would it be back home? Eleven hours on. Have you had breakfast yet, Father? Porridge, tea, bit of toast. Maybe Eti's cooking some eggs. There's a formal feeling in this room; you'll know what I'm talking about. The old lady is aware her sands have run thin. Their family name is Flinders like the explorer who circumnavigated Tasmania, but no relation or they would have mentioned it, I imagine.

Sailing in the southern ocean, Matthew Flinders was as far from his home as it is possible to be.

In the next few weeks I felt as if there was just too much space in front of me. What was I going to tell them next? When would my footing falter? When it did, they'd turn on me. Have me for dinner.

The house was full of unused rooms, furnished in heavy Edwardian detail. But the morning room, with its bay windows and its sofas where the dogs sprawled out, was cheerful. After Helen arrived home from school, Alec, in a display of heroism, made a pot of tea, added biscuits he'd purchased in the village, and served them to her.

If the old lady was asleep, I was welcome to partake.

Over tea in the spring afternoons, I was introduced to the optimistic Alec-and-Helen version of European history. The Renaissance was wonderful because it told us about the real nature of man; the Reformation was wonderful because it proclaimed man's right to seek his own path to God; the French Revolution was wonderful because of liberty, equality, fraternity.

Alec told me about Cardiff. "By far the best place to learn about silicosis."

"Sounds awfully jolly," said Helen, putting on a stage voice: the toff.

"Ra-ther," he answered, going along.

He realized I'd at least know what silicosis was. Small bits of coal dust make it past the nose, mouth, and throat down into the deepest part of the lungs.

"I think I'll leave you two to it," said Helen. "I'll see how Mother's getting on." She bounded up the stairs, the dogs following.

Alec talked to me about silicosis, about the miners.

I told him about my school teacher, Mr. MacDonald. Under his tutelage we grew up believing Keir Hardie, the Labour leader, to be far more important than any of the English kings. I added the accents: the teacher from Scotland, the Aussie kids from the bush.

Alec called Helen back down the stairs. "Get a load of this. The saga of Keir Hardie, told at the far end of the world."

I sat in their pleasant morning room, in my lavender uniform with its wide royal-blue belt, feeling pleased with myself, and very uneasy.

UPSTAIRS THE OLD LADY had begun to lose her way. She became bloated rather than sunken, small and round and puffed out like a pigeon. Alec sat on one side of the bed, beside the green light. Helen sat on the other side, by the windows, and they spoke of small things: the village gossip; the weather; the cricket, how England was going to win.

The old lady struggled bolt upright. "Gin," she cried, "where did they put the gin?" Sister and brother tiptoed out into the corridor, to hold each other and suppress giggles. The old lady's face clouded over. "Why are they laughing?" she whispered, in a plaintive voice, her old arms reaching out for mine. "What is there to laugh about?"

"You mustn't mind them," I said, "they're just having a bit of fun."

Bolt upright again. Looking around, face filling with fear. "Gun? Gun? Who's got a gun?"

The days fell into a rhythm. In the morning room sister and brother played with the dogs and had long, argumentative discussions. Helen placed in my lap a book by George Bernard Shaw. "*You will like it.*" She immediately took it back to find a passage. "When the class barriers are removed," Helen read with great seriousness, "women will have more husbands to choose from."

The pair of them laughed.

After dark, Alec wound up the phonograph and we danced, unskilled foxtrots up and down the corridor. Silly popular songs. Sister and brother danced with each other, then I danced with each of them, singing along to the words. *Button up your overcoat. Dah dah, dah dah di dah / You belong to me.*

Tiring of that, we relaxed in the armchairs and they talked about their brothers, Rolly and Marcus, who had been to the Great War. Rolly was the brilliant one; Marcus ran away from his dire boarding school. Hid out in Spain with their Uncle Fred, who was in raisins. Stayed in raisins until the blight got the grapes.

"Father was beside himself about Marcus running off," said Alec.

"He finally dragged him back to take the public service exams," said Helen, who must have been all of eight or nine when this happened. "For India," she added, putting on a deep pompous voice, "or *at least* Egypt."

"Words fail me," put in Alec, in the same tone.

"Then hostilities broke out. Saved by the hell. He was sent to France instead."

"Grubby little trade war. Nine, ten million lives."

There were two parts to this family: Rolly and Marcus; Alec and Helen. A difference of only half a dozen years between Marcus and Alec, but effectively a whole generation.

The old lady was going back, further back. "I'd been away," she said in an aggrieved voice, "and *she* had a new sweater. They were waiting for me at the railway station, and she was showing it off. *I'd been sick in the hospital and Mother bought her a present.*"

"Mother's talking about her own sister," Helen said, and wept.

Alec put his arms around her. "I've sent for Marcus."

Their mother had reached the stage where time held no meaning. There was movement in the house throughout the night. By morning, we were all tired. The old lady was hanging on for the return of Marcus.

In the early light I walked along the dyke through the beech wood with Alec and he told me what happened to Marcus in the war. Alec was carrying a basket because we were out to find mushrooms. Helen had plans to cook these up with cream. She was a completely amateur cook; a woman from the village took care of all the routine kitchen work.

As we left the house we discovered that overnight, the anemones in the garden border had come out.

At Neuve-Chapelle in northern France, Marcus had been buried alive. "One morning just after breakfast," Alec said, "a good breakfast of eggs and bread and tea, Marcus was walking from the mess back to his lines when a shell exploded. One moment he was walking along; the next moment the ground was heaving in a slow, deliberate way. He felt he was balancing on the back of a camel who'd abruptly decided to kneel."

"What happened?"

"There were other soldiers around; they'd been walking in a group. Several of them were buried; it wasn't just Marcus. He could hear men above, digging frantically. His ears must have been filled with dirt and of course he couldn't see a thing, but he could hear the voices above him."

"Unbelievable."

"Quite. When they dug him out, he opened his eyes. What he saw on their faces was disappointment. They'd been hoping to find someone else, you see. One of the others."

"Did they find him, the someone else?"

"Marcus never knew. They carted him away before he could find out. His face was torn up. His cheek was like a chocolate whose soft centre had oozed out."

I felt guilty, hearing this. It was his brother's story, not his.

HELEN AND I SHARED confidences too.

On evenings when Helen and I had the morning room to ourselves, she'd fetch a bottle of sherry and glasses. Tuck her feet up on the couch and offer me a tailor-made from her cigarette case.

We were ready for discussions I found alarming and irresistible.

"What made you become a nurse?"

"What's this, the third degree?" At first I'd try to fend her off. "I was unaware of having much choice in the matter," I admitted. "You could stay home and keep house, get a job in a shop in town, or go nursing."

"Underneath," Helen persisted. "What idea did you have about it? What inspired you?"

I explained about my mother, who plunged a newborn into a bucket of icy water. "She brought a baby back to life. She had the gift."

I also told Helen about my training at the Royal Prince Alfred in Sydney. The head matron's voice, hushed, intent: "It is a fine art to understand the suffering of others. Perhaps the finest of the fine arts."

Helen, like Alec, talked to me about Marcus. "When Mother was well, Marcus came home at least once every two years, for a visit. Ever the dutiful son."

Did Alec rate as a dutiful son? He had taken time off from his studies to be here.

"Mother insisted it was high time Marcus found himself a suitable wife. The trouble was, Mother could never bring herself to approve of the girls he took up with. Not that there was anything the least bit wrong with them, but they weren't 'out of the drop drawer.' Mother thinks we should be living as we did when Father was alive. For her it's not yet 1914."

"What did Marcus do when your mother disapproved?"

"He'd brazen it out for a while. Insist on bringing them to tea a second time. But sooner rather than later it would fizzle out. He'd lose interest. Leave the girl, return to Spain."

"Your mother won?"

"I'd say so. Not that he'll have to worry about that anymore."

We were silent, thinking of the old woman dying in the room above us.

"If he'd really wanted one of them," Helen continued, "he'd have stuck to his guns and not bolted. He must feel lonely, out there alone. I become quite impatient with him at times, lord knows why he insists on burying himself out in Spain."

Helen poured more sherry into our glasses.

"Have you ever taken a lover?" she asked. I was shocked by both the question and the boldness of the language.

She let the words sit there.

"What's it like?" I ventured.

"It's like ... well it's like that bit in the Messiah: *Wonderful.*"

Back when I was in training, I'd seen the flushed faces of other nurses when they emerged from the laundry room.

Of course, I wondered. I looked at Alec every single day and wondered. Not just wondered. Wanted.

A HOUSEHOLD THAT IS waiting for a death is a particular, exclusive place, with ripples of expectation, and conversations that would otherwise be impossible. In some ways it's like a house in which an infant has been born. Like the two of us now, awake in the sleeping world, you suckling and eager.

One afternoon, after I'd been up all night as well as much of the morning, I walked with Alec along the river path. We were in the wood, beneath fast-moving, damp clouds. When we came out of the wood, the path took us by farms, where we heard piglets.

"Listen," Alec said, excited. "Dear little grunters."

He suggested we take a punt, on the river. "What do you say we go on the river? Come to think of it, I'm dying to go on the river with you."

"Do we have time?"

"Yes, we must, we must."

Electric blue dragonflies hovered over dark green water. "Marvellous," Alec enthused. "So early in the year."

He was standing in the punt. I sat facing him, looking up. He wasn't wearing a hat and the sun was on his brown hair.

"Shall I tell you something?" he asked.

ALEC, AS A SECOND-YEAR medical student, had gone with a Welsh fellow to Wales during the great miners' strike of 1926 — the twelve-day general strike, after which the miners held out for another six months.

Students who supported the strike made this kind of journey; it was common enough.

Their destination was a village in the centre of Wales, largely Welsh-speaking, where his student friend had family connections. Twenty years ago, the men of the village had started going south to work in the mines. Coal paid more than slate.

What struck Alec about the village was the pale grey slate of the cottages, the darker grey of the roofs.

The villagers had names like Huw Bee Hive and Owen Milk Cart. The pub — run, to his surprise, by Evans Potato Field — opened quietly on Sunday night. After most of the village had attended chapel they came back to the pub, which had its front doors locked. They came in through the garden, until all had gathered, including Davies the Copper.

It was November; the miners had come to the end of their hope. A man from the village who had gone south to the mine had been shot.

On Monday he was buried.

Alec heard the singing from the hills before he saw the people. Men, serious in their thin dark blue serge suits, were carrying the coffin on a bier. Down they came, and he and his friend took off their hats and stood in the doorway, watching.

The strong sorrowful singing grew when the procession moved from the hills into the village. Then abruptly the singing stopped.

In slow silence the men filed down the narrow single street, past the deserted Anglican church with its lych gate, to the small, white-washed chapel at the far end.

"What were they singing?" Alec asked his friend. He'd assumed it was a song about the strike.

"It's a hymn." His friend was embarrassed but hid it well. "Quite well known."

As the men entered the chapel, they lifted their voices and began again. Alec's friend translated the lines:

Come no more the voice of the tyrant
To wake them to weeping again

Alec and his friend walked together to the chapel. Everyone in the village was there, and miners from the south as well. After the burial, the singing continued in the cold night. The hat was passed for the miners, who would be going back south.

When the mourners had left the cemetery, Evans Potato Field and his wife welcomed all comers. The pub had a good fire going and food and drink was on the house. Having cleared the plates away, the publican's wife came in and sat at the far end of the room. Alec watched her hand two ladies glasses of dandelion wine, pale as straw.

The following morning the publican's wife stood over the miners as they ate their breakfast. They were going back, walking south. She knew that they wouldn't eat on the journey; they'd be saving the sandwiches for their children. Again, Alec watched. In addition to the sandwiches the publican's wife packed several large cloth bags with a rabbit, a partridge, cheese, sky-blue duck eggs, brown chicken eggs, and jars of her own jam.

As he left the village, Alec had the impression he was sailing, his life utterly light and clean and clear. Even the smallest detail stood out with its own specific weight and dignity. "I felt as if I had been created at that moment. I was like a calf that stumbles to its feet for the first time, and finds it knows exactly what to do."

After the punt, when we were walking home, Alec turned to me and smiled. Really smiled. Our walking together felt different this time. I knew it was because he'd told me about himself, in Wales.

We returned to the house, wrapped up in this mood.

Helen was pleased because she'd cooked a leg of lamb by herself. We could smell the meat in the oven as we came down the hall.

"Marcus is coming," announced Helen. "The letter arrived today."

"When?" Alec cried out, flapping his arms.

THE NIGHT MARCUS ARRIVED, very late, there was much noisy opening of cake tins. The three siblings were excited to see one another.

Marcus had a brown cowlick that jumped forward when he was agitated. His hair, unlike his face, was all his own. He wore thick glasses that made him look a little like a mole.

In the happy fuss of unpacking, Marcus produced a bag of aniseed balls. His sister and brother fell on them. Like little kids, they fooled around, pushing them to the front of their mouths, showing the black balls to one another and giggling.

On his left cheek Marcus wore a tin contraption to hide from the squeamish the fact that part of his face was missing. These devices were made by an Englishman who lived in France. Helen had bought it for him in Paris, and you saw them more often in France than you did in England. The English, more provisional in many ways, were likely to make do with a scarf.

Even though it was dark, Marcus stepped out with a torch for a look at the garden. Came bursting in to report, "The pussy willow has kittened."

I smiled at "kittened."

We sat at the kitchen table, drinking a little celebratory whisky. Alec, Helen and I were smoking, but Marcus couldn't because of his face.

Helen insisted on dancing. "Now there are four of us, it's perfect," she said, as if that settled the matter.

We scampered down the corridor, messing up the runner rugs. Marcus and Helen. Alec and me. Alec and Helen. Upstairs the old lady was dying. Downstairs we were dancing.

"Bye, Bye, Blackbird."

"You're the Cream in My Coffee."

"Button Up Your Overcoat." Our favourite.

Marcus had sat down. I wondered if he'd even heard these songs we were dancing to.

"No sleeping on the job," cried Helen, pulling Marcus to his feet.

"I'm all right," he said. "Really, I can watch."

But Helen made Marcus take my arm, and we danced a little. Marcus looked as if he were being extra tolerant.

Alec and Helen, claiming to be puffed out, stood in the doorway and watched. At the end of my dance with Marcus, Helen clapped.

A FEW DAYS AFTER Marcus arrived, the mother abandoned speech. She had been waiting for her children to gather, and they'd come. The old lady had hydrangea eyes that must have served her well when young. Her mouth opened and those blue eyes stared.

The children were taking turns. Helen did the first night shift, following by Alec. Marcus would relieve Alec at 3:00 a.m. Alec would leave the room, but not to go to bed. Often I'd come out to find him sitting at a small hall table in the dark.

I was waiting for him to mention our afternoon by the river.

Since the coming of Marcus, Alec had been distracted. If he wasn't going to say anything, should I bring it up? Start off with something lighthearted — he'd called the pigs dear little grunters, remember? That was an afternoon when something shifted between us. He'd said, *we must, we must.* You don't forget that, I told myself.

Or do you?

In the longer and longer evenings, my walks were often with Marcus and the dogs. When he wasn't sitting with his mother, Alec was suddenly busy elsewhere. He had studying to do. Helen claimed to have tasks back at the school, and jumped on her bicycle to prove it.

I cannot remember the first really personal thing Marcus said to me.

We were walking together. He poked in the undergrowth with a stick and talked about ancient Britain. The dyke through the wood had been built by the Romans, he claimed. On the ground the brown beech leaves were still sodden, but there were copper buds on the trees. By their trunks, fresh sorrel and woodspurge. "See," Marcus said, "the woodspurge has flowered, three cups in one."

The may trees were already in bloom and the cow parsley was coming out.

Marcus was serious about naming the names.

Someday, I thought, not too far from now, they'll find his tin cheek in the ground and have to ask a curator of a museum what it might be.

At the far end of the dyke was a place where high old cherry trees intermingled with the beech, giving off a light of their own. Marcus's face looked green, the green whiteness of spring.

THE OLD LADY HAD reached her last days. She began to exude the botanical smell of a slow bed-death. At last she descended into that place of strenuous breathing, during which the body undertakes its exhausting, final check round. Room by room, she was shutting her life down. After the effort, a shallow breath, a small whistle. Another door closed. Then again, the throaty struggle.

I was on one side of the bed, Alec opposite me. I had sat at other beds before, in just these circumstances. So, no doubt, had Alec.

On the bed-table was a small light with a pleated, rose-coloured shade. The eiderdown was the standard pink satin. The rosy light fell upon the eiderdown, giving the room the subdued intensity of church.

It was late, after midnight. The "still of the night" is an accurate phrase, I thought. So is the term for the jagged breathing the old lady was doing: Cheynes-Stokes respiration. Chains being dragged across a cement floor; a stoker in a steam engine lifting the heavy coal, heaving it into the fiery mass.

Alec reached out his hand to me.

I took it.

Joined like that, our hands on the pink eiderdown, we listened to the heavy breaths, then the lighter ones. Deep, shallow; deep, shallow.

Alec looked at me, his glasses round on his serious face, his brown eyes big. He smiled.

Then it stopped. The breathing stopped.

What happened seemed to last forever. A powerful sense of knowing melted through me. It was growing in my heart; it was moving up to my head. Steadily, I was filling with a vast, ironic sense at the pleasure of knowing — although what I knew was nothing in particular.

On the other side of the bed, Alec was still looking at me, his smile widening.

I realized I must be smiling too, a loony, giddy grin.

Both of us understanding, as we grinned, that this was something not our own, that it came from the old lady. We'd just happened to be sitting here. We were in its path, overtaken.

It was easy, now. He was going to mention our day on the river, how he'd told me about going to Wales.

Behind us, the door opened.

Alec withdrew his hand.

Marcus had come into the room.

MARCUS, TOO, MUST HAVE been swept up, because he leaned down and started to kiss his mother's forehead in an unguarded, almost unbalanced way. Kiss kiss kiss: quickly, quickly. This was not a family given to wild expressions of emotion and at no time had I sensed in either mother or children the desperation of unbearable loss.

The kissing must have reached his mother, because she stirred. Her face twitched. Her back muscles tensed and her body rose up slightly, fell.

Silence. No breath.

Marcus stepped back.

Then she gurgled, a low rumbling in her chest like a distant lorry. Finally, her laboured, stentorian breathing broke out again.

"False alarm," Alec said.

SHE DIED IN AN early summer dawn.

I stood with Alec and Helen at the front of the house, looking out towards the beech wood. In the moist heavy silence Helen and Alec talked in a formal way about the things they needed to do — whom to call about the body, when the service should be, who should receive a telegram.

At some hour of the long night before, Marcus had gone out for a walk, tripped, and lost his glasses. Marcus came around the path from the back and soon the four of us were down on the ground, searching for the lost glasses. Alec found them. A joint cheer arose as Marcus put them on.

Helen and Alec went back into the house. Marcus and I were alone together.

I became acutely aware of the glossy look of the Portuguese

laurel, the busy activity of birds in the wisteria. A morning like any other.

"It's a strange thing, isn't it?" said Marcus.

I nodded.

ON THE DAY OF the funeral Helen was worried because there were people coming for lunch.

After the undertaker visited, I tidied the old lady's bedroom. Since the death nobody had spoken a word about the green light above Roland's chair.

I opened the window wide.

As soon as the funeral was over, I'd be expected to leave myself. I'd made no plans. I leaned against the window frame, rolled myself a ciggie and shed some selfish tears.

In mid-morning Helen came downstairs in a formal black dress and argued with a woman from the village about how many loaves of bread would be needed. The woman from the village, stiff as a pillar, waited confidently for Helen to crumble and accede.

At the wake I was someone in the background. As aide to anxious hostess Helen, I kept the tea towels damp over the sandwiches until they were ready to be passed around.

When the guests had left, Helen, Marcus and I were to take a walk along the dyke, into the beech wood. Alec had been walking earlier and reported that the beech trees were darkening into their full summer green.

We were on the point of setting out when someone else arrived in a taxi, a childhood friend of Helen.

"You go on ahead," Helen said, to me and Marcus. Waving us away.

IF THE CHILDHOOD FRIEND hadn't arrived late, if it hadn't been the day of the funeral, it wouldn't have happened.

At the end of the dyke Marcus and I admired the beeches and the old cherry trees. It was dusk and the sun was golden. Marcus reached over and ran the back of his hand down my cheek. This felt like an experiment in which he did not quite believe. He was tentative but in a touching way, like an undomesticated animal approaching food put down on a plate.

Back at the house, Helen had just come out to say goodbye to the friend (an elegant woman in one of those sideways-perched hats that were high fashion at the time). She was waving, but her eyes were on Marcus and me.

Moments after that, as the taxi was going down the gravel drive, the words came up: *Marcus has willed himself into it.*

Helen was still waving.

And Alec is letting it happen.

I'VE COME TO A part you will find puzzling; I don't claim to understand it myself. As my daughter you're bound to find me a dangerous fool. For how can you not fear being caught in the immense wheel of repetition? The mistakes of the mother descend, carrying the daughter under.

In London it wasn't easy to find work but eventually I obtained a position at Barts — St. Bartholomew's Hospital — and moved into the nurses' residence on Charterhouse Square.

Alec had likewise promptly departed, for Cardiff. He did not write — a fact which did not much surprise me, although with each post my hand searched the recesses of the wooden postbox in the nurses' residence. I had casual news of him, from Helen when she came to London, and also from Marcus.

The major development was that Marcus had not returned immediately to Spain. He stayed on in London, where he studied each day at the British Museum, having taken rooms nearby.

A few words here in my own defence.

First, the music. One Sunday afternoon Marcus invited me, in his diffident way, to an afternoon concert in the park. We sat in deck chairs, smelling the summer grass and listening to the music, which began with a fragment here, a fragment there. Not in the least like music I was used to; it was confident, strong and strange, but almost disjointed, open. It was speaking directly to me about my life. Part of me was back home in Cliffend with Father, back there permanently. Another part, the daily self, was here in London with Marcus, who was totally lost in the strings. Yet another, the fugitive part, was thinking of Alec up in Cardiff (grey; slag heaps; coughing). The fragments of the music gathered weight in my chest, substantial as the billowing clouds above us, promising rain.

Afterwards we found a tea room, ordered cakes, and talked about Marcus's life out in Spain. I found being with him quite easy. Marcus was not in the least interested in digging out whatever I wished to keep hidden; he left me free to harbour my own uncertainties. One thing I will say for Marcus: he never made a fool of himself by snooping about, assessing, or trying to reassure.

I realized, of course, that in his own way he was courting. He had set his sights on me; the advance was steady, if inept.

Then there was the physical energy, which caught me completely off guard. At this time I was filled with desire that had grown up in the presence of his brother. Alec had turned away, but the desire remained, an insistent hunger.

I wanted, I needed. And Marcus happened to be in London. This was my chance. Sooner rather than later, as Helen had said, he'd lose interest, go back to Spain. So where was the risk? Deep inside a voice asserted it would serve Alec right.

Underneath these rationalizations, something else was going on. The day of the music in the park, after the tea, Marcus and I walked together through the London streets. For hours, until darkness had fallen. At one point in our walking Marcus abruptly turned to me, embraced me roughly, urgently, and for a few seconds my eyes caught his. He immediately looked away, but not before I'd glimpsed a terrible yearning. And I believed I could be the one to assuage it.

That moment, over so quickly, shaped the path of our lives.

Marcus arrived at the nurses' residence on a Saturday afternoon when he knew — because I'd told him — that none of the other nurses would be present. I was standing by the upstairs window, waiting. At the end of the street, a group of men were playing brass instruments. They wore brown suits, some with empty sleeves, or pant legs taped up where a leg was missing. Beside them a dog, also brown, scratched himself. This was how they made their living: they played and sometimes people would throw money down to them.

The dog saw me watching and became fully alert. Maybe people threw tidbits for the dog as well.

In front of my window, Marcus stood, peering up.

The musicians, the dog, and now him.

I forced the window open and threw my arms into the air, waving. I was aware as I was doing this that it was foolhardy, rash — and in its own way, awfully compelling. Even as I was thinking this he saw me, he was lifting his hat, the silk hatband glinting, catching the light.

In through the back way, up the utility stairs, creeping with shoes off, a dash for my room.

Being a nurse, I'd seen the naked body of a man before. Thought myself experienced.

This was vulnerable in a different way. After he'd left I examined my face in the mirror. I've noticed that look since, on couples who announce their plans — a grateful, embarrassed confusion. Often mistaken for love.

In the weeks that followed, I was overwhelmed. I had been craving precisely this intimacy without having reckoned on its force. When Marcus, above me, departed into a place of self-absorption, I found I was free to ride inside my own body, ride right up to its summit — unaware, at the time, of how this could be more a matter of good fortune than inevitability.

My body, aroused, demanded more.

Helen took control of the details. She organized a woman in the village to make me a frock with a drop waist that was already going out of style. Not that either Helen or I cared much for fashion. I told

Helen I would have been just as happy to show up in my nurse's uniform and saw her smile. Maybe she thought this augured well for what lay ahead: a life out in Spain with her unworldly brother Marcus.

We didn't wed in haste; I wasn't pregnant. I stood in my wedding dress in front of the altar at St. Bartholomew the Less — in the Barts hospital grounds — secretly bleeding according to regular, uninterrupted schedule.

I'll show you the picture one day. Me in my twenties dress with a floppy felt hat, which you will certainly find ridiculous. We'll look at that photo together (I don't imagine your father will show much interest) and you'll come up with the obvious question: Where was Alec? Didn't Alec attend?

Helen was not sure Alec would be able to make it down from Cardiff. He was so very busy, she assured me.

A low-key Thursday-afternoon wedding. I didn't sweep in, wedding march thumping. I think the organist may have failed to spot me — probably because of that hat. I simply walked up the aisle with "Sheep May Safely Graze" creaking the preliminaries. I was on the arm of a boyfriend of one of the nurses. There had been a general rallying around. Because I had no family here, somebody had to be found who could "give me away." The giver-away turned out to be a tall New Zealander doing a residency at Barts. He had some wildly Scottish name I cannot recall. He introduced himself to me as a selfless volunteer for any social gathering likely to involve malt whisky.

Reaching the front of the church with the obliging Kiwi, I concentrated on not thinking of Father. I knew if I did I would surely cry.

I stood at the altar below the stained glass windows, which were unusually light and made the place feel quite airy. Throughout the service I was not looking at Marcus; I was examining those windows. There's a baby in each. In one the Virgin Mary, up in heaven, is holding the child aloft like a trophy. In the other window, someone is carrying him down on earth. I decided it was probably St. John the Baptist.

IN THE END ALEC did make the journey. He showed up at the wedding with a mob of friends from Guy's, who mingled cheerily with the Barts contingent, including the New Zealander, all of them intent on the booze. Also in attendance were a few of Helen's school friends, and Flinders family relatives.

Marcus, I noted, didn't have an entourage of his own.

Alec stood at the altar beside his brother. Officially, Alec was the best man, but I'd say he gave his brother away.

As for Marcus, I have no idea what he was thinking as he waited for me. Did he hear my footsteps coming towards him? Did he have any premonition whatsoever of the damage I was to inflict upon him?

Three

Catalonia, 1931–1934

IT IS A ROMAN road that sweeps upward from Port Bou, part of the ancient link between Gaul and Tarragona. So said Marcus on a hot, thundery summer afternoon as we were crossing into Spain. We were nearing the end of our honeymoon, an event I already knew to have been a failure.

We had come by car, not train. We'd driven through the solemn fields of France in somebody's borrowed cream Talbot. I cannot remember whose car it was, but I do remember Helen making the arrangements about having it dropped off in Barcelona and being extra triumphant. I was surprised and encouraged to discover that Marcus could, in fact, drive.

Marcus and I travelled slowly along the coast. In the evenings he read to me from Martial about the pleasures of wintering in warm Tarrraco. "It was the fashionable place to be," Marcus explained, "one of the Emperor Augustus's pet spots. Theatre, chariot races, gossip, Romans from Rome."

"You'd be moving with the quality," I put in, for something to say.

Tarragona was almost home territory for Marcus. His uncle had been in the raisin trade and had maintained a house there. When Marcus ran away from his boarding school — it was something sensitive, clever, English boys did at the time — his uncle took him in. Free to roam the pinewoods and scrub, Marcus had time to consider how an aqueduct made up of a series of double arches embodied the principles of order, arrangement, symmetry, propriety, economy.

"I remember," he said, "the day I realized what happens when the height of a structure is suited to its breadth, and the breadth is suited to its length." He'd felt a wild swooning, better than alcohol. After almost a thousand years, the engineering along the Via Augusta retained the power to stir an adolescent.

We travelled as far south as Tossal de Manises, down the coast from Alicante. What Marcus wanted to see was the small acropolis, the temple and thermal baths of an outpost fort. In turn Greek, Carthaginian, Roman. Nothing beyond the Visigoths was of any interest to my husband. No, that's not quite true; his library included a fine nineteenth century literature collection in English and French — all of it presumably read.

In our journeys we paid particular attention to the ruins of the Roman baths. I learned how the heating was piped into the baths, how the rooms maintained their different temperatures, how they used mud instead of soap.

"Must have been a right little germ-fest," I said. But Marcus was preoccupied with his Roman colonials sitting around their cold baths, clean and relaxed.

DURING OUR LONG HONEYMOON, Marcus forgot why he had married me. His mother had been dying and he'd been obliged to return to England, where, by happenstance, he appeared to have acquired a wife.

Bitter, and far from the whole truth. There were times when we made love — not just desultory coupling, but love.

The first time Marcus made love to me after our marriage was in Northern France, where we visited the graves. It was fashionable at the time; the trains ran excursions from Britain to the Great War graves. Not that we were on such an excursion; we were on our honeymoon.

We stayed in an old house with water meadows in the back, pear trees by the window. Behind the house, the high grasses dripped green and cool as a cathedral. At the front, the grasses had withered and dried to the colour of hay.

The more we saw of the graves, the more tender Marcus became.

The room, probably permanently damp, was cool in the unusual heat. In the evening we watched the shivery stencil of leaves on the ceiling. It was not yet dark.

His mouth tasted of apples.

The war grave cemeteries were flat, with raw paths. The sky, too, was flat, holding the heat. In the fields you would come across old boots, mess tins; you could see the trunks of trees riddled with bullets. In one tree, a field telephone was still attached.

The women of the house gave us fresh pastries and hot chocolate in the morning, calvados in the evening. "A bottle full of summers past," said Marcus, being courteous and appreciative. "Goes down like air."

The women looked at Marcus with the contraption for his cheek, and clearly longed to put their arms around him and kiss him as one does an adult son. No doubt they were beginning to see many such men coming for the graves.

THE SECOND TIME MARCUS made love to me was in Alicante.

Alicante: the pier with music and the pastel hotels and the walk by the waterfront. Rows of palms, four deep. At the end of the avenue, the *Paseo de los Mártires*, was a shining marble pillar with a statue on it: a woman's figure, Liberty.

In years to come I was to return to Alicante and recall this visit as if it had happened in another world to a woman quite unlike myself.

We walked the long way down to the docks and warehouses and out to the mole leading to the lighthouse. There were, in Alicante, colonels from India and retired British manufacturers, just as there had been in Tarragona. Marcus took great care to avoid these people.

At the time of the paseo, shutters were being opened, awnings raised. Groups were sitting on the stone seats along the avenue, the sun was setting, and in a pavilion at the start of the mole, music played. Crowds relaxed on the wrought-iron chairs at the front of cafés, talking happily. The heat lessened and a small breeze came in off the water. The hotels, painted green and blue and pink with cheerful fake facades, looked soft in the evening.

That night I lay in bed and watched the flash of the lighthouse. I was waiting until the light shone into our room, on our ceiling. We were in one of those pastel hotels, with the shutters open wide to the night sky. Marcus removed his shoes and socks. He took off his cheek contraption. It linked around the neck like a small horse collar. I listened for the sound of him putting his shoes outside the door, and the sound of the contraption being placed on the dressing table. I was in bed looking out at the sky, waiting.

I think that time Marcus actually saw me. Me, the flesh of my arms, my breasts, my belly.

Afterwards, I became aware of the slap of dominos.

The shouts of late bathers.

The night watchman with his heavy keys.

A horse being led out. Hooves clattering over stones.

The night watchman, again. Whistling.

Having his call returned.

WE VISITED BARCELONA NOT long after the World Fair, and the affluent parts of the city had the comfortable feeling that accompanies recent success. We stayed for weeks; we were in no hurry. We saw the Stone Quarry and the Sagrada Familia. Marcus pronounced that trying to turn stone into water was a doomed project. (Later, Alec told me you only had to look at the spires to recognize the pines bending in the strong wind — just the way he'd seen them, looking up, as a child on holidays at their uncle's place. The trees kept the shape of the wind long after it had left them.)

In Barcelona, Marcus strove to do what he believed honeymooners ought to do. Tea at Casa Llibre, up in a blue double-decker streetcar through the suburbs — Josepets and so on, up to Craywinckel — sitting on the streetcar's upper deck. The cable sizzled so close overhead we ducked in unison. The conductor pushed his cap way back on his head and laughed.

The homes on the high hills had extensive gardens not that much different from the ones on Sydney's upper-crust north shore — hibiscus, bougainvillea, palm trees. In good humour, Marcus pointed out the houses climbing way up the valley, the pine groves to the south, the blond-brown city below. On a clear day, Marcus said, you could see all the way to Majorca. The day we were there, the sea was grey and cloud hung midway to the horizon. He told me that the Mediterranean smelled more salty than the Atlantic.

At Tibidabo Avenue we took the funicular up to the top for lunch in the restaurant, and took a trip in the stationery airplane. I have a photo of Marcus and me in the airplane; everyone had a picture taken of that. I'll show it to you and you'll spot the staged smile: a happy woman on her honeymoon. Unrecognizable.

WHEN MARCUS SPOKE OF his village, his head bobbed and his cowlick jumped. "You will find that so little has changed," he said, as if this were a splendid promise. Since 4000 B.C., he meant.

Marcus's village felt more marine than terrestrial. It crouched in a defensive position, although it didn't need to, because this village had found for itself a miraculous pocket of warmth. Untouched by the incessant winds of the region, it sat on the edge of a south-facing bay, sheltered by its cliffs.

The week after we arrived, Marcus set off with his spade over his shoulder, walking up the steep hill path. At the top of the hill path was the road where once a week a bus came from inland. He climbed on the bus and it took him off to his ruins.

I was left in a white cottage above a blue sea with nothing to do but look. Behind the cottage, dark vines climbed the hills up to where the cork trees grew. The mountain gorges were filled with the tough green of ilex and juniper while on the clifftops, thyme and rosemary clung to the soil. Below were the red rocks, with a few tenacious salt-stunted pines sticking to them. Then the water.

Marcus was the single village foreigner and everyone knew about him — how as a child he'd lived way down at Tarragona, how his uncle had gone broke in the raisin business, how he'd been in the Great War and was swallowed up by the earth. They knew *L'anglès* was crazy (fingers to forehead, turned like a screw; rolling of eyes). Poking about in ruins. My husband — what a strange term that seemed to me — loved this village: every blade of grass, each summer sunflower, the tribe of slim cats, the butterflies in the bushes.

But did he love me?

MARCUS'S COTTAGE WAS SMALL. At the front, running the length of the house, a combination living room, dining room, and kitchen. Two tiny back rooms, the larger of which was the bedroom. Out of its narrow windows, I could see a few compact vines and two squat fig trees, and beyond, the neighbour's house, with its small courtyard.

Next to the bedroom were stairs that led down to the library.

Years before my arrival, the village mason built the extra room at the back of the cottage and Marcus installed his library of books. The library was a white cave of a room, with wavering, uncertain plaster. Because the house was built on a slope, you walked down a set of shallow outside stairs to reach the library. Or, if you chose, you could walk straight out onto the library roof. The roof was flat, to catch the rain. We kept some deck chairs out there, for the view.

The library was the only room Marcus had decorated in any way, with painted plates, bits of Roman plumbing, shards of pots, old coins, daggers, and a fine selection of ancient bones.

A single picture on the wall showed a slender young Marcus standing in front of a mass of thorny bushes. Beside him, an older man in white trousers pointed in triumph at the ruins of the *piscine*. Marcus, seeing me looking, explained that the man was an archaeologist from Italy, a renowned scholar and a dear friend of many years.

A library and a view: two signs of Marcus's insanity, which the village accepted with complacency. None of the locals would conceive of a *view*. In rare moments of leisure, the villagers sat at the doorway of their houses, looking out into the street.

(When I was living in the cottage with Marcus, I had no idea that my future there would include days of wild perfection. At that time, I would have found the prospect entirely improbable. We should take heart from that, don't you agree?)

MY FIRST AUTUMN IN the village stretched out, full of clear air, charged with heat. Then overnight the weather crumbled, caved in. We woke to a grey sky and chilling winds.

That was when Marcus began to sleep in the library.

"I find it warmer in here when winter comes," he said. In the library he'd laid a fire of lovely dry wood and rosemary twigs.

"It's not winter yet," I protested.

He'd made up the couch; it was quite deliberate. The sheet was folded back neatly over blankets. An English pillow on top, taken from the bedroom.

I sat facing away from the couch, in a chair in front of the fire. "This is inviting," I said, bright and determined. "The rosemary twigs."

The village ran on kerosene and candles, so we sat in the lamplight, the fire in front, the dark behind. There might be some kind of mistake, I told myself. About the couch.

"Are we expecting someone?" I asked.

IN THE VILLAGE WE weren't entirely cut off. You could take a boat around the cliffs, inside the reef, past the headland, to a town where numerous tourists came for the summer. They shouted to one another on the cliffs and swam in the ocean; they stayed at the inns; they bought as mementos shells and little horses made out of cane leaves.

This town also had a small permanent British population. Naturally the ex-pats knew about Marcus the archaeologist; he was famously anti-social. In addition to the retired businessmen, there were a number of ex-pat artists. They seemed to sleep through the morning and drink themselves blotto each evening. I decided they must scramble briefly outdoors in the afternoon, because in small rooms they offered, for tourist sale, sketches and oil paintings featuring the town. The towering citadel was a favourite, while the more talented aimed to capture the shape and colour of the medieval town walls, with the little rocky port below.

The artists, the retired manufacturers, the tourists — all inspected the new wife Marcus had acquired.

Who would have thought?

LAIA AND HER HUSBAND Ramon were our neighbours. Laia came over in the mornings, to clean. She threw cleaning liquid over the tiles and swept the kitchen out. It reminded me of the way, in the country towns of Australia, the pub's tiled floors and footpath outside were hosed down early in the morning. "You'd think we'd been getting drunk and throwing up," I said to Marcus.

Marcus was making toast over the small stove. He was planning a jaunt to one of his favourite ruins, up at windy Ampurias. "You remember," he said, coming to the table, "They're excavating the second settlement. Where Scipio landed in 210 B.C."

"Scipio? Oh *that* Scipio."

"Actually, yes. There was more than the one."

I watched Laia walk down the stairs to the library. She was going in there to tidy up around the fireplace. I listened to her footsteps. By now she'd have seen the couch, the unmade bed for one.

I understood that Marcus meant to go to Ampurias alone. He had always gone alone, why would anything change now that he had a wife? I stared at my plate, listening to Laia tidying up. I found this business of Laia doing the housework to be absurd. When I protested to Marcus, he looked long-suffering in a kindly way I found particularly maddening. Apparently, I'd much to learn, ignorant newcomer that I was. He paid for Laia to help out. She *comes with*, he explained.

I could picture Marcus at Ampurias, which we'd visited on the honeymoon. He'd pointed out the massive walls and its single gate, then forgotten me as he picked his way along the paths between the vanished houses.

She knows, I told myself. She knows by now that we aren't a proper married couple.

After Laia left, Marcus took his cup of tea with him into the library, where he was reading in preparation for his upcoming trip, quiet as a spider. (We drank English tea which we bought in large square tins in the tourist town.)

We'd been there, at the Ampurias dig, on a windy warm day. I'd walked down by the bay and looked out at dark rocks lapping up the blue. Behind me, where men dusted away at the earth, careful as surgeons, there had been some kind of vine, unfolding, shining, paintbox green, so new as to look absurdly out of place.

In the cottage I watched Marcus pack his rucksack, sling a spade over his shoulder. I waved as he headed up the hill to catch the weekly bus. He was going up the path, going to the dig.

A pattern had been asserted. Reasserted.

On winter evenings marcus strolled down to the inn at the square while I read by the fire in his library. At the inn, he played cards, he played dominoes, he drank. The bar on the square had its local patrons: fishermen, the mason, the carpenter, the storekeeper, and one military man dismissed on full pay. If Marcus came in with his face flushed and happy, I knew the fishermen had been talking to him, including him, sharing the rough red that tastes of licorice.

"Fishermen," he told me, "know how to listen to different parts of a storm." Marcus admired the fishermen because they lived as their fathers had, all the way back to when the Carthaginians and Phoenicians pitched up here.

"There are hills in the sea," he explained. "Valleys, mountains, plains. But you have to be a fisherman to see them."

As long as we talked about the things that interested him — the village, the layers of history — we could carry a conversation. With him talking and me asking questions, we could fairly rattle on, as if we were content.

In bed on a winter's night, I'd listen. To the village dogs, roused from their rag baskets by human movement. To the sucking of the mud as someone walked by in the rain. Very late, I'd hear owls, calling to one another, an exchange of secrets. And as the year turned to spring, the call of the rock plover: crisp, demanding, plaintive.

In the morning, if it were a Wednesday, I'd hear a young man's voice and a light, leisurely clip-clip on the hill path. Bernat from the inn with his donkey, Ines. They were going up to meet the bus.

Ines was delicate and careful. Watched where she put her feet, taking her time. When she was concentrating, her large ears stood to attention. Nobody was allowed to rush her, including Bernat, who had once betrayed her in a dalliance with a bicycle and sidecar.

In one of the larger inland villages, Bernat bought a second-hand bicycle plus sidecar, a magnificent, cumbersome, black contraption. But the hill path proved too much for the bike, let alone sidecar. Both were swiftly retired to the courtyard of his home down at the square, and covered with an old blanket. The sidecar became the favourite sun spot for the town dogs, with much competition for the seat. And Ines was restored to her rightful place at Bernat's side.

I woke one night towards the end of that first winter — a serious fishing night. By this time Marcus had come home from the inn and was asleep in the library. I put on my slippers and dressing-gown, took a blanket, and padded out to the roof.

I sat in the dark and watched the boats. They were preparing to go out for tunny. Getting ready, the fishermen were silent, lugging oars, and lines wound on thick cork centres. One of them carried a long gaff. They put their equipment in the boats then came back up the beach for the live bait. They staggered a bit because the bait bags were heavy, filled with water.

There were six big boats — old wooden rowboats. Laia had told me that although each of the men owned a share in the big boats, there was one man who was the leader. I could see the bob and toss of the lamps. Only rowing would be permitted tonight, to sneak up on the tunny. They would put their nets down over on the far side of the bay, beyond where the cliff tumbled to the sea.

I stayed on, watching the boats and dozing. They came back in at about eight in the morning.

Dressing quickly, I took myself down to view the fish. I fancied I understood something about fishing. I knew how mullet looked back home, on their winter run. Mullet, called sweetlips in the shops. They lost their golden shine when they were pulled out of the sea. Mullet were like those frescoes Marcus told me about. Underground, the frescoes retained their ancient colours, but the moment the excavation was successful, the air rushed in and they began to fade.

The fishermen had enjoyed an excellent night and were rolling cigarettes and talking to one another in tired, pleased voices. They were throwing the plentiful catch into a flat-bottomed skiff. As soon as they'd finished, one of them would take the skiff around the cliffs, through the shallow waters inside the reef, past the headland, into the town, where the fish would be sold through the federation to which the fishermen on this coast belonged.

The remains of the catch, the fish they didn't throw into the skiff, was carried in wicker baskets to the centre of the village, where the fishermen conducted a small, informal market beneath the palm tree in the square. Everyone took pride in the palm tree; it was rare in these parts; it showed what a blessed, warm spot this was, tucked away out of the endless wind.

The catch of the morning included not only tunny but meros: whopping steel-coloured sea bass with disdainful, turned-down mouths and poppy eyes. You'd never see the locals eating them; their oily, flaky flesh was much too valuable.

As soon as I arrived to admire the meros, I became aware that the talk had ceased.

One of older fishermen stepped forward, reached out in a courteous fashion, took me very lightly by the elbow, drew me aside.

"What's the matter? Is everything all right?"

"Yes," I told him. "*Tot va bé.*" Everything is all right.

"Your husband, has something happened?"

"My husband is fine, thank you."

The fisherman stepped back, puzzled. "And you, are you well?"

I told him I was in the best of health.

When I'd walked away, conversation started up again. Two of the fishermen grabbed the basket. With one hand on the basket, the other on their hips, cigarettes in their mouths, they headed for the palm tree in the square and sat down beneath it in the morning sun.

After the boats had come in, the village widows would go to the beach and stand about, carefully casual, as if they weren't waiting for anything. Fish would be left behind in the boats, for the widows to retrieve without being watched. Shoving them quickly into their aprons.

MARCUS'S COTTAGE HAD BELONGED to the family of Laia's husband, to an uncle who ran away to Cuba at the turn of the century. The uncle's fishing gear awaited his return in a small shed attached to the outside of the house. Marcus opened the shed and I stepped in, touched the heap of nets and the trident, covered with fine white dust. "Waiting," Marcus said, "for Neptune to call."

The villagers called it the Englishman's cottage. I was the Englishman's wife.

At the beach, when the fishermen were messing about with their boats, I'd hear songs that Marcus said were Cuban. One of the singers had a wonderful, solitary voice, with a tone of immense longing.

The local women, mending the brown nets on the beach during the day, did not sing. But the women down at the inn sang. They sang in the house above the bar and in the impressive garden they tended beside and behind the inn. *Yai yai yai* in the garden, in their large white aprons. They'd wander off into complicated melodies that at their end came round again to that cry, which could feel like a complaint or a cheer, depending, I supposed, upon the mood of the singer. When Marcus wasn't there, and Laia had gone home for the day, I'd listen. I had scant else to do.

I would think up excuses to walk down to the cove, to the shop on the square. The shop looked like a ship's chandler with a few things added. Braids of garlic, candied pine nuts, onions in sacks, cans of olive oil, flour, and all manner of hardware for the boats. I pointed, carefully, and Pere, who ran the store, followed my finger.

Apart from his ancient treasures in the library, Marcus kept his house completely bare. I thought this was his personal style, but when I'd seen inside other houses in the village I realized it must be the custom of the region. I had expected interiors of dark, heavy clutter. About this, as about so many other things, I was proven wrong. Laia's mother-in-law's house had bare walls and only one wooden statute in the kitchen. It was some saint whose name I didn't recognize, which she addressed as if it were a family member.

Laia's mother-in-law lost her husband in the freak storm of

January 1922 — a storm that carried local fishermen almost as far as Majorca.

So much surprised me in this place. But one question I kept returning to. Tell me, why would a man, married little more than a year, no longer wish to sleep with his wife?

WHEN I FIRST MET Laia she struck me as a beautiful young woman: trim and strong, with a small, determined face.

I didn't do much of the cooking. Our kitchen was small, with black and white tiles and an alcove with a charcoal burning stove. Laia's the one who bought the fish and cooked it rapidly. The fish she most often served were like sardines only twice their size.

She showed me what to cook for the evening meals, when she didn't come over: cold potato omelette that Marcus liked.

"I can cook," I told her. "I've been cooking since I was a kid."

For more fancy meals, there were rabbits, caught in the forests above the village, cooked in wine corked the previous November.

Laia spoke easily with Marcus, but my attempts in her own language didn't make sense to her. She'd shake her head, and I'd wonder if it might be some kind of deliberate policy. Then I discovered she'd worked for a French family in Girona; she could speak French. With shared excitement as we puzzled over my abysmal Australian highschool French, Laia and I began to talk.

She wasn't from here.

That was the first thing she said to me, directly.

NOBODY WHO LIVES BY the sea is parochial. There were, in this village, connections all the way to the Caribbean, to Africa. And the local inn was run by a man called Pau, whose mother came from across the sea, from Ibiza. The store owner, Pere, was his brother. Both sons had married into the Ibicenco wing of the family. The garden of these women was full of sweet potato vines, and in season, red capsicum and shining dark aubergine. At the side of the inn, they'd built an arbour of white grapes, and in the front, facing the square, they'd planted petunias, phlox, asters. I was told no other village on the coast boasted such vegetables and flowers, and that the abundance was made possible by its south-facing cove, its unusual and wonderful warmth.

Sometimes Laia's husband Ramon would walk across to Marcus's cottage. He'd sit at the table beside Laia, talking to Marcus but aware of her. Although he was short, he had a large head and thick black hair that stood up in waves, adding height. Whenever he came close to me I could feel the marvellous confidence of his physical presence.

I gathered from Laia that his mother, who seldom emerged from her house, wielded power in the village. She and a few of the other older women arranged the marriages. They had some say in when the weddings should place and even when the children should be born. Ramon and Laia had broken all the rules. Ramon had found Laia on a rare trip inland. *Bam.* He wooed her; he brought her home. As for children, well, she and Ramon made *those* decisions as well. Laia told me this, her face alight and her hands clenched, a lovely prize fighter. Their determination had been doubly vindicated. Ramon and Laia had twins, the first in the village for over fifty years. Little arms batting at the air, Jordi and Josep were the bright future. Laia treated the twins with an easy kind of triumph. Giving birth to two at once, to hear her tell it, was a breeze.

If Marcus was away at a dig, she'd bring the twins over and we'd put a rug out on the roof. They were growing so fast; before you knew it they were able to sit up, looking slightly grumpy. Little pudges fairly crying out to be tickled and coaxed.

We sat on the library roof, Laia and me and the twins.

Laia told me about the village, the way things worked, who held power, who was feuding, who had married whom and why.

"And you?" she asked, looking at me. *What is your husband up to, being away so much? What is going on between you two?* Laia let the unsaid word float across. We both looked at the gulls, sliding about in the air.

I SAW THEM ONCE, Laia and Ramon. Marcus's cottage was built on land a little higher than theirs and I'd found the place — on the stairs that led down to the library — where you could glimpse right into the back of their courtyard. Laia had come up quickly behind Ramon, hugged him, and next thing he was leaning, bracing himself with one hand on the wall, laughing. She'd put her right arm around his hip, and was touching him. She was laughing too. Her left hand slid down inside his trousers and she played with him from behind. They became more serious, more absorbed and intent. He tensed; he let out an animal cry. Naturally, they believed themselves to be completely alone. I watched, a spy plunged into corrupt longing.

LIKE THE OTHER HOUSES in the village, the inn had its plaster white-washed annually in May. The first spring I was there, the vigorous whitewashing lifted my spirits. It was accompanied by a secular fiesta in the square, complete with drums and flutes, and some serious singing.

Laia told me about the fiesta and invited me along. Marcus was away. For weeks, he'd been preparing for his expedition. He travelled by boat to Ibiza, where his old friend the Italian archaeologist was excavating some ruins. He would return laden with parcels for the Ibicenco women from family back home. As for me, I found I was quite enjoying his absence.

Laia came to the cottage to fetch me. She was carrying a baby on each hip, humming. I felt like humming too. It had to do with its being spring, with the whitewashing, but mostly it had to do with walking down to the square beside Laia, my new friend.

Laia's husband Ramon was already in the square. With his fisherman's sloping shoulders, strong short arms and lady-killer eyes, he was a catch. One look at Ramon and you knew why Laia, who wasn't from here, who came from Girona, who'd worked for a French family, who was quick and bright and worldly, had gladly become his wife.

He called across to her. Laia heard his voice and the colour of her face deepened.

At the fiesta the men sang. Some of the fishermen sang the Cuban songs learned from their fathers, with Bernat banging away tunefully on a drum. Two men who were visiting from Aragón sang with their heads very close together, noses almost touching. I kept waiting for the women from the inn to sing, but they didn't.

Here I am, I told myself, at a fiesta in a truly beautiful place, with a friend by my side. Perhaps things were going to turn out all right between Marcus and me. It wasn't as if we were throwing plates and shouting. On the contrary. Maybe that was part of the problem. But I wasn't going to cut and run; I didn't want to leave. I was stronger than that. And I had to admit Marcus was scrupulous in his conduct towards me; when I goaded him he did not take the bait.

Marcus will come round, I told myself. He could be quite sweet, really.

At the height of summer, Marcus and I made our happiest trip — over to Genoa and down the spine of Italy, with the climax being Naples, where we visited with Marcus's friend, the eminent archaeologist.

From his picture on the wall of Marcus's library I'd imagined an aging scholar unimpressed by worldly pleasures. I shivered at the prospect of being presented to the great man. What could I say to him?

I was quite unprepared for Leo — he immediately demanded I call him Leo — who greeted both of us with glad arms, flinging open an old-fashioned cape, brandishing a silver-tipped cane. He whisked us off to a grand hotel, where he discretely ordered elaborate food and drink, all the while talking, laughing, radiating an infectious bonhomie. I had the immediate impression of a man whose kindness was instinctive.

He flipped open a gold cigarette case with his thumb, offered me one. Not feeling in the least under scrutiny, I relaxed.

Marcus, bathing in the warmth of Leo's favour, looked quite overcome with relief.

We were to see the majestic sights Naples had to offer, Leo declared, and Naples had every delight a traveller's heart could desire. With Marcus on one arm and me on the other, Leo sprinted us from one of the city's funiculars to another, singing shamelessly. At the summit of the Chiaia funicular, we had our pictures taken by a street photographer: Marcus and me, Leo and Marcus, and the three of us together.

I found Leo wonderful, and said as much to Marcus, whose face was already flushed with pleasure.

Right away the pair of them left town on some urgent archaeological business, but Leo sent a driver to escort me to Pompeii and Herculaneum, so my traveller's heart was busy.

Having returned to the city, Leo invited us both to his home. Up seven flights of steps to elegant rooms for an impressively lengthy dinner coordinated by a manservant who glided in and out of the gloom, wordless. From the dinner conversation I learned that Marcus and Leo had been together, numerous times, not only at archaeological digs but also in the cities — Paris, Madrid, Rome, even London — although Leo had not visited Marcus's English home, and had not been introduced to either Alec or Helen.

After dinner Leo played us the Neapolitan tenor, Gigli, and I listened for the first time to a voice of silver honey sing "Caro Mio Ben." Gigli Primo, Leo announced, patting his chest in an excited way, was soon to be leaving America, sailing home to his own people.

For the end of our visit, Leo planned a picnic. A launch took us down the Posillipo coast to the Imperial Villa — a first century Roman villa whose buildings had been mapped shortly before the Great War by none other than Leo himself. Once ashore, Leo and Marcus shared the carrying of a large wicker basket, while Leo pointed out the monument dedicated to the nymphs, the temple, the odeon, and the main dwelling.

On two blankets in a pine grove with a fine view of the sea, Leo unpacked the luncheon treats and we settled in as if we too were personal friends of the Emperor Augustus.

Drowsy from the over-abundance of food and wine and the strong heat of the day, we lay back and dozed. At some point I awoke briefly. Marcus had his head resting in Leo's lap. Leo was stroking Marcus's hair and the two of them were murmuring in voices of relaxed content.

Marcus, sensing movement, began to sit up, but Leo placed a light restraining hand on his shoulder.

I closed my eyes.

Going back in the launch, I considered this scene. I decided I must have imagined it — a midsummer afternoon's dream.

On the day we left Leo presented Marcus with a record of Gigli's "Caro Mio Ben." Marcus carried the record home with him as if it were a gift of the gods. Down in the library he played it often, by himself.

HAVING BECOME THE ENGLISHMAN'S wife, I put in a small garden and took up watercolours. I ordered paints and a large drawing block. Enjoying the smell of the paper, the childlike paintbox, I had an excuse to walk around the cliffs. I had an excuse to stare.

I tried to paint the view across the bay: red cliffs and pines, and on the edges exposed to the wind, clinging shrubs. The narrow pebble beach at the cove, and by the cliffs, brown seaweed, heaving. Down by the square, the single street of white houses and the flash of women's flowers. The palm tree.

I was busy at the paint box. The journey from eye to hand, a complete disappointment.

The walls and roofs of the village had a contingent of lean but healthy cats, the majority with coarse, pale ginger fur, almost beige. Cats are difficult to paint, way too fluid.

I tried again. Told myself to focus in, go small.

Shallow water over stones, a thin ribbon of amber. Boats, bright yellow and purple, hauled out. Brown nets, drying. A few slender logs, bleached pale grey. A cork tree with its odd, shaven bark.

Maybe I should forget scenery. Try people instead. I started a sketch of two *Guardia Civil*, based on a snapshot I'd taken on one of my journeys with Marcus. I had the Guardia wearing their grey-green uniforms with touches of red braid.

Laia came over, demanded to see. Frowned. "The hats are wrong," she pointed out. "You've put the hats on back-to-front."

IT WAS LAIA'S CONVERSATION, not my painting efforts, that redeemed the day. She'd arrive, and after a bit of housework, agree to sit and drink coffee, which she loved.

"You know how it is," she confided. "No husband will sleep with his wife on the night before fishing."

"No, I don't know how it is," I said. "You have to tell me."

She hesitated, decided to push on. "It's to save his strength."

So that's what Marcus is up to, I thought. Saving his strength for the Roman ghosts flitting about their porticos. If he doesn't want me for sex and he doesn't need me for housework, what am I doing here?

It was Laia I relied upon for the details.

The cork mansions in the hills behind us had seen better times because cork was being replaced by bottle caps. A few of the villagers — never the fishermen — would venture into the oak forest to trap rabbits and return with tales of charcoal burners.

With the coming of the Republic in 1931, men returned to the village, those who'd had to make themselves scarce during the days of Primo de Rivera. He'd been the dictator just before the Republic, Laia explained. He was forced to resign. They also had a monarch before 1931 but he abdicated and then the Republic was declared. The Republic was formally known as the Second Republic, because there had been another one some time ago. It was almost impossible to figure out.

In the Republic, said Laia, children were able to attend school —
not the religious schools, which had been only for those who could
pay. What's more, they were being taught to read and write in their
own language.

"Divorce," announced Laia, "is going to be legal."

"Divorce? I thought people here would be dead set against anyone getting a divorce, given the religion."

Laia laughed. "Not that I'll be wanting one."

The priest lived at the top of the village on the other side of the
cove, beside a white church and a white cemetery and a stony pasture where white goats were tethered. The priest was a foreigner, by
which was meant he spoke only Castilian. His flock was drawn for
the most part from the hill farms.

Drunk or sober, fishermen avoided the church. On feast days you
might see the fishermen parading around the palm tree, brandishing
brooms, pretending to chant and having a grand, irreverent time.

"Ramon had to be pushed into church to marry me," Laia added,
as if this were a huge joke. I concluded that Laia had, as the British
say, "married down," swept into the arms of the fisherman. I wondered how her parents felt at the wedding.

Marcus married down as well, but not because he was propelled
by passion. What, then?

"You've seen the housekeeper?" Laia asked, lighting a cigarette,
taking time to savour the first puff.

I'd seen the priest's housekeeper moving painfully about the yard.
She did not leave the house and yard; certainly she never came down
into the village.

"Where do they get their food? Whatever do they live on?" I spec-
ulated. "Goat's milk and manna from heaven?"

"You know she's his mistress, don't you?"

"No. You're joking."

"Housekeeper," Laia snorted.

The thought of anyone as ancient as the priest having a mistress
as decrepit as the housekeeper filled me with wild giggling.

Laia, too, swung in her chair and laughed. "Love," she said, throwing her arms up in mock horror, "crops up everywhere."

Grows like a weed. Except not here, not in this house. In this house lives a man who looks at his wife with courteous, unexpectant eyes.

Laia leaned across the table, and in whispers explained about the sea sponge that couples use as a contraceptive. My language was unequal to this, so she filled in with gestures. Up with the sea sponge; open for the man.

I found it a bit shocking; I looked away.

"I hope you don't mind."

"No, of course I don't mind; I'm a nurse, remember." The birth rate in fishing villages was low. Children were an asset where there was land to work, but a luxury for fishermen.

"I was a theatre nurse," I said, defending myself. "I trained back home in Sydney, at the best hospital. The Royal Prince Alfred."

"A nurse of the theatre?"

Laia was looking at me; I was groping for the words. "I'm a nurse — *la cirugía, operar*." And unaccountably burst into tears.

ONE MORNING LAIA CAME over with her apron held up carefully. Opened it to reveal bright black beads in a flurry of fluff. Four black chicks, a present for me. The next time I took the boat around the cliffs into the town, I bought feed for the chickens and some wire; I made a little hen house, put out food. Laia found it hilarious. Didn't I know chickens wandered anywhere and lived on whatever they could find?

Around this time Laia received a sewing machine, a wonderful gift from her parents in Girona. So on my following journey around the cliffs I found the shop that sold dress materials. Yellow cotton with small white flowers.

"For you," I said.

"It's beautiful," whispered Laia (when she was excited or moved, her voice dropped).

THE VILLAGE WAS GOING to have a medical clinic. Twice a month, a doctor would come on foot, down the hill path, his medical bag carried by Ines. The village was astir with a mix of suspicion and excitement. Ramon's mother and the other older women, who knew about herbs and grasses, were definitely unimpressed. Not so Laia. She was at her sewing machine, making herself a new dress with the material I'd bought her.

She was hesitant about telling me, but at last she admitted it: she was going to sit in the front room of the clinic, asking names and putting them on cards.

Laia would wear her yellow cotton dress with the little white flowers, white buttons and a thin white belt. White sandals. An elegant young woman from Girona.

I watched Laia clatter-clatter down the street, waving at people.

At Sydney's Royal Prince Alfred, in the scrubbing room, the chief surgeon held his hands aloft as one of us slipped on his gloves. A surgeon in gloves, hands raised, is a hierophant, a high priest of the body. When all was ready, the surgeon motioned for a moment of silence. You could hear the traffic going by on Missenden Road. He said, "Ladies and gentlemen, let's get some blood on our hands."

Nobody had so much as thought to ask the Englishman's wife. They must know I'm a nurse, I told myself; here, everything is known.

So, I don't speak the language. Well I have news for you: bodies don't *have* languages. Thus spake the eternal sulker; I was by this time mired in humiliating self-pity.

Then Alec arrived.

HE WALKED DOWN THE hill path with Bernat. Whenever Ines was burdened, Bernat would tie the packages to himself with rope. The day Alec came, the items carried by Alec, Bernat, and Ines included books for Marcus, wine in bottles, sausage, Marcus's favourite cigars, and Dutch butter in tins.

The three of them — Alec, Bernat, and Ines — pushed their way through ramparts of sunflowers and swags of blue convolvulus. I was proud of the flowers, having planted them myself.

The bus had arrived late. It was blazingly hot; the cottage burned in the strong afternoon sun. Inside, it remained cool as a cave. I stood at the door with Marcus, smelling the flowers, the hot dust. It was a quiet time, the height of summer, when the waveless sea seemed to have emptied of fish. The village was silent, sunken into the heat. Boats baked in the sun, deserted.

By now I'd been in the village for several summers and my prediction that Marcus would "come round" had gone precisely nowhere. Our best times had been on trips — to Madrid, to the Valencian shore, the Murcian shore, up to France, and over to Naples, where Leo had treated us with such open-hearted hospitality. We had not been back to England; we did not even discuss the possibility of an expensive journey to faraway Australia.

Alec was squinting in the sun. Marcus stepped forward and the brothers grazed one another with a rough kind of hug. A step up from that essentially British greeting, the handshake.

There they stood, looking at the garden at the side of the house. A company of bees was going after mint I'd allowed to flower; a grey-green bird sat on the wall behind the sunflowers, planning its next rapid raid on insects.

The brothers entered the house, to come out on the library roof, for the view of the bay with its horseshoe curve. The green shutters of the white inn below were closed tight against the heat. The air above the sea shimmered. On the far side of the cove were shadows in the cliff face, the deep sharp shadows of summer.

I stood on the roof behind them.

Marcus was the taller of the two. Streaks of grey had begun to settle in his hair. Alec, with his round shoulders and round head, would pass for a Frenchman rather than an Englishman. Marcus was thicker, older, and he had that pinky northern skin that ages so badly in the heat. With his brother, Marcus became almost chatty, full of gossip about what he'd been digging up. They discussed statutes, baths, columns, sarcophagi, tablets, temples. Alec, too, was full of talk about his work. He had completed his residency in Cardiff, and spent some time at St. Thomas's in London. Now he was on his way to the clinical hospital in Barcelona.

Alec walked through the cottage in the way people do when they've come back to a place they know, letting it flood back into them. I'd forgotten that Alec would have come out to Spain in the long summer holidays. Down to the uncle in Tarragona, up to his brother's village.

To make room for Alec, Marcus gave up his couch in the library and moved back in with me. I watched him making these arrangements. I held a book in front of me and said not a word.

The brothers discussed the bus trip, the delays. "Clearly, Primo de Rivera's famous roads did not reach this far," commented Alec. Primo was the dictator who'd been tossed out by the Republic.

I noticed that after the initial excitement Alec began to speak quietly, as if the stillness of the afternoon had entered into him.

I'd been rehearsing his coming, knowing he would notice the hard spaces between Marcus and me. Did he see already that I had become a shallow, resentful wife with not enough to do?

Alec arrived not only with books and food and drink, but a phonograph record and opinions. Mussolini, he said, was in the grip of a fantasy about turning the Med into an Italian lake. The vastly complicated world of Spanish politics was what captured his closest attention; he spoke at length of the players and the parties. The Republic was in trouble: reactionaries were in the ascendant and they were threatening to dismantle the efforts at modernization. Laia would be energized by this kind of conversation; she was always hungry for news. But Laia was at home, probably lying down beside her husband, enjoying a siesta of passion.

Alec and Marcus talked the rest of the afternoon, with me asking an occasional question. From Alec I formed an image of peasants working day-long on the large landholdings of the centre and south, and in the brief, hungry lunch period, sitting down beneath a solitary tree, soberly teaching themselves to read. He had other stories, too, of a well of violence that did not run dry, turmoil, hatreds, and shootouts between *pistoles* in the city.

"The great thing about up here is," Alec said, leaning forward, "the sea was never a landlord. Clancy would know; you grew up by the sea, didn't you?" I flushed, delighted at having a part of my life remembered by him, however inaccurately.

"No," I said. "We visited on holidays. I grew up in the mountains. But from the edge of the ranges, on a clear day, you could see the sea in the distance." The magic straight line, the ultimate horizon.

He turned his attention back to his brother.

Laia had shown me how to cook two or three dishes that Marcus particularly enjoyed. In celebration of Alec's arrival, I skinned and chopped onions and an aubergine, cut a yellow capsicum in strips. I fried the fish, took the fish out, fried the onions, aubergine, capsicum, added more oil, threw in a bit of wine; carefully put the fish back in, using a slotted spoon.

"Mmm," said Alec, coming to look. "How long will that be?"

I could smell him, standing close behind me.

He asked, idly, how I'd been spending my time. Had I been learning the languages?

"A little," I said. "Unfortunately I have no natural talent."

The house inside which I am trapped. *La casa en la que estoy atrapado. La casa dins de la qual estic atrapada.*

Was either of those correct?

Alec smelled of lettuce. A sweet green smell. It was absurd; he'd been sitting on the bus for hours surrounded by sweat and in close embrace with black sausage.

But how do you say, *because I am a gutless wonder*?

Over a late lunch they spoke of village gossip, what Pau was doing down at the inn, how he'd had a small fire. They spoke about the local big shot who owned the cork forest and continued to see himself as above the law.

Alec found Marcus's phonograph and wiped off the dust with the back of his sleeve. The record Alec brought with him had "Smoke Gets in Your Eyes" on one side and "All of Me" on the other. He played the songs; we listened. Then Alec asked me to dance.

I could scarcely open my mouth. It staggered me, the tension I felt, with Alec.

DURING THE LAST OF the day's heat, Marcus, Alec, and I put on our bathing costumes and walked down the cliff path. We paddled into the amber water, pushed out farther, to where it was green.

Treading water, Alec started a game. What are your childhood memories of fruit? Which you do remember, taste or smell? We'd been drinking anisette liqueur that seeped right into the bloodstream.

The teacher's orange in the schoolroom, its lingering smell on the exceptional days when it rained and he ate his lunch indoors. Lemons growing in deserted Cliffend backyards, untended, hardy, and small. Winter greengages, summer apricots, also abandoned.

I couldn't get a word in. Marcus and Alec were busy rhapsodizing about Almería grapes, their texture, their incomparable taste. I lay on my back, kicked off, watching the wake I was managing to make.

Marcus took off for a solitary swim. In a neat self-contained crawl, he made for what we called the red rocks. It was a fair distance but Marcus was a strong swimmer.

I stopped kicking and was treading water.

Alec came over, paddled in a circle around me.

Waited until the ripples from his body reached mine.

He whispered, *How are things with you?*

Touched my back lightly, with his foot.

ALEC AND I WOULD have the cottage to ourselves. We would have the cliffs, the water. On my walks I'd discovered secret ledges, and tracks that led to the sea.

Alec stood behind me as Marcus walked out the door, up the hill path.

When Marcus was out of sight, Alec whispered, "Are you familiar with the phrase, *coup de foudre*?"

"I am," I replied, not turning around.

I followed Alec into the library where he put on the new record. "Why Not Take All of Me?" It was like lying on the edge of an old mine shaft, then falling down, down into the endless earthy dark.

Without a word, we took our swimming costumes and made our way along the cliffs. We found a sheltered spot; we didn't swim. Above us, spine-tailed swifts were snapping up the air. They have short frail legs and tender feet, and must take off from high places.

ALEC WAS LEAVING AT the end of the summer; no question about that. And I knew it wasn't really a case of the madness of love, not as far as Alec was concerned.

But a little bit, surely? A little bit. Yes.

When Marcus returned from his dig, Alec and I moved into the repertoire of deception. I was surprised at the ease with which I adapted to the lies, the double life — polite with Alec when the three of us were together, but hungrily seeking him out as soon as Marcus headed off on some errand. And as I heard the door open again, immediately nonchalant once more, even though my legs were shaking and thighs still damp.

I counted days, I counted hours, minutes.

Alec promised to write. He didn't promise much else.

WHEN ALEC LEFT FOR Barcelona to take up a residency at the clinical hospital, his letters did arrive promptly each week. For six weeks. After that the letters dwindled; they began to arrive once every three weeks or so. By the turn of the year the tone had changed. He'd begun to write of his work, of politics, of the weather. Then the letters stopped.

I should have packed my bags and left.

Why didn't you leave Marcus? This is a question you will be bound to ask.

Not an easy thing, but not impossible. It happened, even back then. Women packed; women left. Knowing it would be ruinous, they marched to the dressing table and swept away the hairbrush, the hand mirror, the clothes brush; they tossed their underwear into the hatbox and slammed the door behind them.

Other women, more decisive than I.

MY LOVE LETTERS, IF you will. Addressed to Marcus and me.

Dear Marcus and Clance: (Alec sometimes called me Clance, to rhyme with chance.)

"Alec is turning into quite the faithful correspondent," Marcus said, and his face filled with a calm, brotherly pleasure.

"Why doesn't he say what he's doing at the hospital?" I replied quickly, to cover my tracks.

> *I was hanging in a square box of a cable car in the round sky and my thoughts were of you in the village. Below, the city stretched away like a garden, its life crowding towards the water. Columbus was staring out to sea, and beyond, painted ships slept upon a painted ocean. Way down there — so far away, it seemed another era — the frill of surf and cabins row upon row looked like lace on a woman's petticoat flagrantly tossed down in the open air, for all to see.*
>
> *Today, I was in the Grande Oriente and I was looking at the sweets on offer: doughnuts bursting with jam, cream horns, nut biscuits, marzipan patties, crystallized scarlet fruit stiff with its own sugar. I was standing in the Grande Oriente and all I could think was of you in the village.*

I should mention that Alec was not particularly interested in food. He ate on the run, whatever came to hand. He ate like a doctor.

In Canaletas, they grilled a sandwich for me over the fire and spread it, still smoking, with the smoothest of mayonnaise. It slid across my tongue like warm silk.

In the Automatic, the lights were low and the tables were set back in recesses and around me people were whispering to one another and the air was warm with secrets.

The Euskadi was full of dark wood, dark mirrors, dark rooms stretching away into shadow, and you will understand why you came to mind.

In the Moka, I can sink back on the couch in a booth; each of the booths has its little individual thatched roof so I'm on my own private desert island. The radio is playing "Dancing in the Dark" and the smell of coffee is in the air. My own coffee comes and I want to drink that smell. I want, more than anything, to sink my face in it.

I helped myself to a recurrent daydream of our life together. Me and Alec. In Spain. An image of the most banal and self-serving kind: we would work together, we would make ourselves useful. Certainly not on the coast, not in my husband's village (the presumption of being useful to anyone as self-sufficient as those fishermen was too absurd even for fantasy). Somewhere distant. Out on the iron-hard plains, where absentee landlords ruled the roost and people starved on dust — but that was somehow in the past. Alec and I were in a room together: a summer night. The air that came through the shutters was filled with the dry smell of wheat waiting for harvest. We lay on our bed in the darkness and knew ourselves to be part of the fullness, fecund and murmuring, all around us.

The stuff of dreams. *Pouf.*

ONE AFTERNOON, ONE OF the many in which Marcus was off on a dig, I slipped into the library. I looked in his desk, found the letters to us — to me — from Alec. I arranged them on the top of the desk, in order. Left them there. Wanting him to find them, to consider them. Waiting for him to return, waiting for the truth to float up. Waiting, and cruel.

MARCUS STOOD IN THE doorway.

Holding the letters.

"My brother," he said. "My brother."

Marcus returned to the library. He replaced the letters on the desk just the way I'd arranged them. Came out later in what he called his swimming trunks. (He kept his clothes in the library.)

"I'm going," he announced.

He walked down the cliff path.

MARCUS SWAM OUT INTO the wide horseshoe of the bay, out to the red rocks, then farther, much farther.

I watched him from the library roof. One hundred feet, two hundred feet from shore. On the other side of the bay, two fishermen, fishing alone in their small dories, noticed him, the idiot Englishman who swam in the ocean. But in February?

Let him swim all the way to Majorca. Let him.

I lay on the bed, thick and tight with anger. When Marcus understood what was going on between me and Alec he said, "My brother. My brother."

What about his *wife*?

I decided I'd confront him when he came home, dripping. Ask him: How can it be a betrayal on Alec's part when you don't want what he took?

THE FISHERMEN, WHO WERE by this time rowing at full speed towards him, saw him go. They had one of those glass contraptions in a wooden frame you place upon the water, to look below.

One of them dived down into the cold, pulled him up.

THEY BROUGHT MARCUS UP the cliff path, carrying him carefully. Marcus lay on the kitchen floor. The water spread and the tiles darkened.

Ramon arrived from next door. He and the other men stood, murmuring only the essentials.

Laia came running. She was the one who touched me, put her arms around me, held me. I was standing, not moving. Looking, not looking.

I understood that there had been some mistake, that he had winded himself on one of the rocks.

He would come round.

I thanked the men and told them that because I was a nurse I could take good care of him. I would need to clear his air pipe. I didn't know the local word for air pipe and realized I was speaking in English.

"I have smelling salts," I said. "I'll fetch some blankets."

They looked to Laia, who tried to guide me into a chair, which I refused. I had urgent work to do.

I knelt over Marcus. Had the fishermen known how to clear his mouth? I put my finger in his mouth, curved it, turned him over, and slapped him between his shoulders. His hands were tightly closed upon strands of strange, pale sea grass, and I longed to open his hands, make his fingers relax, but first I had to get him breathing again. I knew what I had to do: haul him back over onto his front, his face to one side, arms up. I knelt above his head, applied pressure on the lower ribs, then lifted him by his elbows, to expand his chest.

Warm blankets. I must find some warm blankets.

The men held their berets. They stood.

They had seen drowned men before.

IN THE END IT was done. The fishermen left. Pau from the inn and Pere from the store had come with their wives, and now they, too, had gone. The telephone call for the telegram had been sent from the inn. I'd directed it to Alec's home, to this house in England.

In the bedroom we finished the laying out — myself, Laia, Ramon's mother. In the library, one of the fishermen had made sure the fire was going. It flared up, warming me.

I could not sit on the library couch, Marcus's bed. I sat at his desk.

In front of me, the letters from Alec. They were still on the desk, neatly lined up, in sequence. I had put them there like that myself. Wanting Marcus to realize.

The letters, the evidence. I had intended hurt, humiliation. Revenge.

I was Medusa, snakes flying.

Part Two

Saturday, April 1, 1939

A fortnight ago German armies marched into Prague. The dictators are on a roll. Franco in Spain, Hitler in Germany, Mussolini in Italy. I hope that for you these will be names with faint meaning. I wish they could be so for all of us. Hitler is helping himself to Czechoslovakia and Alec believes the somnambulists of Fleet Street (his phrase) may have finally heard the alarm clock.

It is all the more important that Ross reach us soon. He will find us; he'll have guessed I headed for England.

As for you, you're flourishing. Already you're pushing with your hands; you're making little vocal noises. Helen is smitten. Home for a visit — these days she's spending most of her time in London — she can't leave you alone. She likes to lift you up to smell behind your ears. Claims as honorary aunt number one she understands exactly what you're telling her.

In Spain, even in Madrid, it's over. Desperate supporters of the Republic are fleeing to the ports of Valencia and Alicante. Their only chance of escape is to get on one of the boats coming from France to pick them up.

The Spanish Republic has gone down to defeat. But when I was there with Ross, we heard a phrase from a song we told each other we'd never forget: *it cannot be winter forever.*

Ross may be in Spain tonight. May be among those on the run, making for the coast.

What I'd give to know.

Don't think; don't bargain. Never look hope directly in the eye.

Thursday, April 6, 1939

R oss will arrive from the station. He'll come in the front way. I'll hear the motor and run down by myself.

I'll see him getting out of the taxi, on the gravel drive. I'll leave you safe in your cradle. When Ross has been here awhile, then I'll tell him. I'm so afraid he'll feel *stampeded*. I know I did.

As soon as it's the right moment, I'll race up the stairs, gather you up, take you down to meet him.

He'll stand, and I'll place the bundle in his arms. Watch him receive you, light and strange. See him look down into his own eyes, undeniable. The room, this house, the beech wood, all will drift away. Just the singing of birds, high up.

I'll speak your name, hear the question.

"Dolores?"

"D.R.," I'll tell him, "your initials." He goes by his last name Ross, but his full name is Douglas Ross. Dolores Ross. As you already know, I sail under a surname of convenience, but I put your father's name on the birth certificate. The official, pen in hand, asked me the questions and I answered. My last name. Baby's father's last name. The official wrote our different names down slowly, deliberately, taking pleasure in his disapproval. He thought he'd found us out, you see. As if we'd care.

Wednesday, April 12, 1939

I didn't want to take you, but I couldn't leave you and I had to go. Today we travelled by train to London, to an office for refugees, where a woman with links to Aid for Spain has been making enquires on our behalf.

It was a hideous journey. I could cope with lugging the bassinet on and off the train, with changing you on the floor of the Ladies and feeding you in a lavatory stall in order not to give offence. But how you loathed the train with its smell of soot and the banging of doors. How you protested. Refusing comfort, you arched your back, flailed your little arms and legs, and screamed all the way to London.

"Making inquiries" means looking at lists to see if Ross's name is on them. There are lists from the British consul in Marseilles and lists from the Canadian Pacific Railway company whose ships have taken home Canadians — not out of the goodness of their hearts but because someone has put up the money.

No lists available at this time showed the name Douglas Ross. The woman promised she would make further enquires.

With that, there was a knock on the door; a slender girl arrived with a tea tray. The woman behind the desk took a cup of tea but waved the plate of biscuits away in a display of virtue. Yesterday, in the village, I saw a youngster pick all the currants out of an Eccles cake and throw them into a bin. Such wanton waste.

I balanced a biscuit on my saucer beside the teacup, which shook in my hands.

"Do you," the woman asked quietly, "realize that those who came out of Spain quite often travelled under a false name?"

I nodded. Didn't say, *mate, you're looking at one*. My last name has nothing to do with me.

She persisted. "Have you not heard from him at all?"

I told her about the official from the League of Nations who talked to the soldiers at Cassà de la Selva and wrote the letter to me.

She lowered her head and said she was very sorry to hear about that. Then she closed her file and stood up. As if we had come to the end. As if I, too, was supposed to now rise. And meekly leave.

I would not budge.

I put my cup and saucer down on the edge of her desk.

"All we have here is unreliable rumour. Did the League official ask the most basic questions of the soldier who gave him that story? At the very least he should have asked: 'How do you know it was Douglas Ross? Were you there when it happened? If you weren't there, how can you say it's the truth? If you were there, had you met Douglas Ross before? Did you know him by sight? Could you see clearly who it was in that gully? Didn't you say it was dark? Did you go down into the barranco and look into his face? If you did go down, why didn't you search his pockets?' The League official gave no indication whatsoever that those questions had been asked, let alone answered."

Ross would have been carrying letters from me that had at least two addresses on them. We did that because we moved around so much; our movements were unpredictable and every possibility had to be covered.

"In fact, that letter from the League officer who'd been at Cassà de la Selva was no more credible than a barroom yarn, latrine gossip. At home, we'd call it a 'furphy,' after the brand-name on lavatory porcelain."

That's what I told the woman while you grizzled in your bassinet.

It's a relief to have you safely back here, installed in your cradle. I study your sleeping hands: curved, rosy, small, and smooth. You have withdrawn so completely into your own dreaming. What do you hear? You know my voice but don't know what my words mean. Just as well, or I couldn't speak them.

Tell me, would you take the word of a rumour, or would you wait? Little one, you'd wait; I know it. You'd wait and never stop waiting.

You wake, cry out to be held, want my breast. I take no notice of modern insistence on a rigid, scheduled routine.

With you calm and sucking, we snuggle together, cozy, complicit, submerged. You have developed a delicious suck-tug manoeuvre that stirs the honey way down deep. And while you're doing that, you're gazing calmly away from my breast as if another matter is taking your attention, and you are leading two completely different lives at the same time.

As for me, I'm setting out again, back over the dark rooftops and down, down to Spain.

Words are all I have.

Saturday, April 22, 1939

Alec is beginning to pressure me. I should take a boat home to Australia while there is still time. I should take you as far away from the madness in Europe as it is possible to be.

We can't go, not yet. We can't go until Ross comes. And anyway, I don't have the money.

When Ross gets here we'll leave, the three of us on the boat together. I can picture it easily enough: sailing from Tilbury, goodbye England. South and east all the way, down to Gibraltar, Toulon, Naples, Port Said, through the Suez Canal, Aden, Bombay, Colombo, and Fremantle at last. A trip I've made several times, both coming and going.

The last time I made that journey I was returning to Spain. I was travelling with Edith, the other Aussie nurse. Also on board was Ned, who was to become Edith's lover. But we didn't know that at first because he was a stowaway.

Less than three years ago we were on the boat, Edith, Ned, and me. It was another world.

Four

Australia to Spain, September–October 1936

WE FLOATED OVER THE ocean. We went to present our lives.

The hide of us. Who did we think we were?

At dusk the deck chairs in demand were not on the port side, for the sunset, but on the starboard side, to look back at the land. In the new moonless dark, Edith and I watched the phosphorescence: glittery, erratic.

This was the first evening we were truly at sea.

"I think we've lost it," Edith said. "I can't smell anything. Can you?" I sniffed for the famous scent of eucalyptus, which drifts out to travellers long after any sight of land has vanished.

"Nothing."

We belonged to the ship now. Already we had become more aware of its steady vibrations, of the way it lifts and falls regularly, like an obedient patient instructed to breathe.

For the first ten days, we'd known we were close to home. The *Oronsay* docked at Melbourne and Adelaide before tackling the rolling seas of the Great Australian Bight. Last stop Fremantle. At each port the farewell speeches flared bright with belief. People stood, shy and game, and exposed what they understood to be their best selves.

Between Sydney and Melbourne I told Edith my first stories. How my mother had been a bush nurse, a midwife. Rode from farm to farm and seldom was a baby lost. Had a black Lab who was fond of placenta, preferring it to liver. My mother died in childbirth with me.

I'd trained as a theatre sister, had worked at the Royal Prince Alfred. But when I came home from Spain a few years ago the Depression was in full swing. They'd shut down three of the theatres at the Alfred. All I could find was work in a home for the indigent in Surry Hills. After that, maybe there would be a place in a country town. A town with a river, if I were lucky.

Pillows. Spittoons. Bedpans. Phone the rellies.

"I was sticking the toast under the grill," I said, "when I heard the announcement on 2KL. The Spanish Relief Committee was looking for a nurse to volunteer. *Relief* committee. Lord knows why they took me on."

Edith looked pleased with this easy self-abasement.

I was flashing a cheesy under the grill, for lunch. A gas grill, with the pungent odour that I think of as a Sydney smell. I'd recently received a letter from England, from Helen. *Alec has gone out to Spain in support of the Republic,* Helen wrote, *as no doubt you already know.* I pictured Helen on her bicycle, taking this letter to the post office. She stood up on the pedals as she rode uphill. And no, I didn't know. I was the last person he'd write to with this or any other news. Helen saw me in that public role: the widow. I could not tell whether this was wilful oblivion or genuine innocence.

In Sydney the man from the Spanish Relief Committee came on the radio and explained that one of the nurses had dropped out at the last minute and gave the number for volunteers to call. When I telephoned I was told to go down to Moony's Club in the Haymarket for an interview.

All I knew about the war in Spain was what I'd been reading in the papers since July. When military generals attempted to overthrow the elected government, they had the advantage of obtaining immediate assistance from the fascist powers, Germany and Italy. Hitler was sneaking stuff in through Portugal while Mussolini had occupied Majorca. The government of Spain, meanwhile, had applied to the French government for permission to import arms from France and been refused. England wasn't interested. With the democracies seated firmly on their hands, Spain turned to the Soviet Union to buy military supplies, which were expected soon.

The men behind the table at the interview clearly found this potted version unimpressive. My medical qualifications, however, engendered genuine smiles of approval, which buoyed me.

We left from Woolloomooloo at noon on a Saturday, a bright spring day. I was wearing a polished cotton suit I'd bought on the cheap at Paddy's Markets. Pale blue with navy piping. Some of the groups at the ceremony on the dock presented us with small silk banners, gifts for their counterparts at the other end. Those who stepped forward to speak said that the Spanish Republic had put out a call for volunteers in the struggle and in its own modest way, Australia was responding. Our efforts were part of a broader movement to defend the Spanish Republic against the military rebellion that was being aided by Hitler and Mussolini. Defence of the Republic was a noble cause, and one that was vital if we were going to stop the spread of international fascism. All of which sounded somewhat beyond the reach of two Aussie nurses.

During the speeches, Edith tucked the banners awkwardly under her left arm. Both of us were holding massive bouquets of red carnations and red roses. My bouquet made a lovely contrast against the blue suit. When the band struck up the song about how *we have been naught, we shall be all*, everyone knew the words except me.

Just before the boat sailed, well-wishers on the dock reached out for the fluttering paper streamers we threw down, and held onto them until they snapped.

Edith, who'd grown up with a slew of older brothers, was much at ease in the company of men. As soon as we embarked Edith sweet-talked the purser into giving us a better cabin on B deck, instead of lowly C deck. She promptly bagged the top bunk for herself.

When Edith was in a good mood she would knock on the bathroom door at the end of the corridor and shout, in a perky voice, "Secret police. Open up!" The men appeared to enjoy it.

In Melbourne we responded to the usual question: *Why are you going?* One young pup, out of his depth, asked me, *What made you want to become a nurse?*

Between Melbourne and Adelaide, I admitted to Edith I was a widow. "I married my husband in England and accompanied him to the northeast coast of Spain. My husband was an archaeologist. Often away on digs."

Sitting on deck, I read to Edith from the ratbag newspaper, *The Truth*. A woman's story. Two nights before the big day the woman's betrothed leaves a suicide note. Following directions, she finds a little heap of clothes at Bronte Beach. With that, her elaborate preparations swirled down the drain: the society wedding at St. Stephen's on Saturday afternoon, the lingerie lunch, the kitchen tea, the going-away hat from June's Millinery — yellow straw with cherries flying out of a nest of pale green ribbons. She stood on the sand, looking. She could see his footprints, walking away. Not into the waves. Back up the beach.

"Not even the drama of grief," I said. "Just a heap of dirty laundry on the sand."

Already we were approaching Adelaide.

At the meetings, we pushed each other forward — you can do it, you can do it. We did our best at the Old Temperance Hall in Melbourne but were somewhat tongue-tired with the acting lord mayor and lady mayoress. At the farewell gathering in Adelaide, when the hat was passed round, a young couple, having no money to give, threw in her wedding ring. I saw their swift excited eyes, the woman fiddling with the ring, tugging it off, passing it to her husband, who at once dropped it into the hat. Having done so, he grasped both her hands and kissed her on the lips.

"Lucky buggers," I whispered to Edith. "Wouldn't you give your eye teeth."

Between Adelaide and Fremantle, as the ship churned in the bight, we had our pick of the best deck chairs. Tucking ourselves into blankets, we stared at the mighty southern ocean, and Edith asked me about where I'd grown up, who was in my family.

BEFORE I SAILED FOR Spain I travelled back to Cliffend to say good-bye to Father.

Father had recently abandoned the barber's shop in order to join forces with his old friends, the teacher Mr. MacDonald and Eti the Belgian. The three of them had taken possession of one of Cliffend's largest deserted houses.

"We'll huddle together," Father said.

While Eti did the cooking in the so-called new house, clearly nobody was taking any interest in housework. I found the meth and the turps and gave the place a good going over. All three of them talked about the possibility of going to the coast to escape the table-land winters, a notion I encouraged. The problem was Eti, who was now down to the one house cow. "I can't leave her," he explained. "She couldn't bear it."

"You've brought a spring to an old man's step," Mr. MacDonald said, delighted with the news I was going to the aid of the Republic.

Father looked gloomy. "You're going back there," he said, as if delivering reluctant judgment.

"I'll be home in no time."

"Somehow I doubt that, very much."

As soon as the boat docked at Fremantle, Edith was whisked away for a meeting to which I wasn't invited. In the evening, a public event, more speeches. Only hours after we'd set sail again, Edith announced that we were not to discuss our final destination. If anyone asked, I was to say we were off to Paris to see the sights.

"That's daft," I told her. "We've been farewelled all along the line. It's been in the papers. What about the band on the wharf at Woolloomooloo?"

Edith gave me a nervous look.

"Not exactly hush-hush," I insisted.

We sat together on deck and Edith let me point out words and phrases that she will need to know. *Sanidad, sanitario.*

"Here are some good ones," I said, "these will come in handy: *No entiendo. No sé.* I don't understand. I don't know."

In the indian ocean, the ship sailed on. I became disoriented by the tropics. I was familiar with the flash of refracted light that reduces everything to angular shapes and deep shadow, but I was used to the evening bringing relief. Here the flat waters stretched like a hot silver iron, pushing heat into my face, sending me scuttling for shade. Almost anywhere would have to do, even the stuffy observation lounge. The cabin, boiling below, was out of the question.

I waited until well after dark before I ventured out on deck. Stood at the stern of the boat to catch the small breeze the ship creates as the waters churn back into their solid, molten state. Coming up the rear staircase, I caught sight of Edith walking, head down, at the far end of the promenade deck. She was in deep conversation with a swabbie, a sailor who cleaned the deck. What on earth were they talking about?

Edith returned to the cabin very late. Smug and secretive.

That swabbie had approached Edith with a purpose. After a bit of chit-chat he took her down the stairs that passengers were not supposed to know exist. Led her into the depths of the ship, to the greasers' quarters and an ironworker who'd stowed away in Melbourne. He'd been smuggled aboard by seamen and was hiding in a dark aft compartment that Edith now confidently referred to as the lazaret. This lazaret was crammed full of Granny Smiths bound for the markets of Europe. The engineers were taking care of the ironworker.

He slept, Edith confided, on top of crates of apples.

Sure enough, when Edith emerged from the depths she had about her the fresh smell of green apples.

Edith turned into a shadow on the narrow flight of stairs to bring treats to her own, exclusive stowaway. At table we saved pieces of fruitcake. One of us kept an eye out as the other opened a hankie — a nice big man's hankie, Edith had come well equipped — and quickly slid pieces of cake into it. The hankie was folded, pushed out of sight, and we sat, sipping our really very bad tea. In the warmth of this shared conspiracy, I no longer minded declaring that we were off to Paris to swan about.

At Port Said we went ashore together for the hectic conjurers, the flare of braziers in the alleyways, the mud dwellings, the fortune tellers. We were ushered into the back of a shop, amid strange smelling draperies. The fortune teller stared at my hand. "I see many people, many crowds, many, coming down the road towards you, coming and coming, without end." To Edith, he said, with a gesture of pity, "I see a long life. A very long life."

"At least he didn't see a journey over water," I said, as we waited on the docks for the launch with its flickering lamps.

WHEN WE ENTERED THE Mediterranean the mood of the boat changed — it became more serious, more vexatious. The Mediterranean was closer to one's own real life. Marcus used to say that blindfolded, he could tell the difference between the Atlantic and the Mediterranean. The Med smelled so much more salty.

Just after Edith won the ladies' finals in peg quoits, we had a falling out.

I'd innocently announced at table that when the ship reached Naples, I was meeting an old friend. I told Edith my plans as we were sneaking fruitcake for the stowaway. The table at large was discussing the night's fancy dress ball, which had a Robinson Crusoe theme.

Edith's head jerked up.

"An older man," I added quickly. "An archaeologist. A friend of my late husband's. A learned man."

"But in Italy," said Edith, in distress.

"Yes, in Italy."

Edith scooped the fruitcake into the hankie. Folded it. Then she fidgeted with the sugar bowl. "I don't think that will be possible."

The nerve of her.

"He was a friend of my husband's," I repeated, firmly. Husbands carry weight, even dead ones.

Edith took to her bunk. Turned to the wall. She'd managed to convince herself that I'd be putting us both in peril. The boat would dock; there would be protests by fascists. If I stepped ashore I'd be taken away; Edith would be the one responsible for the disaster.

"You can't be serious," I said, to her back, which she kept turned to me in protest. "You surely don't think I'll be whisked away, never to return."

No response.

"Believe me," I added. "I'm not that important."

"He was a close friend of my late husband," I continued, deciding to soften my tone. "He's really old; he must be over fifty. He's offered to take me to the temples of Paestum. He knew my husband for many years."

After I returned to Sydney, I'd made contact with Leo in order to mail him a picture from our visit to Naples. (Leo and Marcus have their arms draped around each other's shoulders. Both are laughing. A photo that Leo should have, not me.) To my surprise, Leo responded and we began a courteous, reserved correspondence. Part of me longed to talk to Leo about Marcus, but our letters did not approach intimate territory. It would be easier in person.

I lay on the lower bunk and stared at the bunk above. Edith was up there, mutely sulking.

THE BOAT WAS ON the edge of a storm. Deck chairs were being lashed together. I watched the preparations for the bad weather and smoked a cigarette. A slim roll-your-own. Pillowslips, we called them. I was thoroughly fed up with the singalongs, the dancing, the cards, the treasure hunts, the deck games, the rows between C deck and B deck about the use of the bathroom. By now, the boat was packed. At Port Said, a slew of home-going police from Palestine had embarked. They'd filled the remaining cabins on both decks and were treating the voyage as a prolonged drinking binge.

I wouldn't give in. Let Edith turn her back on Naples and cry, I told myself. Here was a woman setting out for a war who'd curled herself into a ball at the first sign of conflict.

Naples. At the height of my clueless marriage, I sat among the clustered palms, enormous wall mirrors, chandeliers, and statuary, and felt a long way from Cliffend.

After several days Edith uncurled herself, came up on deck; took the chair beside me. I understood by this that she'd forgiven me, or was trying to. Together we stared at the sea and waited for the wide sweep of the bay, the pencil line of beach, the first sighting. The sun was warm, the sky was clear, and I was glad Edith had snapped out of it.

She told me the stowaway's name. Ned O'Brien.

I talked to her a little about my husband Marcus and my brother-in-law, Alec.

IN NAPLES I DID go ashore. Nobody sprang out of a black car and hauled me off. As I said to Edith, I wasn't that important.

Leo looked so much older than I'd remembered. Fragile, bony. Officially, I was the widow. Such a simple, pure thing to be.

A fraud.

Leo embraced me with his usual warmth but asked not a single personal question.

Hungrily, he read the newspapers I'd brought, using a magnifying glass. As he moved the glass along the lines of type, his hand shook. "I've not seen a decent newspaper in months. In this country I'm ashamed to say we have descended into the realm of the comic book."

Leo made the reasonable but incorrect assumption that because I was on my way to Spain, I'd be well informed as to what was going on there. He was particularly keen to discuss developments that he could not mention in letters. What was my opinion of the proposed policy of non-intervention? When Republican Spain faced the military uprising, their neighbours in France initially agreed to send in matériel to help them restore order. But the British Prime Minister, Stanley Baldwin, put pressure on the French Prime Minister, Léon Blum, and Blum changed his mind. Together Baldwin and Blum were calling for all countries in Europe not to intervene. Germany and Italy, while busy rushing in arms and troops to help overthrow the Republic, were blithely claiming that they, too, supported non-intervention.

Leo had been in Spain in the spring. It rained most of the time, hindering his work.

"I felt sure Azaña would have this sorted out," he said, frowning. Manuel Azaña was the Spanish president. A few years ago he'd been prime minister of the Republic. For me such changes were part of the dense labyrinth of Spanish politics.

"In Azaña's government," he went on, "there was not a single minister who would not be characterized as a liberal democrat in the French or English context."

I talked about the boat, about Edith, about our stowaway, Ned O'Brien.

Leo and I journeyed to Paestum and he showed me the temples. Families were out searching the ground for fungi after the last of the autumn rains. He told me the temples have parallel rows of columns bending inwards. "A little perspective," he said, "serves to reassure the human brain."

I had not planned on spending my day with Leo talking about politics, the voyage, or temples.

When it came time for me to leave, his eyes filled.

I promised to write, to keep in touch. And I failed to broach anything intimate, unable to find either the courage or the words.

I WOKE EARLY IN the winter morning: still dark. The noise of the engines had changed (it must have been the change that wakened me). We were approaching Toulon. Now that we were due to disembark, I didn't want to leave the boat. The complexity of life on land, the heaviness of it, would be more than I could bear. I wanted the safe petty world of feuding between decks B and C. I wanted to be able to complain about the claustrophobic socializing. I wanted to be able to walk out on deck, see the endless space of water.

A cold, grey morning. Three men arrived on board asking for us, speaking no English. A slow procedure at Customs, where the Cooks agent made a huge deal about arranging for the baggage to be sent on.

Eventually the men who had come for us took us off to a restaurant, where it was quickly established, despite the language barrier, that Edith was a comrade. I asked for a vermouth even though it was only 9:30 in the morning. Edith drank coffee and swung her legs, waiting.

The moment of triumph arrived when she leapt to her feet and there he was, walking towards us, smiling easily, his hair flaming around him: Ned O'Brien, the stowaway. Up from the bowels of the ship, smuggled safely ashore.

Tall, gangling, thin, Adam's apple bobbing like a fish. The whole restaurant understood right away that *he* was a comrade. With his wild, heroic hair, with his mixture of utter conviction and wishful thinking, Ned O'Brien appeared to be exactly the man of the moment. If you're racing from a tidal wave, if you're dangling from a cliff, if you're fighting tyrants, give us a man like Ned. Inhaling great draughts of warm smoky restaurant air, Ned was so enthusiastic, so clearly a good bloke that the French greeting party relaxed completely.

Someone in the know who spoke excellent English showed up. A farewell was taking place that evening for a contingent of locals who were going to fight for the Spanish Republic. He took one look at Ned O'Brien and wanted to invite the lot of us. After we'd worked out that we couldn't be at the meeting because we had to catch the night train to Marseilles, we were driven to some offices on the boulevard Jean Jaurès and had our picture taken.

At Marseilles we were greeted with vast immediate affection. It was as if word about Ned had been sent ahead. Ned pumped the hand of a French worker and Edith said something admiring about the Popular Front and grinned at the men like a woman drunk with love, which she was.

Some la-di-dah ladies arrived from the Henri Barbusse Society and took me and Edith away to a tea room for a feast of rich fancy cakes. Of course, with this posh lot I didn't dare have a ciggie, although I was dying for one. We did the round of small talk and wondered what was next.

To everyone's relief two more women arrived with a bunch of winter woollies. Not for us. For soldiers at the front. Eventually we were deposited at the Hôtel de la Poste.

Edith lay on her bed, complaining of cramps.

We'd been told to go to a pharmacy on the rue Cerbère for more supplies. She handed me the name on a piece of paper: *Pharmacie La Méditerranée*.

"You don't have to write it out for me," I said. Then I realized she was daunted by the prospect of having to pronounce it. After two days in France it was clear that even fairly recognizable words were hazardous.

"Could you get me a bottle of peroxide?" Edith was what we

called a "bottle blonde." Would there be peroxide still in Spain? Nobody knew.

It was good to be out by myself in the windy rain, but I felt low, alone.

I hauled back supplies of cotton wool, gauze, and rubber aprons. Peroxide for Her Nibs.

IN THE EVENING AT a large gathering at the Cinema St. Lazare, Edith hit the right note by speaking of the importance of supporting "the anti-fascist people of Spain, who are waging a heroic struggle."

The emcee told the story of Ned the Stowaway. In the audience, murmurs of admiration.

Ned explained that he was going to help the Spanish Republic "because he had to." He spread his hand wide in a straightforward gesture. The Spanish Popular Front, Ned O'Brien told the Marseilles workers, had been elected by the will of the people and as such was entitled to the backing of the democracies of the world. It was, when you got right down to it, simply a matter of everyone getting a "fair go." The translator had a bit of difficulty with "fair go" but it didn't matter to the crowd, not a scrap.

After that one of our French hosts delivered a lengthy speech, translated for our benefit. His words were delivered in a hectoring tone I immediately distrusted. I began to listen in a critical way.

Why, in the midst of this fine feeling, was I wanting to take issue, to find fault?

Next speaker: a British journalist. Recently he'd taken a taxi, with several others, from Madrid down to Aranjuez. There they were surprised on the road by a large number of Moorish cavalry who promptly shot the taxi driver. Behind the cavalry came a bunch of Italian whippet tanks. I'd never heard of a whippet tank, but I could guess. One of these tanks, the journalist told us, turned over in a ditch. The journalist foolishly helped the chap climb out. The ungrateful rescued man waved a pistol. He spoke no Spanish, only Italian.

As the journalist talked, the feeling in the cinema was one of closeness, like the very best of getting drunk. We were just after the drink that makes you ready to talk, ready to laugh, when everyone loves you. You don't know these people, not personally, but it doesn't matter in the least, they'd do anything for you, you'd do anything for them. Like go off to a war.

I was one drink behind.

The sentiment continued to gather speed; it built into a swift, strong current. Inspired, Edith and Ned were giving each other looks that I knew I shouldn't be seeing. I studied the floor.

Moorish cavalry. What do the Moors look like? I'd read the descriptions: white Arabian horses with golden hooves and men in orange cloaks. Top of the fascist pops: *I love a parade*. Moor; floor. The floor of the cinema had been varnished a long time ago and the paint was badly chipped. I wondered when they'd next get round to doing the place up. Probably not anytime soon.

Three hundred or more were on their feet. They were singing the "La Marseillaise" and the "Internationale" and giving the clenched-fist salute. Ned O'Brien's hand shot up with ease; Edith's was just as quick off the mark. Eventually, my hand fluttered up, weakly waving. I was hideously embarrassed but very much moved. What starring role was I aiming for? Joan of Bloody Arc?

BACK IN OUR ROOM, Edith had a go at me about that wave. I attempted to defend myself. "I don't feel comfortable; it's like I'm putting something on."

Edith said, smartly, "Nonsense, it's the salute of international democrats."

"So that's what we are."

"I can't think why you want to be so cantankerous."

We lay awake in the dark, the room crackling with ill feeling.

I thought of my father sitting in his barber's chair, reading. He'd like Ned, I decided. In the old barber's shop, Ned would take a seat by the wall and stick out his legs. Ned would be as much at home in Cliffend as he had been tonight at the Cinema St. Lazare. Would that be a sign of wisdom or of ignorance?

It was hard to stay mad at Edith for too long because there was so much she had to hold in. Down in the lazaret with Ned, that was one thing, but up here — out in the open — it would be so much more complicated. Her heart was racing like a bush fire. Anyone who saw her staring anxiously in the mirror would appreciate that.

The next morning Edith was up and out before me. Another cold, windy day. I took myself for a long walk in the old port district, came back warm from the exercise, almost content.

The room had a kidney-shaped, cheap dresser with a mirror. Edith had piled her things there, scattered and messy. An exercise book from back home.

Edith's handwriting was unsteady and rather endearing. At first sight.

She identified me as having "no precise political beliefs."

Under that, a small arrow pointed to some notes:

Years in Spain?
Money to travel?
Husband?

I let her come in and chatter away. She was bubbly. A good morning with Ned O'Brien, I bet.

Then I sprang it on her.

She shot right back. What did I think I was doing, snooping in her personal belongings?

"What are you up to?" I countered. "What's this tommyrot about political beliefs? Says who?"

Edith's eyes brimmed with tears.

"Don't turn on the waterworks," I said. "It was you doing the writing."

She went no-speakers on me. The pre-emptive pout.

On Sunday night, a night when the locals didn't dine out, a man came to take us to dinner before we embarked for Spain. A stuffy enclosed room in gilt and white, very quiet. Edith and Ned on one side, me with our host on the other.

Amazing what you find out when a stranger starts asking questions of someone you think you know. Edith grew up at Manly. Her father played the violin on the Manly Ferry.

I said I was a widow and that my English husband had died in Spain.

Husband?? Make that two question marks, Edith old thing. You go right ahead.

I didn't say how he died.

Our host loved the stowaway story. He asked Ned a heap of questions and I found out Ned had been an ironworker in the shipyards, more often out of work than in. Between jobs he went bush and lived on rabbits. "You felt your insides turning to fur," Ned said. The man was puzzled. Didn't share Ned's low opinion of rabbit.

Edith hadn't looked me in the eye, not since the latest row. She had her hand on Ned's thigh under the table, I could tell by the position of her arm.

Shellfish in cassis, turbot with light wine, small birds roasted unstuffed, browned in their own juices, a bitter salad. Neither Edith nor Ned could have ever tasted anything as remotely good as this in their lives.

Bombe glacée. Roquefort and Brie.

Bordeaux with the birds; burgundy with the cheeses.

My late husband, I told our host, had been in France during the Great War; wounded at Neuve-Chapelle.

Aahh.

The French always acknowledge, are always grateful.

The wine crept into Edith's face, while Ned ate and ate and looked entirely happy.

Our host kept things going by asking questions about the strange reversal of seasons. (You will find that the other hemisphere does excellent service as small talk.)

At the end of the leisurely meal, the head waiter embraced our host and a car arrived to take us to the docks. A night full of rain and I'd drunk too much. The boat seemed to rise out of a mist. A smallish vessel, dirty beige. British.

The car left. Silence in the wet night.

In the saloon we were introduced to the bulldog under the table, and the canary. Ned found the ball for the bulldog and the obese little chap charged around the saloon, spit flying. Ned laughed and handed the wet ball to Edith. She grimaced. He winked at her, took it back, threw it again.

The captain offered Ned the rest of the prunes and custard, which Ned devoured, oblivious of any outrage. After a round of chat, the captain showed us to our cabins. Ned was to have a cabin to himself. "Look," he marvelled, "a reading light. I've never slept in a bed with a reading light."

In my own bunk I told myself to be prepared — tomorrow I would be in Spain. But I fell asleep quite quickly, which I usually don't, after I've been drinking. I woke in the middle of the night, aware I was alone. Edith must have joined Ned O'Brien in his cabin. He would have forgotten about the reading light.

The next morning we were taken off, the boat not having moved. This was how it was going to be, I told myself: decisions made you know nothing about, decisions reversed. You go here, you go there, and do not ask questions. It was going to demand the patience of a domestic animal.

Another day in Marseilles and nobody seemed to know what to do with us. Our host from the restaurant arrived with chocolates and fruit for the overnight train journey to Cerbère.

Ned was to travel as far as Cerbère and then leave us. Ned would walk the passes into Spain, up over the Pyrenees.

CERBÈRE AT ABOUT FIVE in the morning: a bored customs official came though the train, followed by a money-changer.

Edith pulled at strands of her hair as tears began to slip down her face. Looking embarrassed, Ned put an awkward arm around her shoulder.

She wanted so much more than that.

I didn't like the thought of being parted from Ned either.

At this stage the frontier was iffy for potential combatants. It wasn't yet shut solid, but it would be dodgy for Ned to stay on the train.

"Keep safe," we cried out. "Good luck!"

Ned left, and Edith's strength departed with him. Exhausted, she sat in the compartment, not looking out, unwrapping chocolates one after the other and putting them into her mouth. I was sure she wasn't tasting a thing. Waste of good chocolates, I thought.

The train finally crept through the tunnel, with its dark opening. It moved slowly into the large, modern station of Port Bou, and we had arrived in Spain.

We looked about with the curiosity of newcomers. Workers were servicing the Spanish train; we could have been anywhere. On one side of the station was a small church with fine white brickwork on its spire. Ahead, a massif of rock, another tunnel.

In the shed at Port Bou, when I heard again the sharp, rising inflection of the language, when I stepped up to the official, when I attempted a few words and saw his stony face open, I took over. No protest from Edith, who was overawed by the militia interrogators in their blue overalls busy going through the bags, watched by a few leisurely older officials in green uniforms.

I flashed the letter from the British consulate. The officials smiled at my daft pronunciation and gave us good seats.

We waited for the train to shudder away. In front of us, the tunnels in their bed of rock. When we pass through them, I told myself, I will see what the future holds.

The first tunnel, then, gathering speed, the other. Out we slid into steep brown hills, with glimpses of a grey sea.

There it was again.

On these hills were rows of low branches: grape vines, gnarled, twisted, cut back.

A herd of black goats.

Partridges, rising nervously from a field.

Vegetables growing near the riverbeds.

We moved down through the fields of Catalonia in a thick autumn rain, in our hats and gloves, travelling first class to the war.

Workers in the fields waved at the train, joined their hands together over their heads. "An anarchist salute," I told Edith, to annoy, "signifying the unity of all mankind."

Five

WHEN EDITH AND I first arrived in Barcelona we had nothing to do. We were billeted together in a small hotel on a street just off the top of the Ramblas, where we awaited word of Ned O'Brien. On the Ramblas, we watched yellow trams follow one another up the broad thoroughfare. While this was no longer the city of the summer's newsreels, the streets were aflame with declaration.

Those newsreels showed pictures of militia driving recklessly in trucks and fancy commandeered cars, with initials hastily chalked on the side, their flags red-and-black in the hot wind. With a nervy confidence men and women were hanging out the car windows. In blue overalls and short sleeves, they hummed with dangerous, pent-up loyalty. Anyone who watched could smell the excitement of destruction and triumphant, soaring change. There were also pictures of the aftermath: horses dead in the square in the July sun, big bellies rearing up, their legs stiff in front of them, strangely useless.

ATTACHED TO BRITISH MEDICAL Aid, Edith and I were sitting in cafés, idle as tourists. In the Ramblas, crowds gathered around places that had a radio, listening. Whenever there was a broadcast, the air became electric. The news was of the resistance in Madrid. People raised their faces to the sound of the radio as if to sunshine.

For me the political situation was full of surprises. When I lived in the village there was an important Spanish politician called Gil Robles, for whom Alec harboured a particular antipathy. What had happened to him? He seemed to be off the scene completely. I assumed he would turn out to be a mate of Franco's, but apparently not. Very much on the scene was Francisco Largo Caballero, the prime minister. Big bloke, a bricklayer who learned to read in prison. Largo: wonderful name. I couldn't remember him, and decided he must be relatively new.

In the cafés, the talk was of what Dolores Ibárruri made of Largo Caballero. Ibárruri was a small woman everybody knew as La Pasionaria. She was in the government — the Cortes — and a huge celebrity, the carrier of intense, shared hope. When the military uprising began, she'd ended a speech on the radio with the slogan, *¡No Pasarán!* They shall not pass! And now it was repeated everywhere. If La Pasionaria so much as cleared her throat, people went crazy.

The most serious talk was about the Popular Front. The Popular Front had been elected at the beginning of the year and I formed the impression that it was somewhat like a polygamous marriage which made the partners deeply uneasy. Like everything else in Spanish politics, there was little I could hope to figure out that would be in the least bit accurate about the massively complicated Popular Front. Of anything I said, the opposite could also be true. But the Republic needed a united front against the rebels. So it was geraniums on the windowsills and everyone acting matey.

For something to do, Edith and I gave blood. Down the Ramblas, into a side street, past the lottery sellers — blind men with white canes, their tickets held out in front of them like fans — past a church where slogans had been chalked on the walls, into a small clinic deep in blue shadow. A very short young woman expertly slipped a needle into my vein, then into Edith's, speaking in a pleasant blunt voice and staring at us both in that frank local manner. And I realized that the rising and somewhat harsh inflections had, after only three days, become normal and I no longer even noticed them.

We walked back up, saw the sweet sellers — women sitting with legs wide under long skirts, holding the trays on their knees; the cigarette sellers, wooden trays around their necks, selling *Elegantes*; the barrel organ, union initials painted on it, with two organ-men in velvet trousers and old coats. I looked for the cigars Marcus had been fond of — from the Canary Islands — but did not find them.

For a two-o'clock lunch in the roof garden, I met up with Edith at the Jorba, a department store that had been taken over by the workers. The menu wasn't great, but surely that was only to be expected. We ate small curled fish with pointed snouts, picking them up with toothpicks and dropping them into our mouths. The store seemed to be running smoothly, right down to the Ladies toilets on the third floor and the fountain playing on the rooftop, with its large aquarium of lazy fish.

I bought a few handkerchiefs, admired the lace.

"Who needs bosses?" I said to Edith.

She gave me a guilty look.

Off the Ramblas, I recognized the place where they used to roast chicken: a large open-air fireplace with blackened bricks. It was empty. (*What's that divine smell?* I'd asked Marcus, and we both hurried towards the smell, excited. Many times I'd been relaxed with Marcus, comfortable with him.)

My body clenched when I picked out the cafés of Alec's letters: the Automatic, the Canaletas, the Euskadi, and the rest. You could see women here and there but I did not venture inside. One sunny afternoon I got as far as the broad terrace of the Moka. Militiamen sprawled in the chairs, talking, drinking, and watching the crowds, cheerful.

Edith was off somewhere, so I walked by myself and took the funicular up Montjuic. The cable car was no longer running and the coloured water in the fountains had been turned off. That smudge on the horizon just might be Majorca, but Majorca had fallen to the Italians, who were using it for their planes. Down there, where the cable ended, was the beach with its high, narrow shingle.

I'd planned to come up here with Alec. My idea was that we'd take the cable car down to the beach. Swim in the water; go back to one of those cabins that Alec had imagined as rows of lace. Lie on the rough wooden floor of the cabin, both of us wet and warm. A private place.

Part of the way down the mountain, I passed a restaurant where I could smell meat turning on a spit. I couldn't help myself; I ordered a meal I couldn't afford, but felt better for the luxury of it.

There were mild shortages: croissants but no butter, coffee but no sugar.

In the afternoon I visited the Strangers Department of the *Socorro Rojo* and asked in vain if I could be of any help. Back on the Ramblas, store windows were being taped with paper — brown streamers, crisscrossed. I watched a storekeeper unwinding the paper like a long curly snake. His store was busy, selling badges and handkerchiefs and passing out information about what to do in case of air raids. More and more talk about the defence of Madrid, where things were desperate.

In the cafés, we few Australians found one another — usually among the British. Two young Australian women had become regulars at our table. One displayed the tiresome enthusiasm of a child who for the first time in her life was allowed to stay up all night, unsupervised. The other, timid and easily discomforted, held careful opinions, reluctantly offered up. One morning these two were joined by an Aussie cyclist. He'd come to Barcelona for the Workers' Olympiad — a counter to that charade in Berlin — and stayed on. The cyclist had been on the Huesca front. He sat on the edge of the wrought-iron chair, uneasy, ready to spring up.

The cyclist was the one who brought Ned.

Ignoring traffic, Ned bounded across the broad street. Edith, who was preoccupied with trying to decipher parts of the newspaper *Mundo Obrero*, looked up. She gasped.

Ned lifted Edith off her feet, while the rest of us at the table applauded.

Edith was flushed, unable to speak. Her mouth was pink; she trembled like a young colt. "I've been waiting," she said at last. "Every single second."

Ned was keen to talk with the cyclist about the front. At Huesca, the cyclist claimed, he was driven crazy by the interminable ringing of church bells. From the hills above Huesca you could look right down into the town, see people crossing the street, hanging out their washing, going to market. Apart from the bells, it was pretty quiet.

The cyclist told the story about the priest in Huesca who climbed a tree in the morning with his gun and his plug of tobacco. He passed his days taking potshots at Republicans. At noon he recited the Angelus while kneeling in the fork of the tree. Speaking of which, the best way to spot a Moor hiding up a tree was to wait for him to shift his legs. He'd be wearing those white gaiters, you see, and sure enough, at some point he'd just have to cross or uncross his legs. The flash of white gave him away. Both items to bear in mind if you were on the lookout for a priest or a Moor up a tree anytime soon.

The cyclist delivered this as if he'd just come from the Mad Hatter's. Then sat back, enjoying the ripples of interest.

After lunch we got up a foursome: me, the cyclist, Ned and Edith. We hired a rowing boat to take us out into the harbour. Ned and Edith sat behind the rower. Ned tickling, Edith giggling. "Edie," Ned called her. His Edie.

The rower, a local man, was small and ancient and slow. I could feel the impatience of the cyclist beside me. Give him the oars, I thought, and we'd be zooming over the water as in an early film.

Ned and Edith didn't care where they were, what they saw. Everyone has a right to that kind of silly happiness, I told myself; who would not want it?

The rower pointed out the sights: the elaborate modern buildings in golden stone, a hulk that until very recently had held political prisoners, and by the breakwater, rows of the famous local mussels hoisted out to dry. The smell reminded me of Father down at the coast, coming in from fishing, leaving a bucket of saltwater by the door, blue mussels inside.

Back at the hotel Edith put her hair up in nasty steel curlers. Purred around the room. She was going dancing with Ned at the Café Shanghai. I'd not been there.

One day I'll show you the photograph we had taken on the plaça by the fountain in front of the Hotel Colón: me, Edith, and Ned. We're wearing coats but we women have discarded our hats and gloves. Ned's smiling at some joke he's just cracked. We're in front of the fountain, among the pigeons that have been dropping on the banners. Behind us, to one side, you can see two sweet sellers. At the corner of the big hotel, on the round roof that looks like a candle snuff, someone has erected a large hammer and sickle. On the main facade you can make out the big banners of Stalin and Lenin, two stories deep. (The Lenin banner fell down a few weeks later and nobody bothered to replace it.)

At the Hotel Colón guards stood about and sandbags were piled at the windows. Across the front of the hotel a huge sign declared *Partit Socialista Unificat de Catalunya*, PSUC. I'd not heard them mentioned when I was here before. I decided they could not have been anything to speak of a few years ago or Alec would have said something. Marcus never noticed such things, but Alec certainly did.

NED WAS IN AN excited mood because tomorrow he was going out to the barracks. He'd had an argument with someone at PSUC. Got frustrated with the delays and paperwork, sprinted down the road and joined up with the Spanish Workers' Party, the POUM, short for *Partido Obrero de Unificación Marxista* — but nobody used the full name. This was another group I'd not heard of before.

Edith was none too happy with Ned's decision. In recent weeks, the POUM had been under a cloud for supposedly not supporting the war effort. You could tell Ned hadn't heard anything about that, or if he had heard, he'd dismissed it as unimportant.

Edith frowned, decided to say nothing for now.

Ned invited Edith and me to the Hotel Falcon, where the POUM hung out. Patches bloomed high on Edith's cheeks but she agreed to come along.

I recognized the sun blinds with red stripes on the balconies, faded and looking somewhat more battered. It was where Marcus and I stayed on our leisurely honeymoon, but I didn't plan to mention that.

Ned took us up to the first floor lounge, a large room under a sunroof. We had to walk up; the little gilt cage of a lift was out of order. Fug of smoke, much talk, groups in chairs, heads turning briefly to check the newcomers, then turning back.

The lounge had a constantly busy air. Crates, vats of wine, and stacks of equipment were ranged along one wall. Along another, piles of clothing and blankets, with young people lounging on them. Even as we were finding a place to sit, leather jackets with zip fasteners were being handed out, along with berets — winter gear at last. It was a mixture of pub and street scene, tired in a friendly, spirited, very youthful way.

A grey day, and the light coming from the sunroof was weak. Lamps had been switched on. Dark wainscotting against pale walls. A guitar was playing, there were snatches of singing, laughter rising and falling. Pools of yellow light by the chairs. A large wooden stairway, with more wide, dark wainscotting that people could perch on. Some youngsters were up there, swinging their legs and chatting.

At the table, the talk was about the Generalitat, the Catalan government, about this party's man in that government: Andrés Nin, a short thick chap with curly hair, heavy fashionable spectacles, and a fine set of teeth. I knew what he looked like from poring over the papers. There was so much to find out.

At least by now I'd become accustomed to the way in which the radio intoned the word, "Madrid, Madrid." On my first day on the Ramblas, when I tried to catch what was being said on the radio, I'd been left wondering what *Mathdree* meant. The insurgents had reached the western and southern suburbs of Madrid and the capital was under siege. Franco controlled some provinces in the north and south of Spain but Madrid was the prize he so dearly wanted. He was not going to have her; the Popular Army and the *madrileños* would see to that. But the government had moved down to Valencia on the coast because they were afraid the road was going to be cut. I couldn't imagine what it must be like to be in Madrid.

Madrid was the heart of the world.

This is what we talked about, what everyone talked about: Madrid was supposed to have fallen on the first of October, then on the twelfth, then on November the fifth. On November the seventh, Franco announced he would hear mass in Madrid on the following day. The rebel radio station in Lisbon lapped this up, supplying vivid descriptions of Franco's entering the city to rapturous ovations. All of which a famous American correspondent repeated, right down to the dog following the procession, barking for joy.

It didn't happen. They did not pass; Franco did not take Madrid but Hitler and Mussolini recognized him anyway. To celebrate, the rebels bombed the city indiscriminately: civilians, hospitals, anyone. This was something modern, something brand-new.

Madrid was due to be taken by Franco before the new year. Fat chance. Stay tuned.

We sat within our sofa's pool of light discussing this news. On another sofa, a group of people were playing chess. They were talking quietly, their heads together. Their subdued, detached demeanour made me think they might have recently returned from the front. But what did I know?

Edith was lured into conversation by a serious Dutchman. I took him for a German but was corrected with a stiff schoolmasterly nod. He had oblong glasses in steel rims and spoke painfully precise

English. Were we winning the war or losing the revolution? If the revolution were to be lost, how could the war be won? He asked Edith these questions in a calm voice, drawing her in. He started out believing he was talking with Ned, but Ned wasn't up to batting this kind of thing back and forth.

The Dutchman lay idea upon idea, a trim, methodical talker. Not having divined Edith's distress, the Dutchman moved along, unperturbed.

Ned wasn't interested in any of it. He wanted the fellow to talk about being at the front. Had he been to the front? Yes. Doing what? Driving an ambulance.

I wondered what ambulances looked like at the front. I'd seen them here, streaming through the streets: dirty white, with a yellow-and-white pennant flapping in the wind. The effect seemed to me somewhat papal but of course I hadn't said so.

The Dutchman turned back to Edith.

Ned stretched his long legs, looked around, smiled at a tall woman, signalled for her to come over. She was in those blue overalls called "monos" — they were going out of style, being replaced by khaki uniforms. Under her overalls she was wearing a postbox-red sweater. Her lips, too, were bright red. She had her tasselled militia cap on, and beneath it her fair hair was sticking out. A serene face. The effect was one of faux innocence, and very attractive. To dress like a tomboy was to draw attention to one's feminine beauty. Ned was happily distracted from the serious chatter. We pushed up along the sofa to make room for her.

She waved her hands when she spoke. A gesture, I decided, that began as an affectation in adolescence but had by now become habit. She told me that before the war she lived each summer in Sitges. I imagined her in a garden thick with heat, her face sunburned and northern. Why had she stayed on? Had she been married herself, perhaps? I wondered what we might have been able to talk about if the others weren't there.

Some incorrect response from Edith became too much for the

Dutchman to bear. He stood up quickly. Announced he was going in search of something for us to drink and didn't come back.

Edith was sitting with her legs crossed. Ned reached down, and, in front of me and the lovely Sitges tomboy, caressed Edith's ankles, first one, then the other. Edith blushed fiercely, pushed his hand away. Ned sat back, laughing, pleased with himself.

I found the bar and bought glasses of wine, which we drank before wandering off.

While we'd been sitting there the sun had come out. Its light fell through the skylight in straight shafts, so that when I looked back into the room, the blue cigarette smoke was illuminated. The room floated in a smoky dream.

Sitges had already attracted another group of admirers.

I would see the Dutchman once more, just before I left Barcelona for Aragón. A funeral procession was in progress, a modest affair. He'd climbed on the hearse, and as it moved along slowly he was making a speech. Climbing on a hearse to make a speech was not that unusual. He talked, he exhorted; no doubt it was meant to inspire himself as much as others. It was raining and windy and the locals hurried by.

A FEW DAYS AFTER our trip to the Falcon, I was grilled at the Foreigners Bureau and it became clear to me that Edith had been dobbing me in, snitching.

I was questioned by five men. A long desk in a grand room ruined by the addition of tacky low partitions. An important hum.

Two Poms sucking on pipes, acting very much in charge, did the talking. Also present: one small Frenchman who despite his casual clothing looked exactly like an anxious banker, and two Catalans, sitting as pissed-off observers.

Why had I come back to Spain?

I had come back, *I didn't tell them*, because I drowned my husband here and his brother Alec was somewhere in Spain. And, *I didn't ask*, if you lot are the spooks around here, would you mind telling me where Alec is right now?

What had I been doing, going out on my own, unaccompanied?

Ah, so Edith had snitched on me about that, too.

Walking to places I had seen with my husband. On our honeymoon.

Stick that in your pipes.

I RETURNED TO THE hotel, lay down on my bed, and lit a cigarette. At least I could count on Edith's not showing up; she'd gone off with Ned somewhere. Without a word to me, Edith had arranged for us to come over to the Hotel Pasionaria. (Pasionaria, I kid you not.) We packed our bags; I trailed after her in the street.

The Hotel Pasionaria turned out to be a former convent and cold as both poles squared, cramped with many children and few mothers, all of them kicking up a constant ruckus. At the Hotel Pasionaria you could enjoy the deep freeze along with the piercing distress of refugees.

Don't even daydream about a hot bath. Fully clothed, I climbed into bed and thought of Edith and Ned out together. I pictured Ned laughing, Edith's face turned up. I pulled the blankets over my head, sank into the shell of my body, and dreamt.

The woman from Sitges wears bright red lipstick and wide shoes, like boats. She has just been addressing a huge crowd to wild applause. Now we are in the Falcon only it's deserted; she's playing the piano. She turns and says, "You killed your husband, didn't you? From the moment I saw you, I knew."

IN BARCELONA, A FUNERAL for some Bavarian shot in the defence of Madrid, much quoted as having said, "The road back to Berlin is through Madrid." How did that start, saying the road to one place was through another?

A massive funeral, with people lining the pavement and filling the balconies, and much singing of the national songs, the anarchist songs, the communist songs, everyone together in the streets. The flower shops in the Ramblas had been emptied. The man being honoured was a German in the International Brigades who fell in the defence of Madrid. A former member of the Reichstag, he'd been in Dachau, in solitary. He'd strangled the guard, taken the guard's clothes and escaped to Prague.

As we walked in the funeral procession, this story was told again and again.

In battle he had the calm of a land surveyor, they said. Outside a village northwest of Madrid, he lay on the ground, his wool-lined jacket open, a small hole through his sweater above the heart. He'd exposed himself to fire because he'd heard someone wounded, crying out for help.

Cheering and being cheered, I was to march with the women's international contingent. I looked around for the woman from Sitges, but didn't see her. Huge flower wreaths — red, yellow, and purple for the Republic, red and gold for Catalonia. Lots of chrysanthemums, which were in season. Many other wreaths in red alone, some red with the hammer and sickle picked out in white.

Not like Edith to miss this kind of bash. She was going to be late because she was seeing Ned off to the front. The barracks were way out on the edge of the city; she'd have to cadge a lift back.

A group of Germans marched smartly by, some with shaven heads, some with walrus moustaches, singing the "Internationale" in their own language, then shouting *Rot Front!* The crowds sang the perky "El Himno de Riego." They sang the broad and sturdy Catalan national song, "Els Segadors," the reapers. They sang the little hurdy-gurdy tune that passed as the POUM anthem.

We were in our various sections, waiting to join in. Children first in little militia caps, followed by cavalry, with the horses stepping sideways, tails swishing, uneasy at having to pace so slowly. People reached out their hands to touch them. A big velvet muzzle pushed itself into my hand and I was startled by the reassuring warmth. Behind the horses, militias, only a few stepping as if born on a parade ground, the rest slouching, talking, turning around to greet friends, all with the ease of a street party.

With our banners, with gigantic wreaths, singing our secular hymns, we lifted ourselves up, right up, into that place of dissolving. So that when, in front of the Hotel Colón, the corpse, carried proudly aloft, was addressed directly by a loudspeaker, I floated into the words.

The English memorial for Marcus had been nothing like this. The vicar mounted the pulpit and the words he spoke hung untouched in the frozen air above us. I in my guilt did not once look up to claim them. At that service I buried my face in my gloved hands. The gloves had been cleaned and smelled of petrol.

Waiting to join the march, I watched the local *milicianos* trooping by, belting out their songs. They were wearing monos, the workers' overalls. In between blasts of "A las Barricadas!" the cheap material brushed against their thighs as they marched. The onlookers heard the swishing and started imitating it, making the sound with their tongues: swish, swish, swish. For some reason up ahead, the procession had come to a standstill. One group started singing "Sons of the People" loudly. The group in front responded with the "Internationale." Who could sing the loudest won, like a contest in the stands at a football final. It ended with cheers and tasselled caps being thrown in the air, people joking, the retrieval of caps, followed by some chanting. The procession moved on.

This was my second funeral in Spain. Marcus was buried here. We had held the memorial for him back in England. Marcus's body was interred alongside his uncle's in the English part of the cemetery at Tarragona; the service in England was a gathering for the family.

During the arrangements and the burial in Spain, Alec treated me with the utmost, frigid courtesy. From Tarragona we travelled by train to Madrid in order to catch the plane to London. I remember waiting for the plane in Madrid, acutely thirsty but unable to stir myself to find a drink, unable to move from the chair in which I slumped, cowed by the steel-and-glass modernity of the place. The journey — from the village down to Tarragona, up to Madrid via Valencia, over to London, and finally onto the train and home to sodden countryside — was undertaken by Alec and me sitting together in mute proximity. So much as an accidental slight touch of arm or thigh was greeted with a shudder of withdrawal. In public places, Alec would open a door for me and stand well back. The inquisition did not start until we reached English soil. *What lies did you tell him?* Alec demanded. Within days his questioning had swollen into full prosecutorial rhetoric. *What lies did you heap upon him?*

AT THE END OF the Ramblas I caught sight of Edith in the crowd opposite. Her face weary in the cold sun. I thought she'd said goodbye to Ned. But she announced, "He's fallen ill. Of course he couldn't go off like that."

In recent days she'd been increasingly unhappy with Ned's decision to go off — her term — with the POUM. Daily, the POUM seemed to be losing official favour. Edith would make a fine politician of the lower ranks — ear to the ground, alert to the scuttling that precedes a fall.

"What's wrong with him, exactly?"

I'd guessed right away Ned wasn't ill. They'd had some kind of row; he'd given in, and she'd emerged victorious but exhausted.

"I told him it would be for the best if he didn't go."

"And?"

"I'm moving him over to the Pasionaria."

"He's stricken with illness but fully able to make the move?"

Already the uplifting feeling of the funeral had begun to slip away. How could it evaporate so quickly?

It was by then early evening; the clear air of the city was growing chilly and along the Ramblas, birds were making preparations for the night ahead, gathering and chittering in the trees. For them, the day had been like any other day. The road back to Berlin may be through Madrid, but the dead Brigader wouldn't be among those making the journey. As for the birds, none of this would ever be their concern.

With our hands in our pockets, Edith and I walked back to the freezing hotel.

Ned moved into the Pasionaria. Before you knew it, Ned was off to Albacete, where the newly organized International Brigades were headquartered.

Game, set, and match to Edith.

LYING ON MY BED in the Pasionaria I considered the send-off for the Brigader. You couldn't do much better than that.

Anything would have been better than the memorial for Marcus in the English village church. A nerveless afternoon. Rain, quiet but incessant, robbed the village of colour and light. At the wake people stood in the front room in their hats and overcoats, hastily tossing down whisky to keep warm, with the relatives giving me the dead-fish look. The wake hadn't lasted long.

Alec and I climbed the stairs to his old room with its smell of books and damp. He switched on the lamp. We took off our clothes, got into his bed.

For a few seconds during the wake I'd been standing near Alec, and the decision had passed between us, to be quickly hidden in the offering of sandwiches. I could tell by Alec's face that he meant it as a closing act of retribution.

Fine.

His weight above me, tense. But dogged.

Shove the spade into the heavy moist soil. Push with all your might, don't quit until it budges.

"Anyone who doesn't want to have sex after a wake might as well end it right now," Alec said.

Burn one's bridges behind you, the classic strategy of retreat. Fire on the water, smoke, mist, clouds, blotting out the sun.

A FEW DAYS AFTER the Brigader's funeral I was at the cinema. Some people I met at dinner had suggested a nine o'clock flick. The film blanked out with a whine and a printed notice came on the screen. *You are all asked to keep calm and follow the attendants down to the cellars. The film has been suspended.*

We sat in the darkness. The flash of cigarettes being lit. Then the crowd rose and I trailed along with them, enjoying the shared excitement. It felt like the familiar good cheer of a casualty ward. The crowd took me not down to the cellar but out into the street, to a navy blue sky and a city in darkness. The only light was the shaded one that showed the way to the new *refugio*. A dim hand pointed downwards: this way to the underworld.

Someone lit a fresh cigarette, was sworn at, put it out. Cars with faint blue headlamps moved down the avenue. Above us, broad bands of lights swept across the sky, crisscrossing. The white scissors of lights were like archways, like a line of poetry recited at school: *I saw eternity the other night / like a great ring of pure and endless light.*

Next day there were stern warnings from the authorities in the paper. That was a practice, a drill. People had not been frightened enough.

THE WAITING IN BARCELONA continued.

"Does nobody want us?" I pressed Edith. "What are the procedures?" Of course it was Edith who was doing the arranging.

"I believe word will come." A flat response.

"Word will come," I mocked. "A messenger with wings?"

"We need our safe conducts." Our travel permits.

Word finally did come. Edith, having scurried off early one morning, returned in a major tizz. We were to pack our bags immediately. That day we too were on our way to Albacete.

The lorry arrived. Up climbed Edith.

"You stay there," she said, "hand me my baggage." Like an obedient lamb I grabbed her bags, heaved them up. I should have being paying more attention to her face, her nervous voice.

It must have been pre-arranged. Because as soon as I'd passed up her bags, the lorry started its engine, pulled away.

Leaving me gawping on the pavement.

I WAITED AT THE Hotel Nouvel, where the British Medical Aid Unit was headquartered, indignant sentences brewing up in my head. Edith left me stranded and I'd come to find out why.

I demanded to see the man in charge. Took a seat along the wall.

The afternoon passed. No, I was not leaving. I would continue to wait, thank you.

When the man finally gave in and agreed to see me, he was in turn polite, stern, hostile. Although my accent buoyed his British confidence, I was proving difficult to dismiss and it was the end of the day.

A man of resources, he dipped into his repertoire. There was a dance this evening at the Café Shanghai, which, as I would know, had Barcelona's best dance floor and a fair orchestra. Would I care to, after we dined?

Two can play at the appeasement game.

We walked together, out into the street. It had begun to rain, a downpour, and we were forced to run across the square. The rain and the running lifted some of the heaviness in me. After that, the dining and the dancing came more easily.

His arm had to reach around to my shoulder blade; we were the same height exactly. I placed a firm hand on his shoulder and he was left with nowhere to hide.

Not one your English roses, mate.

"I need to get out to a forward hospital," I told him. "How come you aren't making good use of me?"

No, he was not at liberty to discuss my posting, lack of. For my information the lorry Edith left on had broken down near Valencia and anyway, women weren't being allowed anywhere near Albacete. He could not imagine where I picked up such a notion.

I smiled; we danced.

He tried to grip me with a different kind of authority. I slid away, felt a flush of mean pleasure. But by the end of the evening I'd extracted both a promise and a temporary position.

ON A FINE MIDWINTER day I took the tram up into a fancy residential district, found a grand house bright with red-and-white banners, a sanatorium. Its large square entrance hall had a ceiling going up to a painted dome, a distant, overcrowded heaven.

My temporary task was to instruct *enfermeras*, nurses in training. I was to teach them to recognize and treat the infections that come with being hungry and exposed to cold. I would be working under the direction of a French doctor who lectured the trainees about the patients he was treating.

Pneumonias mainly, and this morning, a tuberculosis case that had hemorrhaged. After he'd spoken he looked to me for some words about the treatment of pleurisy.

We were teaching in a long room from which the former owners had removed the paintings but left the elaborate frames. "Be sure," I told the trainee nurses, "to secure the drainage tube in position with a safety pin." The vast empty frames along both walls gaped with silence; they overwhelmed. I heard my voice going up into squeaks. *Safety* pin, indeed.

After the class, the French doctor led me out to see the garden. "This is the garden of everything," he promised. Clipped yew hedges rubbed up against palms, woodland nymphs gazed into coppery pools, a gravel sweep led past raised flower beds down to an extravagant swimming pool, tiled cream-and-blue, and drained.

On this sunny cold day a contingent of staff had dragged chairs into the depths of the pool. They appeared to be keeping this hideout for themselves — no patients or trainees in sight.

"Come on it, the water's splendid."

I could tell, from the Frenchman's careful way of hauling his left leg down the steps, that he was a veteran of the Great War. About the same age as Marcus.

It was very still inside the pool, a suntrap completely sheltered from the wind.

"This feels like being in a warm bubble," I said.

"A bubble will burst," the French doctor replied. "While it lasts, however, it is a brief moment of perfection."

I wondered if I should ask him about his past, about the war, where he came from. But he had closed his eyes. Beside him, I sat back and closed mine.

"Soon," I heard myself telling the French doctor, "I will be on my way to the front. Have you heard they're starting a hospital at Grañén? In Aragón. The British Medical Aid Unit." He wasn't responding, so I didn't go on, as I'd planned to, about how I was looking forward to really getting my hand in.

This became our pattern. Together we adjourned to the swimming pool in the early afternoon. The French doctor sat back in his chair, still as a lizard. I sat beside him. After a week of shared silence, the French doctor began to talk. Keeping my eyes shut, I listened to his voice, which was no louder than a whisper (sound carries so easily in an empty pool). He touched my arm and he spoke to me about the wide, shallow dish of Aragón.

IN A TOWN IN a high valley there lived a mayor who had grown up without knowing the warmth of a full belly. As a child, as a very young man, he'd worked in a seed shop; he'd lost his job. He was a clever youth, but a hungry one. He began to work in iron.

When the impossible happened, when he became the mayor of the town, he called upon some friends of his, ironworkers, to make a wide, shallow dish. There was nothing ordinary about this round dish, which was easily ten feet across. It took four men to carry it. They cranked it up on the back of a lorry, threw in hessian sacks of rice, and drove around the neighbouring villages.

The arrival of the lorry was a signal for the men of each village to set out into the countryside: chicken were beheaded and plucked, goats were slaughtered. In the open, muddy space that served as the village square, a fire was set and lit, and tended by children. The dish was lifted to hang above the flame. Olive oil splashed into the dish. In went the rice. Wine, chicken, the goat — cut roughly into large slabs — all were tossed into the iron dish.

When night fell — and the nights were cold in the high valley — the fire roared and a delicious smell rose. It drifted into the small group of houses. The animals on the ground floor smelled it. Above them, women in the open windows smelled it.

When the food was ready, the villagers gathered. Women and old people came down the stone stairs, carrying small, triangular lamps, lit with olive oil. That night everyone in the village knew how it felt to fall asleep warmed by food.

Hearing this story, I was standing at the edge of that village, watching from the shadows. Alec was there beside me, and Marcus. It was Marcus who pointed out the lamps.

WHEN I FIRST PITCHED up in Grañén it was a quiet sector of a quiet front. Aragón had been a battleground early in the war but now Franco and his fascist pals were concentrating on Madrid.

A fine day with clear light, a cold wind. Round haystacks, white houses, stands of small pine trees. Up into gorges, the steam train labouring, then out into higher, agricultural country, with fields of sugar beet.

I was expecting an open carriage thronged with militia, but the train was modern, with corridors and compartments. Such trains were made in Belgium, Alec had told me. Only a man would bother knowing that.

In the compartment: several old women in black, a young woman with a toddler, and a big-boned middle-aged man with a withered foot. The toddler, a little girl, was stringing words together and pointing. From time to time, she cried out in triumph at her success.

The people inspected me with direct looks. I told them I was a nurse. All of them smiled at the word *enfermera*, repeating it. Then, *enfermera australiana*, with a small intake of breath, to indicate wonder.

By mid-afternoon we'd reached a city where the air was filled with the smell of beets. Huge mounds of dirty brown lumps were piled up beside the beet factories. Mother and child alighted. After much delay the train left the station in the evening, only to come to a halt again at the outskirts of the town. The thin blue light came on in the compartment and the locals passed around their black bread and a few bits of sausage unpacked from handkerchiefs. I had two hard-boiled eggs and a half a dozen dried apricots, which pleased everyone enormously. As we ate, the blue light flickered and failed. At first we greeted the sudden darkness with laughter, as if it were part of some fun we were having being together and by now, so well acquainted.

After we'd finished the shared food, the laughter drained away and the compartment grew stuffy — cold but stuffy. Darkness persisted. We waited, patiently at first, for waiting had become a familiar task. Then with resignation, we slid down in our seats. Our breathing was making a mist on the windows. The man's head was leaning heavily against me, his mouth open, and he'd begun to snore. Probably he'd been up long before dawn to reach the station to make this journey.

Smells took over — sweat, garlic, bad teeth, black tobacco, and the anxious smell that comes from living with constant tension. Already I had my own word for this smell: threadbare. The smell of thread-bare was a tired smell and in those times you found it throughout the land.

A half moon was making its way among many clouds, so that the compartment was occasionally filled with its shadowy light. In the small hours the train jolted into movement and at last we shuddered into the high valley of Grañén.

Six

AT THE FARMHOUSE THAT served as the hospital, it was not yet light. The profound quiet of a rural place before dawn. The mud in the courtyard was slippery. Flagstones were stacked in readiness for laying.

The Poms had set up mattresses on the floor, with nurses and doctors separated by a big Union Jack. (The Spanish doctors had another dormitory.) I lay on the floor and my body knew it was not in a city. I slept more deeply than I had since I stepped ashore in Toulon.

In the morning, I found a tough sparse country that definitely had the feel of home. A dry land; it showed its shape, and I liked it. Stubble still on the ground from last year's crop, low bushes, some irrigation. Snow on the distant mountains, but no wind and the sun felt warm. Beyond the muddy courtyard with its heaps of flagstones, I could see a group of olive trees and lemon trees, small and hardy and strong. The ground beneath the olives had been carefully worked in preparation for planting. An encouraging sight.

They were making a real dormitory for us, with beds.

There were three other nurses, from England. In a week or two, when sufficient time had passed, the conversation would move on from complaints about the daily routine into personal territory.

I'm a widow. Lots of widows in this country; presumptuous even to mention it.

Then wait for it.

How did he die?

There will be a silence, a gap.

GRAÑÉN WAS A HOSPITAL with few patients, which was maddening. Two in the ward had gunshot wounds in their hands from their own rifles misfiring. An abdominal case. One jaundice. I'd thought I was coming to the front, not a backwater.

At some point everyone sent to Grañén wondered why they'd been set down so far from any front lines. Turned out a couple of chaps in the British Medical Aid Unit selected the site by consulting a Michelin guide while sitting in their new offices in Barcelona. Staring at the map, they noticed it was on the railway and halfway between two cities, Lerida and Zaragoza.

They pointed with soft fingers. That's the spot.

I'd long ago acquired the ability to slip into groups of people without sticking out — it's something you learn quickly as a nurse. All medical staff shared the same dining room, but the locals sat at one end, speaking to one another, mostly in Catalan. One of them had worked at the clinical hospital in Barcelona. I asked, of course. Did he happen to know an Englishman named Alec Flinders? No, he did not.

In the dining room the radio was the centre of life. Having failed to take Madrid by frontal assault, Franco aimed to cut the roads into the capital. No dice. There were rumours that Mussolini and Hitler were telling him to get a move on with Madrid.

Franco's next bright idea had been to attempt to cut Madrid off from the rest of the Republic by sticking Musso's troops in up around Guadalajara, northeast of the capital. But they were forced back — we captured a heap of prisoners and equipment, all Italian. Now, a ton of evidence proved that Mussolini was in fact waging war on the Republic, but nobody in Britain wanted to hear a word of it.

The very latest was an attack against the Basque country in the north, along with renewed and wider bombing. Franco was going after Bilbao, its steel industry and its important port. With the bombing, I decided they were aiming to instill terror; they were trying it on.

We listened to the news, the Catalan doctors translating. Madrid bombed. Barcelona bombarded from an Italian warship. Bombs on Valencia and bombs on Port Bou.

Had Marcus's village been bombed? Surely not. What would be the point in that? The cottage would be there, just as we'd left it. The big iron key still in the door.

After the radio and its news, one of English team read aloud from a book by P.G. Wodehouse. I suspected he found it a relief to be, in this place, reading of English toffs making fools of themselves in castles. I found it irritating and precious. Set Wodehouse down here and he'd be rah-rahing for Franco in two seconds flat.

I could do it, I decided. If I ever needed to, I could reach the village. Barcelona to Blanes, a bus to Lloret, another to Tossa, then a boat around the cliffs inside the reef. That would be the best route. The cottage would be there, exactly the same. Marcus's books in his library, his Roman artifacts.

As soon as I arrived in Grañén I found out that the mayor was furious with the British for having descended uninvited. The English medical team called the mayor "Pancho Villa."

"Who's this Pancho Villa?" I enquired of one of the doctors.

"Famous Mexican revolutionary. You haven't heard of him?" He strolled off, whistling "La Cucaracha, La Cucaracha."

It was understood that Pancho Villa was incapable of meeting our entirely reasonable demands. One of the English doctors announced he'd a mind to take the little blighter out and give him a good thrashing.

The mayor probably did have quite a bit of power behind him. Here the towns and villages elected representatives to a body called the Council of Aragón, which was running everything from schools to trades. Maybe they wanted to run the hospital as well.

Out walking, I waved to a group of men ploughing a broad field with single disc ploughs and donkeys. They waved back, giving me a surge of happiness. At the edge of a muddy field, a mob of white pigs looked unaccountably pleased with themselves. Maybe they'd located a cache of truffles somewhere. Farther along, a farmer was planting sugar beet seed. When I waved to him, he came over and showed me the rough, bumpy seeds. They lay in his hand, a rugged farmer's hand. He smiled down at them. He knew how to make them grow.

The church dominated the village, as no doubt it was meant to. You could see it from any point of the flat high countryside. On my return to the village, I paid a visit. The church's medieval altarpiece, undamaged and beautiful, was a painting of the dead Christ being lifted tenderly down from the cross. I wondered how many local people still slipped in, to bring him up to date on what was going on. These days the church was being used as a granary; you could hear scurrying. The church mice had died and gone to heaven.

At the end of my walk I had to return to the hospital. And really, there is nothing more enervating than a hospital with not enough patients. Afternoons and evening were the worst. I wrote letters. A package arrived, with tobacco.

I was out in the country as often as possible. It gave me chance to think about things other than the war news on the radio.

Daily, I took long walks along the Huesca road. Occasionally I could hear a rumble of artillery, but very little was happening on the Huesca front. The mountains to the north, with snow on their peaks, turned to lemon and purple and floated in the cold air. I thought about the village, and what happened to Marcus. If only I could go back to the time before Alec came. That was when I should have packed my bags, left, gone to London, started again. I should not have stayed until Alec arrived; I certainly should not have stayed after he left. Now that I was back in Spain, I found I wanted to be in that cottage again; I wanted to walk from room to room, to acknowledge somehow.

I took to the Grañén countryside immediately. After the stony heaviness of the city, it was wide open. Even so, it was profoundly different from home. Everything here, including the mountains, had accumulated centuries of having been known. In Grañén I felt the same way I did in Marcus's village. There, every winter storm, every fish, every bud, blossom and fruit was tied up with so many years of living, a human story being told, a story going on and on. Sometimes at night, when the villagers slept, I felt that they carried the whole thing in their heads. All of this was so unlike Cliffend, where you understood right away, no question, that you might reel off into space any time and nothing would be altered. Neither your presence nor your absence were of any significance whatsoever to the earth or the sky. I missed that. I missed the wild country at the back of beyond.

A BARCELONA DOCTOR WAS leaving. We held a celebration for him: rough sparkling wine, nuts, a few dried black figs. One of the English doctors played the piano. His personal favourites were dreadful, arch ditties from Gilbert and Sullivan in which the foreigners were ever so funny. On this occasion even he knew better and he gave us what we wanted: the new songs: "I've Got You Under My Skin" and "The Way You Look Tonight." There will never be better dance music; it simply isn't possible.

Nobody wanted him to stop. The pianist groaned, let himself be bribed with cognac, played until dawn. We were exhausted, happily and completely unfit for emergency arrivals, should any show up.

Spring brought the pleasant smell of turned earth. Around the ditches, small brown birds had begun to flit about, excited to be back from somewhere. In the fields behind the hospital, a crop showed its tender bright yellow-green. Beyond the fields, almond trees in late, high-country blossom. The radio spoke of the bombing of a town in the Basque country on market day. No anti-aircraft guns in this town, no machine guns, no batteries. In the afternoon, the two-engined white planes came first, then the three-engined black ones. German and Italian bombs fell like grains of sand until the sky pulsed with flame clouds. The fascist version was that the Basques had dug fake bomb craters in Guernica and poured gasoline into them to make Franco look bad.

When we received some head wounds from a shell bursting up at Huesca I felt relieved. At last, I was able to be of use.

A few of the doctors had been in Madrid, where they'd witnessed the random bombing. Something beyond known boundaries, beyond belief. Occasionally they spoke of it, in low, puzzled voices. I was learning to listen for that particular tone of voice.

It was so new: the dining room, three stories up, still set for dinner; the exposed bathroom, a towel flapping in the wind; a baby's small mouth closed tight on a severed breast; a foot in its boot up a tree; lantern rows of bodies lined up on the pavement for collection.

One of the English doctors sat at the piano, made up a song, "Down at the Old Foot-in-Boot." I was also learning to listen for the bad jokes.

Meanwhile, I had the valley of Grañén to look at. Wide, rolling away to the blue hills, and in the distance, mountains with snow. You could try not to listen to the radio; you could try not to find out.

Over a small supply of nuts and anise, the doctors spoke about Federico Duran-Jorda, the Catalan doctor who established the Barcelona Blood Transfusion Service. In Madrid, the Canadian Norman Bethune was doing the same thing. The radio told us that this Bethune made a speech in Paris about what happened to the refugees on the road from Málaga to Almería. Refugees: a mule, pots and pans, a bit of furniture. For the ambitious, a mattress. Walk two hundred kilometres, dodging *avion*. When you finally reach Almería, Italian planes arrive right on time to bomb the place to pieces. Marcus and Alec used to rabbit on about the big purple Almería grapes they'd eaten as children but could never find again. So sweet, they'd agreed, with the exclusive nostalgia of siblings. No other grape could match them, said Alec. Nothing, claimed Marcus, nothing would ever come close.

Apart from making a grand speech in Paris, Bethune was on to something useful with blood. In the dining room the doctors tried to remember what they'd learned in medical school about blood groups, about refrigeration. We heard the Canadians were setting up trucks so that they could carry the blood.

A Catalan doctor had witnessed a transfusion. "A dead man," he said, "came back to life. Like in the gospels, only it actually happened."

"He wasn't really dead, surely. His system just got the jolt it needed." I thought of my mother, who brought the baby back to life.

"The heart," someone said, "didn't Aristotle say the heart is the centre of the body, where the soul lives?"

"Better leave souls out of this."

"Have you heard? Apparently a Russian in Moscow successfully resuscitated a young man who'd slashed both his wrists. Injected him with blood from a cadaver of a sixty-year-old man who'd died after being hit by a bus."

"Would you say the young man got lucky?"

"The sixty-year-old certainly didn't. He caught the bus."

"You'd hardly expect a suicide to sit up and say thank you all very much."

"You never know. He might. Cry for help and all that."

The doctor who was superb on the piano struck up a tune and sang, "It must be omin- omin- ominous to be hit by an omni- omni- omnibus."

I did not make friends with the medical staff, not in any personal way. I kept my own counsel.

As the days grew longer, the radio spoke of how the Non-Intervention Pact would be put into practice. After the news we sat at table, talking. The British government didn't give a stuff; no surprises there. Blum of the Popular Front government in France may have tears in his eyes but was keeping the frontier closed. Those two sterling non-interventionists, Germany and Italy, would have their warships patrol the coast north of Málaga. To keep the peace.

"Very droll," said one of the English doctors.

One night some men from the Durruti column were brought in. They'd been riding on a flatbed of a railway truck; Italian planes had come over. They'd been standing up, waving at the planes, assuming they were their own. It's an odd thing, when a man's body is roasted it grows smaller, it shrivels, but the eyes remain the same: man-sized.

In Barcelona, the Catalan president, speaking in the plaça de Catalunya, asked a huge crowd if they would promise to endure every sacrifice and put every effort in the defeat of fascism. "Yes," shouted the crowd. "Yes, yes, yes." "Catalans," he told them, "your promise has ascended to the infinite; it has been heard throughout the world and by generations to come. Remember this! *Visca la Llibertat!*"

Listening to the speech, I felt large and restless; I think we all did. We drifted out onto the terrace to stare up at the night sky, with its endless stars.

"Look," said someone, "there's Vega."

"No, not overhead, you dope, not yet, you have to wait until midsummer. Over there. The bright one."

"The starry heavens above me."

"You didn't know the Great Bear is the Big Dipper to the Yanks? Where have you been all your life?"

"The Irish call it the Starry Plough."

"I believe in France it's the Casserole."

"I could kill for a fine French casserole right now. Great hunks of boneless beef, cream, wine."

"I rather wish you wouldn't."

"What's that over there? Cassiopeia?"

"Might be. Shaped like a W?"

You couldn't see the Great Bear from Cliffend but Mr. MacDonald had talked about it, how it was highest in the northern sky when it first woke from hibernation, its paws in the heavens.

WITH THE SPRING, THE pace of the town quickened. Militiamen poured in, then just as swiftly poured out. Something was happening and naturally we didn't know what.

Relations with Pancho Villa and his people were growing worse by the minute. The butcher was refusing to sell meat to the hospital, which perhaps didn't matter that much because in the kitchen the women were refusing to cook. The power went out. No question of anyone agreeing to turn it back on. "I think they may be trying to tell us something," I ventured, and got glared at. Such sentiments constituted unreliability, no doubt.

Maybe Pancho had told us something, because there was talk of us packing up and moving. As for the English doctor who fooled about reading P.G. Wodehouse, he'd begun to speak in loud, precise vowels to the locals, whose eyes continued to slide about. And in that country, if a person does not look at you frankly, if he or she does not gaze right through you to that far place where nothing much matters in the long run, you should realize you are in trouble deep.

What snapped us out of the domestic bickering was a series of small Republican offensives against the insurgent forces to the east and north of Huesca. The war had finally come again to Aragón, a quiet sector no longer.

Just after a brain case died on the table, we had a man with wounds through the right wrist, also wounds from left hip to right scrotum. I worked on debriding wrist, hip, scrotum. Debriding is just a fancy name for cleaning the wound; it is absorbing, intense work.

Later, I assisted with several casts and ended up covered in plaster myself. Let's get plastered in Paris, we said to one another, for a laugh.

Around this time we had our first prisoner. There are technically accurate terms for this but I would say he had been flayed alive.

A contingent of enthusiasts arrived from England. After dinner we held a dance in their honour, and they made speeches about the unique gallantry of the Spanish people. Some of the visitors quizzed us nurses about our reasons for being in Spain. It was a relief when they departed, off home to pen expert opinions.

I'd other things to worry about. I'd been examining my face in the mirror — an ancient, wavy affair above the cupboard optimistically referred to as "the dispensary." The whites of my eyes had turned yellow.

At first I thought I'd just gone off the food. Beans swimming a marathon in olive oil will do that for you. Usually my stomach could take anything. This time, however, it was in full revolt and showing no sign of letting up.

Yellow mucous, yellow urine.

"I'm full of bile," I said, making of joke of it. "My bile runneth over."

A sick nurse: a contradiction in terms. I made up my mind to go back to Marcus's cottage in the village by the sea. Stay there until I recovered.

"I can take care of myself," I explained.

I would take some leave. I had a bolt hole I could get to.

Seven

Catalonia, May–August 1937

THE VILLAGE WAS VERY quiet; no signs of the war, although a few of the houses had been painted a dark brown, a disconcerting sight among the white. The cottage was the same. Like the others, it crouched on the cliff, facing away from the ocean. The large iron key in its lock, never used. I pushed open the door.

I didn't take the route I'd planned. I came by the weekly bus that crept out from inland. The bus was stopped regularly by village committees to whom I proved of no particular interest.

Usually the bus would be met by Bernat with his donkey, Ines. Instead, I walked down alone, clutching my stuff.

I arrived carrying toothpaste, Band-Aids, Aspirin, and tobacco. I'd also brought tins of sardines, a luxury in a village that lived on fresh fish. Unsure of how long I'd be here, unsure of what may or may not be needed. I moved through the rooms, smelling the cottage: the plaster, the dreadful cleaning fluid used to wash the tiles, the sea smell, the damp of a house that has been shut up —

and a startling smell of stable. That was new.

Another surprise awaited me when I stepped out onto the roof above the library. Down at the bay people were fishing with lines. Line fishing was what total amateurs did, people from the villages inland. Much frowned upon by the local fishermen. *The man who fishes with the hook eats more than he catches.* So said Laia's mother-in-law. No villager would eat such fish, Laia had explained, because they'd been caught on a line and were filled with pain at the moment of death.

Something must have changed.

Although Bernat wasn't there to meet the bus, by now the whole village would know I'd arrived. When Laia came bounding in, I rushed into her arms, joyful.

I did not ask, Where is your husband? Where is Bernat? Why wasn't he there with Ines? There would be few young men in the village by now.

She did not ask, Why have you returned?

She ran next door to her home, returned with weak coffee, and sat at the table, facing me, eagerly rolling herself a cigarette. Her mother-in-law was not so good, but the twins — I should see them — growing so fast! But will it be safe? They turned yellow when they were newborn; Laia was terrified.

"They will be fine," I reassured her. "This is totally different. When babies have jaundice it's just their livers starting to function, that's all."

I could see she didn't quite believe me.

We drank our coffee, we smoked. I was exhausted, yes; the bus was tiring. Was I happy to be back?

"To see you," I said. "I'm so happy to see you. When I first came here, I don't know what I would have done without you."

She'd received a letter from Ramon. From Extremadura. She leapt up again, hurried next door again to fetch it. Why would they send a fisherman to landlocked Extremadura? Way over there near Portugal. I knew there had been fighting in that area, and at Badajoz, which had fallen, a massacre of civilians.

As soon as I'd drunk the coffee I was dropping with fatigue. Laia touched me on the arm, smiled. She would come over later, she promised, she would bring me water with lemons floating in it.

Laia's mother-in-law was herself ill, but sent over a message. There was a bird, mother-in-law advised, a bird with long legs, very long beak, and yellow eyes. If I were to look into the eyes of the yellow-eyed bird, I would recover.

"It's here only in the winter," Laia added. "It wouldn't be around now." She tucked her hair behind her ears, as she did when she felt embarrassed. She had come with the lemon water, but without the little ones.

"Please don't worry," I said, "there's no risk of the twins becoming ill. You can bring them over. I'm dying to see them."

I undressed and slid into the bed, feeling the cottage taking its shape again. The only puzzle was that odd new odour. How had the cottage developed the rich smell of cow byre? It was late spring but in the damp sheets my body felt cold. When you re-enter a house, my father said, you become the person you were when you lived there before.

In the library I sat on the couch where Marcus used to sleep. His ancient treasures were still there: plates, pots, coins, daggers, bones.

I was an idiot not to have realized right at the beginning that a wife wasn't what he wanted. Back with his family in England, Marcus succumbed to the force of custom and to expectations, his own and others. I suspect he believed marriage might lessen the burden, but the weight only grew heavier. Without me, Marcus would not have taken such a swim. Would not have lived his last hour lashing the water with his arms, taking himself out too far.

Searching beneath the phonograph, it didn't take me long to find the record.

I hurled the Gigli at the wavy plaster wall.

Made of brittle shellac, "Caro Mio Ben" broke into several large pieces. An aching howl arose from the back of my throat as I selected one of the pieces, threw it again, harder. Picked up the smaller pieces, and threw those. In a fury, I kept at it until every piece of the broken record lay in black shards on the floor.

The room remained eloquent in its silence.

ONE MORNING WHEN I was slowly recovering from the jaundice I woke early from a dream, convinced of its reality.

A young man is sitting in a kitchen. A familiar scene: herbs drying, a woman frying an egg. I can tell by the white walls and the sea smell that it is a cottage on this coast, in a village like this one. An old man in a chair. Two other men, also elderly, have come to the door, where they stand, watching.

At the table, the young man is wrapped in a blanket. In front of him is a glass from which he has recently drunk cognac.

The dream had two distinct chords. The woman at the stove, the older men: excited in a quiet way. The young man: uneasy, embarrassed.

Down a hold covered with a sheet of oilskin, he has arrived on the Catalonian shore. Part of the morning catch, smuggled in on a boat that would have slipped away last night from a port just over the border in France. He has come for the Republic. Now that he's made it, he's overwhelmed by the strangeness of the place, daunted by the welcome. He's also very tired.

I lay in bed, staring at the uneven plaster on the ceiling. I woke some more and the room asserted itself. Bed, chair, window, and that pervasive barnyard smell — all as they were last night. I was losing the dream. Already it was sinking; if I didn't try to remember, daylight would cover it over until it had never been.

When I woke fully I realized with pleasure it was still there. I tucked it away, like a small round pebble to keep in my pocket, for comfort.

I was getting better. I could still feel the tenderness of my liver, and I tired easily. But the worse of it — yellow eyes, yellow skin, deep yellow urine — was fading.

"I'm so much better," I told Laia, "I could eat a horse."

"No horse flesh available, but an omelette?"

Now the children were allowed to visit. They ran through the house on sure little feet. I waited for the right moment to scoop them up, to savour the heft of them.

"I could eat you," I told them in turn, with growling sounds. "Eat you all up."

They shrieked happily.

Here in the village, food was not yet totally scarce. The big boats did not go out but the boys and old men fished from dories. I'd seen the regular line fishing, which Laia clearly did not wish to discuss. Vegetables from the garden, rabbits and pigeons in the cork forests. No sense of excess, but then there never had been.

Having declared myself recovered, I started walking about the village again. That's how I happened to be down at the square when Pau fell off a ladder and sprained his ankle.

He was up on the roof of the inn, attempting some repairs. A short, square man, Pau was flushed with effort and wiping the sweat from his forehead. He waved; I waved. I walked on.

Next thing I heard was yelling. The women of the family were running to his side.

Coming back down the ladder, Pau slipped.

He called out to me. I was startled by this, and hurried over. By the time I reached him, he was downing cognac rapidly.

"My foot, my foot," he groaned. "Englishwoman nurse, my foot." As he said those words, a flood of surprised pleasure spread through me. Pau was asking for my help.

The ankle was swelling up fast.

I raced up to the cottage, grabbed my bag, hastened back down.

I bound the foot, gave him an analgesic.

The ankle healed beautifully and Pau made a story of it — everyone who frequented the inn heard what the Englishwoman nurse had done.

THE UNTHINKABLE WAS HAPPENING down in Barcelona and Laia was bursting to talk. Supporters of the Republic appeared to be fighting amongst themselves. Shooting and arrests; a fierce battle going on at the telephone exchange; barricades in the streets; a general strike.

Even more amazing were the rumours of fighting at the Generalitat, the seat of Catalan government.

"How can this be true?" Laia's tone was pleading.

Something must have gone terribly wrong, but what? Laia looked to me.

How could I not be better informed? Laia understood without hesitation how factions within the Popular Front jostled and disagreed, passionately — but this fighting was incredible, unbelievable, crazy.

Laia began to walk with her arms folded close about her. She opened them only to her children. Lifted the twins up and held them too tightly. They squirmed and demanded to be put down.

The inn had a radio. As women we did not go there to listen, but Laia picked up details from the Ibicenco women. And the old fishermen took their boats around the cliffs, inside the reef, into the town. News walked on water.

So it was not that we did not hear what was happening early that May, down in Barcelona. It's that what was happening made no sense at all. Most disturbing to Laia was the fighting between the federation to which the fishermen belonged, and the Catalan government, the Generalitat. Laia was intensely proud of both.

"Do you have any idea what's going on?" Again she looked to me, but what could I say?

I really didn't know.

In angry frustration she asked, "Don't you care?"

I bowed my head and wept.

That night Laia left her sleeping children, marched down to the sea and stood on the shore. Erect, with rigid folded arms, she stared out as if challenging the darkness.

I SEARCHED FOR SOMETHING to distract her. "You know that smell?" I said. "The smell that's strongest in the library?"

She flushed, reached for a strand of hair to gather behind her ear.

"Ines," she said, her voice dropping. "She needed" — Laia was picking her word with care — "protection."

I could actually see Ines as we spoke. She was down in Bernat's courtyard, beside the abandoned bicycle with its sidecar and the gathering of village dogs. Ines stood and dreamed and looked in need of no protection whatsoever.

"They were coming for her, you see. They were taking domestic animals for the war. To carry things." And to eat.

The news moved from one headland to another. Officials were coming into the villages, requisitioning mules, donkeys, horses. For the women of this village, who had already given their young men, this was crossing the line. Enough. No more.

"She had to be hidden," said Laia. "We needed a place."

. The Englishman's cottage, close to the hill path. The officials would walk right past it, their eyes intent on the houses in the cove, the village square, the palm tree, the inn. They would be looking down the hill, not sideways.

At the back of the deserted Englishman's cottage was a big room. Perfect. The women were up before dawn on the day they knew the men would come.

"Did she eat any of the books?" Ines devouring Marcus's Homer: a tempting thought.

"Impossible," declared Laia, becoming cross. "Ines wouldn't dream of such a thing."

In barcelona, events continued to unfold with the improbability of nightmare. Troops were on their way from Valencia, government troops, thousands of them, elite Assault Guards. But why were they being sent in? Who asked for them? Who were they mobilizing against?

Laia was appalled. "If they are *our* troops," she said, with a tremor in her voice. "Why are they fighting *us*?"

First we heard there had been a truce, but then we heard the militias were being disbanded. I thought of the German woman from Sitges in her monos and tasselled militia cap. What would she do, where would she go? She couldn't return to Germany; that much was certain.

The Republic was to have a new prime minister. Juan Negrín was going to replace Largo Caballero. Negrín had been finance minister in the Caballero government. Before he entered politics, he'd been a professor of physiology at the University of Madrid. Now he was about to tackle the body politic of Spain.

I still couldn't figure out what was going on in the Catalan Generalitat. Above all, I didn't know what was happening to the federation through which the fishermen sold their fish.

One evening pau's wife came up the hill to Laia's with an unusual request from the farms.

"They must be desperate," Laia told me. "Farm people never ask villagers for help."

A prolonged labour that had been going on for three days. Now the woman was at the end of her strength. They knew Grandmother was ill and could not come, but could Laia? Could she bring the Englishwoman nurse?

"Do you really think they've asked for me as well?" I was gathering my bag and two of Marcus's shirts. My bag contained only a small set of instruments and a few painkillers.

"I think you're the one they're really asking for."

Laia sounded anxious, as well she might. "They've heard about the ankle," she continued. "You know Pau's been boasting about it at the inn."

"An ankle is one thing," I said to Laia, "a baby quite another."

Laia and I set out. We'd a good eight-mile walk ahead of us. Directions from Pau about where to go. It was a track, uphill. As we walked, the dusk thickened. I realized the woman must be doing badly, or the women of her family, without doubt accustomed to attending births, would have known exactly what to do.

Glimmer of farmhouses, smell of fields, the deep quiet of hills by night. An owl called, as if to itself.

I carried my bag; Laia carried the shirts. I worried that my bag was not much more than a basic first-aid kit; I was ill equipped for a midwife's tasks. The shirts had been hanging in the closet — nobody had touched Marcus's clothes, naturally nobody would.

"We'll put those on when we get there," I said to Laia. "Mainly to reassure myself."

"They won't reassure the farmers."

Without moonlight, we were feeling our way, eyes on the rocky ground. Finally we located a collection of stone walls, then a high wall of white plaster, a wooden gate, a small yard, men with wary eyes.

"We have come from the village," Laia said. "I am Ramon the fisherman's wife and this is the Englishwoman nurse."

A flutter of black clothing, a back room with low cane chairs, the bed.

The young woman was trembling with exhaustion. She had clearly endured tremendous bouts of diarrhoea. Drenched with sweat, she lay in a bed that had not been fully cleaned up.

I put on my white cotton shirt, Laia puts on hers. We shared a grin: this is pretty silly. I made a point of us both washing.

The women dressed in black muttered amongst themselves, then began talking all at once. Laia translated for me, but their hands told the story without ambiguity. A first baby. They thought the baby must have been the wrong way up because it was taking so long, but it wasn't. They'd been giving the mother castor oil to drink, but her labour appeared to have come to a standstill.

"See if you can find out from her," I told Laia, "about the three days of labour. Ask her what's been happening."

Laia conferred with the young woman, whose replies were constantly interrupted by the women in black.

One of the women offered olive oil.

"Olive oil is to encourage labour," supplied Laia.

"Yes, I understand."

I looked the young woman in the eyes; she was afraid of me. I took her hand, and with Laia beside me to translate I told her that I knew she was in great pain, that she must be tired, that we were here to help her have her baby, and that she was going to be all right. I smiled at the young woman — no more than sixteen, seventeen — and she wept for the sympathy, for the frustration, the suffering, and the fear.

I felt the baby. "The baby is fine," I said.

The baby was alive. That's pretty much the sum of what I knew.

Dilated about two inches, cervix swollen and hard. Surely it was not a good sign to be so hard? I took the olive oil, smoothed it across the perineum. A wave of approval swept the room. So, I'd done one thing right. Somewhat buoyed up by this, I gave the young woman an analgesic, the strongest I had, ground up quickly in water.

After that, my hands were busy. What was going on with the baby?

The shape of the pelvis told me the baby had turned, was head first. So what was amiss? There. Got it! The baby's head was tilted to one side.

Calm down, I told myself.

The head was sideways and needed to be face forward. I stared at the woman's abdomen. I must shut out all distractions and go back, back to the year I did obstetrics.

Now think. How do you manoeuvre the baby's head into position?

Two steps. First with Laia's help, I must coax the mother onto her hands and knees and with my hands on her lower back, sway her hips. I'd seen it done once and it worked. I remembered because at the time I'd felt hideously embarrassed. The doctors, a crude male lot, had called it "the racehorse position."

Then I had to help her upright so I could rotate the baby's head, gently, gently.

Bingo.

Beginner's luck, really.

The cervix was slow, slow, but it did continue to dilate. One year of obstets does not a midwife make. It was light by the time the baby's head crowned; summer sunshine was streaming into through one small, high window, making a shower of dust motes.

Laia and I were tired, the mother was beyond tired, and the women in black were taking turns to encourage the mother, who was oblivious to all of them. If she had favourites and enemies — and she must, because they were family — if she was obliged to please one or held grudges again another, it was of no concern. She was being swept up into demanding territory. On she laboured, struggling and struggling. Then cried out she was parched, she needed a drink.

I thought she might be sinking but she carried right on.

Her energy was building so wildly that Laia, myself, and the women in black were carried along with her. She was a mighty ocean liner. Time jumbled and it was happening all at once. The baby grabbed the current, rushed out wet and slippery and in one piece, bloody marvellous. A boy. Before you knew it, he was letting out cries of complaint.

Almost immediately, he opened his eyes.

We washed him, dried him, and put him on his mother's chest, with the ladies in black mewling their delight, agitated, wanting to get at him, hold him.

The baby quickly became alert, quiet, looking at his mother. And now the two of them were putting out into the room wave after wave of full, heavy fresh-minted tenderness. We hugged, Laia and I, and the women in black hugged everyone, even me.

I had to rouse myself out of this and start thinking about the placenta. The placenta, favoured food of my mother's mutt, Blackie. My own mother was a bush nurse familiar with remote farms. She must have seen triumphant mornings such as these. But when her own turn came, the ending was different.

The women of the house, much relieved, began to take over, to do what no doubt they had always done: knead the mother's abdomen.

Out the placenta came. It seemed massive to me.

All eyes were back on the baby.

Having looked up, he rested. Smacked his lips, began to mouth his fingers. Saliva poured down his chin. He pushed on his mother's chest. His hand moved from his mouth to her breast, and he touched her with tiny wet fingers. I'd had no idea that could happen so quickly. Back when I did my year of obstets the baby was invariably whisked away, to be returned at a more convenient time.

Turning his head from side to side, the baby was approaching his mother's breast. With mouth wide open he made several attempts until — success — he was set fast upon her.

"Time we were on our way," I said. Laia and I took off our bloody shirts, looked normal again.

IN THE FRONT ROOM, the men thanked us formally. Now that it was done, they wanted us gone. One of the younger ones was clearly the father — he was getting thumped on the back and was hanging his head, proud and sheepish.

How drab and apart they seemed as they filed into the cleaned-up bedroom where the birth had happened. The women, being joined by the men, were like drunks when someone sober has arrived in their midst.

As we left, the family was beginning to pray together. Something struck me as odd about this scene.

"I suspect the Almighty is about to receive the credit," Laia said.

The moment we were out of sight of the house, we began to whoop and carry on. "What do you make of that, eh? Pair of crazy amateurs."

Up there on the hills we were being buffeted by a big wind, practically pushed along. Laia and I flew down the rocky track, silly as goats, laughing and talking about the birth.

"The head, the head," I cried out. "I couldn't believe how I managed to gentle the head around so it was in the right position."

"Little devil couldn't figure out which way to go. Left or right?"

"But as soon as he came out, he was oh so very sure of himself, wasn't he?"

Laia recalled her double birth: Jordi taking his time, followed by Josep, who raced out to catch up with his brother, determined not to miss a minute. Ramon, coming into the room, breathless.

Speaking of her own babies excited her further and Laia did a little dance on the path, waving her shirt around. She was flashing the bloodied shirt in mock-matador fashion, shouting, *the head, the head, the birth, the birth*, teasing me, a foreigner who had such daft ideas about this country.

Skittish and tired, I chased after her; we fell on the ground, panting.

That's it! Back at the farm house, the men were all ages.

"Why are those men still up in the hills when there are so few left in the village?" I asked Laia.

She paused. Stood up, folded the shirt. The game was over.

"They are not with us ..."

Ramon and the other fishermen had gone to fight in defence of the Republic, but up in the hills they supported the other side.

For the final miles we said little. Back at the village we crossed the square, climbed our path. Laia hurried; the children would be wondering where she'd got to.

I curled up in a chair on the library roof, exhausted. My thoughts were with my mother. That night I'd learned more about her.

LAIA NEEDED RAMON. SHE resented being weighed down by the strength of their love. How could she be expected to shoulder that alone? His bland brief message said: *I am well, how are the children, how is Mother?* "What am I supposed to reply?" she protested. "He lies, I lie. Well, not lies, but not the truth."

She resented me, too. Knew that I would walk off up the hill path. Not yet, but one day.

I stayed on in the village many weeks longer than I should have and we played with the children, Laia and I, with the Republic in a shambles and her husband absent in far Extremadura.

Laia was planting a serious vegetable garden where once I'd grown flowers.

I should mention that the soldiers were paid at the same rate, six or seven pesetas a day, I forget which. Ramon would have sent his pay home, but it wasn't much.

The children's favourite game was a vigorous version of hide-and-seek. First, I had to recite the silly lines, none of which the children understood, apart from the name at the end:

Two old chairs, and half a candle
One old jug without a handle
These were all his worldly goods:
In the middle of the woods,
These were all the worldly goods
Of the Yonghy-Bonghy-Bò,
Of the Yonghy-Bonghy-Bò.

Then I had to say, in loud, threatening tones, "Who's the Yonghy-Bonghy-Bò? Who's the Yonghy-Bonghy-Bò?"

"You are," they squealed.

"Well then," I said, "I'd better count to ten before I start to *eat* little children." This was the signal for Jordi and Josep to run and hide.

"Yonghy-Bonghy-Bò is coming, ready or not."

I pretended to search, getting more and more mock-angry.

"Nothing to eat *here*," I shouted, kicking a cupboard and moving on to the next possible hiding place.

"Not a *scrap* to eat here." Kick.

Sometimes they gave themselves away with giggling. I'd approach the hiding place, make a display of sniffing. "What's this I smell? Flesh? Fodder? Tasty young child flesh? My favourite. Yum yum yum."

On it went, until they scooted past me, making for the path that led to their home. As soon as they'd gained the path, they'd reached safety

Time for them to cry, "We won; we won; *we* won."

By MIDSUMMER LAIA HAD begun to talk to me again with real ease. My ignorance back in May was forgiven. We discussed everything: food, the shape of our lips, what was happening in Catalonia and the rest of Spain.

I, too, had grown more confident. "I cannot imagine anything better," I said to her, "than being with people when they are most in their bodies."

Laia hoisted Jordi up on her shoulders. Something Ramon would have done.

Josep looked up at me, hopeful. "Come on, you," I said.

By now these two were rather heavy. We talked amid a clutch of moving limbs. "If you're going to be carried, you have to sit *still*," Laia insisted in vain.

She'd known all along, of course. The men from the hill farms were not fighting with Ramon, Betran, and the others.

"Would you have done anything differently? If you'd known?"

"No," I answered. "I would not. A body in my care, however briefly, is a body in my care. That's an absolute."

"Doesn't that make it too easy?" Laia's voice was tentative, weary.

"It does," I agreed. "A luxury most don't have."

Aloft, Josep, and Jordi had begun a sparring match, distracting us. "What else could we have done?" she asked.

When she was working for the French family in Girona, the master of the house had read from the great French authors to help Laia improve her language — not whole sections of books, she explained, just bits and pieces. We hunted about in Marcus's library and finally Laia found the passages she wanted. Her favourite was Zola, whom we read for the smells, the food, and his frank kind of sex. She translated passages into Catalan so that I, too, could improve my language.

No tree could be seen against the sky, and the road unrolled as straight as a pier in the midst of the blinding spray of darkness.

We spent much of the day in the garden, where, with help from Ines's manure, Laia was cultivating aubergine, tomatoes, broad beans, artichokes and capsicum that were so healthy, full, and fat that they impressed even the women down at the inn.

As we weeded and dug and separated, Jordi and Josep played with the soil, tunnelling in it, eating it when Laia wasn't looking.

At my kitchen table, with Jordi and Josep banging saucepans, we drew up lists. *Very hard to get*: sausage, salt, flour, rice, coffee, sugar. *Somewhat available*: garbanzo beans, figs, almonds, oil, a rabbit when someone goes into the forest. *Available*: potato and onions, cabbage.

Very soon we'd have our own glorious harvest to see us through the rainy months. Laia was full of plans about what to do with the booty of the garden: what to dry and hang, what to soak in brine or store in oil.

"It's only until the men come back," she said. Until Ramon comes back.

Because everyone knew the men of the village would come back when the job was done, walking down the hill path, glad to put it behind them, glad to be home, away from the rest of the country, which had proven one more time that it could not be trusted to properly manage its own affairs. The men would row out in the big boats; the fish, who'd been on holiday and quite unsuspecting, would come. In number, the fish would come. The Republic would go on. Despite the intrigue and grief and improbable changes on the government side, it would all go on. As for what would happen in those other far countries, who could say? We didn't care, we couldn't care; life was here.

Laia and I were consumed with food — not with eating it, but with how to obtain and sustain it. What else could we find? Sparrows, not much of a feed, a pheasant if you're in luck. Fish, pulled from the sea on lines, small rock fish full of bones, despised but eaten now by all who can catch them. The occasional pigeon. In a scrape of rocks on the cliffs, plover's eggs but only in season.

Laia cooked a dish of red capsicum and garbanzo beans laden with rosemary. Delicious. Laia announced she could live on this forever, but worried about the children, who needed meat, which did not exist in the village. The only animals were the cats and dogs, who'd gone from thin to ultra-thin, and Ines the donkey. No question about eating any of them.

I should have been working in a forward hospital somewhere, but there I was, discussing food with Laia. "Don't you people make potato bread?" she queried. "Do you prepare it the same way as I do?"

It was rumoured to have been a wonderful year for wheat in Aragón but none of it was finding its way to the village.

"When Ramon comes back," Laia said, "we'll eat a sausage this long" — spread of arms. To bolster her case, she searched in the library, came back, and read me a passage from Zola:

Strings of sausages and saveloys of various sizes hung down symmetrically like cords and tassels, while in the rear, fragments of intestinal membranes showed like lacework, like some guipure of flesh.

"Oh my God," I breathed.

"That's what we'll have," she said, happily. "Gluttony is the one sin god forgives."

In the evening, I sat on the roof, drinking a little rough red. Food may be scarce but we had wine. The moon was up. Earlier I'd gone over to say goodnight to the children but they'd already been put to bed. Laia, too, was asleep. Small mouth, small body, curled.

Glowing and excited, Ramon used to pick her up, twirl her round. Over his shoulder, where he couldn't see, her eyes would be open wide, amused. *I love him, love him, but make no mistake, I'm nobody's fool.*

Love, charity. Faith, hope, and charity, the big ones, the virtues. Three sisters. One could whistle and one could sing and one could play on the violin. Faith is the bossy one, the eldest who believes she has to lead the way. They say the greatest of these is charity, but hope's the one that will see you through the hard times.

Laia loved Ramon. The children of course. Presumably her parents up in Girona. Her sisters and brothers. How many did she have? We'd talked about them but I couldn't remember. I wondered if she loved Grandmother, Ramon's mother.

Hope was the middle sister. Quite a surprise she made it into the top three, I decided. Hope, my mother's name. Hope: a fine name for a bush nurse.

Hope was Laia, waiting for Ramon.

But Ramon had gone. Down in Barcelona it was impossible to know what had become of hope.

When I was running out of all possible excuses to remain in the village, I received a letter from Ned. Gangly, red-headed Ned, who loves Edith, which is a huge mystery in itself.

These days it was Pau who walked up the hill path while the village waited. Waited through the erratic arrival of the bus — watching Pau as he came back down the path, lugging on his back whatever had been delivered — waited until he had reached the bottom of the path, had gone back into the inn.

The village was silent, strained with listening.

After Pau sorted the mail, what he did was this: he stepped out into the square in front of the inn and in a vast town-crier voice shouted the names of those for whom mail had come.

Nobody waited for mail like Laia.

On the day the mail was due to arrive you would find Laia in her front room, on a wooden chair with its high back, her hair loose, distracted, staring ahead. Anyone looking in would understand that images of Ramon were settling around her. One by one, they came. His hand was resting on top of the chair, just behind her neck. She felt the fast-thick thudding of her own heart. Her eyes closed. She was waiting for him to tip back the chair, for the repeated words, always remembered.

It was not Laia's name that Pau called. My own name bounced around the cliffs, floated on the water.

Alec? My father? Helen?

A letter posted in Spain, but I did not recognize the handwriting. Even before I opened it I was thinking, this is it, this will mark the end of my time in the village. And what came into my mind, surprising me, was the thought: I've been happy here with Laia and the children. I've been almost content.

My name had been called in the square and there it was: a letter from Ned.

Dear Clancy:

How goes it? Bet you didn't expect to hear from me. I'm not much of a hand at writing. I'm in Valencia with a few hours to spare before we set off again for Madrid. This time my load includes books, newspapers, and writing sets with paper and ink. So I thought, why not give it a go?

This brings me to my news. Driving up last time, I was taking a library of books from hospital to hospital. Blow me if one of the hospitals wasn't Grañén where I believed you were. That's what Edie's letters said.

This driving business is a lark. I suppose the men need books. And I'm not always carrying books. As for the run from Valencia to Madrid, it's helping. Everything those people need has to be brought in from outside.

So this day I was ripping along and there were some women in a field, all eyes on the sky. How do you tell an enemy plane? See if it drops bombs on you. (Joke.)

So I leap out and I'm looking for a ditch. I've grown to really appreciate a good ditch.

The planes were coming over one by one. Like kids lining up for the diving board. They were going for Grañén. It was my next port of call. You know the way it stands out on the plain.

None of our chasers in sight. Nothing to do but watch. Heinkels by the look of them. They took their time dropping their loads, enjoying themselves.

As soon as the fascist planes had cleared off I hopped back in the camion and hot-footed it over to Grañén. Turns out it's an all-Spanish place now. I asked after you but they said no, I should try Socorro Rojo. So that's what I'm doing now.

I ran into the hospital to see if I could help at all. The hospital was standing but parts of the roof had fallen in.

The school took the direct hit.

I saw these little slit trenches by the ruins of the schoolhouse, slender things not much bigger than a gutter. The nippers must have run from their classroom and jumped into the trenches, light as butterflies.

Before this I hadn't been in the actual business. Write with your news. Remember me to anyone who might know me.

> *Yours affectionately,*
> *Ned*

I HADN'T BEEN IN Grañén when parts of the roof fell in and the school took a direct hit. I'd been playing with the children, talking with Laia, pretending I could forget.

I was sitting at the kitchen table, the letter in my hand, when Laia came in with the children. Saw my face.

"Does this mean you're going?" she asked in a flat voice.

I looked at her. Jordi and Josep, one on each side. They'd picked up on their mother's mood and stared at me with smooth, accusing faces.

"Say it," Laia demanded.

Eight

THROUGH SOME OFFICIAL OVERSIGHT I was given an entire room to myself. Time to think. Time to write to my father, to Laia. It was quiet in the room. If I wanted to, I could go to the kitchen, boil water, bring it back in the jug, wash my socks and underwear. But I didn't have the energy for any of that; what I wanted was sleep.

After I emerged from the village and asked to be sent to the Aragón front, I was dispatched without delay to a real field hospital in Alto Aragón. That was almost four months ago. The front had been a moving line high in the hills, and when the front collapsed, we rushed to escape. I came down to Valencia, where I was supposed to stay until reassigned.

The room was one of two pieces of enormous luck. On my way to Valencia I'd run into a Frenchman in the Regiment de Tren, the transport regiment. We got talking and it turned out he knew Ned, he was in the same outfit. Even better, they were currently stationed in Valencia.

I sent Ned a note and arranged to meet him.

So beautifully silent, this room was in a farmhouse outside the city, a rather splendid farmhouse with a passageway through it that opened into an enclosed courtyard. Being at the back of the house, I looked directly into the courtyard. Beside the bed there was one bentwood chair and — clearly a new arrival — a packing case upon which sat a basin and jug, and a bunch of candles tied with string. This must be the best room in the house, because the courtyard cut the wind. For a while in the afternoon it was sunny. The sun came directly into the room and warmed the air.

I decided I might as well stay here in bed because the next day I was going into the city to meet Ned, who was at an autoparc on the other side of town.

Valencia had become another city in darkness, one blue light at the corner. Dark, cold, depressed. A few weeks ago, the government moved up to Barcelona. Solid city buildings stood empty, their lower windows boarded up. The sandbags, which always seemed useless to me, now looked exceptionally so. I realized there must be plans for these buildings but so far nothing had happened and they stood like a hole in the centre of town, giving the place such a sad air.

We were waiting for the rebel offensive against Madrid, expected any day now. The doomsayers in the British press were busy shouting that the Republic was done for. They had their own reasons for saying this but if Madrid were taken, they would be right. To top things off, olive oil of all things was becoming scarce, although they said this year would yield a bumper crop.

I HITCHED A RIDE in the back of a truck. The truck-bed looked dubious, so I stood, fingers curled around the bars that held the canvas. I could feel the metallic cold coming in through my gloves. Freezing.

Ned was already at our meeting spot, leaning against a wall, one leg behind him, propping him up.

He waved his arms wildly, sprinted over to seize me as I jumped down, and lifted me off my feet. Big bear hug. He fell into step beside me as if I'd last seen him only days ago.

Quickly, we filled in the major blanks. Ned was still using up his luck driving the Valencia–Madrid road. As for Edith, shortly after she gave me the bum's rush in Barcelona, she returned home where, I gathered, she stormed about the countryside showing the film *The Spanish Earth* on an old sheet and extracting donations from all comers. I pictured Edith up on a packing case addressing the crowd both before and after the film.

"We're going to work our way down," Ned explained, as we hurried along in the cold. By this he meant going from the Victoria to the Metropole, and then on to the Regina. The little plates that came with the drinks grew progressively more slender but Ned's energy was undiminished. By the time we left the Regina I was leaning against him in the wind and the rain. "*And we're bound for Botany Bay*," sang Ned, tunelessly. We were bound for the inevitable Shanghai bar: low ceilings, low tables, smoke-filled, crowded, rowdy, edgy, drunk-happy. Ned introduced me to his mates, who turned out to be Irishmen from the Connolly Column with names like Danny and Liam and Frank. "Wild boyos all," promised Ned, cheerfully.

The wild boyos were well advanced. They'd reached the point where they'd open their coats, show you their hearts. Danny was a printer from Dublin, Frank hailed from Cork. Liam had a donkey at home. When he looked at a donkey here, ears pinned back, straining under a load, he saw his Little Nell. I began to tell him about the remarkable Ines, but the talk moved on.

In Dublin, Danny inked the plates for the Irish version of the much-reproduced poster of the little girl looking up at the planes. Identified only by her morgue number, her head is propped on a cloud pillow, while towering high above her, planes fly in menacing, precise rows. A child to remember because of those open, dead eyes.

We talked, oh how we talked.

The future of the Republic? And which one would that be? Ours or this one? Their reasons for coming. If Franco were defeated,

Mussolini would collapse. And if Mussolini collapsed, it would undermine Hitler.

The high spirited hubbub continued: So what was the current British Prime Minister, Neville Chamberlain, up to? Speaking out of every orifice, starting with both sides of his mouth. Deals with fascists were addictive; Chamberlain couldn't get enough of them. *Lie down with dogs, rise with fleas. O for a voice like thunder and a tongue to drown the throat of war.* Crazy bugger, Blake. The government's packed up shop and gone to Barcelona, what do you make of that now?

At evening's end we stumbled off to where the Irish had finagled a place to lay their heads. The boyos were not in the least disorganized. Before they set out in search of whatever entertainment came their way, one of them soaked a pot of porridge. The Irish porridge parties, Ned told me, had quickly become a feature. If you were lucky — all women were lucky — you'd be invited. The Irish salted and ate their porridge as it came out of the pot, precarious on the primus stove, and if you could find a tin and a spoon, you were welcome to as much as you liked.

More talk, a bit less wine, and the night wound down at eight in the morning.

We stepped out bleary-eyed into the rain and right away realized by the number of people on the streets that something had changed. Despite the weather and the hour, fire crackers were going off down at the central markets. I grabbed the paper, read the Spanish, translating roughly for Ned.

The government has made a massive strike to free the provincial city of Teruel from the fascists. With tank forces and infantry, the government has advanced. In the first wave artillery support was not used in order not to warn the enemy.

Success, and in the nick of time. So much had gone against the Republic, but now we were finally getting a break.

More fireworks, more people, and Ned and I were hugging strangers in the street.

"They've done it! Now we'll see."

"So many men, a surprise attack, such confidence."

"They've pulled an army together that is capable of this," said Ned with a vast grin, Adam's apple a-tremble. I knew what he meant. Just a few months ago the disarray seemed permanent, fatal. Lately the slogan had been "fortifications against a fascist offensive," with the goal of holding on through the winter.

"For the government to turn around and go on the offensive itself," he marvelled. "No more standing about like a bandicoot on a burnt ridge."

The city was alive again, bursting with gossip not just about the offensive, but a possible victory.

"This is more like it, eh?" Ned put his arm around my shoulder, held me in a friendly way. "What do they say? They shall not pass. *¡No Pasarán!*"

"*We* shall pass," I replied.

Snow was falling up at Teruel; it was cold at the front. A blizzard had swept in but the infantry continued to move forward.

We raced for the papers, we gathered round the radios. *Lightly wounded men rose from the snow to rejoin the advance.* (A likely tale.)

Ned and I moved about the city with the Irishmen, who in the way these things happen, had become our daily companions. Ned and the Irishmen talked. Mostly I listened.

"They've entered the city; they've taken control the lower floors of buildings."

"It'll be the knockout punch, I tell you. A heavyweight has entered the ring."

"Eat your heart out, Jack Doyle; ditto, Joe Louis. Rat-tat-tat-ta-tum. Here we come."

"You'll see what this means. The government will get the weapons it needs."

"The democracies will extract the digit. Finally. They'll pressure Germany and Italy."

"You daft git. They've shown themselves to be useless as tits on a bull, and besides, Italy's just walked out of the League of Nations."

"Franco was sucking on dreams of Madrid but now the bastard's got to deal with Teruel."

"Must confess I'd never heard of the place before this."

"At the very least, the heat's off Madrid."

"Madrid, Barcelona, Valencia. The heat's off all three."

"Heat's off *in* all three. Freeze your nuts off."

CHRISTMAS EVE WAS COMING. I invited Ned to spend it with me, in my room. Grey again, really unseasonably cold for these parts; the sky held snow. But the news remained good and was getting even better. In Teruel, government troops had taken control of the main part of the town; they were in the governor's office.

Early in the evening of Christmas Eve we hitched a ride from town on a lorry and it felt comforting to be back in the rural quiet.

All day Ned had been carrying a parcel wrapped in newspaper under his arm. When we reached my room he presented it to me.

"What's this?"

"Santa," he said.

"Santa's reindeer pranced in early this year?"

"Not really. Back home it's already Christmas Day."

I opened the parcel and found a wide brass bowl. It felt heavy.

"Just the thing for charcoal under the bed," he explained. He must have organized it from somewhere with the Irishmen.

"This is wonderful," I said. "Where did you get it?"

"Never you mind. Let's have it filled."

"No, wait. I've something for you, too." I produced a little box of tea one of the Irishmen had given me. *Bewley's* on the label.

We made our way to the kitchen, carrying the brass bowl and two mugs. A crush of other residents had gathered around the stove and the open fire beside it. The talk here, too, was of the victory. I was pleased that most of it was taking place in Spanish and French or Ned would immediately begin making friends and we'd be there all night.

I pushed through to the stove, boiled some water. At the fire, Ned raked out ashes and hot embers into the bowl as if he'd been doing it all his life.

"I see you've become practically a local."

Back in my room, Ned carefully placed the bowl on the tiles under the bed. I swirled a little of the precious tea in each mug.

"Now," he said, "we'll be ever so cozy."

The tiled floor was freezing, the wind blew in at the shutters, and we hurried to climb into bed. Nothing the least bit romantic about this. A bed was an asset and there were rules for how to share it. Take your shoes off. If you've extra socks, put those on. Any coats and jackets that aren't wet go on top of the bed. Hop in wearing your sweater and long pants.

Ned complained about the bolster being hard, but we settled in.

"How do you like this?" asked Ned. We were sitting up in bed with our mugs of tea.

"Very domestic," I replied, wrapping my hands around the mug and bringing it up to my face, to enjoy the warmth of the steam. I'd been wanting to have Ned to myself, so we could gossip properly.

At the Madrid end of his run he would see, strung out along the road, refugees fleeing into the city. He passed other trucks that had come with food. The refugees milled about in the rain, shawls over their heads so they looked like shabby bundles on legs. As for Madrid itself, you should see it. Trams running, cinemas open.

I bet he tells Edith the upbeat things about Madrid. I bet she repeats them. She didn't visit Madrid but that wouldn't slow her down, not one little bit.

In October Ned drove all the way from Madrid to the lower Aragón, taking troops to Fuentes de Ebro. In addition to the constant rains, this was a dreadful autumn for the Republic, with one setback after another. Fuentes de Ebro was a fiasco; what was supposed to be a quick and decisive offensive turned into a dragged-out defeat.

The more Ned spoke, the more relaxed he became. I realized it must have been a long time since he'd talked in any personal way.

"We've been busy of late. The side roads are crap but the main roads are pretty good, really. The stones laid down, topped with bitumen. You can put your foot to the floor. As soon as you've done that, you come round a bend and a donkey is mooching along with the bloke in the cart behind him fast asleep.

"When we're on a run we sleep in the truck, eat in the truck and the rest of it. At fifty miles an hour believe me, that last bit can be tricky.

"Driving a truck is not what I thought I'd been doing, but they asked who could drive and I had to open my big mouth. They got me to drive a truck forward about twenty feet, no more. Then put her in reverse. That was it. On the spot I was put in the Regiment de Tren, the transport regiment. Anti-fascist on wheels. At your service.

"The blokes in the autoparc are okay. French, mostly, and quite a few Yanks, because ninety-nine percent of the locals don't drive, but I expect you know that. We're part of the Spanish Army and I'm a corporal. In case you think I'm putting on the dog, all the drivers are corporals so it doesn't mean a thing.

"We do have a few chumps who came along for the ride on the ocean blue. Now they're here, those bastards want to turn right round and go home. You can pick 'em because they're the first to start whingeing.

"At the beginning of the summer we were up behind a place that had a lot of little hills, lots of grass, at least more grass than in much of the country. Gum trees. Naturally I headed for a gum tree to sleep under, it smelled like home. Then after that, we were in a posh resort outside Madrid. It was broken down of course. Slept on the roof. I reckon I can find my way round the northern stars by now but I miss seeing the Cross. Edie assures me it's as bright as ever.

"Have you heard from Edie by any chance? Her speaking tour was a huge success. You know what she's like. The moment she stepped off the boat in Fremantle it was on to Perth, Kalgoorlie, Adelaide, up to Broken Hill. Everywhere she goes, it's *Defend Democracy, Spanish Relief.* Here's me snoozing away under a gum tree. Her hero at the front.

"The moon is a good part of life. On the night-time route from Valencia up to Madrid we often keep our lights off. Of course, whenever you hear a plane at night you switch off. By day you keep an eye out for anyone in the fields. If they're looking up, it will be a plane. Park the *camion* beneath a tree if one is available, crouch down in a ditch and become well acquainted with an excellent piece of Spanish earth."

CHRISTMAS MORNING, AND IN the kitchen a bit of carol singing. Ned and I contributed a song in English: *I saw three ships come sailing in / On Christmas Day, on Christmas Day / I saw three ships coming sailing in / On Christmas Day in the morning.*

On this Christmas Day in the morning the talk was of Teruel. True, a few weeks ago some in the room had only vaguely heard the name, but now everyone knew the victory at Teruel would be huge; it would take Franco's attentions away from Madrid and pre-empt him from attacking Catalonia. The Republic might have lost its Basque industrial base to the rebels, it might be under what amounted to a blockade by sea — thanks very much, you non-intervention hypocrites — and it might be getting screwed by the French who couldn't make up their minds whether the border was open or shut, but up in Teruel the Republic was able to defeat fascist troops, who had Hitler and Mussolini's arsenal streaming out their backsides.

Ned turned to me. "What's the Spanish word for hope?"

Ned was talking away, making friends, language having proven not much of a barrier after all. I fell into a half sleep by the fire.

I saw three ships. I saw my father at the shack down at the coast, the bright heat of the day, the blazing cloudless sky, the even greater heat of my aunt's kitchen, the chook, the threepence in the pudding. I saw my father run into the surf.

Back in my room we divided a small piece of *turrón* and four dried apricots. Christmas dinner.

"With apricots," I told Ned, "you have a choice. You can either cut them into small pieces or you can have the entire half. Stick it in your mouth, turn it to the inside, poke your tongue into the sweetness."

"Give us a half," he said. "Let's go all out."

BY SOME MIRACLE THE sky cleared and in the afternoon the sun emerged. We pushed the bed into the patch of sunshine and lay basking.

"Do you ever want to leave the autoparc?" It was not a casual question. With the territory we had in common, Ned and I went way beyond the standard chatter.

"It's okay, I reckon. Sometimes I get a whiff of holding the horses at Agincourt."

I decided I'd been mistaken about Ned. When I met him for the first time, he had the fabulous aura of the stowaway, with heaps of physical presence. I'd seen him almost as a comic book figure, the first to scramble up the barricades.

I got it wrong. There are men here who have come for the fight, because fighting is what they do. But Ned, with his easygoing temperament, has not deliberately sought out danger.

"Your driving work is vital," I said. "Imagine what things would be like for Madrid without the road in."

"How about you?" he asked. "Do you think of leaving?"

He deserved more than a pat reply, but what came out was not particularly articulate. "At this point, no. As they say in my trade, be as close to the wounded but as far from the battle as possible."

Our second and final evening. Come morning Ned was due back at the autoparc.

With the night the rains came again. We lay unable to sleep. "We've had too much rest," I said. "We're not used to it." I began to sing, "We've had too much rest on Christmas Day, on Christmas Day in the evening."

"Impossible. Nobody can have too much rest."

In that loose place in front of sleep Ned started to talk about driving just last week, and hitting ice on the road. It was night-time; he had the lights off. He'd never driven on ice before but at the first patch he remembered he was supposed to pump the breaks. He did that and he was out of it.

And immediately into it again.

The second time on the ice, the truck slid out from under his grip. He felt he was on a sailing ship and wind had silently filled the sails.

"I thought, I'm going with the sails, the sails can take her, there's nothing more I can do."

I turned my face to him and his tongue was in my mouth; it tasted of apricots. He stroked my face and my arms and I took off my sweater and eventually we took off our layers, and made a very quiet kind of love that calmed us both.

WITH A SENSE OF respite, of reprieve, I made arrangements to set off for Teruel, up in the snow.

Also on the road to Teruel was Douglas Ross, Mac-Pap.

Part Three

L ittle one, I'm shimmering.

The morning post brought a letter for me from that woman we saw in London, the one with the refugee group connected to Aid for Spain. Just a note and a clipping from a newspaper, the *Toronto Daily Star*, about a Mac-Pap who'd been stranded in the south. In late January he was picked up by a coastal steamer out of Valencia.

You realize what this means, don't you? I was right! There are Mac-Paps cut off in the south. The article concluded that seventy-five to one hundred Canadians likely still remain in Spain or in France. As soon as I read that, I realized, *that's it*. Somewhere in that generous number is your father; I *know* it.

I haven't told anyone yet. Whenever I say Ross must still be in Spain or France, Alec and Helen look stricken and start treating me the way hospital visitors treat an invalid — with solemn, ineffectual concern.

Only you and I know how it feels to burn with patience. You have his mouth, and there, under clown cheeks, I've located the line of his jaw. You have so much of him in you.

I hold you aloft, up against the undiminished sky. He is present; right now he is standing behind me, so close I feel his warmth. I only have to turn around, ever so slightly, and there he is, arms open wide.

This is the first time you've taken flight. You cry out in ecstasy. When Ross comes, he'll be the one doing this. He'll be tossing you into the air.

I'm the one who needs to keep my nerve.

Friday, May 19, 1939

Went up to London today and disgraced myself. Took you along — you've just reached the stage where you can pick out strangers and don't want to have anything to do with them. It was a repeat of our previous visit: both of us miserable.

Back to the office of the woman who's been making enquiries on our behalf. I was in a foul mood because of the train trip, which, of course, you detested.

I sat in front of the woman and wondered why I was relying on her. Too much of a vicar's wife: brimming with good intentions but unfamiliar with organizing anything beyond a jumble sale. What I wanted, I told her, were the names of her contacts so that I could contact them myself. I put this as tactfully as I could manage, with heaps of if-you-please and ever-so-grateful.

She wrote out a bunch of names and addresses. Then she said, "It seems likely to me that he may have already gone to Canada."

That did it.

I was on my feet, screaming scorn — and appalled at myself, my rudeness, my lack of self-control. "He wouldn't go on to Canada. He'll come through France to England; he'll be in touch with me right away; it will be the first thing he'll do."

Seems likely. How dare she *seems?*

Hearing my fury, you were all tears. You didn't subside into panicky hiccoughs until we were settled in a little city park we've claimed for our own, with a pond and few passersby. But the way you recover is amazing. Before long you were crowing over your rattle.

We have the name of a group in Canada, Friends of the Mackenzie-Papineau Battalion, in Montreal. I'm going to write to them today, ask them to put me in touch with some of the boys in British Columbia. There will be Mac-Paps in British Columbia who can tell me more, there must be.

Somebody, somewhere, has accurate news of Ross.

Thursday, May 25, 1939

We've developed the routine of passing our evenings together in the morning room. I install you on a field of cushions, where you alternately sleep or hold court. We gather here, talking, reading, scribbling, admiring you, and listening to the radio. Alec studies the papers, in which the news is dire and the public mood one of revulsion. The port city of Danzig is next on Herr Hitler's list and he means to have it.

Like an ordinary inhabitant of the British Isles, I'm sitting in an armchair calmly reading the newspapers as if they were the sole source of my anxiety. Danzig, the editorial informs us, is a free city with Polish access to the sea guaranteed by the Treaty of Versailles.

Spain was not worth defending, Czechoslovakia was not worth defending — Poland, apparently, will be.

When the dusk grows thick we sit on without the lamps. Outwardly, I am not in the least hysterical. Inwardly, I'm catching the next boat to France; I'm down on the Spanish border, screaming demands. And I wouldn't care what happened; I would not care. I'd lie face down on the ground, shovel earth into my mouth.

That is of course quite out of the question; I'm in England and I must *carry on*. What a ghastly expression.

I must wait by pretending not to.

Sunday, June 18, 1939

I wrote to those people in Montreal, the Friends of the Mac-Paps. Hadn't heard back so I wrote to them again. Asked them to send me the addresses of some of the BC boys so that I could contact them directly.

If none of them has news of Ross, I could at least ask them to help me locate his mother's address. Maybe I could write to her, ask if she's heard anything. My letter would be discreet — I wouldn't tell her about me and Ross. Wouldn't enclose a picture of you in my arms. Christ, she might have a heart attack.

Given the time that's gone by, I have to admit Ross may be still in Spain rather than France, and to be honest, it's likely that he's injured. There are many who would have taken him in, who would have shielded him. I know how brave these people are, how determined. I lived among them.

Friday, June 23, 1939

Alec is becoming more mobile each day and I'm glad for him. He is able to drive again. With him off on various errands, and Helen up in London much of the time, it's just you and me in the big house. This is their home, not ours.

I feed you, hold you, change you, comfort you, but inside my blood has turned to lead. Whenever you're sleeping, I lie down too. I want to sink down, down, down, into a place of utter silence.

That's what I want. I can take no more.

You wake up. I'm on duty again. You're learning to play. I put a towel over my head. *Where's mummy gone?* I whip the towel off and you point and gurgle and rejoice. *Mummy's here. Yes.*

Every experienced nurse is a practised deceiver. Smile for the patient; do not disclose. It's an accomplishment I honed in Spain. There you had to learn to pack away the most appalling news and get on with things.

Mummy's here. But where is your father?

Soon, soon, things will come right. I need to hold fast to that. I need to remember that in Spain, in the least likely of places, happiness rose up in me like light, like music, like a bird in flight.

Nine

I WAS GOING UP the mountain in a high, fur hat.

We'd made our way up from the coast, through orange groves covered with snow. It was quiet in the muffling snow and at this time the bombers did not come by night. Took us twelve hours to drive the first seventy miles in the truck. Often, we'd had to get out and push. Holes in my shoes and my feet were wet. It was the first day of the new year and we were heading for Teruel. The driver had brought us as far as the truck would allow, with only a little piece of chain for the tires.

I knew what lay ahead: smoke from a faulty stovepipe, iodine, burned alcohol, the sweetish iron smell of blood and the even stronger smell of ether.

The Republican Army had taken the city. Finally, after a string of defeats, success, a breakthrough. Now reinforcements were making their way up the icy roads. Spaniards, Germans, Poles, Finns, Czechs, Canadians, English, French, Americans. Teruel, in insurgent hands since the early months, had fallen to the government forces — a tough but encouraging victory. The city was evacuated of civilians, although some chose to remain. As thousands were coming down, we were going up.

In one of the small villages en route our truck was forced to wait as more important military convoys took over the road. The stream of evacuees and civilian traffic swept down against the tide of trucks, artillery, tanks. In the push on the road through the village, those who were going up and those who were coming down had brought each other to a standstill.

The driver backed the truck into a narrow side street, left us there while he investigated. A Scottish nurse and I sat in the freezing cab, watching the night come in and worrying about our shoes. I didn't know the Scottish nurse; I'd met her for the first time that morning.

"As soon as we can we'd better organize some boots," I told the Scottish nurse. That's the term we used, "organize." As in appropriate, steal.

We spoke as strangers do, bland questions yielding equally bland responses.

"Who've you been with?" I asked.

The Scottish nurse said something about the British battalion. Before long she pulled out a picture of a man. Quite a bit older, hair thinning on top, wrinkly smile in a sunburned face. He was a cook and she'd known him for seven months. Last February, the cook had been at Jarama, just east of Madrid.

"How long have you been here?" she asked.

"A year and three months."

"But I thought you spoke the language."

"A little, just a little."

"More than that." She wasn't going to let it go.

"Before the war, a few years ago, I lived here with my English husband, an archaeologist."

My small command of words, my crumbs, were now invested with absurd value. Imagine for a moment an army whose members cannot speak to each other, where even signs are treacherous, where one person's gesture for "stay down" was another's for "come forward."

"Did you come as part of a contingent?"

"Just one other nurse," I replied. "And a chap who joined the IBs." Edith and Ned.

The two of us sat in the bluish dusk, waiting. The Scottish nurse embarked on what must be the cook's version of Jarama. The British volunteers were vastly outnumbered by Franco's crack troops, backed to the hilt by artillery and tanks. On the third day the British line broke; they retreated. But they discovered they were the only ones who stood between the rebels and the Valencia Road. So that night, they crept back. Franco's troops, believing these exhausted men to be fresh reinforcements, took fright and scarpered.

The Scottish nurse did not embellish; she did not cast her boy-friend in any heroic role. But surely defeated men could not set out again, by night, without first having had a good feed?

A few single candles appeared in the stone houses on either side of the street. Neither of us heard the steps of the truck driver. When his face filled the window, the Scottish nurse let out a yelp.

The village was a railhead. At the station, one of the railcars was being used as a hospital; the other was serving food. We should go there and eat now, the driver said, because we would have to walk the rest of the way up. How far? He wasn't sure. Five kilometres? A few miles? Nothing much. Uphill, though. No worries, I told him. We were strong. We would manage.

Beans in olive oil, dubious coffee, and a bonus — English biscuits, vanilla creams, one each. I lifted up the top side of my biscuit, ran my teeth over the sweet creamy filling, slowly scraping it off.

"I could devour a whole packet of these," I said.

The Scottish nurse giggled, pulled her biscuit apart and tasted the filling, too. We compared the teeth marks we'd made. When we finished with the filling, we each ate the biscuit very slowly, one side at a time, taking tiny bites. "They've put vanilla essence in the dough as well," the Scottish nurse said. She was right; it lingered in our mouths.

"Lovely," I agreed. "Isn't it just lovely?"

Not far from the train's hospital carriage, three local men were digging. They had only one spade and were taking turns. The ground was difficult for them; it was slow going, the spade ringing on the frozen ground. Beside them, several blanket-covered mounds were collecting shrouds of light, thin snow.

"I'll go take a look," I said.

The moment I stepped from the railway carriage, one of the diggers picked up something on the muddy snow behind him. He spoke a few words to the others, which I could not catch.

My first thought was, he's bringing me some small wounded pet. *No, please no. I won't be able to help. Not here, not in this mess.*

The man was wearing the usual clothes: corduroy pants, a woollen belt, an old jacket. I took a step forward, my feet aware once more of the chilly ground. He presented the furry bundle. As soon as it was in my hands I realized with relief that it wasn't alive.

A high black hat made of fur, with a grand brim. A man's hat. Not his own, nobody like him ever wore hats. A bit of booty. Organized, most likely, from one of those who had been coming down from the city we'd taken. He looked directly at me. Brown eyes, dark, like a furry animal himself. With those eyes upon me, I felt a surge of warmth in my body.

"Take it," the man said, giving the hat to me. In the local idiom, he added, *I give it to you.*

It was too big. But that was an advantage, having it around my ears and halfway down my forehead. I turned to the Scottish nurse, who had come from the train, "How do I look?"

The man stood to one side. Not smiling, serious. This hat was a gift because we were nurses, we were on his side, and it was cold in the snow.

It was like wearing a large kitten on my head. I'd never worn fur in my life. Not much call for it, back home. "What do you think? Haute bourgeoisie?"

A FEW HOURS INTO the early winter dark the flurries thickened, and we continued to climb. The snowfall grew into a whiteout. We pushed our bodies into the weather, breathing heavily. Then halted, gasping. It was like being at sea, out on the deep ocean without any boat.

What time was it? Must be going on ten. I did my calculations. At home that would make it morning, very early, the start of a mid-summer's day. Father, down at the coast, might be awake already, feeling the heat beginning to stir. How are you this morning, Father? Are you in fine fettle? If you've been awake even just for a little while, I know you will have thought of me. It's quite tough going here, Father, but I'm doing all right, I'm going to make it; you can count on me.

If we stopped, if we let our guard down, we'd slide to the bottom of the mountain and have to start the climb over again.

"Bracing hill walk," said the Scottish nurse, bending double and puffing.

In the dark we could see the lights of the dressing station. The Americans. They'd gone ahead. Set up this station below the town.

Seeing their lights meant one thing: not far to go now.

IN THE HOT, SHARP comfort of the dressing station, I began to relax in painful relief. The Americans had the best coffee, which they'd brought over with them and went to great lengths to brew. I felt the hot liquid pour down my throat, inhaled its warmth.

One of the American nurses found us chairs by the stove.

"Goodness, how do you do it," the Scottish nurse marvelled. "Coffee *and* chairs."

"Happy New Year," the American nurse said, smiling.

"Here's to January," said the Scottish nurse, "the month that looks both ways."

The American nurse's face was blank.

"Janus," the Scottish nurse explained. "The Roman god who looks both ways: back into the old year, forward into the new."

I planned to slump there forever, warmed by the American nurses' stove, sipping their amazing coffee, relaxing in their most wonderful chair.

"There's no electricity up there," said one of the Americans. It was shoptalk about what to expect; I was barely listening. Speaking of the doctors, she referred to an American medical professor, an older and much respected man. I nodded; I'd heard of him. She mentioned the Spanish doctors at the field hospital up ahead, the medical students, and the nurses in training. Then she spoke the name of the English doctor on the medical team.

Hearing Alec's name, I stood up. *Nobody associates that name with you.* I'd gone back to my maiden name. I was Clancy Cox.

I sat down again, careful not to look at anyone.

The American nurse, sensing some change, moved away from the stove.

Setting out again, we walked, not talking, our mouths covered in scarves, the hat about my ears. We pushed hard against the wind, into snow that seemed to envelop us. The Scottish nurse was almost running to keep up because I was lurching rapidly, as if propelled from behind by some powerful hand.

Dr. Alec Flinders. *Alec.* So many times in Spain I'd wondered where he was.

AROUND MIDNIGHT WE REACHED the edge of the city; we found the building that housed the field hospital. Candlelight shivered in the gloom.

A mansion, the country home of a rich man from the coast who would have come up here in the summer to escape the heat, and in the autumn, for the fishing. At the front was a portal where carriages would have driven in. I searched my mind for the correct term but could not find it.

We knew it must be the right place because there were two big muddy ambulances parked out front. Ambos. That's what we Aussies call ambulance men. The ambos were sleeping, curled up together for warmth, in one of the front seats.

Concentrate, I told myself. Stay alert.

My feet were so far away from the warmth of my head. In its fur hat, my mind felt detached, as if it had decided to have nothing more to do with the rest of me.

The portal led to a stone staircase. Narrow by local standards, about three feet wide. The wooden banister had been chopped away to give the stretcher-bearers room to manoeuvre. Beyond that, a landing and a frosted glass door with a thin light shining behind it.

What would Alec say to me?

We walked up the stairs and the Scottish nurse pushed open the door. The air was thick, suffocating. On the far side of the room was a stove with a stovepipe repaired with brown adhesive tape. I wanted to fall forward into that warm dense air, let myself be carried down in it.

What would I say to him?

Once the room must have been a parlour. Long French windows, shuttered. The walls were painted with hunting and fishing scenes. The owners of the house, up from the city, would have sat in this room with the windows open to the sky, feeling pleasantly pastoral. Recently, someone had been improving upon the wall scenes: tanks had been inserted into the rural setting, and beyond a gathering of deer by a stream, a plane dived from the sky. Whoever made the additions had a good handle on perspective but only a thick black pencil to work with.

On one wall was a whorl of blood. From someone transfusing, perhaps for the first time. The room wasn't empty of course. No room with any heat in it would be empty. Near the stove, on straw mattresses, men lay in states of shock. The staring, the trembling, none of it remarkable.

There was a room behind, which we entered next. A long room, another parlour, a summer room: an old sofa, an armchair, a few other chairs. A huge armoire, crammed with medical supplies: drugs, serum, anaesthetics, dressings. The sight of these supplies was at first reassuring, then alarming. What were we expecting?

This was the receiving and classification room, where someone like me had to pick and choose which men were so badly wounded that they won a place by the stove in the front room. In this room there were windowpanes but the glass had been knocked out. Some shelter was provided by boards, held in place with the same adhesive tape they'd used for the stovepipe in the front room.

Men were fully clothed, except where they'd had their clothing cut away for bandages. Many still wore muddy boots. They registered that two women had arrived; a few raised their heads. The ones who had the energy to be interested were drinking something from cups made out of condensed milk cans. No light, only candles. The town's electricity line had been knocked out, just as the American nurses had warned.

The doctors wouldn't be here. Not in the classification area.

We glanced down a stone corridor to our left, seeking someone in charge, someone who would show us where to hang our coats, where to plunge our hands into a bucket of freezing well water, where to begin work.

We reached the dining room. A makeshift operating theatre had been set up. More candlelight. I could make out a dressing table, two surgical tables, and an autoclave — a sterilizer — that burned alcohol. I stood by the wall that had a rack hung with coats, hats, uniforms, and long white gowns. I moved back against the wall.

In the far corner of this room a little black kitchen stove had a bucket of water on it. A local nurse was bending over the stove, coaxing it to burn. Smoke poured from the ill-fitting stovepipe. Like the one in the parlour it was mended with brown adhesive tape.

They're making good use of that tape, I told myself. The stove didn't belong in this room; someone had dragged in it here.

The doctor was not at this moment working.

I hadn't looked at him, not yet. I was still wearing the high fur hat. I knew I must look like the wreck of the Hesperus, coming up in the midnight and the snow. I was thinking I should stay here by the wall, make a joke about turning myself into a coat rack. At the same time I was considering the stove. I bet the alcohol for the autoclave was running low. They were sterilizing with boiling water.

Black-and-white checkered tiles on the floor. The wood for the fire, stacked by the stove, consisted of rungs of chairs and other bits of furniture. It was once a coal stove, but clearly the coal had run out.

I could have stood like that, taking note, forever.

Alec gave a small shrug to indicate he'd registered the arrival of nurses, he was expecting nurses. He had the polite face that meets a stranger, a mild, unseeing gaze. With that we were dismissed, to find our way.

I stepped out so that I was no longer protected by the coats on the rack. I took off the hat. And he looked up.

I watched his face fill. With surprise, then with a terrible weariness.

I saw him draw back. Pull his body up. He couldn't afford to go further into what he was feeling, not there in that place, not with what he had to do. He nodded, acknowledging that yes, he knew me. Nothing as dramatic as denying me thrice.

Beside the coat rack was a barrel containing tubes of saline solution wrapped in pink wax paper. My eyes stayed with the wax paper.

Moments passed, a wide, slow time.

The local nurse, the one who had been tending the stove, came over to show us where to go.

Nurses reporting for duty.

WE WASHED OUR HANDS; we got down to work. It did not take long to tour the wards. No heat, stone floors, no glass in the windows, shutters. Few blankets, fewer linens. Mattresses — most of them straw, just one wire-spring, a few cotton-stuffed — laid directly onto the stone. Automatically, I performed the inventory that nurses do:

half a dozen pillows for fifty men, only two enamel bowls, four buckets. Four bed pans. No cups, plates, or saucers.

I was assigned to the classification room. I moved as many men as I could into the front room where the stove was; I didn't want them in the icy wards, not when they were so vulnerable to shock. I worked through the night, concentrating so as to blot out Alec.

My first night in Teruel. In my mouth the name rhymes with fare-you-well.

The nurses' quarters consisted of some beds at the back of the men's ward, with only a sheet between the men and us. Mattresses on the floor. One of the local nurses had dragged in a drawer from a wide cupboard — no doubt she'd organized it somewhere in the city. It looked exactly like a coffin. Just the thing for a proper nap.

The local nurses were having a meal, which they immediately offered to share. Some condensed milk in a can and a slice of grey bread, which tasted so much better than it looked. I examined the available mattress. Touched it; it was wet. I turned it over; the Scottish nurse tossed a sleeping bag on the dry side. In the weeks to come, the Scottish nurse and I would take turns in the sleeping bag on this mattress. We aimed for six hours sleep after forty-eight hours work, which was standard.

I WOKE TO THE light poking its way through the shutters. When the planes came, there would be no point in hiding, no way the men could be moved to the cellars in time.

I crawled, fully clothed, out of the sleeping bag — an American sleeping bag, hugely valuable, a gift to the Scottish nurse from her British boyfriend the cook.

Looked out the window.

This was an old city, built on a rock at the junction of two rivers, a deep gorge on either side, with an ancient town wall overlooking the gorge. Cathedral spires, and in the middle distance, red cliffs, eroded to look like organ pipes. To the west of the town, a great bare ridge.

At the foot of the house — the back of which dropped down very steeply — a river flowed sluggishly. I could see a little garden leading down to the river, partly tiled. The plants winter-dead. A sundial without the dial.

The snow created an equal, even light; the river would look the same at eleven as it would at three. Hard to say what time it was, impossible to sense the passage of the day.

I found the kitchen, where the medical staff hung out because it had a stove. I gathered from the tension in the room that it was already a day of heavy casualties. The hospital, too small for fifty men, expected two hundred.

In the dining room, now the operating theatre, I found that the others — Alec and two student doctors — had already *stepped into their pelts*. This is a term I used secretly, only to myself. It is how you turn yourself into a theatre nurse. Imagine a fine skin closing around you, enclosing you perfectly. It's clear as glass and nobody can see it, but it's flexible, like a seal's pelt. Essential for being fully immersed. For in an operating theatre your work is alive, pumping and fighting. If you didn't transform yourself, if you stayed in your ordinary daylight place, you'd be useless.

Alec could have been working for forty hours or more. He made the first incision, clipped it tight. A good incision, neither too deep nor too wide. No yellowish fat popping up after the incision, before you got to the muscle. Not much fat on any of these men. Not like when I was doing my training back in Sydney and you got silvertails from the posh suburbs.

Alec clamped the smaller blood vessels, tied off larger ones.

"Knife," he said. He cut through the fascia, holding the muscle with the back of the knife, deft, almost casual. Then he drew back the sheet of peritoneum. "Retractor."

It was so cold that when Alec made this incision, vapour from the wounded man's abdomen rose into the room.

Probing the white twisted sausage of intestine, Alec was distant, focused, removed. He started work on a resection. This can't be hurried; there wasn't much for the rest of us to do but watch.

As he worked, Alec talked for the benefit of the student doctors. "In our line of work," he said, his tone conversational, "you basically have a healthy man with a hole in him. What is the first and acute danger? Shock. What does he need? Stabilization. Then what? Debribement — removing all the dirt and the foreign bodies, every last bit and piece. Then what are your choices? Tie off the wound? When would you resection, like this? Tell me, in what situations would you consider keeping the wound open, doing a cast?" For the students he was speaking a mix of Catalan and Castilian, batting along. His ability with languages seemed impressive to me but in fact he was probably pretty dreadful. As a child he'd spent his summers at Tarragona, as an adult he'd completed that residency at the clinical hospital in Barcelona, but he was very far from being a fluent speaker.

Safe inside my pelt I could listen to his teaching voice.

Only when he'd finished, when he was putting the stitches in, from a far place I could not yet pay full attention to, my mind resumed its tick-tick-ticking. Had I really fooled myself into thinking that Alec would rush to shower me with forgiveness?

Later we worked the two surgical tables at once: a femur with gangrene; a nose reduced to blood pudding. At the other table, perforations of the intestine. One of the student doctors recognized this man. He'd gone to school with him; the fellow went about in shirtsleeves in all weathers. Alec ignored the personal, out-of-place remark and the student blushed, looked ten years old. Then Alec gave a brief grunt of concentration to suggest he was so intent on the work that nothing had been noticed.

Easy to understand why the student has slipped up: here we did not have the luxury of the covered body, with the iodine stain bared for the incision. Instead, we had the man entire. Only his head, behind the ether mask, was partly shielded.

After the theatre, I worked again in the classification room, in the rush and the muddle and smell. An inoperable stomach, a hopeless head.

Three men together. One had a hole in his chest, was frothing blood when he breathed; shrapnel has probably invaded his lung. His companion appeared to have lost his sight, but it could be shock; the third had a thigh wound of no importance. They had been together in their field kitchen when it was shelled.

After them, a heavily built man, brains showing through his skull like a soft fist. On his colourless face, freckles stood out as if they'd been recently attached.

The afternoon brought more stomachs, legs, arms, hands. And the worst, the head injury cases. By the end of my shift, forty-nine men had been classified.

At some hour of the night I took a break. In the kitchen the Scottish nurse and two of the Spanish doctors were sharing a marvellous prize: a tin of salmon. Fried potatoes, garbanzos.

A candle on the table in the centre of the room, a pool of golden light, like a medieval painting.

"Come," said one of the Spanish doctors. "Come and eat."

THE NEXT TIME I woke I sensed the pace had slowed. It was snowing so hard the fighting had stopped. The classification room was empty. Time at last to organize the wards. The Scottish nurse was already there, showing the student nurses how to change dressings, do injections. There was a shortage of trained local nurses because this used to be the exclusive domain of those in holy orders.

Minor surgery was done on the wards. Without any anaesthetic, the American medical professor was expertly removing a small piece of shrapnel from inside the lip of a German man, who was being horribly brave.

The Scottish nurse announced she'd a bee in her bonnet. Stoves for the wards. That's what was needed.

I set off with the Scottish nurse and a student doctor, out into the snow and mud, across a square to an ancient stone house with a coat of arms painted on a dirty whitewashed wall. This was the sandbagged office of the board of aldermen. The aldermen, wiry tough men, had recently returned from hideouts in the hills. For the last eighteen months Teruel had been on the other side. When the city was taken back from the rebels it was mostly emptied of civilians. I'd been told that of those who remained perhaps half were with us.

"Stoves," I said, with the student doctor elaborating, "we need stoves for the wards."

These tough men reminded me of old gold miners out in the bush back home. I'd tell Father about them; it was something I could put in a letter.

I smiled at the men. "Can you get your hands on some stoves?"

Kerosene stoves arrived, four of them, insufficient but miraculous. With the stoves, a bag of improbable, bright oranges.

The night after this I was in the kitchen when the Scottish nurse, with Alec, staggered in carrying enamelware: buckets, cups, pans.

Laden, triumphant. They had raided stores in the abandoned city.

Soldiers were doing this too, when they got a chance. The soldiers' clothing and personal equipment were random at best. A soldier might have one blanket, rolled up and carried over the shoulder, tied at the ends with a bit of string. He might or might not have an oilskin or an overcoat. Some, having arrived for this winter battle in rope-soled sandals and short jackets, raided the town and plunged about in patent leather shoes, fancy vests, opera cloaks — they wore anything they could find.

"Look-look-look what *we've* got," the Scottish nurse cried in a mock sing-song voice. "Look what Doctor Alec and I found."

"There was a cellar down below the store," the Scottish nurse went on. "A cellar with supplies. There's a network beneath the city, tunnels carved out of the rock."

What else would they be carved out of? Dr. Alec wouldn't be asking me on any such expeditions.

"Freezing," supplied Alec, and added in a spruiker's voice; "Ladies and gentlemen, step right down. This way to the cold circle of hell. Now featuring housewares for diverse needs and every taste."

They were planning to return for more buckets, more cups.

Alec stood beside the Scottish nurse, laughing, not looking at me. This enamelware was truly a superb find. They continued to clank about with it, stamping their feet and puffing.

The Scottish nurse was in high spirits. "Alec has been telling me," she announced, "about the lovers. The two lovers that belong to this city."

"Has he now?" I countered, to give myself time. "What's he been saying?"

"A case of tragic first love." .

"In that case, better keep it brief."

Alec had moved behind me and was bent over, noisily organizing the enamelware into piles. He began to speak while he was sorting.

"This girl and boy had loved one another since childhood, but the boy's family had come down in the world. The girl's father told the boy he'd have to leave and make a name for himself before he could marry his daughter. The boy agreed to stay away for five years. So he did, and the day he came back to the city, having made his fortune, the bells were ringing. It was for the girl's wedding. She was a young woman by now. Turns out there had been a mix-up about when the five years ended. The upshot is the young man died of despair. So the woman shows up at his funeral in her wedding dress, kisses the corpse, and dies, too."

One of the local doctors had come in and was listening. He caught on, grinned, said something brief and rapid.

Alec translated: "'The lovers of Teruel / She was a dope and he as well.' That's what they say around here."

"It's where Shakespeare swiped the plot of Romeo and Juliet," Alec explained. "A most excellent and lamentable tragedy."

"Far-fetched, if you ask me," I said. "Not to mention the surplus of juvenile angst."

"Didn't have time to make up his plots from scratch," Alec added.

"Their corpses are still here," claimed the Scottish nurse. "In a church somewhere. Entwined, no doubt."

"Not entwined," Alec corrected. "Entirely suitable for public viewing. A case of single beds, side by side."

Beds of stone.

"Wherefore art thou, Romeo," said the Scottish nurse.

"My only love," replied Alec, still organizing his piles of enamelware. "Sprung from my only hate."

"What a load of rubbish," I said.

Early that morning I'd had to take a body down myself. I gave him a quick wash. Bound his jaw. Tied his name to a tag with a short piece of string around his ankle. What we knew of his name. I used another short piece of string to tie his legs. (Be careful; don't waste string.) The morgue in one of the cellars was nothing formal: hastily erected rough pine shelves. We'd have covered the bodies if we could, but they didn't feel this ghastly cold anymore.

That morning we had about six in the morgue. From time to time somebody came — I didn't know who — and took the bodies away for burial. I imagined some sheltered spot, near a building or beneath a tree, where the ground hadn't yet frozen.

I'd turned to leave the morgue when, on the shelf nearest the door, I recognized a thick head of hair.

I was looking at Ramon.

I'd noticed him by accident. I could just as easily not have glanced his way.

Ramon and Laia. I stood by his body saying their names. Laia and Ramon.

How could Ramon be lying naked and dead when Laia was in the village, waiting for him? Needing him.

Laia and Ramon. Impossible not to realize that for those two, lovemaking was yummy and urgent. Walk into a room and you'd feel their hum, back and forth. (It had filled me with loneliness, so many times.)

Hair keeps on growing after a man is dead.

And yes, I had to assure myself, it was Ramon, it was.

I didn't touch him or stroke his face. Later I wished I had, because that's what Laia would have wanted. He was there on a shelf, and it was hideous and strange. Even to look at him felt wrong somehow.

The blood in my head drained away. I leaned against the doorway, dizzy with questions. Who would tell Laia? How could she bear to hear the words? What would happen to Laia and the children? What would she do? Who would comfort her?

I left the morgue knowing I must put this right at the back of my mind. I could not afford to think about it. I needed to close the door, walk away, climb the stairs. I had work to do.

THE OPERATING ROOM FILLED with the wet, clean smell of plaster. Alec and two students were making a Trueta cast, talking quietly. The students knew about Josep Trueta, of course. One of their own, a brilliant Catalan surgeon. Alec was removing tissue from around the wound. He was asking questions. What dual problems does the closed plaster technique address? By leaving the wound open, one of the students told him, you secure drainage while the cast manages the fracture. What other advantages are there? Alec prompted. You prevent the reinfection that can come from changing dressings, another answered. Don't worry too much about the pieces of bullet you can't reach, Alec advised. Just make good and sure you have taken out every single piece of organic foreign matter. Every bit of dirt, every sliver of clothing or wood.

He fished around in the wound and right on cue, came up with a splinter. Held it up for us to admire. A murmur of good-natured approval.

THE BOMBING HAD BECOME more severe and we were working flat out. We didn't discuss what was happening in the battle; we did not speculate. The local doctors knew much more than we did and kept it to themselves. I understood well enough that at first the battle had been about opening another front to distract the insurgents from concentrating on Catalonia. It was also forcing Franco to take his eyes off Madrid. It had something to do with the road to Zaragoza — we'd been trying to take Zaragoza since the very beginning.

But it was becoming clear that what started out as our victory may be turning into yet another defeat. I'd been in the kitchen and the local doctors were eating in silence. Not eating, actually. One of them was sitting with his head in his hands, while the other looked blank and miserable. The day after that, the pair of them pulled me aside to say we must make plans to move the worst cases out. Then they both hurried off.

Now the entire medical team had begun to speak, in a carefully off-hand way, of what to do: arrange to have the patients put onto the slow, wood-burning train down to Valencia. Head injury cases first.

IN THE KITCHEN AGAIN. It was the only social place and we kept the stove going one way or another. That day we were burning solid blocks of wood taken from an ancient door. They gave off a strange smell.

When I arrived Alec was there; he saw me sniffing. "Hundreds of years of varnish," he said. "Varnish, vanish."

He was cleaning the stem of his pipe with a surgical needle. Looked at me, motioned for me to sit.

"Grub's gone," he said, his tone almost friendly. "All gobbled up."

For a few moments we were silent. "So," Alec said, suddenly putting his hands in the air, as if acknowledging surrender. "We've got it over with. We've met again."

I said nothing. It was a truce, of a kind.

NEXT MORNING, ROSS WAS brought in.

He came from the battlefront north of the town, where his battalion was dug into an open field. The Canadians were fighting in snow, sleeping in snow, unable to light fires because of the danger of enemy artillery fire.

Ross had frostbite. His leg was white, with waxy skin, hard to the touch, numb.

"Frozen body tissue," I told him. He knew this already, but I believe it helps to hear the words spoken aloud.

I applied warm compresses; wrapped him in blankets that were not that clean.

His leg warmed, his skin blistered, turned red, then blue and purple. He tried to bear down on the pain, to keep it under his control. One of those pale faces that flushes deeply. The thought flit through my mind that I liked a man's face that shows itself, vulnerable.

I made a sterile dressing, placed it between his toes. "It's best if you keep still," I said.

An open face with a rather large forehead, serious blue-grey eyes, and a restrained, intelligent manner.

"Try not to disturb the blisters."

Later, I was touching his leg and an image flooded up: a clearing in a dark forest. The grass — no, moss, or what felt like moss — was spongy underfoot. The trees were dominant, huge. The bark of one enormous tree was very deeply grooved, dark brown. Beside it was a different tree with bark that looked furry, the colour of a red setter.

He lay there on the spongy ground, pinned fast by a log. He was listening to someone who was running, crying out for help.

I must not let this distract me.

I put my hand on his leg. "Can you feel me now?' I asked. "You can, can't you?"

He nodded; again his face flushed, this time with relief. He was getting better, ready to talk.

Our first, entirely unremarkable exchange of words:

"What part of England are you from?"

"I'm not from England. Australia."

"Haven't met many Australians."

"Not many of us here."

"When did you come?"

"A little over a year ago."

"But you speak the language."

"Just a little. I lived here before, you see. On the Catalonian shore, with my husband. When he was alive."

"Oh. I'm sorry."

He introduced himself. Douglas Ross. Formally, he extended his hand, and I shook it. He gave an ironic smile, acknowledging that this was an after-the-fact introduction; we'd already touched.

"That's a Scottish name, Ross, isn't it?"

"My mother is from Scotland."

"Your father, too?"

"Canadian. Died just after the Great War. In the Spanish flu."

"Ah. I'm sorry. Do you remember him?"

"I was too young." He propped himself up on an elbow. "They call me by my last name, Ross. Don't know why." He said this lightly, an invitation to move away from the heavy stuff.

"It could just as easily be other way round," I replied, going along. "Ross Douglas."

He grinned. "The first shall be last and the last first."

"Exactly."

Ross had come up with the Canadians in the blizzard that welcomed in the new year.

"We spent New Year's Eve in a barn. Wrapped ourselves in straw, it was so cold. Buried ourselves up to our necks. Straw's scratchy but it keeps you really warm. Best sleep I'd had in weeks. When we woke, the land was covered with snow. We struggled on in the snow, me trailing along with the bogie of the Maxim."

He paused. A Maxim is a gun. So he was a gunner of some kind.

Bogie of the gun. What was that, exactly? Funny word, bogie. At home a bogey hole is a place to swim, a swimming hole among rocks in a river.

"Funny how we call it New Year's Eve. My mother, she calls it the Old Year's Night. Only she pronounces it 'auld.'"

Mother was showing up already.

"We slept in the straw on the Auld Year's Night," he continued. "I can't remember when I was last so toasty. The straw had been threshed. They do it right there in the barn, you know: winnow the grain, thresh it."

When I touched him, his nerve and bone and muscle were going through my hands and I saw his face when he was out there, away from the hospital. In the thick of battle, he had the sick determination of a child on a high diving board.

That's how it was. I touched him; I knew him. There was nothing in this of the long arc of learning the other's tone or gestures. No preliminaries, no doubts.

Naturally, we did not speak of these things.

I did not ask, what exactly happened back home, in the forest? Who was running for help? It's got something do with why you're here, doesn't it?

EARLY DUSK, NO MORE risk of air raids. Ross was tense; he was leaving the hospital, going back to his lines. I'd had his clothes washed. I took his jacket and burned the seams myself, with matches.

I told him I was going to go over his head again with paraffin and vinegar to ward off the return of lice. It's well worth doing for this reason alone, but that's not what I was after.

Rubbing him, I could feel his thoughts.

Out there on the front lines he didn't move around; none of the Canadians did. It was the Americans who crept into the town, raided the shops, desperate for additional clothing; it was the Americans who found a hat shop and wore sombreros. The Canadians, in open terrain to the north, stayed put.

At first when the frostbite started he was mad at himself for being clumsy with the gun. Then the shivering stopped. He noticed his muscles stiffen, his breathing slow down.

I rubbed him with the paraffin-vinegar mixture, letting my hands do their work slowly. He made a small noise.

Foxy, his little dog back home, was licking his head to wake him up.

The shell that was coming in whined higher, faster, waiting to explode. When it hit, the shell had a deeper sound. It was like being hurled into thunder. Then the air filled with smoke, hissing.

One of the boarders in his mother's boarding house came home with clippers he'd borrowed from a barber and gave their little dog Foxy a summer cut. Snip, snip, and the fur showed golden, sandy and grey, with a darker ridge following her spine. The unclipped tail remained a fountain, splashing over with pleasure.

On the third day about two hundred bombers and fighters came over, flying low and tight, thrumming and vibrating. If he'd lifted up a shovel he would have hit them. They looked right at him — and didn't see him. It was the strangest thing.

For a while there were sardines, tins of them, with the name in French along the side. Then they ran out. Was that before one of the boys — Yorky, was it? Yes, him. Yorky went out late one afternoon to lay a line for a phone and didn't come back. A flamingo sunset. Hard to look at it, though, because the cold made his eyes water. He'd been told about cold eyeballs when he worked in the woods with the Finns. You'd think the cold would kill the lice, but oh no, those sons of bitches simply lapped it up.

As I combed his hair it turned dark gold with its slick of oil.

The exploding shell created a thick parcel of fog around itself. The flames leaped up above the fog. He could see the shadows of the flames against the snow.

The shelling hammered so long it seemed as if the walls of the sky would surely crack.

When he felt small, eaten by cold, the trick was to think of seeing his bedroom slippers. Just seeing them. Plaid, with a hole made by the big toe. Neat, side by side. Warm, dry and ready.

His hair was soft; the skin behind his neck was soft. He could be taken for a Russian. For anyone they thought might be a Russo, the enemy reserved special attention.

I didn't know a thing about military strategy, but a drover's blind dog could have worked it out by now: Franco was completely free to bring in all the matériel he wanted while the democracies stood meekly by. We made one bold move, only to fall back. At first Teruel looked like a decisive victory. It didn't look like that now.

THE FREEZING WARD AT the front of the house must have been one of the bigger bedrooms, perhaps the master bedroom. Ross stood beside me and we looked across the narrow valley to the steep clear-cut range beyond. Patches of red earth showed up in places where the snow had been blown away.

An ancient aqueduct stretched across the gorge.

The news today had not been good — the rebels were trying to take the high ridge to the west of the town. It had an odd name, *La Muela*, the molar.

We stood together, looking out.

On our side of the gorge, at the edge of the old town, was a wrecked stone building. Behind it, a grey-green tangle of bush that I decided must be holm oak. The field had a stone fence about my height, and a broken wooden gate. Just inside the gate a large grey horse was daydreaming, unconcerned.

Soon it would be dusk.

As we watched, a red cat came out of the ruined building and sat down in the snow beside the horse. Ross turned to me and grinned — for the colour of the cat, for the quiet horse in the ruined landscape.

Earlier in the fighting, one arch of the ancient aqueduct had been blown up. The broken arch lay on the ground, a pile of rubble.

"I wonder if it was Roman?" Ross asked, of the aqueduct.

The broken arch wasn't what you looked at; what took your attention was the emptiness of the air where the arch had once been.

"Yes, it probably was Roman." Marcus would have known.

"Such a long time ago."

I longed to touch him. Was he thinking about the ancient Romans, or was he thinking about the barn he slept in on the last night of the year, or about his slippers and Foxy back home?

He turned to me. Quickly touched my hat. *Where did you get that?* A gesture that the smile about the animals made possible.

I took off the hat. He let me smooth his hair, and I put the hat on his head. On him, it didn't fall about the ears. "A man's hat," I said. "Fits you perfectly. Take it."

Even as he was protesting that he couldn't, he felt its fit, its warmth. "Take it," I repeated.

"I couldn't." He removed it.

But after he'd dressed in his shabby uniform, he let me pass him the hat. He stood clutching it in his hands, shy about making any kind of display of himself.

"Put it on," I urged. "You're going to need it." And he did.

I LISTENED TO THE sound of his boots on the stone stairs. I stood at the window; watched him go, walking away in the great silence of snow.

Ten

Catalonia, March–April 1938

I KNEW I'D SEE Ross again. I didn't experience this knowledge as a great rush; I felt no suddenness or shock about it. It was there, a given, the way things were.

About the last days up in the snows of Teruel, I have nothing to say. I never will. It is time excised; it cannot belong. Teruel was retaken. We were unable to move all the wounded men out, and for that there are no words.

I left Ramon behind, in the ground.

AFTER TERUEL I WAS stationed at a small hospital just south of Barcelona that specialized in cases of gangrene. Very soon the hospital was due to be relocated to a larger place farther down the coast. I wasn't sure why this was happening; I suspected the doctors put in the request and it slipped through without anyone paying attention. But I wasn't complaining, because I was working with an excellent team.

The two doctors were older men, Belgians, veterans of the Great War and vastly experienced.

I didn't know what happened to Alec after we fled Teruel. He was still there when I left with the abdominal cases. Nor did I have any news about the Mac-Paps.

THE IDES OF MARCH, 1938. Before heading to bed, I set out for a walk behind the hospital, to a small hill of pines and scrub. About nine-thirty at night.

I was standing on the hill, leaning on a tree, having a cigarette, and not thinking about much when something extraordinary happened. In the darkness, frogs began to croak. Birds, settled for the night, woke and flew about in the air, disoriented. Dogs barked, calling to one another, their tone rising and rising. Then the trees began to protest; the sound in the branches was exactly like the tearing of linen. The ground rattled. My initial thought was that I was being engulfed in an earthquake, while part of my mind was declaring that it couldn't be an earthquake, not in Spain, and another part was busy announcing that animals were the first to know.

In the distance, green signal flares of anti-aircraft batteries exploded. That's when I realized it wasn't an earthquake. The fascists were bombing Barcelona.

The bombing continued until night frayed around the edges.

THEY BOMBED BARCELONA EVERY three hours for three days and three nights. The figures are not completely accurate, but we rounded them out.

Fascist planes poured over from Majorca and tumbled their loads willy-nilly into the centre of the city. It was part of an experiment, to see if such things could be done.

What I did not know when I stood on the hill, watching the signal flares and feeling the animal distress, was that Alec had returned to the hospital in Barcelona where he'd completed his residency. Between raids, hospital staff rushed into the streets to gather up who they could before the next wave. Coming back at last to casualty, all was speedy and strangely bright: the red blood from a living arm, the whiteness of the dressing, amazing.

Another raid, and out they dashed again.

NOTHING HAPPENS IN SHOCK — not sympathy, not understanding, not compassion. Everything goes into suspension, everything including fear. The brain, small, detached, without emotion, observes. Observes the vibration in the air, the slow bending of trees in the strange hot wind, the way a building groans. Observes the body parts crowded together in a basket, bumping about as the truck runs over something in the road. Observes the relief when the sound of bombers dies away. The relief deepening.

Crunch of glass beneath the feet. Stone, dust, wood, paper, household implements. A body on the park bench with its drying blood is being inspected by a sparrow, head on one side.

ALEC WAS SEVERELY INJURED; he would live.

His sister Helen wrote to me with the news. Alec's hospital had contacted her and arranged for Alec to send a personal telegram. *Vital organs OK. Entombed in Plaster of Paris. Cure by decay.*

A Trueta cast, like the ones he himself had applied many times. I'd heard that in England it was already popularly known as the Guernica treatment.

They're supposed to be sending him home, Helen wrote, but could I find out what's going on and would I let her know?

A wall fell on him, a brick wall; it collapsed as a result of the bombing. I was irrationally comforted by the fact it was something as ordinary as a wall.

AFTER THE RAIDS, THE British consulate moved from Barcelona up the coast to Caldetes, with its lovely, irrelevant beach. At Helen's request I visited the consulate to inquire about the formalities of transporting Alec home to England. I sat in the consulate office in my one and only costume of pale blue with navy piping and told them he was my brother-in-law.

DON'T THINK FOR A minute that this cleared the path, finally, for Ross to arrive fully in my life. Nothing at that time, in that place, was simple.

The next thing I did was get married to a stranger, the German.

HELEN STARTLED ME WITH a request. She was coming to France and hoped to meet with me.

Helen had turned her attention to aid for Republican Spain. She'd come into contact with a group in Paris that assisted the wounded who were being sent out of Spain but who had no home they could return to. Such men were by this time scattered from Bordeaux across to Montpellier. Helen had a plan. It was, she explained modestly, the least she could do. What she had to offer these displaced men was a way to slip them into Britain, and thence on to more friendly countries such as Mexico.

Already her group had managed to find others who were willing, but — how should she put this? — I was an ideal candidate.

I TRAVELLED UP TO Perpignan to meet her. Helen was overdressed for the warm southern spring: hot, excited, and totally out of place.

Like everyone who was free to leave Spain for a short period of time, I was immediately distracted by the presence of so much to eat and struck by the marvel of not saying, *last night we were lucky; we ate mule.* Naturally, I had my shopping list from the medical team and everyone else who'd heard about the trip. Not only drugs and medical supplies but bobby pins, shoe polish, hair shampoo, and all the chocolate and coffee I could carry.

With my shopping well under way, Helen and I rounded up a driver and we set off for Hérault. It was a day when spring was at its most confident; the salt marshes shone silvery-bright. Leaving the main road just before Montpellier we turned inland, pushed up with the wind behind us, and rounded the bend into a small hill town overcome with the exuberance of cherry blossoms. We rolled down the windows and trailed our hands in the rush of sweet air.

I thought of Alec, lying in a London hospital and missing out on this. In England the buds would still be tight on the trees.

"How does it feel to be riding to the rescue?" I asked.

Helen giggled. Pleased to be there, to be travelling in a car in the springtime, in a strange country, able to commit herself, to be generous, to be involved in subterfuge.

Last night Helen outlined her strategy. First, she talked about the wounded Brigaders who'd come out of Spain, whose home countries had fully fledged fascist governments: maybe up to five thousand Germans, three thousand Italians. No welcome mat back home for any of them.

The British government wasn't dusting off the welcome mat either. They'd allowed some groups to bring in Basque orphans but weren't a scrap interested in adult refugees. But given the deteriorating situation in Europe they were relaxing their requirements somewhat. If a British subject could provide sufficient guarantee for her new husband's support during a period of temporary residence in Britain, he could become a transit emigrant with definite plans for onward emigration. In short, I had to promise to support him, then send him on his way.

None of it had to be for real, Helen reassured me. Neither the marriage nor the plans. All I had to do was sign. As for the guarantees of support in England, she and her organization would be taking care of that.

Trust a member of the Flinders family to round me up for this.

And of course, I didn't really have to take him all the way home. The organization Helen was working with was in contact with a similar group in Mexico, a country that was receptive to the difficulties faced by refugees. Once he reached Britain, arrangements would be made to pass him along, although that might take a little time.

While marriage by itself would be insufficient — under a daft 1914 British law I would technically become an alien by marrying him — it was a pre-requisite for offering those guarantees and signalled the solidity of my intent.

I'd had one bizarre marriage, I decided, why not another? At least this one might be of some use.

WE REACHED A TURNOFF, motored along a cracked concrete road between vineyards where the buds had already burst, and lurched steeply down between rows of plane trees in new leaf to a dilapidated villa in the Italian fashion.

The villa, clearly uninhabited until recent months, was completely surrounded by vineyards. Rampant greenery was in the process of consuming the villa, swallowing it whole. The stone terrace was stained green from the copper of the vats, and baskets for the grapes were stacked high against the balustrades. In the clearing — you could no longer call it a garden, but the grass was lush and fresh — geese were leading clutches of goslings.

Inside the villa we found men with wounds that had healed; the place was a holding pen humming with frustration against the pretence of convalescence. For these men, the budding and burbling of a new season must seem like a taunt. They knew exactly why Helen and I had come, and greeted us formally. One of them led us to chairs on green-stained terrace. Coffee was produced.

We brought out the first necessities of any visit: cigarettes, tobacco, shaving brushes, soap. These were followed by second-order necessities: paper, pens, ink, and postage stamps. The third order of necessities, newspapers and books, we had forgotten.

After the coffee and the gifts and the thanks, down to conversation.

The Non-Intervention farce, compared with which, what we were up to on the terrace was as nothing.

The jumpy response of the French government. Even with a French wife eagerly awaiting, there were hoops, obstacles, road-blocks. The officials didn't like the idea of these men moving in for good. Given arrangements for a third country, however, these same officials would be waving you on, all the way to the Channel.

The men's problem was a modern one: they had no proper papers. Many had come as tourists for the Paris Exposition; some had come for the Olympiad in Barcelona. All they had were honourable discharges from the Brigades. Once the war had been won, these papers would be valuable indeed, but not yet.

Helen was at her most polite: brisk and very British. She offered the deal. Further shaking of hands, filing in of documents, and a peculiar atmosphere of restrained, humiliated gratitude that was difficult to bear.

HELEN AND I ESCAPED for the evening and the driver took us back down to Montpellier. At dinner, with the courage of wine, I asked her about Alec.

Alec was healing. He was forced to lie on his stomach but could manage books. Last seen reading *Daniel Deronda*. One mirror provided him with a view of the room and another provided him with a view of the window.

"He says he's learning to view the world aslant."

Alec would be good at that.

"One of the doctors is a fellow from his Cardiff days."

They could have cozy talks about silicosis.

Alec had fobbed me off on Marcus because he wasn't ready for encumbrances during his residency in Cardiff. Then he'd come out to Spain and we had a summer dalliance. Who could blame him for that?

Me, for one.

Not blame, perhaps, but resent. Certainly, resent.

"What do they say?" I asked. "The doctors?"

"They say he's a blithering idiot for having gone out to Spain."

"But the prognosis?"

"Time." In time, he will heal.

I imagined the room in the London hospital — him lying there with his mirror view of the cupboard, the zinc tray, the door. From the other mirror: the window, tight buds, and the liver-brick of an adjoining hospital wing.

"Wings," I said. "Not the best term for parts of a hospital."

Helen looked up, briefly puzzled, uninterested. "You're the nurse. You should know."

I took the last piece of bread. Not a single scrap of fine French food would ever go to waste, not on my plate.

When Alec was waiting for the narcotic, on the jumpy edge of pain, that's the time he might think of me.

"Did he say anything about me?"

Helen would have been full of her plans, would in her enthusiasm have mentioned me, the star candidate.

"He sends his regards."

Regards. Unadorned.

The next day we returned to the villa where the Brigaders were penned up, and this time we took newspapers and books. Again we sat out on the terrace. In the fresh morning light the vineyards were dotted with shining green pearls.

I heard footsteps, two sets. I looked up.

Irrationally, I hoped to have the one with the smile, not the one with the eyes that popped. But it wasn't to be.

Otto and Hans. Two palpably generic names.

The marriage would be just on paper, of course. Nothing else.

Otto began to give a tidy bow, shook my hand instead. I smiled at him, asked him where he came from in Germany. At the question his neck jerked up, his eyes flickered with guarded interest. Had I perhaps been to Germany in times before? I was afraid I had not.

He looked out to the vineyard, where the wind had come up.

Contained, distant. Tough as fencing wire. Had to be or he wouldn't be here.

I, too, listened to the others speaking. I felt an urge to reach out and take this German's hand, to confide in him, to take the risks you can take with a stranger.

Boldly, I would ask him why he came to Spain. Not what his politics were, but what had entered his heart, what he had seen or heard that started him on the path to this place.

I would tell him why I had come back to Spain. In this country, where I had been idle and cruel, I wanted to be of use. What else? That at the core of me I was a nurse, a real one — he could trust me in that at least. In addition to my work and food and sleep, practically all I ever thought about was my father back home and the disaster of my first marriage, in which I had driven my husband to his death. There wasn't much else inside me, really.

Not true. At Teruel, a Canadian had slipped into a deep place that I couldn't comprehend. But I wouldn't mention him; it was too personal, too private, and inchoate besides.

I sat on the terrace and imagined myself talking honestly to Otto: No doubt you will find me a complete naïf. Yet underneath these layers of ignorance, I do have an understanding I picked up from my father, a man who dwelt at the edge of the world. I found it again in the fishing village in Catalonia where my husband lived. If I were to name it, I would say it was a conviction that grows inside you when you are acquainted with hills that fall away into nothing or with an ocean that takes all. It is this: we are all the same, all worth exactly the same, and those who indulge in calibrations of privilege and wealth are simply up themselves.

This dream about talking to Otto was mere fantasy. Not so much as a mild shiver of mutual attraction passed between us.

At the villa, arrangements were made. A day later, down to the *mairie*, and on an afternoon filled with a steady wind, Otto and I were married by the *adjoint*, the deputy mayor, who was small, round, and pink-faced, with a red, yellow, and purple rosette in his label — the colours of the Spanish Republic. Otto and Hans wore their Brigade buttons. I understood, by the deputy mayor's embraces, his stepping confidently past the reticence of the Brigaders for a kiss on both cheeks, that he was the one who'd taken care of the papers the German bridegroom could not produce; he was the one who'd supplied the requisite lies about the length of time I'd been in the district.

Neither Otto nor Hans really relaxed. No fooling around, no falling into the role of newlywed and best man, not even for a momentary lark, despite the lunch the deputy mayor insisted upon and paid for himself.

Carefully, Otto and Hans savoured their meal; they dwelt over the thick, tasty sauces. I could see the food-warmth spreading inside them, reaching their brain, bringing content. I felt the same warmth inside me. The deputy mayor and Helen were pleased with themselves in additional ways: Helen, acknowledged ace recruiter, and the deputy mayor, successful saboteur of a whole raft of petty laws. Both had managed to assist a stranger, to whose health they were eating and drinking.

At the culmination of the brief paper shuffle at the *mairie*, a document had been put in front of me to sign. Clarice Thaelmann, that's the new me. Ha! Inventing a name to use for the marriage documents, Otto had adopted that of his battalion. As I looked at my absurd full name and began to sign it, unruly laughter bubbled up. Even the first name I never used. If only Laia could have been by my side, how she would have rolled her eyes. How she would have loved being in France, how she would have devoured the food and wine. Laia, who would not laugh with Ramon again.

The Germans were in good enough humour by the time they raised their glasses to *¡No pasarán, Pasaremos! Sie kommen nicht durch!*

Wir kommen durch! The road back to Berlin would have to take a detour through London.

By this point the diners in the restaurant sensed the general air of fellow-feeling at the table. They saw a groom toasting his bride.

Helen gathered up the papers — the essential part of what had happened. She would take them back with her, to prepare for the passage of Otto to Britain.

I returned to Spain, having entered my second marriage on the most contemporary terms, and was assigned without delay to the base hospital by the Ebro.

On the other side of the Ebro, the Republicans were in full retreat and Ross was among them.

Eleven

Catalonia, April–May 1938

ACROSS THE RIVER, WE were waiting for the soldiers to arrive. In a house among hills, now a base hospital, our medical team was ready. Prepared for the occasion, we were restless as hosts awaiting guests.

I prowled the grounds, having nothing better to do. Gravel walks, a pine grove surrounding an ornamental pool filled with rainwater, a line of poplars at the back that acted as a windbreaker. Behind the poplars was a creek and beyond that lay an orchard and vegetable fields. Cabbages, onions, carrots, potatoes, none of them yet ready for eating. In the orchard, beehives among the almond trees.

Yesterday up at the house, men arrived in a lorry with stretchers, which they brought in through the big windows. The best kind of stretchers, with steel struts to discourage lice from bed-hopping. The men were cheerful as they manoeuvred the stretchers, tramping down the flower beds and shouting curses to one another — *I shit in the chalice* and so on. Shocking our friends from the American press, who were here waiting with us.

We were preparing for men in disarray, who'd been out in the fields, unfed, dog tired, wounded. In the impressive rooms of the main part of the house, the stretchers stood in neat rows, at the ready. Blankets and even some sheets had appeared. Not sure how the latter were going to be cleaned. We had no power and an insufficient number of candles, but maybe more could be found.

This morning a van showed up with amazing luxuries: long black coils of sausage and mounds of goat's cheese. When the van came in I stood about with the other medical staff, admiring its contents. We wanted to believe that the food had been sent from France, where last month Prime Minister Blum had finally come to his senses and thrown open the borders. But his government had fallen and he had just been replaced; what would that mean?

The prospect of French food was enough to make us wobbly at the knees. Then somebody turned the cheese over and saw the Spanish name. It came from around Valencia. With this, the little group around the van broke up, disappointed.

If that wasn't enough, it was beginning to look as if we would soon be cut off even from Valencia and its fruitful gardens, its *huerta*.

FROM WHERE WE WERE I could not see the Ebro. One of the men from the American press, newly arrived with a car, offered to take me with him to the river. He told me that upstream near Zaragoza the rebels had opened the floodgates so that the water ran high and fast, yellow with mud.

We scrambled up from the road, climbed over a stone wall, made our way through grey-olive scrub, and stood above the Ebro.

In a long field on the other side, farmers continued to work. Birds were dipping about among the soft spring grasses by the bank. In the distance the river appeared silver in the morning sun. Somewhere downstream, out of our sight, a shattered army of men was making its way across under fire. The notion seemed entirely implausible.

Beside me, staring at the water, the American had the self-absorption of a person who is driven by his work. Storing up details for people to read.

I was looking at the river, feeling the sun on my back, not thinking of anything much, when from nowhere, swiftly, a surge of panic exploded inside me. A torrent was sweeping across my chest and up into my head; blood was pulsing so fast it pushed the breath out of me. Automatically, I took note: dry body heat, hot red face, cold hands, and a desire to stay still, never to move again. I gripped the swirling wall.

I was wearing a pair of jodhpurs Helen had given me. Over my blouse a sweater — also a gift from Helen — of green-and-brown wool, with a leather button so I could pull the collar across my neck to keep warm.

I was hanging onto the wall in these winter clothes, their unbearable heaviness, their heat.

What's the matter?

Tearing at that leather button. Air, I needed air. Unable to speak.

The American took my arm in an impersonal way, like a stranger at a funeral. We walked back to the sunken road, the car. I sat uncomfortably, beads of cold sweat underneath my blouse.

By the time we arrived back at the house, I'd returned to myself.

The American, habitually courteous, did not ask, what was *that* about back there?

AFTER A LUNCH OF oranges stewed in wine, I showed the American around. We started with a trip to the impressively well-stocked wine cellar.

Neither of us mentioned this morning, up at the river, but it had thrown us together. For the short time he would be here, it would be me he sat with, talked to. Tomorrow or the day after, he'd be gone, off to somewhere new. But for now the big American would be the one. We would expose parts of ourselves, then we'd move on and never see each other again.

We traded our first round.

He wrote under his middle name but his first name was James; everyone called him Jim.

I'd lived in Catalonia, had been married to an Englishman, an archaeologist.

Before this? In the war?

I was at Teruel. A score; he was interested in anyone who'd been up in frigid Teruel.

Any Mac-Paps, did he know any Mac-Paps? Had he in his travels happened to meet a Canadian called Douglas Ross?

No.

I told him about what happened to my brother-in-law. How he hurried out into the streets of Barcelona after the March bombing, became trapped beneath a falling wall, and was now in London, lying on his stomach.

Together we discussed the house, which belonged to a well-known Catalan painter. The main part of the house would be called Georgian in England but had local touches such as the tiled front hall. In recent years the place had been modernized, with large glass doors at the hall's far end.

"We haven't cleared much out because we'll just sort, operate, and move along."

Dominating the wall of the front room, looming above the stretchers, was a series of paintings of a young woman's head. The face was by turn innocent, flirtatious, but always with a direct and challenging gaze. In every version her long hair, which streamed behind her as if underwater, was crammed with twisted metal.

"A modern painter," Jim said. "Must have loved her once but he left her behind."

I would be working in the older part of the house. Smaller rooms, painted chocolate brown, heaving with furniture. In addition to my regular duties, those with serious battle wounds that had reached the stage of gangrene would be under my care.

I was so lucky — luxury of luxuries — I had a space to myself.

Just a bed crammed in by a wall behind some cupboards, but hang a blanket in front and *voilà*, private quarters.

We inspected the rest of the rooms of the older wing. Cupboards crammed with chess pieces, dominoes, tennis rackets with sagging catgut, sets of cards, wooden toys, scads of trashy novels in French, and boxes full of velvets and wild feather plumes that children must have used for dress-up. Clearly these people paid a great deal of attention to keeping themselves amused.

"Do you think they played charades?" I asked.

"Not sure. It seems like a very English game to me."

"In this house you can feel that people have been happy."

He smiled.

We shut the cupboard on the velvets and the feathers. Dust flew up.

DINNER. SOMEBODY HAD GONE down to the cellar and brought up bottles. Stories circulated, as they do. About a doctor on the other side of the river, operating in a tent during a bombing raid. Knelt on the ground with his hands in the air, to maintain asepsis. When the bombs finished falling, he stood up and immediately resumed operating.

Big Jim the American was talking about Madrid, the support of a million people at the end of a single road, and the way orderly life goes on. The key, he claimed, was the fundamental steadiness of the Spanish government, which for sixteen months had ruled an area greater than England and Wales, defending a front over a thousand miles long against the insurgent Spanish troops, bolstered by the Italian Expeditionary Force, German forces, and Moors from the colonies pressed into service.

Big Jim, champion of the Popular Front. Leave out the murky bits; might as well.

Anise. And the conversation became bleaker. Some might say, more honest.

Now we were talking about the retreats. This spring had been a nightmare. The fascists, with heaps of men and equipment, were able to mount their big offensive and it had proven too much for us. Weakened by the loss of men and matériel at Teruel, the Republican Army had been scrambling. And the Soviet Union, which used to contribute equipment, was sending way less and in fact seemed to have lost interest.

More anise.

Some young slip of a thing with a Home Counties accent started in on the *automutilados*, how they must be treated as deserters. Not a nurse, this one. I suspected she may have taken a tour of a London hospital one Sunday afternoon before transforming herself into a nursing assistant. There were more of these assistants about. Had we come to end of qualified nurses? And what would she know about self-inflicted injuries? Tennis elbow, that'd be the extent of it. The Belgian doctors I'd been working with could tell her a thing or two about *automutilados*. During the Great War, the trick, they said, was to run a coin around the wound, make it pay. Prolong infection, prolong your life.

"What we need," I told Miss Home Counties, "is not penalties for self-inflicted wounds but soap, enough to eat, and adequate quinine." Miss Prim, that was me, up in the pulpit, putting an end to girlish chatter.

I turned to the American, Big Jim. After Teruel, I told him, I'd gone to a small hospital just south of Barcelona. When my work here was done, I was due to move to another hospital on the coast, with the same doctors. They were Belgian, quite old, and obsessed with gangrene. These doctors, I explained, were somewhat disappointed that gas gangrene wasn't what it used to be. Gangrene had been a huge deal during the Great War because of the trenches. The doctors, I added irrelevantly, had a truly marvellous supply of laudanum, much more handy than the morphine tablets one has to mix with water, suck up into the syringe.

Listening to this babble, Big Jim became quite talkative; impossible to make a fool of himself, he'd decided, not with me. He'd lived for many years in Germany, had been married there. I pricked up my ears at this. Did he marry a German? No.

He spoke of what was happening in Germany. It was incremental, he said. Little by little, everything that matters has been chipped away. The first step, he declared, was way back, with the reintroduction of the death penalty. He drew his fingernail sharply across his own throat. In the candlelight his throat was pink and the fingernail left a thin white mark.

"The majority did not vote for Hitler in the 1932 elections. So where, you ask, has the majority gone?" Big Jim leaned forward.

I hadn't asked, but Jim's a sweetie so I didn't mind.

"I'll tell you," he offered. "I'll tell you how it's done, in five easy steps."

"January 1933, the little man becomes chancellor. Has it handed to him by the ruling elite. Most in his cabinet are conservatives, not Nazis. February, Reichstag fire. Commies cop the blame, and he's rounding up opponents, murdering them casually as a schoolboy at play. In March — same month as the election — he pushes through an act that gives the cabinet full legislative power, assent no longer required from the Reichstag. On the first of April, he launches an official national boycott of Jewish businesses. This peters out within a few days because of public lack of enthusiasm.

"Doesn't matter; he's on a roll. The very next week, legislation is passed for the 'restoration' of the civil service. Jews and sundry opponents of the regime lose their jobs. So it goes. You can say, oh no you don't, but if you've lost the power, my friend, you're getting out of the rain by standing under a drainpipe. By midsummer all political parties other than the Nazis had been disbanded and the trade unions were no more."

He would have written a piece on this, just as he would have written those comments about Madrid. People in New York or Chicago would be reading Big Jim's columns while eating their breakfast cereal. Did his opinions make a whit of difference?

Jim continued to speak of Germany, where he'd married his wife, who turned out to be French, and a musician. By this time I wasn't really listening; I was enjoying looking at him. His hair was a deep red but you could see streaks of grey at the temple. Still handsome, he would have been an exceptionally striking younger man. I wondered briefly what it would feel like to be enclosed in his arms. He didn't hug me up there at the river, he just took my elbow, steered me. He could have hugged me but he didn't.

Big Red Jim, I bet they called him. Big Red, hopping about Europe.

His conversation hopped back to Spain, to the Republic's appeal to the League of Nations. "They put their case in Geneva with level heads even though they felt betrayed, just like Haile Selassie."

I wondered what he made of that strife last May in Barcelona. Too tired to ask.

We mooned in our glasses, pretty much drunk. Candlelight flickered on the watery anise.

"Who," Big Jim asked, "could ever forget the eloquence of Haile Selassie, the Lion of Ethiopia, speaking to the League?"

Time for bed.

"Italy had invaded his country without declaring war. Britain and France promptly recognized the occupation."

"Cowards," I agreed idly.

We'd be up all night at this rate, I decided. Jim was a man of our times, one of those chaps who couldn't resist the smell of history cooking up.

I decided to tell Big Jim a story of my own to head him off at the pass. How I'd crossed the frontier into France, met my sister-in-law, and married a German. I promised it would be just the main part, not the family details. I explained that as a nurse I was free to cross the border, and was not subject to military regulations.

"We're going to be such wrecks," Big Jim said with a grin. "Big day coming tomorrow. I feel it in my bones."

"Let's press on regardless, shall we?"

"That's the spirit," he agreed. "The spirits."

I AWOKE DRY-MOUTHED WHEN it was still dark. We were on double-hour daylight saving, so eight in the morning was really only six. In the dream I'd been clawing my way into the ground, hard ground without shelter, and nothing was as it should be. I was also talking to Big Jim. "Fever is not an enemy," I was saying to him, "fever is on *our* side."

I shook the dream away.

Something had happened in the night. I knew even before I emerged from my bed behind the cupboards that the garden would be filling up fast.

Overnight, they had begun to arrive. Some still wet, in tatters, some wearing old clothing peasants had given them, all exhausted.

Men so tired their tongues hung out.

I DRESSED QUICKLY, HURRIED to the main wing.

This was no longer a garden with an ornamental pool in a grove of pines. It had become a shabby, sprawling, all-night outdoor market. In the grove, on the gravel sweep, men had claimed their own particular places to stretch out. While most were making mounds of sleep, some were stirring. Picking lice, repairing shoes, washing their clothes in the pool, even drying them on the bushes. Already there were disputes over who owned what patch; there had been a knife fight in the garden over the unripe vegetables.

Each man had made his way to the hospital to fall upon the bread, the cigarettes. A lucky few had struck camp in the tiled hallway, where they were beginning to smell.

Those able to swim arrived first. Next to come were those who'd walked to Tortosa, where a bridge was still standing. Tortosa was a pile of rubble; the Italians had been bombing it for the past three weeks.

"Why didn't anyone wake me?" I complained.

All through the morning the battered ambulances were making deliveries. These ambulances crept along in green-and-yellow camouflage. Not a pane of glass in any window.

I was busy and free from thought. Cleaning pellets of shrapnel, dirt, and cloth from a man's face so swollen he would be unrecognizable even to his family, I was completely absorbed. Time had become irrelevant.

You could say I was happy.

FOUR DAYS LATER THERE was only the smell of trampled grass, stains on the gravel where small fires had been lit, bundles of old clothing, discarded equipment, empty tin cans, ruined boots.

Like locusts they came; like locusts they moved on.

Camps were hastily organized up the valley, closer to the river. Quickly, as if by instinct, men searched for and found whoever was left of their company, their *peloton*. Down some rock-and-clay gully they were building shelters — no more than a rough roof made of scrub, with pine branches if possible, and a bit of straw for the ground if they were lucky. Somewhere to lie down, somewhere to enjoy the luxury of a Chesterfield or a *Gauloises Bleu*. Somewhere away from the eyes in the planes.

They waited until a soup truck came up, and the truck bringing mail. Already they were giving the gullies the names of streets back home.

Big Jim took me up with him. I watched him moving amongst the men, asking questions, listening. His Spanish was atrocious, French so-so, German presumably excellent.

I saw him approach the soldiers with deference, more than a little embarrassed. It was genuine but also effective. Men turned to him, their faces opened, they talked.

We came back to the hospital, with Big Jim full of the stories he was about to file. "This is a super-serious army," he said. "Wounded, these boys stagger across the river in defeat, and the first thing out of their mouths is, 'What's Neville Chamberlain saying? What's happening in Austria?' They ask these questions and I don't have the heart to tell them that Chamberlain has been busy cooking up a pact with Mussolini.

"If the Republic can hang on," Jim added, brightening up, "the democracies will come in against Franco, sooner rather than later; they will be forced to. France first, then England will follow. I have no doubt that the Republic will hold. Madrid, having come this far, will never fall, never." Big Jim was packing his bags, moving on. Next stop, next article, Madrid revisited.

Big Jim was a great bloke, he meant well, knew heaps. But the first thing a wounded man says is *¡Mamá!* Help me. *¡Ayúdenme!*

THE WOUNDED WERE BEING moved on, the medical staff going with them. We were down to the last of the stragglers.

The news was staggering. Good Friday, April 15. In the afternoon, the rebels entered Vinaròs on the Mediterranean. They'd reached the sea. The Republic was cut in two.

A flare of anxiety as the white-and-silver planes came directly over the hospital — and kept on going. Late in the afternoon, another *avion* alarm. They flew over; keeping high; we heard bombs in the distance.

We were in a tremendous rush. No time for paperwork, no time for anything. Just get the wounded on their way. The main bridge at Tortosa had been bombed but a secondary bridge was still in working order.

In the late afternoon a man was brought in by ambulance.

SOMEBODY FOUND ROSS ON the other side of the river and ferried him across. A massive wound in his left leg. Muscles shattered from the top of his shin bone to just above the ankle. The first six hours are critical for a wounded man, but Ross had been out there four, five days.

The enemy was already well entrenched at the river, but Republicans sneaked back, picking up latecomers.

"One of ours," the stretcher bearer said.

Right away I recognized him.

Tied to his belt: a jam jar with a few papers in it, one tin can for a cup, and my hat.

"HE HAS BEEN UNATTENDED for too long," the surgeon said.

Touching Ross, I was aware of the frightened flutter of his heart.

The skin of the leg was bronzed where it had been shattered. Local swelling. A thin froth erupted from the wound; it smelled sweet. I felt his taut white skin, marbled with blue. Cool to the touch.

The surgeon, who was swift, experienced, examined the swollen muscle. He was having problems probing with his scalpel. The muscle did not contract.

"Oedematous," the surgeon said, stating the obvious. Swollen, distended. The mighty fortress of our long words.

Parts of the muscle were beefy red. Other parts were black.

After the surgeon was finished, Ross would be mine, to watch for sepsis, for fever. I looked at the fine long bones of his feet. He still had his feet; he would keep them both, I promised myself. He would not become a cripple, he would not.

The surgeon snipped at the dead muscle: we were down to business.

As we worked, we talked back and forth, the kind of conversation we had at dinner. What will it mean, the rebels having reached the sea? Maybe all of the Republican forces will need to be withdrawn to this side of the Ebro. I repeated the words of Big Jim: what we have to do is hang on. England will follow the lead of France and there will be an alliance, at last, against fascism.

Finally the surgeon was satisfied. "He's all yours."

Part Four

Twelve

HE'S HERE, IN MY care. Every scrap of my training, every single thing I've ever learned, will go into making sure he comes through.

Is he stirring? I'm sitting at the other side of the narrow room, beside a fireplace roughly boarded up. I'm keeping the curtains pulled; the light might disturb him, frighten him.

Yes, he has stirred. He's opening his eyes.

"I've been waiting for you to wake." I feel like someone who's been swimming beyond her strength and has finally reached the far side.

Another nurse puts her head around the door. "Your patient has come round then, has he?"

"You're a lucky lad," this nurse continues. "We thought you were a goner, didn't we? How's he behaving? A real pain in the leg?" Jokey good-sportish voice, packed with deceit.

I wish she hadn't come in. I wish she wasn't carrying on like that.

As soon as she's gone, I talk to him about his leg. I'm going to syringe it every half hour. I'm going to take the best care of it.

"You mustn't worry," I say, sounding worried myself, "as soon as you're well enough, I'll be taking you to the coast. The doctors there are the best, they really are."

He wakes again.

I sit beside him. He's too tired to speak. Together we examine the picture on the wall next to him. Somebody's getting married. They're standing on the front steps: the bride, the groom, and the relatives. A boy in a white collar and a big fluffy bow. Bet they had trouble persuading him to wear that. Everyone looking important about having their photograph taken. This picture is quite old. You can tell by the men's horseshoe beards and high collars. Speaking of horses, at the edge of the picture the mare has craned her neck around, to make sure she's in the photograph, too. Looks like a mare anyway. Quiet and relaxed.

I offer Ross a little food. I was able to locate only a few chestnuts and a half glass of red wine. I see Ross wants them but can't bring himself to eat or drink, too much bother.

"You must try," I say, quietly. "We don't have a great deal of food at the moment; it's been sent on."

"The others have gone," I add.

I talk to him again about his leg. It's important he has the facts; he deserves to know what's going on. I tell him I will be draining it of fluid, syringing it every half hour. The affected tissue has been cut away successfully.

"Tissue?" he asks in a dreamy voice.

"Everything is going well. All will be well, you'll see."

"Grab a bit of ground and burrow in."

"That's right," I say, smiling. "Burrow in." I pull the blanket up to the top of his chest.

He looks at me again. "What time of day is it?"

"Afternoon."

They came at last to a land where it was always afternoon.

"My name is Ross," he says, politely.

"I know."

ROSS IS ILL, WITH the deep passivity of a wounded man who realizes he can stop making an effort.

The Tortosa bridge, the one that's still working, has been hastily covered with planks and turf, to strengthen it. It has borne the weight of trucks, an army in full retreat, and refugees. We join them in the push north, inching along the terrible road to Santa Barbara.

Ross is at the front end of the morphine, chatty.

"Knew this Swedish guy wounded at Teruel."

And I remember Teruel, the view from the window, the high fur hat. The sound of his boots on the stone stairs.

Does he remember me?

"This Swedish guy," he says, "he got wounded at Teruel. Was it ever cold. The Swede was sent down to a hospital on the Med. Quartered in a villa, flowing veins all around."

"Flowering vines," I suggest.

He has to stop, to consider. "Right. Like I said.

"The Swede came down from Teruel in late January. When he woke in the hospital he looked out and saw the ground covered with white. What he first took for snow turned out to be blossoms, white blossoms. He couldn't believe it. Blossoms in January."

A story often told, sucked up by men who were miserable and cold. For a Swede, for a Canadian, January blossoms would be miraculous indeed.

"The dining room was this glass verandah out over the sea. The Swede said you could hear the water splashing about under the floorboards while you ate your breakfast. When he was feeling better, he'd walk down past salt flats to the sea. Ate fish for dinner caught that very day."

"Sounds like Benicàssim." The International Brigades had a large convalescent hospital at Benicàssim, on the coastal road north of Valencia.

"That where we're going?"

The wonderful vague protective happiness of the drugged. Doesn't feel particularly worried about anything. Not at this moment. He's with the Swede, opening the window on January blossoms.

"No, my friend, it's not. We're on the other side of the river."

Is he aware the Republic has been cut in half? I haven't talked with him about that yet.

"I don't think they'd let me into Benicàssim," I add. "Not sure I'm completely to be trusted, you know, not even now. Not out of the top drawer, you understand."

He's not listening, which is just as well; it wouldn't make any sense. He's falling asleep.

It happens quite often. Lucid enough that first time at the base hospital, when he was looking at the wedding photo. Since then he's been slipping back and forth, coming to terms.

HE IS LIKE A man underwater who comes up for air before going back down.

"Your hand is in mine," I tell him. Maybe he hears me, from far away.

He speaks to himself, to the shadow in the room.

He reached the river; he'd almost made it into the river when the rifle went off.

He'd joined up with the telephone guys and right away he'd asked about Tony. Tony was with a telephone unit, so it made sense they might know him, but they shook their heads.

(Who is this Tony? I will have to find out.)

The telephone men were carrying their wire and the switchboard, which they stored carefully when they hid. The switchboard had *Made in Madrid* printed on its side. It was their most important possession. Because they were telephone men they were carrying the phone and wire; they weren't carrying guns. He got to carry the single rifle. It had belonged to someone else before him and when they handed it to him, he didn't ask questions. That was back before they reached the river.

They followed the North Star. They were moving across the hills by night, following the star. Like the wise men, they joked. Bringing their switchboard. They took turns carrying the switchboard. It was light enough to carry by your side. There were no lines ahead of them; they were taking the wire to lay some lines. He just tagged along.

He was walking with the telephone guys. They'd been walking about thirty hours. He figured out why they didn't want to let the switchboard go. It kept their spirits up, held them together. As long as they had that switchboard, they had a purpose. They weren't part of a collapsed army scampering north in defeat, they were telephonists planning to lay down lines wherever they found the next front. Besides, the switchboard was so lovely and modern. Weighed no more than eight, ten pounds at the most. It had little lights, and when it was set up, it could connect you with up to twelve different companies. All you had to do was hit the button, switch over, and the call was put through.

As he said, he was carrying the rifle because he'd tagged along with them. At the river, he was scrambling down the bank when it misfired.

Someone lifted him and that was when he knew he was dead. Those old ancients who talked about the Shades turned out to be correct after all; it was dreary. Nothing special.

Funny those ancients being the ones who'd got it right, not the clergy, who'd promised St. Peter at the gates. So much for those Sundays at Holy Trinity. Which was a pity in a way. His mother was going to be disappointed. When she found out it had all been for naught, she'd feel let down.

He was in the water and it was very cold and then he was lifted up. You had to cross a river to reach the Shades, didn't you? Didn't somebody come in a boat and row you? It all fit. He was being rowed across. The rower was winded. Didn't say a word. You could tell he was a big man by the heavy way he breathed.

It was the rower who took people across the river; he tried to remember the rower's name. He also tried to remember the name of the river — a short name, just a few letters. But for the life of him couldn't remember it either. Four letters.

THE TWO BELGIAN DOCTORS — bald, small, stooped, and sufficiently alike to be mistaken for brothers — greet me briefly, examine the patient without fuss, and let me decide where to put him.

In the smallest ward I can find, only four beds tucked in beside one another.

With vindicated melancholy the doctors pronounce that being cut off from the south will lead to shortages of supplies.

This hospital is the very best I could ask for: experienced doctors, Frenchmen in the kitchen, Dutch and German nurses, apart from me. I am the lone Englishwoman, although I take pains to point out that I'm not English, not in the least.

Ross is not fully aware, has not yet really arrived. I try to follow his faltering sense of time and place. When he speaks, images float within a vague shell of chronology.

One of the Belgians explains to Ross in English, "The necrotic tissue has been cut away and the leg appears clean."

"What's necrotic?" Ross asks. He's looking at me.

"Dead," I say. "Not like you. You're very much alive."

"I am?"

"'Fraid so, my friend."

The doctor continues. "The wound will be drained of fluid and closely watched. We shall see how the smaller arteries and the veins take up the work of the larger ones."

How, not *if*. With this optimistic verdict, the doctor leaves.

"I'm going to have you outdoors in the sun," I say. "Keep the wound exposed constantly, so it will stay dry, let the air at it. You'll just lie back and look at the sky."

"The sky," he says.

"Your job right now is to take it easy," I tell him. "Sit in your chair, read, talk if you want, snooze, enjoy the sunshine in the garden. Do you think you'll be equal to that task?"

Suddenly, he's awake and conscious: a good sign, an excellent sign.

"Nurse," he says. "You're so demanding."

Almost flirting.

FOR THE PAST THREE days Ross has had a high fever and a dangerously low heart rate. The cause is not his leg; an infection is attacking his chest and lungs.

I've been beside him non-stop, trying to keep him talking, so he won't pass out. He rides the fever with an uncomplaining courage that makes me all the more determined. He must not, he will not, weaken to the point where a new infection attacks his leg. Not on my watch.

Today he is calmer, his heart rate is climbing back up; he still has the chills but I tell him they're natural; he's out of the woods.

I ask him casual questions, mostly to keep him alert. When did you come to Spain? Where have you been? (Too early to embark on how we first met, up in the snows of Teruel.)

He arrived in the summer of last year. Trained at Tarazona de la Mancha, the headquarters for the English-speaking troops. Last autumn he was with the Mac-Paps in Aragón. Took part in the doomed assault on Fuentes de Ebro in October.

But what he wants to talk about is how he retreated to the river.

Back on the hill on a night with no moon. If there had been a moon the soldiers in the road would have seen them. He and the telephone guys were hiding in an orchard on the hill, sticking out like a dog's balls.

Had he mentioned the orchard before?

"Don't stop," I urge him. "Tell me about the orchard. What did it look like?"

Stubby little trees, close together, thick with leaves and just as well. The orchard saved their skin.

In a village before darkness fell, one of the telephonists had bought a wheel of cheese from a woman. She had a store that like everything else in the village was under bombardment. The back of the store was open to the sky, although from the front it didn't look too bad. The cheese was her last piece, but she insisted she wanted to sell it.

The rest of them stood in the road, nervous, listening to the exchange. The one who was buying, being tired, knocked over a chair on his way out, and he stopped to pick it up. Despite the fact that the store was only half there, the chair must be righted.

They were in the village and buying the wheel of cheese, then they tramped down the road and they heard tanks, so they hopped it into the fields, climbing up well above the road.

They'd gone to ground in an orchard; surely he'd mentioned the orchard? In the moonless night he could see tracer fire — it was tracer fire for sure. He must have lain down on the ground and drifted off because when he woke there was no sound of tracer fire anymore; it was intensely quiet. He could feel the wariness in the men around him.

Enemy soldiers, below them, were walking along the road. Not marching, just walking along, probably three or four abreast, at least one company.

In the darkness he was convinced the soldiers on the road who were closest, turned, looked up the hill, right at them. Nobody breathed. As he sat there all he could think of was a Tom and Jerry cartoon, with the smell of cheese rising like a white ribbon. Although the ribbon was wafting down to the soldiers, finding its way to their noses, he and the others would be safe, protected as they were by their talisman, their switchboard with its nifty set of lights, *Made in Madrid* on the side.

And this really did happen because the man who bought the cheese said he'd paid thirty-five pesetas when usually it would have been two, and when he knocked over the chair in the store he apologized and picked it up. You don't get that kind of detail in a dream.

HIS CHEST AND LUNGS are recovering; he's at the stage of paroxysmal coughing but really he's coming through well. He has no secondary infection in his leg. The words continue to march out of him; the narrative is a shambles but he is unable to stop.

He'd been in company number one. They came down late and were sent out from Batea; a guy called Crane was in charge.

This was before he tagged along with the telephonists. Crane was tall and pale and skinny just like a real crane. He was a Yank but he was with the Mac-Paps.

They had a gun. It wasn't a Maxim, it was something else, slightly more modern, smaller. Some Russian name. Taboski? Tabruski?

"I don't know the name," I answer. "But Tabruski sounds better. I'd put my money on Tabruski. What were you doing with the gun?"

They'd set it up to cover their men and Crane was a smart one, he chose some boulders, massive things. They put their gun in there so that it poked out, just right.

He felt pretty safe even when they were taking fire, because Crane had found them this lovely ledge with these fine boulders to hide behind. He made sure he had his high fur hat on, regardless of the weather.

"What was Crane like?" I ask. "What sort of fellow was he?"

Crane laughed out loud when he first saw him in his hat. His *hidalgo* hat, Crane called it. Soon everyone was calling him "the Don." Crane started it. They could laugh, but it was his own exclusive secret weapon.

He couldn't say how long they stayed there tucked away among the rocks. He used to watch the stars and one night he recited to Crane a verse he'd learned at school: *As the stars shall be bright when we are dust / Moving in marches upon the heavenly plain.*

No need to become maudlin, Crane said. But it wasn't maudlin; it was something bigger.

If you're down a hole deep enough, Crane claimed, you can see stars in the middle of the day. Was that just a story or was it true?

"I'm not sure," I say "I think it may depend on how deep a hole you're in."

They remained among the boulders until one morning the runner reported the rest of the men were gone. They didn't have anyone to cover for anymore. They were stuck in their secure position. Everyone else had left.

Crane — who'd have made a pretty good runner himself — flew off to find out what he could. Should have seen his face when he got back.

He knew Crane would bring them through. You'd think he could really fly, no kidding. When Crane brought them safely out from behind those boulders, when they caught up to the rest of the company, one of the commanders began yelling at Crane for getting left behind. The words were just starting out of his mouth when a mortar came, flaring orange like an exploding flowerpot, and you should have seen that commander scamper. No more complaints out of him.

In the muddle Ross fell in with the telephonists. Never found out what happened to Crane. A man like him, he had his head screwed on right. He'd be okay. Wouldn't he?

I HAVE TIME NOW, to study him, to soothe him. I carry with me some eucalyptus oil I've had since I left Sydney on the boat. Pour a little into warm water; wash his feet. This is an old nursing trick. The smell is soothing, promises something is being done.

I clip his nails with small scissors. Rub some of the mixture into his feet, avoiding places where it would sting. Slide the oil in between his toes.

He sighs his pleasure.

A hand reaches down towards me, falls onto the bed. A man's hands, thin long fingers, rather elegant. Unkempt nails.

I continue. Sweep upwards with the eucalyptus oil, taking my time. Finally I reach his armpits.

"So what are you?" I ask, fooling. "Rank or file?"

"Rank, for sure."

"Right on the money," I say, pretending to sniff. "Definitely rank."

Cleaning him with the oil. Anointing him. Tickling him. "I do believe we have a live one here," I say. "A lice-free soldier."

The other men in the ward laugh. Because none of this has been going on in private. They're Spanish Army in here: Aragónese, Catalan, Asturian. They don't understand the words but they know exactly what's happening.

I should feel uncomfortable — a woman, in public — but I've lived so long without privacy, it doesn't seem to matter much.

He sleeps.

I touch his hair on the pillow.

Out of the corner of my eye I see two of the men exchange obscene arm gestures, grinning.

HE COMES BACK TO ordinary life; he's young and basically sane, so he comes back.

He shits green slime, as men do when they've been out in the mountains, unfed and ill. I quickly slide the bedpan in under him, catch the slime. I do this numerous times a day. No hierarchy of tasks for nurses here, there are so few of us, we do the lot.

You wipe the man, he lies back, and you whisk the pan away, saying little.

But with Ross something adolescent has swept into our exchange. I hold the bedpan aloft in mock triumph, he demands to see. I lower it to him, as one might offer a plate of food.

"Green," he whispers, making a disgusted face.

"Slime time."

We giggle, out of control. I put the pan on the floor, unsteadily.

"I do believe you're crazy, nurse," he says. "Unhinged."

"Speak for yourself, greeny guts."

The entire ward is watching. "Entertainment's on the house," I cry out. "No extra charge."

THIS HOSPITAL, ONCE A tourist parador in the days of Primo de Rivera, stands by the sea at the end of a sandy plain, where a mountain finally rears up and the coast becomes rocky.

The nearest town is set well back from the coast, so the hospital has a feeling of being remote. It would be an ideal place for an infectious hospital, but it isn't. Here the men who've been victims of gangrene sit on the terrace, much as the tourists would have done, and admire the scene. This countryside has none of the natural abundance of Benicàssim, remembered by the Swede and passed along to Ross. The hills behind the plain are olive-grey and pale with dust, aloe, and juniper. But the garden, within the walls, is intense with cultivation: fat little palms, roses, lemon trees, arches with vines, the works. All Ross has to do is watch his leg take its time to heal, making sure the foot will be fed with blood.

I have him here with me, in the warmth of the garden, at hand whenever I'm able to find a quiet moment.

"I was looking out for you," he says, in his calm voice.

"Now that's what I like to hear." My own voice, light in return.

"So this is what good fortune means."

Much pleases him: The pyjamas he wears all day with a sweater over the top, his slippers — both items of immense luxury. The fig trees leafing out. The fresh smell of myrtle. Breakfast on the terrace. A view of the rocks, the morning ocean. Checking the tides: in and out, soft and regular as a cat. The mountain to the immediate south. Off to the north, the sand dunes, with rockrose coming into brief flower beside the tough daisies.

I HAVE A BREAK and can visit him in the garden. I stand watching him from behind. He hasn't heard me yet. Slender shoulders, that fair hair. I must find him a sun hat. I walk towards him and he turns his head.

"What is your pleasure m'lord?" I ask, putting on a silly voice. "Dost thou desire to remain in the direct sunlight or shall we make our retreat into the shade?"

He swings his hair away from his eyes. With his mouth partly open, he smiles, and my heart tumbles.

We sit together and he begins, consciously this time, to offer himself to me.

WHAT KIND OF A man is he? The only child in a house without a father. I was an only child in a house without a mother, I tell him. A motherless daughter, a fatherless son. Aha! A match, you see. A palpable match.

The fatherless son, held close. The boarders in his mother's boarding house treated him differently from the way they treated each other. The friendly jeering, the affectionate jabs — he was a bit of an outsider to all of that.

"My husband," I tell him, "was a man who at heart did not wish to live with a woman."

He has a hard time looking at me when I say that.

See, in these matters I do not take care of you. We are adults, you and I.

ROSS AND I ARE quiet talkers, like fishermen on the way to the catch. He returns, repeatedly, to the orchard on the night with no moon, to the river where the rifle went off.

This time he has broken off, agitated, unable to continue. The book he'd been reading before I came over slides from his lap, lies on the ground.

I pick up the book, hand it to him.

We sit in silence, slow down time, and he quietens.

"Tell me," he says, reaching out, taking my hand, keeping it. "Tell me about where you come from."

I come from Cliffend, a deserted mining town, a ghost town.

"You don't feel like a ghost to me," he says.

"That's because I'm a ghostess."

"The ghostess with the mostest."

"Seriously, what does it look like, this ghost town of yours?" he prompts.

One of the other nurses is coming across to where we're sitting. "You're wanted," she says to me, curt and businesslike.

I promise him I'll be back as soon as I can.

"Most wanted," he calls after me.

WHEN I RETURN TO the garden, he's waiting.

"I've been thinking," he says. "About when I see you walking towards me."

"What about it?"

"Some lines go through my head; I was forced to learn them at school. Found them the other day, in a book here."

"Tell me."

"It's very old-fashioned but you'll get the gist. The poet says he hardly has the skill to utter even one of the feelings buried inside him. But once in a great while — it's extremely rare — he meets another person and it's like a bolt's shot back. He finds that what he means, he can say.

And then he thinks he knows
The hills where his life rose,
And the sea where it goes.

"That's how it is," he says. "Seeing you."

We're under the trees in the garden; others are here too, and anyone could be looking down from the open windows.

"For you and me both."

He laughs in glad embarrassment.

"I think of nothing else," he says.

"Nor do I."

"I want to know everything about you." His eyes hold mine, won't let go, and there it is at last, the emphatic energy of desire.

"Start with Cliffend. Aren't those the hills where your life rose?"

CASALS IS COMING TO play. Not here, but in one of the tawny towns inland. He regularly plays for the soldiers. Just before the fascists reached the coast he was down near Valencia.

Ross has heard of Casals. When the war began, the *Orquesta Pau Casals* was in Barcelona for the Workers' Olympiad. Hearing of the insurgent uprising, and told to go home for their own safety, the orchestra and chorus stayed on, singing Schiller's ringing words in Catalan. *All men shall be brothers.*

Now on an afternoon in May, Casals is coming and we are invited; everyone who can go is going.

From our hospital and from others in the area, some of them new and temporary, soldiers and medical staff arrive for the concert. There has of late been a huge effort to move the wounded from down south around Valencia, which is where the convalescent hospitals were concentrated before the Republic was cut in two. They are being brought north by boat, in danger of being bombed by the Italians based in Majorca.

We're in a large room of the town hospital, which probably had once been a convent, and this perhaps the refectory. Windows open out onto a cloister, a courtyard. Trees in full fresh leaf cast a green light from the courtyard garden.

I sit with Ross. He's in his chair, which I've been pushing. I've found a small stool so I can sit beside him. His hand comes down, reaches into my lap. I take my jacket off so it covers his hand and mine. Nobody knows but him and me.

Casals plays by himself. Just his cello. Casals with his eyes shut. Short, rather dapper, a balding head. Thighs open to the instrument. We listen to the opening cadenza, and then he takes us off into a broad river of music, strong and frank, and it's all in there: lies, foolishness, vanity, hunger, revenge. A melody edges on into the strangeness of things, coming at last to an open place that sounds like joy and sorrow fused, nothing less.

While he is playing, outside in the courtyard there are small birds in the trees, calling to one another.

CLAPPING. THE GREAT MAN rises. Pulls out a clean handkerchief and wipes the dome of his head, shining with sweat. Lights his pipe.

I join a group of smokers out in the cloister. Cadge a cigarette for Ross, then run to the toilet with urgency. Throughout the playing I've been feeling an unmistakeable moistness between my legs that I have not felt since Grañén. With the poor food and irregular hours, my system had shut down. It is the same for many of the other nurses, and in fact rather convenient. One less thing to worry about. But now, after all this time, I'm bleeding. I need to do something about it right away or I'll have a stain spreading on the back of my skirt.

In the unattractive surroundings — one grasps exactly why the British call them bogs — I fish out fingernail scissors from my purse, cut a square out of my petticoat — good job I'm wearing a skirt for the big day out — and make myself a rag.

AFTER THE BREAK ROSS and I sit not touching.

Casals starts with nothing, so slow and uneventful the listener grows restless. Is this going anywhere? Shall these dry bones have life? God yes, and listen, here it comes, gathering and gathering. Part intimacy, part swagger, part lonely excitement.

Am I capable of entering into what I feel with Ross? Do I have the nerve? I'm glad we're not holding hands; it gives me space to concentrate.

The music is precise and lush at the same time.

Why him and not another? But it is so. I must not, I tell myself, I must not let my pride make me hide away, fumble, let this pass. Courage, Casals tells me. Face it. Don't be a fool, don't for a moment think it's going to be simple.

In the room: silence, applause, tentative chatter, relief. He plays every single day, we tell each other. Never even heard a cello until he was eleven years old. Found the Bach suites in an old shop down by the harbour in Barcelona; they'd been seldom played. Spent a decade making them his own. Who can imagine?

ON THE WAY BACK to the hospital, in the back of the lorry, we are quiet, dazed by the music we've heard. When we come to a railway crossing, the lorry stops. It's waiting for a train, and likely to be waiting some time. Usually in the back of a *camion*, especially when there are delays, there will be songs. Today it's the Germans — the only ones who can cope with the enormity of Bach — who begin to sing. The rest of us listen in silence. They are the peat bog soldiers, "Die Moorsoldaten." They've brought this song with them from the Emslandlager, the German concentration camps of the past four to five years. A predictable rhythm tramps in four-four time and the song is grim, but also hopeful in a surprising way: *ewig kann nicht Winter sein*, it cannot be winter forever.

You can do what you will, you can clamp the French border shut again, you can cut the Republic in half, but all men shall be brothers and it cannot be winter forever — especially not here, in the warmth of May, with Casals streaming in our brains.

I've been taking scant notice of the lives of others, patients or nurses. When we get back from Casals I leave Ross in the garden, head off to the staff office. I find the air thick with anxiety. While we were in the town, listening to Casals, the hospital was visited by the police. SIM, that's the acronym. The military intelligence, *Servicio de Investigación Militar.*

Everyone tight-lipped. The SIM took away the Asturian in Ross's ward, despite his condition. He is accused of something which is, of course, undisclosed. I know this has begun to happen but until now it has not happened in one of my hospitals. It has not seemed quite real.

The doctors and the nurses are huddled together, talking back and forth in strained voices, going over the details again and again.

A German nurse is slumped in a chair, choking on tears. "He is a good man," she cries out. "I know he is a good man."

I stare at her grief, shocked. I can tell by her tone that as Ross is to me, so is the Asturian to her. I've been so wrapped up in my own life I've not even suspected.

"There has been a mistake," one of the other nurses says, to comfort. "You'll see, there has been a mistake."

"He is a good man, a good man, not a spy, not a wrecker," the nurse continues to protest. He is my man, she says. *Mein Mann.* Not just her boyfriend, it turns out, her husband. How can this have happened without my even noticing?

I think of that other German, the woman from Sitges whom I met at the Falcon when I first came back to Spain, with her bright red lips and her overalls. In my dream she knew what I'd done to my husband Marcus. Her lot are now officially wreckers, a danger to the Republic. If Edith hadn't grabbed Ned by the scruff as he was on his way out the door to the POUM barracks, Ned would be a wrecker as well. Which just goes to show.

In the evening, amid ongoing tears, the German nurse's anger is stirring. "What Judas," she asks, "what *Judas* has done this?" She is packing her bags, wild and disorganized. She's walking out. Medical staff are free to leave if and when we want; nobody can stop us, or at least that's the idea.

The Belgian doctors are imploring, "Don't rush off, don't be rash."

She can go, she will go. But where?

"The entire Republic has become a whispering gallery," she shouts. "A shithouse whispering gallery."

NEXT MORNING, I ENGINEER rearrangements. The other men in Ross's ward are to be moved to a larger ward, but Ross is to be held back.

I will have him to myself.

I claim my justification: it will not be for long. It will be only temporary. Perhaps a few days at most, because of the recent changes.

There's a new, large-scale push to ship the wounded out of the country. This hospital is no longer to be a home for those recovering from gangrene. Soon we'll be having every Tom, Dick, and Harry coming through on their way out. The doctors shake their heads in sorrow. Their skills will no longer be needed.

The place will be full of strangers.

"Be careful" the doctors say to me. "Be very careful."

We will have the rarest gift, privacy.

SIESTA HOUR. SHUTTERED GREEN silence in the ward that holds only Ross.

I slide alongside his good leg. We make an awkward shape on the hospital bed.

"This must look pretty weird," he says.

"Who's looking?'

"Trapezoid? Rhomboid?"

"Haven't a clue."

"X marks the spot."

His body is cream fading to apricot.

What's this, dark and sweet?

He gasps.

Swimmers out in the breakers, straining, brimming. Then I'm on my own, arching into the deep of him, shuddery in the legs, arms, stomach of him.

Drowned creatures washed ashore. Clear, smooth, whole, and splendid, home.

We have forgotten the lives we had. We have begun.

Now THERE IS NOTHING Ross will not tell me. He talks about where he comes from: New Westminster, in British Columbia on the west coast of Canada. He talks about his best mate, Tony Rabich. Tony is older than he is; he lived in his mother's boarding house. For a while they shared the same room. Tony found him a job in the woods at a time when jobs were impossible to find. He was with Tony in the logging camp. When he lay trapped beneath a rolling log, Tony was the one who saved him. He came to Spain with Tony; they were in training together at Tarazona.

He tells me about his single attempt at sex here in Spain.

Before they were sent to Aragón, they had leave in Barcelona, him and Tony. It was his first time in the city. One of the lads they met up with took them to an attic which turned out to be a restaurant and they had the best meal you could imagine, with people playing the violin really well and singing. He didn't know such food was still possible in Spain — egg and onion chopped together to start off with, all the way through to fruit compote at the end. After the meal they'd found two young Spanish girls and it was okay for Tony but not so good for him. The girl who was with him took her clothes off and she was wearing this black flannel underwear. Not what you think of when you say "black underwear," just homey and threadbare. She stood in her black pants with her thighs pale beneath, completely mortified and pushing herself into it.

He tried but found he just couldn't. Not like that. But that look of failure on the girl's face. So afraid there wouldn't be any money to take home now that it hadn't happened.

"Don't think about it," I tell him. "At least don't think about it right now. Tell me something that makes you happy."

"That's easy," he says, and opens his arms.

WHEN I'M WITH THE doctors I become a stranger to him: serious voice, all business and the occasional flash of professional camaraderie.

"I much prefer the woman without clothes," he says.

"Temporarily clothed all right by you?" The doctors have just left.

But when I syringe his leg, it is no longer as a nurse. All the while I'm working, he murmurs about his hunger for my lips.

"My lover, my friend," I whisper to him.

"I'm starving," he says.

"Out of luck until two o'clock," I say. "Have a smoke instead."

WE ARE TOGETHER EVERY day, in the afternoon. I'm the one above; it's because of his leg.

Lying beside him afterwards, he claims to have the goods on me. He's been watching me, he says, and now he has a name for me when we make love. Not for the beginning and middle, he says, he's still working on that. For the end.

Picture the highest falls in the world. Huge falls, towering, magnificent: the waters fall and fall, a thousand feet, two thousand; the waters fall so far that before they reach the ground, they turn to mist and drift in the sun. What began as a mighty roaring becomes soft as air.

"Angel Falls, they're called."

"As in the rain from heaven?"

"Nah," he grins. "As in some guy called Jimmy Angel, a pilot who flew around down there."

"Sounds like a gangster to me."

"Angel Falls," he repeats, "that's you, just after."

ONE MORNING IN JUNE the tissue that was damaged simply sloughs off.

All the dead tissue on his leg drops away, leaving the skin with a lean, tender look, the leg still emaciated. He will learn to walk on it with his cane; it's a medical victory; it's our victory, our faces are flushed with it.

Now we can be certain we have a future to contemplate, we're incoherent as drunks. I promise him a warm world where there are no hard winters, no more battles for him, no more wounded soldiers for me. I promise him the coast, where my father is coming down to the beach to greet us.

Imagine: we've been out in the bay, rowing, and the moon is rising behind the shack. Soon it will be shining on the banana palm.

These are not impossibilities, I tell him. They are ordinary life, like oatmeal bikkies and tea with two sugars. Cookies to you.

We inspect each other's hands: this line, that line, each laid down in preparation for the intersection, when our hands first met, up there in Teruel in the amazing cold. We press our hands together, trying to match the lines.

Two things, he tells me, flashed in the Aragón sun: the buckle a Lincoln took from a dead man; orange peels lying on the ground, inviting, tasty.

I tell him about Cliffend, about the aunts in town, about my training in Sydney. A girl from the bush, I didn't mix much, I wasn't a social success, not being what they called "a joiner." Instead of sitting around giggling and washing my hair with the others, I'd walk into the city to the library in the old Queen Victoria building, spend ages selecting a book, walk back, lie in bed, reading, alone.

Above the entry to the nurses' home, was the motto: *Be silent, listen, observe.* Part of learning to be a nurse, I tell him, was acquiring a sense of being set apart from others, separated from normal time. At any hour of the day or night, you could be working.

"Just before dawn I came out of theatre after a surgery of over eight hours. I walked into the medical staff hallway, looking for the trolley. Around the clock, the trolley provided thick black tea and door-stop slices of bread spread with butter. Took the tea and bread into the courtyard and sat by the fountain. The fountain was silent; it was a decade of drought.

"Birds were already stirring. On the road outside, a few cars and carts were starting to go by. I sat at the edge of the fountain, eating the bread and butter, drinking the tea. The sky whitened, the birds began sweeping about in gangs, and — I was half-dead with fatigue I suppose — I had the strangest feeling that I'd been lifted up into that shouting sky and at the same time I was resting there by the fountain, happy amid the din, seized with a sense of having earned my place in the world. My work gave me a reason to be."

"Now you have another," he says.

I TELL HIM ABOUT last autumn, up in Alto Aragón, where I was for once working with an all-Spanish team.

It rained in Alto Aragón — such a cold, steady rain. The sky cleared and I could see fresh snow on the peaks. When we had a push on, the goat track that posed as a road was clogged with mules and vehicles going up to the front and bringing wounded out. Trucks and ambulances tended to bog down but the mules could get through.

"What was the field hospital like?" Ross has a knack for figuring out exactly what I want to talk about.

"Nothing to it. Take a stretcher and a trestle and there's your operating table. The one thing that has to be carried out as if you were in a hospital is the preparation of the man's skin: shaved, cleaned with soap, then sterilized with spirits and ether. As long as the man's skin is clean, it doesn't matter if the kitchen floor is made of earth and the walls are dirty.

"A boiling saucepan on a primus stove will sterilize instruments in five minutes. Any item that has a lid can be pressed into service. You need some kind of portable instrument table, set up and swabbed. Gloves, towels, and dressings, sterilized and stored in drums. Stick the drums on the table, lift out the gloves with sterile forceps. You have to be a fanatic about the routine: hand washing in the basin, with frequent changes of water. Make sure everyone washes for at least five minutes. Pour spirits over their hands. Then you can put on their gloves.

"For meals, we operated *al fresco*: a cooking tent and an eating tent. The surgeons arranged for a larger farmhouse further down to act as an evacuation centre for those who were able to be sent on. Before that, we had nowhere to put them. You want to move the post-operative cases out as soon as possible. The exceptions are the abdominal wounds and the head injury cases; you can't move those along quickly.

"The Spanish team let me have full rein and in turn I asked no questions. I couldn't help contrasting the smooth way in which we'd taken up residence in this field hospital with the endless trouble the British team seemed to have in Grañén.

"From time to time, bands of men on horses came to confer. These militia men brought the surgeons a big, calm mare, a lovely dappled grey with a silver mane and tail. She quickly became quite the expert at inspecting my pockets. The surgeons made good use of this mare, riding to the surrounding villages. A few days later the local people would contribute what they could: a goat, carried across an old farmer's shoulder, bread heaped on a cart.

"The men who arrived on the horses had to be anarchists or POUM remnants. Perhaps they'd become part of regular units or perhaps they were operating on their own. I didn't need to know. How the comrades of yesterday had officially turned into villains was a mystery to me.

"I walked whenever I could, especially when we had a break in the weather. Found a stream where I watched the birds. They were all alike: chipper little fellows not much bigger than a house sparrow in shades of grey, with a sturdy beak.

"One day I was working with a Spanish surgeon. Outside it was raining but in the kitchen, the surgeon was delicately bringing parts of the large bowel above the site of the injury out onto the surface of the abdomen. I was completely caught up in the probing and lifting but also perfectly aware that this moment carried inside it the past, with the wave of blood when the abdomen was opened, and the present, with the kitchen smells of garlic and olive oil competing with the open ether. Further out, beyond that, was the round of practical, grinding details — the gloves in the drum, the water that needed to be changed yet again, the lack of any clothing for the wounded men — we had only blankets. Out farther still, it was raining, there was mud and retreat, and beyond even that, the air was filled with the confused abstractions about what was happening here. Against all this, within all this, was an act of skill and delicacy that may yet save a man's life."

I have an urge to tell Ross everything.

"We had two nurses. Both of them grumbled about me behind my back. I was the tyrant-in-charge. I was constantly after them about the primus stove. I could hear them thinking, *On the prowl, the old battleaxe.*"

Ross smiles.

"It's hard to make a primus burn slowly but that's what must be done, and a primus that is made to burn slowly will become clogged. It's a doomed cycle if you're not constantly on top of it."

"I can't think of you as a tyrant," says Ross. "More like a softy toffee." He reaches out, touches the back of my neck.

"Oh but I am. I don't mind taking shifts in a bed, I expect to. But I do want to be told about it. I found one of those nurses curled up in the bed I was due to use. She'd claimed it for herself without so much as a by-your-leave. I stood above her and shouted, 'Get out!' I even pointed to the floor, like some corny creature in a cartoon."

"You had to leave in a hurry." He says this as a statement, not a question.

"At the end we had to pack up on the double as the front collapsed. We came scrambling down the mountains, stopping frequently because of the wounded. We were forced to rest on a track by a creek, and the man who'd had the abdominal surgery died overnight, leaving me with an overwhelming sense of failure. The surgeon's best skills had come down to nothing."

AT THIS HOSPITAL WE'RE exposed, right on the shore. Tonight there is a chilly strong breeze off the water, despite the season. It kicks up the sand so it stings. We're on a long pale peninsula of land here, flat, not the kind of coast I'm used to in this country.

I walk along the grassy edge of the beach where tough plants are beaten down by the wind. Off duty tonight, I can stay as long as I like. I looked in on Ross but he was sleeping.

I find a shallow dune that provides a minimum of shelter, sit down in the cold, head on my knees.

Soon I will confess to him. About what happened with Marcus, and Alec. I sit in the dunes, rehearsing. I wanted my husband to vanish; I wanted his brother instead.

Begin again.

I didn't know him, my husband Marcus. Didn't see what was in his heart. Alec came to visit on his way to a residency in Barcelona; it was my moment of rescue. When I realized I couldn't have Alec, I turned on Marcus. In the library, I arranged Alec's letters by date. Left them there on the desk.

I stand up, search for stones; throw them into the sea.

TWO LETTERS.

Laia writes. After she received word of Ramon's death, she took the children to Girona, to her parents. I can understand why she needed to go, but Girona is less safe than the village. The village will still have vegetables in the garden and fish in the sea; not even the fascists can take the sea away.

Ned writes. He's being transferred to an artillery battery. He doesn't know what lies ahead, but he reckons he's going to give the battery his best shot, joke. Able-bodied men are being taken out of the autoparc and reassigned because the army is regrouping.

This is when I make my first mistake. I read Ross the letter from Ned.

OUR ONCE REMOTE HOSPITAL at the edge of the sandy plain has become a staging point. We are no longer certain of having the room to ourselves. Medical staff and their patients are arriving almost daily, having come by boat from the south. How quickly we have come to accept the division: the north, the south. Patients will be moved farther north, then across the border.

As for the need to care for gangrene, our team has been officially abolished and soon the Belgian doctors will be leaving for Barcelona.

The news is full of the bombardment of Granollers. Many dead and many wounded. The hospitals in and around Barcelona are responding as well as they can but much of the medical aid and the majority of the doctors are at the front.

I watch Ross listening to the news, becoming infected by it. I am so thankful Ross won't be going back to the front. Soon, we'll have to decide what happens to us, where we go from here. I don't want to rush him. I will be sorry to leave Spain, because the needs are great and becoming greater. But now there is Ross to think about. Where can we go? To England. Then what? We don't have to think seriously about this until we're finished here. It won't be long.

The new arrivals bring their modest treasures with them, including a phonograph. They set it up on the terrace, with its view of the rock, its suggestion of holiday ease, and we listen to the clarinet and sax of "The Night is Blue." I stand up to dance with Ross.

"Hand in hand, by the edge of the sand, we danced by the light of the moon," I say to him.

He shambles about on crutches, frustrated. "I would go hand to hand with you if I could, but I can't." An irritable tone I've not heard before.

The majority of those on the terrace are messed up in one way or another, so it's pretty much a *danse macabre*. The wounded men are being sent out of Spain at a time when nothing has ended, nothing is settled, except for the fact that we are losing. I suspect many of them came here with a sense of seizing fate by the throat, and now they are going back, diminished, and not just physically.

The singing that follows the dancing starts out in fine fashion, with "Viva La Quince Brigada." But it fizzes out in bouts of banality. The contribution from the English-speaking contingent is "I Do Like to Be Beside the Seaside." Even after that, the night continues, and a fractious mood develops. Nobody is willing to be the first to say, enough, I'm going, time to turn in. Arguments break out over trivial matters. Before I realize what's happening, Ross and I have slid into a foolish disagreement about some item we read in the English newspaper, the *News Chronicle*. We debate details neither of us can fully recall. He claims he remembers and I don't, which I maintain isn't true.

Exhausted, with ill feeling ripe in the air, the group finally falls silent, looking out at the sea. Across that sea, and up in the heart of Europe, a wave of darkness is on the move.

TONY RABICH COMES TO see Ross.

I meet him twice. Once when he arrives. Then again, after he's spent five hours with Ross.

When a solider shows up, Mac-Pap insignia on his shirt, asking to speak with Douglas Ross, the news reaches me immediately. Even though this place is now overrun with strangers just passing through, everyone appears to be well aware that I'm the one who'd want to know about a Mac-Pap visitor.

I intercept him in the upstairs hallway, offer to take him to Ross. We skip the formalities of introductions; I assume he's already had to announce his request several times. So I don't realize at first who he is.

I leave them together, go on with my work.

They have sat in the garden together, had lunch together, and now I'm walking across, on my break, to spend some time, a social visit. What I see is this: Ross relaxed and expansive, Tony Rabich entirely at his ease.

Ross introduces us.

I see the flicker.

Tony had met me as a nurse taking him to his friend. Now he's looking at me anew, Ross's girlfriend.

Not what he'd been expecting.

The flicker: she's old.

Thirteen years older than Ross, in fact. Tony doesn't know the years, and nobody stands there and counts them out.

Tony offers me his saga of how he swam to Spain. It's the story of the sinking of the *Ciudad de Barcelona*.

Before the war, the *Ciudad de Barcelona* plied the Barcelona–Ibiza run, and it carried Marcus on the overnight trip so he could grub about in the ruins of Sa Caleta with Leo. Not that Tony would be the least bit interested in that. I had at the time not been particularly interested myself.

I sit beside Ross, my stomach tight as a brick. Tony is busy describing the various ways in which men drown.

Tony claims to have staggered ashore alongside the Yank who arrived with a pound of Maxwell House between his teeth. I've already heard that yarn about the Maxwell House. Listening to Tony, I'm less convinced than ever that anyone would go paddling along with his teeth clamped on a pound of coffee when a torpedoed boat was going down. Tony swears it's the level truth.

Ross is so close I'm longing to reach out and touch him, but I don't. Animated, cheerful, he hasn't picked up on my mood. So far, so good. *Bring up that smile*, I remind myself, *keep it going*. Ross is with an old friend who not only knows his home but has shared it. What Tony says, what Tony does, counts.

After Tony leaves, all the talk is of Tony.

Tony says something big is being planned. Nobody knows for sure when, but soon. It's an open secret: a new front, a dramatic offensive. They're going back across the Ebro. Tony says he's in training and he's pretty sure that's what they have in mind. Tony says it makes sense when you think of it.

I don't say anything. In thirteen years, you learn something.

THE END, WHEN IT comes, is abrupt.

The hospital is being closed. I sit in the office with the Belgian doctors, who are reviewing a form. If they sign it, if I sign it, Ross can officially be under my nursing care.

I'm going to miss these doctors. An agreeable, avuncular warmth surrounds whatever we do together. Today, however, the doctors are remote, worried about their own future.

"We must write in here where you are going to be with your patient."

Before the strain of this upheaval, they would have said, with knowing smiles, "*your* patient."

My patient and I are going to have to find a place to stay, and record it for the authorities. At this point, I've one priority only: to be alone with Ross, to get him away from the swirl of war. Myself, as well. After that, who knows?

Ross has made no mention of leaving the army, leaving Spain. All around him, here at this hospital, men are on their way out. They've done their bit; they're going.

As if the doctors can hear my thoughts, one of them says, "I see the patient has made no mention of applying for a discharge."

No, indeed, he has not. The patient has recently been visited by his best mate, Tony. And Tony is much more than a comrade-in-arms, Tony is from home. Tony is a brother.

No, the patient is not thinking clearly. Neither is his lover.

If he had applied for a discharge we'd be leaving the country. A plane to Toulouse, the shock of city lights, the surprise of abundant food. The guilt of having walked out when needed.

"I know of a place," I say. "I have somewhere here I can take him."

I let them write in the details. In the back of my mind a voice starts up: *You're taking him back to Marcus's place? What do you think you're doing?*

"For how long? The form asks for the length of his convalescence. We have to give them a time. What is it you have in mind?"

What do I have in mind after the village? I don't have anything in mind; we haven't discussed it. London is the obvious choice. In England I legally have a husband, the German whose real name is certainly not Otto Thaelmann. I haven't even told Ross about that yet. I will have to find work, of course. Ross and I have talked about living at the beach back home, but only in a daydream way, nothing practical. No wonder we haven't thought this through; it's much too complicated.

"Shall we say, four weeks?"

Four weeks with Ross in the village.

"Yes," I assent. Let's say four weeks. Tell them four weeks." Four whole weeks.

To REACH THE VILLAGE, we need to go through Barcelona.

This time the city fails to exercise much pull on me, which I note with some surprise. I'm busy making lists, standing in lines, buying things at wildly inflated prices. A small can of olive oil, tobacco, and the barley concoction that poses as coffee. I try for salt and sugar but without success. While it still prides itself on its nonchalance, the place is much changed. A quieter city, although the cinemas stay open and the opera continues. On balconies everywhere, rabbit hutches have appeared: food on the hop. The flower market still operates, the trams run, people hurry about, aware in a new way of the blue sky — the rapid upward glance. *Too high.* Fine; carry on.

The medical staff I have lunch with bemoan the changes. Time was when the people would, during air raids, remain seated on the trams, chatting, waiting for the power to come back on. No more. Now it's everyone out, down into the *refugio*, grim and quick about it. I remember the buoyant cinema crowd at the first emergency drill. Advised to follow the attendants down to the cellars, they surged outside instead, to watch the searchlights sweep the sky.

After a little hospital shoptalk, the bombardment is the main topic of conversation. Each night the Italian bombers are at it. Back again next morning, bright and early. Nip over from Majorca, drop the bundle, home to the island, liquid lunch, lazy afternoon.

This is what the medical staff keep coming back to: the maddening monotone of the engines; the close air in the shelters; the way the mind struggles to paper it over, doing a wildly amateurish job.

I am out of touch with this, not part of the shared experience.

"We're leaving for the village," I say. "We're not staying here." I'm glad to escape, to return to Ross.

IN BARCELONA WE HAVE our first row. While I've been busy buying supplies, he's been limping about, making inquiries. One evening he approaches the topic obliquely. "It's true that they are taking all the able-bodied men out of the autoparcs." A statement, not a question.

I curse myself, curse Ned, curse Tony.

"There is no need," I say. "You've done enough."

"I've done next to nothing. As you above all others are in a position to know."

"You're in no shape."

"I will be. Or I will be enough."

"You won't be. Not really, not for ages, not for years."

"Now you're exaggerating."

I go silent.

"It's not that I'll be doing anything particularly dangerous. Your friend Ned was in the Regiment de Tren and he did OK."

Fine, let's both talk about Ned. Let's neither of us mention Tony.

"That's Ned. This is you. This is *us*."

"The autoparc isn't going to change anything."

"You know as well as I do there's talk of ending all International Brigade involvement. They're thinking of sending the IBers home."

"We'll burn that bridge when we come to it. Isn't that what you like to say?"

"I'm going out for a walk. I can't take this any longer."

"If you want, we'll walk. A nice hobble will do us both good."

"I said *I'm* going for a walk."

AFTER FIVE MINUTES OF brisk walking I turn, hurry back to the flat. Up in the little cage of a lift, into his arms, then to bed.

And now he is tracing my face in profile. His fingers move over the dome of my skull, onto my forehead, down my nose, over my lips.

"This is the best time," I say lazily. "Just being here with you like this."

"I wait upon your pleasure."

I take his hand, press it to my lips. "You do indeed, my love."

"*Enchantée*," he says, in a silly voice.

Idly, we pretend we're an old-time couple, reviewing our lengthy past.

"At Teruel I stood at the window to watch you go. It was snowing."

"Before that. Where were you, back in June of last year? When I was on the big boat to France?"

"I was in Grañén. I had jaundice and because of that I returned to the village. Have I told you about the jaundice?"

"Yep. Were you in the village all summer?"

Having left my lips, his fingers have resumed their travelling.

"Pretty much."

"You were in the village when I came to Spain on the little boat."

"I know. One morning I awoke from a dream and you had arrived on the Catalonian shore."

"At the end of the summer, you went to Alto Aragón."

"And you were in Aragón in the fall."

"Fuentes."

His fingers investigate detours. He pauses, "We could have met in Aragón and not have waited until Teruel. We were only hills away."

"How many hills are we talking about here? It's a pretty big place."

"Pretty nice shape, I'd say. Not too big, just right. I'll take two of those, yes please."

"On New Year's Eve you slept in the barn, in the hay. You were on your way up to Teruel."

"Where were you last New Year's?"

"Valencia. That's where I ran into Ned. I was sent up to Teruel from Valencia. Going up, the truck got stuck in a village and we had to walk the rest of the way in the snow. That village was where the man gave me the hat."

"Our hat."

"Quite so. You're *tickling* me."

"Is there anything else I should know about your life in Spain before me?"

"What's this, the inquisition?"

"I'm not the inquisitor, I'm the grand tickler. Any intelligence the tickler should be extracting before abandoning his post?"

"Quite possibly."

"And what might that be?"

"I'm not sure I can tell you."

"Sure you can. Fire away."

"Well, last April, not long before you were brought into the hospital, I crossed the border and married a German IBER who'd been wounded. I'd never met him before. It was just for the documents, you understand. To allow him into Britain."

"Jesus, woman."

"It's only an arrangement on paper. It's so he'll have somewhere he can go. Mexico most likely. You mustn't let it worry you."

"My girl's just told me she's married. Why should I let a little thing like that worry me?"

His fingers have stopped their journey. He's sitting up.

"Will that mess us up when we go to England?"

Ha! There, he's said it. *When we go to England.* All along he's been thinking about leaving, getting out. He's planning on us going.

As for the marriage to the German, that might indeed prove a problem — but surely I can get round it somehow. I'll have to.

"Nothing," I tell Ross. "Nothing will mess us up."

In the dark we make a cave of the sheets, our hearts wide awake.

THE BUS TO THE village takes forever and the threadbare nature of the Republic — barely limping along — is brought home to me by the hours we spend waiting in the dust for a replacement bus that does not arrive. Following that, there are two more days of delays caused by *avion* back in Barcelona, with ongoing bombing that disrupts everything. The heat of summer is upon us, bouncing relentless from the rocks. On olive-grey terraces, aloes and vines bake in the sun, and the ocean's coolness is dwarfed.

It is a splendid relief to arrive.

The women from the inn are up working in Laia's vegetable plot, my old flower beds. They inspect us — anyone coming down the hill path is of huge interest. They stand up, arms going promptly into the small of their backs. I don't think the women are particularly excited to see me. Ross, however, they look upon with immediate affection: a son, somebody's son; he is a prize.

It feels so strange, with Laia gone.

Exhausted by the journey, Ross sleeps for fifteen hours. "I quite like watching people sleep," I tell him, when he wakes.

"How about hearing them sleep? Enjoy the snorers, do you?"

"Yes," I insist, "the little gasps, the shifts in pace, it's like they're on a road, going up, down, up, down, steady — then suddenly, a surprise."

"I can't say I share your enthusiasm. You're the one person I want to see sleeping, curled up into yourself; I long to be in there with you."

"Dark places, my friend, dark places."

"I'll take my chances."

Ross MAKES HIS WAY down to the inn. He now uses only a single cane. In the miraculous way people have, the men communicate with him despite the language. They welcome him; they drink together. Soon Ross is regularly playing dominos and coming back with the smell of the men about him, reporting on their conversation.

"*Bon dia*," he cries, when he sees one of them. "*Com estàs?*" "*Bé, gràcies.*"

The days begin to jumble one into another, each lovely. But even here, news of fresh bombing arrives, brought by boat around the headland. Badalona is bombed, and Blanes.

We go out in a dory, easy to push off, with its flat bottom. A sweet little boat, yellow with purple trim. Ross is rowing.

"You look as happy as Ratty," I say.

Ross sweats heavily. I tell myself to sit still and let him do it. Dignity must be allowed to trump pain, that's what I was taught.

We put in a line, don't catch anything; doesn't matter. We have peas from the garden to eat, peas so soft we gobble them raw.

Accustomed to me again, the women from the inn have grown more friendly. There are three more Ibicenco women than when I was first lived here. (Last summer Laia told me they'd come in September of '36.) Sisters or cousins, in black with white aprons. Ibiza is in enemy hands; who knows what may have happened to the husbands?

I sit with the women beneath the wide gnarled stock of grapevine at the side of the inn and have conferences about what can be grown. I am invited to admire their fine sweet potatoes, the laden fig trees, the peppers hanging in the kitchen. It's not like talking with Laia, but I am grateful.

Ross AND I swim out on the slack tide into the empty sea of summer. Swim back, lie in the shade of a rock. He holds up his fingers. I look between them up at the sky.

With difficulty, we climb the cliff path. "There's no rush," I say. "Here, nobody rushes."

I watch him in Marcus's library, looking at the books.

He comes with me to the bed where I slept so seldom with my husband, where I slept a few times with Alec. I wait for him to ask, *Why did you bring me here, to the house of your husband, with whom you were miserable?* Or he might say, *if it weren't like this* — meaning the war, the shortages, the difficulties of finding a place to be together — *would you have brought me?*

No.

And I would not have brought him if Laia were here. I would not have flaunted such happiness.

Ross arrives home with fresh gossip from the inn. This spring, Ross tells me, the men rowed out in the long boats with nets: old men, and some of the young ones, little more than children. He has plans to go out with them in their dories, not far from shore, with the lighter nets. How he knows these things, can make these arrangements, is a marvel to me, a form of magic. Perhaps one or two of the men speak to him in that stiff, schoolbook Castilian they learned as little boys, those who had a few years of schooling.

I watch his breastbone lift as he talks; the tan of his body looks healthy. He browns up quickly, leaving those white places under the arms, where the sun does not reach.

He does go out fishing one night, returns with a scant catch. It's still summer, I tell him, what does he expect? In the morning, tired but pleased with himself, he stands on the roof of the library wearing navy pyjama bottoms. I sit behind him, watching, aware I have done this before.

A commotion on the hill path. A couple of men from one of the inland villages are bringing down a dead horse. Beside the inn, out of sight of the beloved Ines, it will be carved up, exchanged for some of the few fish brought in overnight.

Ross leaves the library roof, goes into the house, to bed. I follow him. He is humming a tune; he often sings to himself these days. Pop songs, hymns, anything. I never heard him do this at the hospital. Being here suits him, I decide. A house suits him. That this cottage belonged to Marcus doesn't appear to disconcert him in the least.

We lie in bed listening to the work on the carcass. "I wonder who's doing the sawing?" I ask, idly.

He stops humming. "Would it be the men from the inland village? Are there rules that apply? My carcass; I carve."

"I don't really know. I lived here for a few years, but I don't know the first thing about it."

"You know the essential things," Ross says.

I touch him beside me. Feel the blood in his body, close to the skin, excited.

The essential things: no future, no past. No fading into night; that's hours away from now. There is only the present, his warm body in my hands. I have him with me. He will dwell in me all the days of my life, I think, reaching for archaic language to explain the moment to myself.

Without him there would be nothing. Without him, my life would be a cold wind in a dry valley.

WE SWIM FROM A narrow cove. A stony beach, but a good entry. This was the cove they used when they brought Marcus ashore, when they carried him up the cliff path.

I haul out, sit on the beach, watching Ross swim.

So much has fallen away, sloughed off.

Ross is coming towards me out of the sea. It turns shallow quite suddenly; one moment he's swimming and the next moment he's on his knees, and then with an awkward scramble he's upright.

"He is risen," he cries out. "Alleluia."

I hand him up a towel, his cane. Water gleams on his skin.

We sit side by side looking out to sea. In the distance, birds are flying. They would be crying out so as not to lose one another in the immensity of the air. We cannot hear them; the sea takes away the sound.

Ross has a way of turning towards me so my face is on a level with his shoulder. I lick the salt taste of him, warm in the sun. He takes my hand, extends my arm, runs his finger along the soft skin inside, slowly, up and down.

I know what we're up against. My father used to say it: the stars move still, time runs, the clock will strike.

WE FALL INTO FLAGRANT, cosy laziness. Lie abed until mid-morning, me darning his socks, him reading. In Marcus's library, Ross has found a book of poetry by A.E. Housman.

"Too modern for Marcus's taste. Show me."

I put the darning aside, take the book from him, read the dedication. *To my brother Marcus from your loving sister, Helen. Christmas 1923.*

I give it back; he finds some verses he remembers.

On the idle hill of summer / sleepy with the flow of streams / far I hear the steady drummer.

"Learned that one at school. My mother claimed it was her favourite. She loved it when I'd recite."

I don't think much of *summer / drummer*. Yet who could blame a mother for feasting on her son's voice?

The darning needle goes up and under, up and under, then back the other way. Soothing. Father showed me how to darn; Ross tells me he doesn't know how. His mother darned not only his socks but those of the boarders as well.

"This does not bode well," I say. "I would have denied the existence of a man less domesticated than my father, but I appear to have found him."

"What's there to be domestic about? At the beach we're going to live on fish and bananas, aren't we? I can cook a fish. I can peel a banana."

The banter reminds me of the big dusty cupboard with the family playthings, back at that base hospital near the Ebro. A house devoted to pleasures. They knew about the idle hill of summer. "You looked like a drowned rat," I say. "That day the ambulance brought you to me from the River Ebro."

"Clearly irresistible."

"Like something the cat dragged in."

Ross LEARNED ABOUT THE melons the night before, down at the inn. Pau said he was to come and bring the Englishwoman nurse with him. I was pleased with that.

The Ibicenco women grow melons amid their sunflowers. They want to give us some.

Seated on low chairs, we sip sweet wine. I very much need Laia here, to help me through. Afterward, the two of us could have gossiped about who said what.

Pau, having poured the fingers of wine, stands in the doorway, from which point he can keep an eye on any possible customers at the inn and also manage the conversation. The stories are told again of Pau's foot, and the Night of the Baby. No doubt there is also the Day of the Drowning, but it will not be featured when the Englishwoman nurse is about.

After the formal pleasantries, we go out into the garden, and one of the women lifts the sprawling floppy leaves of the melon vine, exposing the plump riches beneath. "So many," exclaims Ross.

"Impossible. Marvellous." In the house he was quiet but in the garden understands exactly what is expected of him.

We carry the fat little melons up the hill. Still warm from the sun. As soon as we're inside the cottage, we relax. Ross is holding two of the melons up to his chest, humming. He tosses me one.

"Don't do that," I cry out, catching it. "Don't you do that again. I'll drop it, ruin it."

Still fondling one melon, he pretends to be a crooner. "*These foolish things,*" he sings, "*remind me of you.*"

I collect the melons, put them into the long string basket, stand on a chair, hang the string basket on a hook.

I step down.

He's been leaning against the wall, watching me. Together we look at the melons hanging there, round and quiet. "No harm will come to them now," he murmurs.

I decide I can tell him, right then, about the letters from Alec that I'd arranged for Marcus in the study. Tell him about Marcus, about Alec, and what I did.

Not expecting pardon.

I have been wanting to tell you this. And I realize it is a terrible, perverse kind of pride, hugging guilt to oneself when I can see, all around us, what is happening to others.

Now look at me. Look at me, Ross. What are you going to do?

IN THE SPACE AFTER love, after the warm fatigue, the room rights itself, and time flows back, speechless.

NEWS ARRIVES. A LOCAL boat sputters around the headland from the town; a newspaper is carried to the inn. Ross goes down, brisk with his cane. Comes home bursting.

We've gone *back* across the Ebro. Like Tony said. We might have been smashed in Aragón last April, but we've regrouped and have gone on the offensive. Surprise and speed are on our side. That'll keep their minds off attacking Valencia; we've got the bastards on the run. Already we've moved up towards Corbera and Gandesa, this time it's going to be different, you'll see.

The river has been crossed.

Now the men at the inn speak openly to Ross of the war. Every one of them, I gather, is a sturdy optimist. We've suffered some defeats, granted, but it will come right; we're the ones with *élan* and energy; we've not lost yet, far from it.

To my ears this sounds like Christmas and the first days of Teruel.

Ross waits, restless, for the next boat that brings the newspaper. The paper provides the details: at one o'clock in the morning of a muggy summer's night, an army slid in silence into the river. Swimmers pushed bundles of wood in front of them, enclosing ammunition and rifles. A flotilla of small boats — like the dory we use — also slipped across. Before dawn fragile bridges were in place, to take the tanks and more matériel.

And the nightmare was unfurled, one more time.

When will he be going back? Two more weeks. He plans to go hobbling about in some support and supply role in an autoparc. He won't be able to drive with that leg; they wouldn't make him do that, surely?

Autoparcs, however well hidden, can be spotted from the air, are targets for *avion*, sitting ducks.

Bitterness has entered into our lovemaking; we can't wipe it out entirely. Around us, the war is once more at high tide. So many already know this, will know this — the sheer numbing exhaustion of it all.

WE COLLUDE TO IGNORE the immediate future. Speak of the time beyond.

We will go to London first, then to Australia. That's the plan. No idea where the money for the voyage is going to come from. I will find something to do; we will save the fare. One of the BC boys worked in the luggage room at Waterloo Station before he came to Spain. That would be a start, Ross claims.

He does not suggest we go back to Canada, to New Westminster, to the boarding house. I think he is unable to imagine his mother opening the door to him with me by his side. Not yet. So Australia it will be.

I dig in my bag for the letters from my father, all of which I carry with me. My father's latest — written before the Ebro offensive — is to the point, if not encouraging. "The professedly double-edged embargo really cuts only one way. It keeps the forces of the legally constituted government unarmed for the benefit of the well-armed rebels."

Ross and my father. The thought of those two together fills me with pleasure. Lying beside Ross, I stretch my legs in the bed, curl my toes.

"A long way from Europe," I promise Ross.

"The farther away, the better."

"We can go to the beach."

I have something to tell you, Father. Something of the greatest importance. I've met this man, his name is Ross, and you will like him, I'm sure of it. You will really like him.

In no time Ross will be going about barefoot in a dirty old sweater, having lengthy state-of-the-world discussions with Mr. MacDonald. Mr. MacDonald will insist upon it, will be unable to believe his good luck.

"You could go crabbing in the mangrove swamps."

It will be my home, not his. In Canada, his mother will be waiting. And possibly much else.

"You could fish seriously if you wanted."

I talk about the winter mullet, huge shoals moving up the coast. The scouts come first, nosing about, seeking out the right places; then a great whack of them arrives. Men are throwing out nets. They watch the floats narrow as the fish surge in. Later, the men strain against the weight of hauling them in, stunned by phosphorescence as mullet leap in the nets. Another shoal and then another, they come, accompanied by birds and sharks all the way up the coast.

I tell him about the surf where it turns the colour of green glass. The sand below, clear as old floorboards. Out beyond the bar, there is deeper water, and visible, colourful life.

"Is it like here?" he asks.

"It is and it isn't. It's like here, only ..." I spread my arms.

Open, no cliffs, a few low headlands with feathery slim she-oaks, tea-tree in flower. Big broad beach, wide sky. The sun very strong, the blue clear light intense.

"Just you and the sky and water and the edge of land. Hard to explain."

But he's nodding his head, he does understand.

"It was like that, too," he says, "on the island where I went logging." A place dominated by huge mighty trees, hundreds of years old, enduring, steady. A landscape sharply observed by raven and eagle. The sea, cold and quiet and dark green, full of its own complex authority.

"Here they have been fishing since the days of Carthage," I say, thinking of Marcus.

"Carthage," he repeats.

Carthage was razed, ploughed over; nothing left.

OUT WE GO IN the dory again. All appears to be as before, but his mind is on those other small boats that have crossed the river, that have reached the far shore of the Ebro.

Impossible not to think.

He rows. He still isn't strong, but he's coming along. We're low in the water but very stable. "Would Mrs. Mole fancy a row?" Mole and Ratty are messing about in boats.

I shake my head. Today I feel too tired.

A calm sea. A day when you think there could be nothing around the headland, nothing but more tranquil hours.

"Look at you," he says, "taking the morning sun."

With my eyes closed, I listen to the oars, to the sound of water. In rhythm with his rowing, Ross sings snatches of a hymn: "*Soar to the uncreated light,*" he intones. "*Drink of joy from deathless springs.*"

"It's what we'll do," he adds.

"Sounds good to me. When do we start?"

"Not long now, Mrs. Mole."

"How much of that religious stuff do you believe?"

"Some of it remains mighty attractive. Not the bit about adoring on bended knee. But blessed are they that mourn for they shall be comforted, blessed are the merciful, blessed are the peacemakers. We could do with a dose of that all round."

"Do you think anything comes after this, when we're gone? Do you think people meet up in an afterlife?"

He stops rowing. Reaches over, touches one of my breasts.

"Being here with you now is everything. That's what I think."

"No pie in the sky by and by?"

"This *is* the pie. The best I've ever had."

"How come a boy like you, who attended church on Sunday and can remember the hymns, how come you've left that behind?"

I shouldn't have asked. It was Tony. Over on the island, logging, he and Tony slept in the forest and figured things out.

WHAT WILL IT BE like when he leaves? The melons will be hanging in their string basket but he won't be here. I won't be able to come up, put my arms around him, feel his lean belly. I'll have only the smell of him: on the sheets, on his towel, on my body.

He rows. We're not going anywhere; we're just here to be out on the bay, together. There is that moment of silence before the oars enter in a silky rush. At the upswing, water drips. The oarlocks creak. A day of no wind; a little laplap; the dory glides.

I have no strength. My breast feels so tender where he touched me.

A heaviness of the limbs, a yearning to stretch out, to sleep. Why would we ever leave the village? Why not stay on? Let us lie here forgotten. Let us lie in bed until the world comes to its senses. The way things are going, it might be years.

"Let's never leave," I tell him. "I can't bear this day to end."

"This day will not end," he says. "It will happen forever."

Thirteen

Republican Spain, August–September 1938

WE MADE OUR WAY to Barcelona, where through some medical contacts I located a room for us in the city, which was by now brimming
with refugees. We would have a few nights together before Ross was
assigned to an autoparc.

A maid's room, a single bed at the top of a house. It seems to me
that we lay there, entwined, for three days, without once leaving. We
must have gone out in search of food but I cannot remember.

On the fourth morning just before seven o'clock, this ended.
Ross was due out at his barracks. Since that hour, I have in every
essential way remained in that room, in that bed, with him beside
me, within me.

BACK IN THE VILLAGE, I couldn't do much. Anxiety about Ross was
making me nauseous. At first after I'd thrown up I'd feel better,
clearer. Then my limbs would again fill with lassitude — yes, that's

the word — a heavy longing to lie down, to play over in my mind the hours Ross had been with me. I was tired, so utterly tired. Tired of ever climbing up the climbing wave. The voice of my teacher, Mr. MacDonald, rose up in me. *Pull yourself together.*

Any idea of going back to work sickened me. I pictured myself standing by a doctor as he re-sectioned a piece of the large intestine. Watched him scoop the bowel out so that its twisted length lay harmlessly on the patient's white belly. Nausea rose up in me. Having been with Ross, his skin clear, clean-tasting, smooth, sun-healed, I could no longer face a body that had been torn open.

THE BUS ARRIVED IRREGULARLY, at most once a fortnight. It brought the mail.

I waited for Pau to call my name in the village square.

Waited to open a letter, to read and reread it like a thirsty animal. Aware that I was waiting exactly as Laia had waited.

To comfort myself, I spoke with Ross constantly in my mind.

Maybe he was up behind Marçà somewhere — for security reasons he could not give me the exact location. It was common knowledge that the camps were at Marçà, it was from Marçà that they'd made the Ebro crossing, to push the offensive.

He was with another man — I make him into a Frenchman, a crazy little chap from just over the border — Michel, Mich. Like hunter-gatherers, Ross and Mich were driving from village to village to scrounge food. Wine, honey, and nuts were the best prizes by far. We'd lost the provinces for wheat, cattle, milk.

Mich was an ace mechanic as well as driver; he could make a truck run on string.

Ross and Mich were taking the food they gathered to the men who'd been forced to fall back again to our side of the river. When Ross was at the camp, he was able to fit in a swim in the water tank. Up behind the water tank a group of Poles were busy making lousy cognac. Everyone who bought from them was led into thinking they were the only ones in on the game. This increased business.

Rumour had it that the International Brigades were being pulled out altogether. The line of thinking was that if the Spanish prime minister could go to the League of Nations and say that there were no foreign troops on the Republican side, then Franco would pull out the Italians and the Germans. Dream on, Ross said. All the talk about pulling out the IBS was just a diversion. We needed the democracies to lift the blockade. That in itself would be enough for the Republic to win the war.

The best thing was this: Ross was due for leave in two months at the outside. Come early November, I would be going to Barcelona to meet him.

THE BUS CAME. NO letter from Ross.

I SEARCHED FOR ANOTHER way to push myself through the interminable hours.

What I came up with was this: I would write down everything Ross had told me about himself, arranging the details in some kind of rough order. This would serve to steady me because it was not wishful thinking; it was real.

Seated in the library at Marcus's old desk, I began.

I'd pressed Ross for the details. Although I'd never been to his country, I wanted to see with his eyes, to hear with his ears. And he wanted that too; he was possessed with a yearning to tell — not just anyone, *me*. Call this for what it is: love.

ROSS'S FATHER WAS A doctor who served in France during the Great War and met his mother while on leave in England. She came from Scotland but was living in York. They fell in love and were married in 1916. At the end of the war, his father brought his pregnant

Scottish bride home to New Westminster. In the first year of peace, his father contracted flu from working with the victims of the pandemic. More people died of the Spanish flu than in the Great War, Ross's father among them.

That's what people said about the Spanish flu: *more people died*. It was as if his father — and the rest of them, fifty to one hundred million — had done something perverse: waited until just after the war, then detracted from the tragedy that deserved to hold centre stage.

His mother was alone, with an infant. She had no relatives in all of Canada, let alone BC. She took in boarders, she taught piano. She played cards, she sang songs, and when she cleaned she claimed to go like a bat out of hell. Sweeping, polishing, plumping up cushions that had an embroidered cathedral on them, *Ypres* in yellow thread below.

She ran a first-class boarding house. Good food, and the rates were reasonable. The books that had belonged to Ross's father were kept in a wooden cabinet with glass doors, in the front room. A new boarder would stand, looking at them, either impressed or intimidated: "Got a fine lot of books there, Mrs. Ross," or "Can't say I'm much of a one for book learning myself."

When a boarder came home drunk she knew how to jolly him along, how to steer him smartly to his room, and when to lock her own bedroom door.

Ross MUST HAVE BEEN about seven, eight — little. He'd gone one Saturday morning with his mother to the butcher's shop. Except they hadn't stayed in the butcher's shop; the butcher removed his apron and signalled to the young assistant to carry on.

"I had to bring the boy," his mother said.

The butcher disappeared into a back room. Ross could hear water running. The man was washing his hands.

After that, the butcher took them outside, then unlocked a door immediately to his right, a door with dark brown varnish. Up the stairs they went, in silence. The butcher first: big feet, heavy tread; his mother in her lisle stockings, high heels, Sunday best; and Ross. The carpet on the stairs was worn, tacked in at the edges so it would not come up. Some of the stair rods were missing.

At the top of the stairs the butcher ushered them into a room. The upper room, Ross thought, and wondered how the phrase had come into his mind.

They remained standing. The man didn't look like the butcher now because he wasn't wearing an apron. He put a roll of music on the old-fashioned phonograph and wound it up.

"Jesu, Joy of Man's Desiring." The music played. All the while the man was looking at his mother.

They didn't have a cup of tea or anything, although his mother had told him that when visitors came, it was what you did. You asked them to sit down and then you asked them if they would like a cup of tea and they said yes and you made it and brought it in on a tray.

The man played the music again and they still weren't sitting down and there was clearly going to be no mention of tea. Ross could tell by the doilies and vases with paper flowers in them that it wasn't a man's room.

He recognized the music; it was a hymn. He'd heard it at Holy Trinity, where he and his mother worshipped on Sundays. They stood up and sat down, and then they knelt. His mother listened to the same things he did but after they left, she never said a word about any of it. That didn't mean it was unimportant to her. Quite the contrary; it was so close and deep it should not be cheapened by chatter. They went to this church because it was the one his father had attended. Left to her own devices, his mother said, she would not have gone to the Anglicans; she would have chosen the kirk. He was glad they went to the church of his father; he'd seen what she called the kirk and it looked plain and drab, as if it had fallen on hard times and could not afford even a scrap of beauty.

When they'd come to the end of listening to the phonograph the man descended the stairs first. He held the door open and just as they were going out, the man pushed a white paper package into his mother's hands. Blood blotted the edges.

For years, packages in printer's paper were regularly delivered. The roast for Sunday dinner led to leftovers in white sauce and parsley on Monday, stew on Tuesday, sausages on Wednesday, meatloaf on Thursday. His mother showed him that things could be made to last.

A practical woman, his mother.

TONY HAD A TRUNDLE bed in Ross's room; you could roll out the bottom bunk as needed. The arrangement was a stopgap measure until Tony's leg healed up. All the other rooms were taken. Out of work, Tony had been riding the rods through the Rockies. He'd broken his leg in a fall from the train.

During the day Tony tucked his crutches under his armpits and limped down to the public library to read. At night he lay in bed, smoking and talking.

"We are the ones who ploughed the prairies and built the cities. We can build them again, only better next time. We carry a new world, here in our hearts."

"Warfare from the air has abolished geography."

The words drifted up to Ross from the bottom bunk.

ROSS FINISHED HIGH SCHOOL but he couldn't train to be a teacher like his mother wanted because there wasn't any money. Not in New Westminster, not anywhere. When Tony got a job in a logging camp, he managed to arrange for Ross to go along with him. Over to Vancouver Island, up the coast, on to another ferry to a smaller island, and into the woods.

They were logging the big old trees and the islanders who owned the land were getting nothing for them. (A dirty double-cross by some muckamuck down in the city, loafing in his Shaughnessy mansion.) The work wore Ross out. He was used to sitting in school. The first day he did okay but by the third day his arms and back ached so much he wondered how he'd make it through.

He and Tony worked all day and in the long evenings they took out a boat that one of the island people lent them and they fished, and caught their dinner. Every salmon that goes up every stream in the whole Christly province has to travel up this channel, the locals said. Pinky-red salmon, the best. Cooked over a fire on the beach. If it was raining they turned the boat over and ate under that. At night, they slept in the woods where the ground was soft, thick, and spongy. Best beds in the world, the locals said, in the Doug Fir hotel.

The day the log rolled, Tony flew off the springboard the instant he saw what was happening. Ross had read about such things in the paper — a father lifting up a bus because his child has fallen under it. What Tony did, hauling and lifting, was the act of a madman. When, above him, Tony moved the log that trapped him, Tony's face had turned the colour of liver.

To HAVE THEIR PASSPORT applications endorsed, Ross and Tony were instructed to go to a doctor's office in Vancouver, down by the railway tracks at the waterfront. The doctor knew about the new law that had been passed. He wrote that Tony was going home to the Balkans, to see his parents. And he wrote that Ross was off to Paris to see the Exposition.

Ross and Tony walked along Hastings Street. Paris Shoes, Men's Fine Clothing in blue and red neon, and the sign on the corner in the shape of a star: Star Express. They were headed for the post office to mail their passport applications. They could mail the application in but they had to go in person to pick the passport up, which worked out just fine. Ross didn't want his mother finding an official envelope when the mail plopped through the slot onto the floor in the hallway. She'd pick it up, hold it in her hands, turn it over. When he came in she'd give it to him as if she owned it herself. *What's this?*

Along the waterfront, gulls wheeled and cried, kicking up a racket. Funny thing about seagulls: when they were inland, they mostly kept their mouths shut. You saw them flying about over Central Park, searching with sharp black eyes. They were several miles in from the sea and knew they weren't really at home, so they stayed silent.

When he came to the corner of Hastings and Granville, Ross saw the mountains across the inlet, still with snow on them, and clouds lounging about. In the grey day the mountains were such a deep dark blue. He was going to miss them. Mountains and the sea: they were home.

He looked over at Tony, who grinned, thumped his shoulder in that self-assured way he had, and ducked off somewhere.

AT VANCOUVER'S MAY DAY march the cherry trees were already half in leaf, half in blossom. In the middle of the speeches someone announced in one of those drum-roll voices: *A man in the crowd is this very night leaving on his way to Spain. Let's give him a cheer and send him with our greetings to the Canadian boys over there.*

Ross's heart leapt up like a startled fox and he felt his cheeks redden with alarm. But the man wasn't speaking about him. He wasn't going tonight. He wouldn't be leaving for a few weeks yet.

It heightened the senses to be planning to break the law. The legislation about enlisting in foreign armies has just been passed and anyone with a nose on his face knew it was meant for Spain. He'd read it in the paper: If any person *bla bla bla*, such person shall be guilty of an offence under this Act. An illegally enlisted person. That'd be him.

It was Tony who had the idea. When Tony came back from the meetings he was so fond of attending Ross could practically see the steam coming out of his ears. Tony took things personally; it seemed to be in his temperament. Tony liked to quote that guy who said, "While there is a lower class I am in it; while there is a criminal element I am of it; while there is a soul in prison, I am not free."

Ross told Tony: "Of course you're in the lower class, pal, along with the rest of us. Now you're about to make it into the criminal element as well, what with *An Act Respecting Foreign Enlistment*. They can throw you in prison for going to Spain, so you've an excellent chance of getting to third base as well."

Ross CAUGHT THE TRAM home to New Westminster. The tram rattled across False Creek, up the hill, and swung left into the busy stop at Mount Pleasant. He had a good seat by the window and luckily there was lots of room so he wouldn't have to give it up to the women who were climbing aboard, clutching bags from their Saturday shopping. Their shoes went *clickety-click* on the wooden floor.

Someone at the front of the tram had left a window down and the carriage filled with a harsh rush of freshness. It hurt to open his lungs wide enough to draw it in. But after the endless grey winter days he'd take the steel-blue air anytime.

The tram rattled past wooden houses with laburnum and lilac blooming together out front, past the stores with false fronts and recessed entrances, up and up to the dark damp green of Central Park, with its big entrance gates. As soon as he reached the park he felt himself relaxing. The city of Vancouver was below and behind. He was going home.

Past Central Park and into the farmlands. At Olive Street black-and-white cows sauntered through the pasture, making for a barn in front of an old orchard. The fields spread out after that, and the smell of earth felt heartening somehow. On to Vorce station by Deer Lake Park and the muddy scent of fresh water. Here, if he was lucky — and he had been, sometimes — he might see a deer with big shiny eyes and a damp nose.

Not today. They'd be in the dense bushes somewhere, possibly with young.

Along the ridge spur, then steeply down into New West, a different world again. The docks were busy; he could see the big boats, a dirty dark orange. By the water, just along from the docks, the timber mill was pumping white smoke into the air.

A strong woody smell of pulp and under that, the abiding smell of the big river.

He jumped off and walked along the side of the hill to his house, where the lights were on. Inside, his mother would be making supper.

Soon he would have to tell his mother. Tony didn't have the problem of needing to tell anyone. Tony had family in one of those Balkan countries. He seldom mentioned them.

His mother had wanted him to become a doctor. When she realized they'd never be able to afford it, he was supposed to grow up to become a science teacher. He worked in the woods instead.

Now he was going to a war. Like father, like son.

He wasn't leaving right away. He could promise her that. He was going with Tony, so it would be okay, she wouldn't have to worry.

FOR HIS FAREWELL DINNER, his mother cooked a roast, followed by apple pie and cheese. She gave him a fountain pen, a good one, an American Blackbird. The boarders chipped in. Ross felt embarrassed, unfolding the case from the tissue while everyone at the table watched. He guessed right away what it was. This was the present she'd planned all along, for when he left home to become a science teacher. The boarders knew it was an extravagance; they would have gone for something practical. Boots, maybe even a sleeping bag.

As for the leaving itself, the date got pushed back a week and it was a relief when it finally came round. He'd planned to board the Canadian Pacific train in New Westminster but they ended up having to go down into Vancouver because they were holding some kind of send-off there.

He and his mother and Tony caught the tram and he shoved his valise under the seat. She'd packed a mountain of egg sandwiches, which she was clutching in a brown paper bag.

"You've enough to feed an army in there, Mrs. Ross," joked Tony.

Not the smartest thing to say.

A wet day in June. Just when you think you've said goodbye to the endless bad weather, it comes sneaking back. Ross sat staring over at the rain-blurred mountains, not daring to meet his mother's eyes. Near Olive Street some people were standing about in the field looking at one of the cows. At Mount Pleasant, people were busy going in and out of the shops as usual. But he was cut off from all of this because he was leaving. He wished he was on some errand and would be catching the tram home in an hour or two.

His mother's face was stretched drum-tight, in her brightest public mode.

In the echoing grand hall of the Canadian Pacific station, as his mother trembled and touched his coat one last time, Ross concentrated on not thinking.

Ross travelled with Tony and the other BC boys by train across Canada, then down to New York. Over to France on a boat with underfed waiters in the third-class dining room. The boat took eight days to reach Le Havre and he rented a deck chair that cost sixty-three cents American for the whole trip; it was worth it. He was put at a table with a Dutch family and was relieved to find they limited conversation to pass the butter, pass the sugar. The boys were supposed to make themselves as inconspicuous as possible, but that was a joke. You could pick them out right away, talking in groups, sitting together, arguing, reading and exchanging books.

At the Exposition in Paris, Ross and Tony and some of the others drank champagne out of paper cups. Ross had never drunk champagne before; it slid down his throat like a soft drink. First they tried to visit the Spanish Pavilion. Beside it, the huge German Pavilion glowered down. There'd been some mix-up and the Spanish Pavilion wasn't open yet. Ross was glad he saw it, even if he only peered in through the locked front door. After that they sat on a bench and looked at the Eiffel Tower and he imagined an engineer holding up his hands to the empty sky, measuring. Tony said they built it to celebrate the centenary of the French Revolution: liberty, equality, fraternity. Worth a toast, that was. One paper cupful for liberty, one for equality, one for fraternity. Ross threw up in the bushes and missed the Russian Pavilion.

TONY WASN'T IN HIS group. For some reason they were being sent in two groups. Ross crossed over the bridge with the buildings soft in the evening light. Did the light in Europe look soft all the time, he wondered, or was it just Paris? The train station was massively ornate. One of the boys said it was an example of wedding cake architecture. Inside, the place was busy with porters in their blue smocks. They looked like bit players in the Gilbert and Sullivan he'd seen with his mother in New Westminster. She'd hummed and tapped for weeks afterwards.

The stations had levels; trains were coming in up and down. The train they were taking was in the basement. Ross looked down and saw it, green and squat.

An old guy at the gate took their tickets. They'd been told not to board the train as a group. Instead, they were to go down one by one, mixing in with the crowd.

When the first of the boys went down, the old man took his ticket, looked at him, and shook his hand.

Ross was the fourth of them to pass through the gate. The man didn't hesitate a second. His hand came out, rough and strong.

It was a relief to climb aboard the train, to walk down the corridor, with its dim light.

In the depths of Gare d'Orsay in Paris Ross was on the eight-fifteen for Perpignan and Cerbère. Much banging of doors and shouts of *En voiture* and at last the engine was beginning to heave. An intense feeling floated in the air.

The train pushed its way through the suburbs of Paris. Homes, factories, brickworks, dogs, the momentary flash of lighted windows, people making dinner. In his compartment the other passengers already had the blue light on and were busy laying claim to territory for the night ahead.

He could still feel the pressure of the old man's hand.

FOR SEVERAL DAYS HE waited in a room in Perpignan.

He was supposed to be moved on Monday, but then it was Wednesday, then Thursday. In Perpignan, he'd been warned, there were certainly spies and word could be passed. Again, he was supposed to make himself as invisible as possible.

The room had a bed, a dresser with a basin and jug, and an old cupboard full of empty hatboxes. He kept his clothes on the single chair. An old-woman smell hung in the air: powder, dust, and stale scents. He decided that it was a grandmother's room and that grandmother had died. He was in the old part of the town, where the high houses, in the great heat of summer, huddled together to provide shade for one another.

He looked out his window. Sat on his bed. Walked up and down. Watched the light advance across the ceiling. It was a huge luxury to be alone; he could lie down — although the bed was hard, with no proper pillow.

The other boys in his group had departed for Carcassonne or on to Cerbère; he had to wait until there were sufficient numbers to take another batch across. He was on his own, he gathered, because there had been some kind of mix-up.

The woman of the house brought him a shirt, a loose local shirt of cotton, and cool. He put it on and felt like a schoolboy.

Each day at his window he watched a bunch of dogs — pointers, spaniels — well fed, in good nick. They guarded the intersection at the end of the street, not hesitating to lie down in traffic, which dutifully diverted itself around them. Having rested, they roused themselves and dashed about, conferred briskly, and set out again like successful entrepreneurs.

One night older man in a cream summer suit took him out to dinner at a hotel full of exuberant noise, with people yelling and old men playing dominos, children running about between the tables. Huge posters on the wall in red, yellow, and purple.

"Here the food is good," the man said. "The wine also."

At the next table, French workers. They crossed over the border to fight with their Catalan brothers, the man explained, but came back to work, because they had families here and families must be fed.

"It is as simple at that," the man said, and shrugged.

Ross looked at the Catalan workers. Most of them seemed much older than he was. They crossed the border and fought alongside their brothers. This time yesterday, those men could have been in Spain. Ross felt a shiver start in his stomach.

Ross was in hiding, in a beach cabin. The man in the summer suit had led him to the end of a row of cabins. Square boxes, with a front that was simply a calico curtain in tricolour stripes. A bench ran along the back of the cabin and on it a group of men were sitting. They'd been dead silent as he approached. They shoved up, so Ross had a place at the end of the bench, and then they spoke quietly. He couldn't pick all the languages but either Dutch or German, and of course French.

Through chinks in the walls, he could stare at the sea. At the blaze of noon the white sand blew and the sea lapped in its small constant way, with very little tide. No more than twelve feet away, some children were building a sandcastle, with serious conversation, orders and counter orders. Their voices so close, yet very far away.

The second night, the Frenchmen took turns as scouts.

The boat, lightless, crept up under the pier without the scouts' knowing it. One of the sailors had to come looking for them.

A boat about thirty feet long, with a pointy bow and a pointy stern, painted a dark colour and a light one. The men slid down the hatch, doubled up, and were stuffed into the hold. The hatch cover closed. Ross heard a heavy oilskin being dragged over it. Naturally, the hold stank of fish. He had to concentrate on not gagging.

A single cylinder engine by the sound of it, said one of the men. A make-and-break, said another. None of this sounded reassuring. Ross had only ever used a rowboat.

In the dark, sealed off, they were heading for the coast of Spain. An hour or so later, a deeper throbbing. A diesel engine. They listened.

Ross was conscious of the dry breath in his chest, going out, coming in. Shouting above them in French, then the sound of the diesel, getting more distant. One of the fishermen slipped open the hatch cover and grinned. Sweet salt air rushed in.

Ross was sent to Tarazona de la Mancha, for training. In Tarazona he stood in line, and the man at the table barely looked up and said Ross would work on the guns.

The first and best thing about Tarazona, Ross said, was that Tony showed up. He was safe; he was okay. Tony was assigned to a telephone unit along with Yorky, another one of the BC boys.

"What do you know about telephones?" Ross asked Tony, joking.

"I know how to call the operator."

Ross was put on the guns with some Finns from Timmins, Ontario. He was happy about that, because he'd worked with Finns in the woods and Finns could be counted on to be tough customers. He wasn't the *sargento* or anything like that, just one of the extras. The Mac-Paps had only recently been formed. Before that, the Canucks had been in with either the British battalion or the Abraham Lincolns. He'd heard of the Mac part — William Lyon Mackenzie, who oddly enough was some relation to that son of a bitch of a PM. He didn't know much about Papineau, but like Mackenzie, Papineau had tried to chuck the British out in a failed rebellion, way back a hundred years ago.

They learned to fire the Maxim by pretending to, because there weren't any ammunition belts to spare. The Maxim had thick iron wheels, a metal jacket that had to be cooled by water, and a heavy steel shield. To move the Maxim, they had to take it apart. He helped carry the pieces of the gun to their sleeping quarters, where they practised assembling it.

During the day they were dragging the Maxim up a hill. Their muscles gleamed, their sweat was slippery, they grunted as the gun got stuck in a rut and would not budge. One night they were shown a Russian film that happened to have scenes of horses dragging Maxims. For about a week after the Maxim boys whinnied and neighed at every opportunity.

IN THE EVENING HE had Tony to talk to, and in that way at least it was much like home.

Tony had been on the *Ciudad de Barcelona*. After a lunch of octopus Tony and a lot of the other men had gone down for a rest because they were due to arrive in Barcelona late that afternoon. He'd been below when the torpedo hit. Tony had to rush up on deck, dive in, and swim like crazy to escape the pull of the boat as she sank. The noise was amazing. One of the boys caught below had been a champion swimmer back home in the States; others who jumped had never learned to swim. The night before the boat was torpedoed some Australians put on a wrestling match, and they were quite good wrestlers.

ROSS AND THE OTHERS were assigned to help with the harvest. Many of the locals had gone into the army so the Brigaders were bringing in the wheat. It was heavy work and Ross had to watch himself with the sickle. What made it bearable was the singing, in so many languages. The boys from Saskatchewan sang wonderful Ukrainian songs. Ross wasn't sure what the words meant, but he gathered they were along the lines of the most beautiful girl in the village.

Nobody talked about the men who came back from Brunete, which was supposed to be a victory but didn't turn out that way. Brunete, a series of battles and not just the one, had to do with trying to dislodge the fascists from the western approaches to Madrid. Even after a huge amount of fighting, the battle lines remained pretty much the same. The Brunete men arrived the day after they finished the harvest.

The worst thing about the Brunete men was their eyes. Not the way they looked at you — although that was full of cynical contempt — but the pus that trickled out, that persisted. If you tried to be friendly they'd tell you to eff off. Tony had spoken at length with one of them. Turned out he and Tony came from the same place in the Balkans. Tony said they'd been ordered not to say anything.

They celebrated the harvest with a fiesta in the town square. Maria of the doughnuts and Josephina who ran the pastry stall and the people at the inn set up a low trestle table and put out food and soon the singing started up. Tony, who was good at such things, danced with Maria. After they danced, Maria took his face in her hands and kissed him. Everyone laughed and clapped. Then of course Tony danced with Josephina, who kissed him also. Through all this the men from Brunete stood apart, like wraiths. They didn't talk to each other; they didn't smile and cheer for Tony when the women kissed him — not even the guy from back home in the Balkans. They didn't so much as look at one another to roll their eyes in shared scorn. It was as if each had a moat around him, drawbridge up, completely on his own. Their indifference made Ross feel as if the whole harvest celebration was a sham, but how could it be? It was something tangible. Come winter, there would be grain in the barn.

THE BEST THING ABOUT training? That was easy.

Going to the river.

They walked five miles there, five miles back. The road had a few trees. Small scrubby pines mostly, with a sharp smell that was surprising.

Along the river's border, poplars and some alders. Ross felt the coolness coming as he approached the river. The grass was longer; there were small fields of crops.

He climbed down with the others, took off his clothes and waded into the muddy water, cool and deep. They swam and threw water at each other.

Ross horsed around with Tony and Yorky and the rest of the boys. After a bit he paddled off by himself. In the light breeze the poplars made a papery sound. It was August, but already the leaves were turning.

On his way to Aragón Ross spent two days and two nights on the train, passing villages. At the stations, children clapped, young women waved, while the old were for the most part silent. At one village station some very young men were sitting beside meagre cardboard suitcases, utterly disconsolate. New recruits. Conscripts, probably away from their village for the first time. They didn't look like they'd be much help to anyone. At another station he saw prisoners on the platform, waiting to be taken in the opposite direction, down towards Valencia. They seemed weary and ordinary, unnervingly so. Were they brave, these men? Somebody claimed there wasn't much difference between hysteria and courage. They didn't look hysterical, just tired.

Courage. It was a word Ross had to think about because it didn't feel in the least bit real.

The soot blew into the carriage and his body began to smell of the train. As they travelled north, dry hard country emerged, with the sky exceeding blue and thin clouds that gave the horizon a stretched look. He was reading a book about a pilot in Venezuela, by some Yank. Flew about in his little plane, drinking, discovering mountains and waterfalls. (Only he didn't really discover them; they had a whole pile of names already.) Books were passed around; he'd read anything in English; he had no standards whatsoever.

THEY WERE SENT UP into the hills, where they were supposed to be keeping an eye on the enemy.

Ross walked along the ridges and he had to watch his step because it was rocky. Occasional machine gun fire, but nothing that came their way. They'd dragged the Maxim all the way up but there wasn't any call for it out on the ridges. A few of the fellows who came up later had a cache of rifles, which they handed out.

On the far ridge were insurgents. They weren't bothering him and he wasn't bothering them. Ross found he wasn't thinking about the need to halt the rising fascist tide. Water, food, that's what he waited for. When the donkey came up, that was the high point of the day.

BACK IN CAMP IN Aragón, Ross told me, the Mac-Paps were joined by some Lincolns in a grumpy mood. These Lincolns were wearing battle gear stolen at the front. Trousers, hats, belts. When Ross thought about it for a minute he realized they'd been close enough to the dead to take these things off them.

The bugler was a Canuck who'd come up from Tarazona with them. After the first two days of being awakened by the bugle, one of the Lincolns stole the bugle and crushed it under a truck. Tony was hugely offended. "Who on earth do they think they are?" The bugler had been good, his notes thin and high and sweet. "It was like waking up to a girl," Tony claimed. "Almost."

IT TROUBLED ROSS THAT so much effort had been made to get him to Fuentes de Ebro. The doctor in Vancouver signing the passport application, the boat trip, the training, the matériel, the food, such as it was — after all that, no thanks to him, the line must have gained about one-and-a-half kilometres, which when he worked it out was less than a mile.

On the first morning at Fuentes Ross was lying face down in the dirt, having thrown up. *This is not where you're supposed to be. There has been a mistake.* The speed of fire was so fast his brain couldn't keep up. His body was some crazed animal, pawing the ground and heaving at the same time, but he'd left his mind behind on the truck, looking out, deciding that the plain was bigger and wider than anything he'd expected.

After a very long time, or maybe it was short, the artillery fire lost interest in him. He crawled, stood up, winded, amazed. They would have to go back for parts of the Maxim. Ross was sure that as soon as they approached the truck the fire would be upon them again.

They'd just managed to set up the Maxim when Ross heard someone saying that sooner or later they'd have to move forward. No way he was going to move forward into that. Where was their own artillery, wasn't there supposed to be artillery support? Fish in a barrel. Turkey shoot. Ross had never shot at fish in a barrel or been to a turkey shoot but he was getting the idea.

Noon: the planes came over, one by one, while he watched. He felt a huge shaking as if someone had put him in a box and hurled the box in the air. Again, he was throwing up. His tongue was thick as rope. He couldn't breathe properly.

ROSS WAS WATCHING THE tanks flare up orange and black like a ghastly Halloween trick, when his world shattered. He was lying on the ground again, not aiming, not firing, but holding the ammo and shaking. He was aware of stretcher bearers rushing in front and some of the men from the unit alongside were running forward with their Maxim and two of them dropped like birds but the first guy, one of the Finns, kept right on going. The Finn wasn't in the least hysterical, just gone way beyond anything you'd call normal.

THINGS SETTLED DOWN INTO a terrible tedium. Ross and the others couldn't leave their hole and they couldn't advance under shell fire. On the third or fourth night Ross slid out of the trench to throw up.

Ssch ... sssch, silent, from nowhere. At first his shoulder felt no more than stung.

They came from the dressing station to fetch him and he was being loaded onto the stretcher. He felt glad to be safely bleeding, dizzy, and wet.

In the ambulance, blood was seeping down from the top stretcher, and Ross told himself, that's interesting, that's good, my blood's coming down from above as well. Blood would protect him sure as cotton wool.

They took him to the field hospital where he learned that he had pleurisy in addition to the shrapnel wound, which thankfully was not too deep.

Ross was sure he saw the planes come in around noon, had felt the air torn apart. The others said no, the planes hadn't come until later and they didn't drop. They just turned around and left; it was too late and their own men would be targeted. He decided he must have got the details jumbled up ...

THE BUS ARRIVED.

Pau carried the mail down.

My name was called in the square. At last.

I stood up, hurriedly closed the notebook, left the library. Ran to the square on weak legs, my heart ablaze.

IT WAS ONLY A letter from Helen. I told Pau he must have something else for me. Could he please check again?

Helen's letter lay on the desk for two days, unopened. My mind was with Ross, deeply with him. I could not turn to anything else; it felt too abrupt, too painful, impossible.

When I finally read Helen's letter, I learned that she had become involved with yet another committee. This committee was making contingency plans for the children's colonies, the *colonias infantiles*.

The Republic had set up children's colonies, primarily for the young who had been orphaned but also for children whose parents wished to send them to safety, away from the bombardments of the cities.

I skipped to the last page, to see where this was leading. What she wanted would be buried just before the end.

Would I be willing to take a brief journey by boat? Arrangements have to be made in the south. The problem was, with so much territory having been lost, the Republic's *colonias* were over-burdened. The children were at risk of becoming refugees for a second time.

Helen said she knew I was busy (*busy? hardly*) and they'd had someone in mind but he was unfortunately no longer able to assist. (What happened to him, I wondered.) The plan was to re-house the children near the French border. All that was required was a single trip by boat to organize the embarkation. A British steamer was due to dock in Barcelona is two weeks' time. Its captain had agreed to assist.

Jesus, Helen. One good cause after another. Having extended her hand to men without a country, she was now bent upon saving the children of Spain. I should introduce her to Edith and between them they could put the entire world to rights. Forget your League of Nations; here comes Helen, here comes Edith — all rise, please.

WHEN AFTER A PROLONGED delay the bus showed up again, I felt that surely, this time.

I didn't wait for Pau to sort the mail down at the inn; I intercepted him on the path. He handed me the modest bundle, let me examine it.

Nothing.

Just Helen again.

ARRANGEMENTS NEEDED TO BE made. On a contingency basis, you understand. When the government won the war, the children would naturally be repatriated. Would I be willing to play a part in the liaison and coordination?

Helen hoped to hear from me soon.

Half-awake, I daydreamed of Eti from Cliffend. Eti was at the front, in the Great War. He was coming along in the darkness with a team of horses. Eti was the handler; he rode alongside the quartermaster until they approached the lines. The horses stopped. The quartermaster held the reins. Eti leaped down. Both sides were supplied by night in this way and the wagons were a favoured target. (Eti used to speak to my father of these things, while I eavesdropped.) Before anyone else, the horses could tell. Their breathing changed, that was the first thing to notice. Raised heads, pinned ears, tensed muscles. Some horses would stand stiffly, their necks extended. Others would throw their necks down, stamp. Eti would walk at the front mare's shoulder. He could hear the horses grinding their teeth, feel their shuddering. They'd follow the mare, they'd heed Eti their handler, they'd hold still while the earth exploded.

When I aroused from this waking dream, I struck a bargain with myself.

THEY'D SENT HIM ACROSS. That's why there has been no letter.

Because Ross was on the other side of the Ebro, I should be there too.

If I made an effort, if I journeyed to Valencia for Helen, I'd receive word from Ross.

When I returned, his letter would be waiting for me.

TO THE HOTEL, OUR meeting place, the ship's captain brought his own beer and cheese, neither of which was available in Barcelona. Captain Hughes was a large heavy man with a tidy manner, a completely non-committal expression, and a sweet Welsh voice. His ship, the *Stackpool*, a collier from Cardiff, was part of the British merchant fleet which ran the blockade, bringing fuel to Spain. These trips were made for profit and not conviction, Captain Hughes took pains to point out. For unofficial cargo like mine there was no charge. As we spoke, he'd break away from time to time to scratch his neck in neat precise jabs, a nervous mannerism I realized I was meant to ignore.

Two waiters watched us like birds. The moment we left the table, they'd be over to pocket the scraps.

We turned to my instructions from Helen and her committee. Up to four groups of children, all under the age of twelve. The captain considered the details carefully, without apparent passion. The plan was for me to return to Barcelona with the children and staff from one school; the other schools would have children and staff come down to the docks at times that I was to designate. Two loads from Valencia; two more from Alicante. At Valencia, the captain told me, he was scheduled to take on a shipment of onions.

"What arrangements will there be?" I asked. "On board? For the children?"

"A tarpaulin over the forward hatch."

Fortunately for me, I would not be expected to have much to do with the actual shipment of the children. They would come in a covered truck to the docks. They would be escorted aboard. They would spend the night near the forward hatch, with a tarpaulin for shelter. The steward would try to provide some chocolate, if possible. The journey would be overnight. Even with the steward filling the children's pockets with a sweet treat, it would be at best a time of controlled distress.

I found it a relief to be working, to be planning, deciding what to ask and what not. I hadn't felt this good in weeks. I would have liked to enquire about what plans were in place should things go awry, but the captain's manner did not invite hypotheticals.

"The Non-Intervention officer?" A Non-Intervention officer travelled on each ship in order to prolong the pretence that Mussolini and Hitler were not in up to their eyeballs.

"Sound enough fellow," said Captain Hughes. "Norwegian." Non-Intervention officers were not allowed to leave port.

Do you know ahead of time who you're getting? Does the Non-Intervention officer remove himself to his cabin in order not the witness any unofficial cargo that might be coming aboard? I kept these questions to myself. The captain and the Norwegian would no doubt have come to an understanding.

A tidy man, my captain. I imagined the methodical way he would take off his shirt, place it on its appointed peg. Surely the Non-Intervention officer would be similarly neat. Men who lived on ships would be well acquainted with limitations. It was an understanding that would serve them well in what had become of Spain.

After the meal we talked a little about Valencia, and I told him I was there last Christmas, with a friend, a fellow Aussie called Ned.

"Ned?" the captain queried, a careful invitation.

"At the time he was in the Regimen de Tren. I've met a Canadian who's joined that, too."

"Where is he now?"

"I'm afraid he's on the other side of the Ebro. By the time he crossed over, some of the men had already been pushed back."

"So you've heard from your friend, Ned?"

"Ned? Oh, he's with an artillery unit. Somewhere around Barcelona I think."

"I'm very glad to hear it."

The captain thought Ned was my lover. Amazing, how we tidy things away, having read them exactly wrong.

WE SAILED IN THE evening. The ship was from the same line as the one we had sat in on the dock at Marseilles, so long ago, when Ned polished off the English prunes and custard. Now the ship's mess reminded me not so much of Ned as of Ross. The corned beef, the spuds — this was fare his mother could be serving over in Canada, in her boarding house.

Ross could be sitting here, chatting away to the captain and the Norwegian.

After the evening meal, the captain and the Norwegian produced a board and arranged chess pieces. They set up for a game to take them through the journey. I don't think they were conscious of shutting me out of their routine, which had a domestic, male quality to it.

In the cabin I thought of Ned's pleasure at having a bunk with a reading light, and in a whisper told Ross about it. I was pretending we were a long married couple getting ready for bed, the rhythms relaxed and familiar. Did you notice, I told him, how the captain's nervous tick of scratching his neck has completely disappeared now that he's on board?

At two o'clock in the afternoon of the following day we reached Valencia's harbour, a marine graveyard. Every third berth had a sunken ship in it. Most of the sunken ships were in up to their funnels, but one of them had gone down only to deck level and leaned in a startling way. This ship was one of their own, Captain Hughes said. He gave the name and yes, it was the very same one we'd spent the night on in the harbour at Marseilles.

What of its captain and bulldog? "Safe," the captain said. From the deck we stared across at the wreck, quiet as a country churchyard.

"Last time I was in port," continued Captain Hughes in his lilting Welsh way, "I took a rowboat over, looked in through the skylight. The table was still set but there were fishes among the dishes."

I gave a subdued smile, for the rhyme.

On the battered dock, a *refugio*, smart and new. The captain saw me looking. "The Hotel Chamberlain," he said.

"When you debark," the captain advised, "you mustn't dally. Don't hang about for one of the authority's cars. Present your papers and keep going."

It was a mile to the tram and when I alighted from the tram it was another two miles into the city. I realized that this had been a whole day of feeling better. I quickened my pace, swung my bag as I walked down the avenue. Not many people about, cafés deserted in the afternoon. The branches of the trees had been lopped for firewood.

Look at this, Ross, an avenue of blasted trees, as in the blasted heath. Speaking to Ross lifted me up; I began to run, not because I needed to, just for the joy of it. *We made it,* I told him, we weren't sunk; *we made it, made it, made it.*

I raised my voice, I cried out his name.

I'm running with you, Ross.

I WAS PICKED UP by an official in a battered yellow Ford station wagon, taken to a crossroads, dropped off. Two hours later a springless cart arrived, hitched to a mule.

In English we'd call the children's colony a boarding school, although that term, with its suggestions of stern regimentation, would be inaccurate. So the director assured me. A printer had just left, having delivered the tailend of a long roll of paper off a printing press. The play room was filled with the attractive inky smell of the paper as the teacher tore off pieces.

The children, lined up for lunch, had watchful eyes. There was more to eat than in the north: grapes, apricots, nuts. Afterwards, I worked with the director on documents, addresses, contacts, arrangements.

Business concluded, I was taken to the dormitories to look in on the children as they lay in their little beds, which they were free to arrange as they pleased. They'd pushed the cots together and were tangled in heaps: legs sticking out like the petals of a sturdy daisy. I looked away.

Tears rose up so easily; it wasn't the least like me; it was humiliating.

I found it wearying to be with a horde of children. Laia's two were scrumptious, but I didn't see myself as the maternal type. Never had a doll. Certainly I appreciated newborn infants, with their translucent skin and stunned-fish faces — that was different. For the most part I thought of children in relation to myself, the little princess of Cliffend. I'd stalked about the place, reliably greeted with applause by Father, by Eti. Knowing I could count on their smiles, I came and went as I pleased, a young tame animal.

ALICANTE.

Trains still ran each day to Alicante. Up at three-thirty, off to the station for a five o'clock departure. The packed train huffed along through groves of oranges and lemons. Those closest to the windows talked about the orchards as if they were visible in the dark. The oranges, they said, had formed but were not yet ripe.

I was expecting to stand, but a place was made for me on a wooden seat. Local women were in summer dresses with bare arms and legs although it was autumn by now and chilly enough. As soon as I'd sat down I had to rush to the toilet. Damn. Just when I'd started feeling so much better. The toilet was a malodorous hole in the floor; you could look right through it, see the track spinning away beneath you. Pity the poor blokes who maintain the lines.

We didn't travel right into Alicante as the station had been bombed. We walked the last mile.

I remembered the avenue of palms, four deep, the cheery facades, the marble woman on a statute at the far end of the avenue, the *Paseo de los Mártires*. The column for the statue was still there but the woman's head was gone. Palm trees were similarly decapitated, as if in solidarity. Broken stone benches, empty hotels, shell holes in the roads. Upturned wrought-iron chairs and across the road, a patchwork of stone, wood, glass, and iron.

At my hotel, the Palacio, the chambermaid took me along a corridor on the top floor, past heaps of smashed plaster. She demonstrated how to kick the door to open it, shrugged at the crack across the length of the ceiling. It was a room, it had a bed, what more could I want?

"A bed is all I need," I agreed. "I'm not fussy."

I awoke from a restless dream in which I had been reciting, repeatedly, the contents of a tray: incision knife, tissue knife, one straight scissors, one curved scissors, one suture scissors, mouse-tooth forceps, six small curved clamps, six straight clamps. Tried to shake myself awake, to stop my mind zooming back and forth on a pulley.

Out there somewhere in the dark, not in this building but farther away — perhaps in an office block — blinds rattled like bones. The windowpanes of that building must have been blown out and the blinds left to swing in the wind. The more I tried not to hear the rattling, the more grating it became.

The wind continued to pick up; my shutters began to bang. I got up, crossed to the window, opened the shutters, looked out. Below, an unlit truck was parking.

People jumped down. There must have been some women in the group because there was much laughter, waving and shouting.

Salud simpacticos. A woman's voice.

And where are you, my love, tonight?

THE GARDEN AT THE front of the colony outside Alicante had three beautifully tended rows, all the same size: first, red salvia; next, a row a tough yellow flowers whose name I did not know, and below those, purple salvia. The colours of the Republic flared in the grey light. The place was being closed down and the gardener was going to be out of a job.

Hadn't I heard?

Ana, the henna-haired women in charge, was excited to be the one with the news of the prime minister's announcement.

As she led me to her office — a gracious room with a piano; no doubt once a sitting room — she described how Juan Negrín, the Spanish prime minister, had made the speech at the League of Nations the day before. The decision was to go into effect immediately.

"What's happening?"

"We're withdrawing the International Brigades and all the foreigners in our army." She looked pleased about this, which infuriated me. "Negrín has asked the League to control the withdrawal. He's offered them the proof they need to show the world that the withdrawal will be complete and total."

"It takes two to tango," I said, lamely. I was breaking my own rules, doing this. I shouldn't be arguing with a Spanish woman; I'd no right. But if Mussolini and Hitler didn't withdraw their troops as well, where was Spain going to end up?

"Without the Italian and German soldiers on the other side," she asserted, "Franco will crumble."

"Now there's a lovely thought," I said.

"The pullback has begun. The 15th Brigade is being moved back across the Ebro."

Ross would be among them. This changed everything.

Ross was safe, out of the war. He was coming back to me.

ANA SUGGESTED LUNCH. SHE produced two bicycles and we rode to an inn, to meet some *Brigadistas*. To meet one of them in particular, as it turned out. A Czech, neat in his uniform.

I couldn't eat. My stomach churned with the news. I drank instead, silently toasting Ross. *To my lovely one, whose war is over.* There was nothing to stop us now, I thought. We shall all pleasures prove. The still, clear autumn afternoon felt like an omen of perfection to come.

In the courtyard the talk was of one topic only. Mussolini had already announced he would withdraw his legions only after Franco's victory.

The place filled with men in shabby cloth jackets, shapeless trousers. The Czechs, who wore their little side caps in the Spanish manner, were among the tidiest in a sea of khaki, brown, olive green. Americans showed up looking and smelling like Davy Crockett.

Ana clutched her lover's hand across the table. He looked embarrassed but did not deter her. She again held forth about Negrín's speech.

Laughter, eager voices, smoke, plenty of homemade brandy, bottles of Malaga pulled out from under the bar, wine sloshing onto tables. Much slapping down of pesetas, which were just little pressed cardboard disks. Not that I'll be needing them much longer. It was almost shocking to think about. *Ross, safe. His arms around me.*

The Americans announced they were going to eat themselves silly when they got home. Pastrami on rye. This big. The Malaga ran out but somebody claimed he could find more at his uncle's, or failing that, at his brother's friends. Afternoon faded to evening.

The Americans were able to talk about sailing home to pastrami on rye, but where could the Czechs go? Hitler was busy running propaganda newsreels about the "massacre" of Sudeten Germans and shouting that Czech oppression must cease. Lover boy here could stay put with his girlfriend but what about the others? I felt glad I'd married the German, Otto. The world was filling up with people who had no home to go to.

Another Czech came to sit at our table and began asking me questions, working his way through them in that particular fashion men have when they've decided that you'll do, or you might do, or it was at least worth going down that road to see how far it could lead. In response to his questions I told him I was a nurse, no, not English: Australian. I'd been here almost two years. Before that I'd actually lived here; I'd been married. No, not to a Spaniard, to an Englishman.

"Oh," he said, "you're English."

So many of the men in this room had endless miles to go, stateless in their wretched clothes and rotten shoes. I'd lost the capacity to get drunk in an orderly fashion. Tears threatened yet again. I was becoming ridiculous.

Nobody was paying attention, nobody apart from the Czech beside me, who seized this opportunity to slip his arm around my shoulder.

"Let go of me."

He took his arm away. Five minutes later he placed his hand on my thigh. He was making what he believed to be soothing noises. He must be drunk as well, I decided.

At the end of the long evening, a truck was found to take us back. The two bicycles were slung up. We climbed in, the four of us. At the colony all four climbed down. The bikes were passed to Ana and her boyfriend. She and the boyfriend melted away.

The Czech who'd sat beside me suddenly began shoving my shoulders back against a wall, kissing me while I squirmed. I ducked my head so that his mouth found my hair.

I aimed an elbow. I aimed a knee.

Flutter kick. Flutterkick. Inside me.

Flutter kick, there it was again.

He was yelling at me in Czech. A short, sharp, sneering word. Naturally I didn't know the word but I could make an excellent guess.

I pushed at him, hurried into the school building, found the office, slipped in behind the piano.

The door opened, the lights were switched on. I heard his boots. He took a few uncertain steps towards the centre of the room. Unfocused, confused.

He was turning.

Lights off. Gone.

Safe.

I was gasping, and not from getting rid of the drunk-of-the-night. The verdict had just come down.

And I called myself a nurse.

Sitting on the floor, I did a few elementary calculations. Last period, early May, when Casals played. Last and only period. After that I'd stopped again. Thought I'd just gone back to the way things were, back to what had come to pass as normal. Only it isn't normal, is it?

Possible reasons for not ovulating? Basic question, easy answer. I flew through my exams with the greatest of ease.

First kick? Sixteen weeks along or thereabouts. It could not be; it simply could not.

What a prize idiot.

So wrapped up in Ross I hadn't been paying attention.

THIS REALLY WAS CRAZY, it couldn't be true. But it was. I'd detected that kick before, in other women's bodies. I was like those girls who'd come into the hospital back in Sydney during my obstets year. I knew what I'd thought of them.

I didn't do nuffink, miss. Just that one time at the beach.

Let's have a look at you then.

The voices carried their sense of injured justice, the indignant desire for revenge.

I should try a hot bath, bottle of gin, throw myself down the nearest set of stairs. That's the level of knowledge that had brought me to this. *Be silent, listen, observe.* I had been doing none of these.

My father had told tales from my mother. One was of a girl from a distant farm, eight months gone, apron billowing, claiming she'd been eating too many pumpkin scones. A joke meant for Eti and Mr. MacDonald, not for me. I was sitting on the tank stand, out of sight but within earshot.

They'd laughed in their easy male way. Their bodies didn't get the better of them, of course not.

MORNING. ANA ENTERED THE office, was much surprised to see me. I pretended I'd been perfectly comfortable in a chair all night long. Thank god she hadn't found me behind the piano, prostrate with humiliation.

She gave me her cup of the liquid that passed for coffee. My face was tight, nausea took over and the room swayed. (I'd thought that at least was over, done with.)

Ana escorted me to a narrow bed off the staff common room. "I'll leave you in peace," she said.

I must return to Barcelona as soon as possible. Ross could be there within days. Damn and blast this whole stupid journey.

I needed to see someone, and right away. Who? The medical staff known to me were entirely taken up with the wounded bodies of men. Laia would figure out what to do, or at least I could talk to Laia. But Laia was so far away, up in Girona.

I didn't want to be some ineffectual emissary arranging the evacuation of children. Above all, I didn't want to be a woman who stupidly got caught out. She fell pregnant. That's the verb, isn't it? Out of Eden, after the fall.

I put my hands on my abdomen. Of course, any fool could have felt it: uterus rising, pushing up.

Ana came back in. Parked herself in a cane chair, stuck her feet up at the end of the bed, and started chattering.

So much for leaving me in peace. I closed my eyes, wished she were Laia.

"The talk about the Sudeten Germans being persecuted is just a smokescreen. If they let Hitler dismantle Czechoslovakia and give him the Sudetenland he won't stop there. Next thing he'll want Skoda, and its armament factory."

Ana would have picked this up from her boyfriend.

"And have you heard the latest from the fascist zone? The speaking of Basque and Catalan is prohibited. All names not based on saints' names have been forbidden."

What would happen to little Jordi and Josep? When was this nightmare going to end?

"Is Adolph a saint's name, do you suppose?" I asked.

Ana looked glum.

"Wait," she says, "there's more. They're burning the textbooks used in secular education. Even paintings have to conform with 'nationalist and Christian values.' Goya's *Maja* is to be banned from public view." The nude one, I bet. Arms up behind her head, she's waiting for the bloke to tear off his clothes and join her on the sheet.

Too confused for any of this, I pleaded that I had to lie back, shut my eyes.

In London I should be able to find help with my problem. Barcelona could prove difficult; I didn't have the right kind of contacts. I might even have to try the Belgian doctors, who were now in Barcelona. Admittedly, pregnancy was a long way from gangrene, but needs must. I'd better get a move on; I must be pretty near to running out of time. Past running out of time, actually. Back in London, Helen would help me. And Alec, he'd help me, too. In our few letters back and forth, the truce that Alec began in Teruel had deepened. I'd told him about Ross, and that left him free of murky emotional waters.

Ross and I could catch a plane to France, over to London for a D&C. I could be there by this time next week. I could just make it; scraping in under the wire. Might have to adjust the dates a bit. They'd believe a nurse. I'd find someone; I had to.

Tolerant male voice, very British: *Silly thing went out to Spain and got herself in a spot of bother. One scarcely knows what to say. Had to put abnormal vaginal bleeding, history of, on the dashed report.*

If I hadn't been such a fool and come south, Ross and I could be on our way by now.

WE MADE SAFE DELIVERY of the first of the children's colonies. The boat to Barcelona was not approached; nobody was dragged off to Formentera for interrogation. Children cried, threw up, were offered blankets and chocolate. None of them made much of a fuss. So much had happened to those mites they knew they'd no choice but to be carried along in the current.

A letter awaited me from Father, who delivered gloomy judgment on France and Britain. *By the banks of the Rubicon, they lay down and slept.* Father would have written this ages ago, but just this week Neville Chamberlain announced that somehow war must be averted. The Munich Agreement would do the trick. As for Signor Mussolini, Chamberlain said Europe and the world should be grateful to the head of the Italian government for his work in contributing to a peaceful solution.

The Cortes met in Sant Cugat del Vallès, bleated brave words. Resistance would lead in time to victory. Believe that if you can.

Flutterkick has been at it again. Very quiet on the voyage, awed by all that water. On dry land, more confident, ready for gymnastics.

THERE WAS NO LETTER waiting for me from Ross.

Fourteen

ROSS WOULD HAVE COME with the others, back across the river, back to the camp at Marçà. But there must be some mix-up down there at Marçà because I know Ross would have written.

As soon as Ross arrives, we're going to hightail it to London. Until I hear from him I can't leave. I just can't.

I search for work because we're going to need the money. No problem with my throwing up anymore; the reverse is happening. I've taken to eating every scrap of food I can get my hands on. I'm one in a million in the Republic, putting on weight.

A hospital in a camp for *la guerra inútil* — sacks of bones with enormous eyes. They say little.

Take the Italian there in the third bed by the wall, turned away from me, in a state of exhausted apathy. He's worn and re-worn fear so long it's broken him down. Refusing to eat. He wants no more, he says.

I sit beside him, I lift my hand, lightly brush the air near his face; he does not flinch. My hand creeps in closer, strokes his cheek. He knows I'm simply a nurse, at this moment demanding nothing in particular of him. I offer him a cigarette, sit watching the smoke of his breath.

I'm here only to note his bruises, dress his wounds, let him rest. He can let go of it all now — the blows and the falls, the blurring of speech, blood in the mouth. Let it go. I don't know how it happened, whether it was some of ours or some of theirs. I don't need to know, don't bother telling me. Let it go.

He curls thin, turns away again.

I'm dogged, I keep on.

Look, my hands say, I know you're alone, I know you're done for. You've the smell of a man in the deep lair of his own cave, gone to the bottom of life, looking up. Despite what's happened, it's still there, what's in you. The warmth you have at the core of yourself. It's still in there, isn't it?

With my hands I tell him, yes, you reached the end of the road, you've gone through the silence and you're back. At least you're coming back, that's right, you're capable of coming back and your own body tells you this, not just mine. You already know this.

Take a chance.

You can come back, I tell him. You will come back. You'll see.

In time his apathy lifts, he stops shedding nails, hair, intestines. He starts back.

First, gruel, then something a little more substantial. Slowly, like an animal creeping up on prey, he approaches solid food. Once he's started, he cannot stop.

His indifference to me or any nurse is complete; he's interested in only one thing: nourishment. He eats in such a focused way that it feels almost obscene to be acutely hungry myself and watching. With supreme concentration, he eats.

Outside the camp is a park where I take my breaks. An ordinary park with a raised ornamental pool. Nobody seems to come here except me. It's the kind of park where in normal times families would walk in the late afternoon. The fountain has long since been shut off, and the trees, which used to be clipped, are branching out in all directions. Their boughs hang down over the pool. They're some kind of pine and they've been shedding their needles. For a while the needles float in the still, dark water; then they sink.

I sit on the rim of the pool and look in. Inspect my face, a dark glimmer. I lean over, try to make out the thickening shape of my body.

FLUTTERKICK IS WAITING. LIKE a skilled and ruthless general, it knows exactly how to exploit delay.

Ross love, it's really high time we got a move on. Please write; I so much need to hear from you. I can't tell you how much.

I send off a letter to Ned, ask him if he can find out where Ross is. Maybe Tony Rabich will know. If anyone knows Ross's whereabouts, it will be Tony. I ask Ned if he can at least find out where Tony is.

Marçà is being closed down; they're moving up north to Ripoll. That must be it. How could letters be delivered when they're closing down camp?

Each day I ask around. Does anyone have news of Marçà? Have they by any chance heard of a Mac-Pap by the name of Douglas Ross? Soldiers will talk to a woman on her own, especially when she doesn't say much about herself.

Anyone who's been at Marçà has my total attention. What they want to tell me about is their final parade.

They hadn't asked to leave; they were being sent away. It didn't make a great deal of sense, especially now, after Munich. Chamberlain said that everyone could go home and have a nice quiet sleep but that didn't seem to be in the cards the Spanish people were holding. At Marçà the International Brigades had their parade on a marvellous sunny afternoon that felt like summer even though it was early October. On vines all around them, grapes hung full, driving the bumblebees crazy with excitement. The parade consisted of a certain amount of marching about, entirely useless but you get the idea, followed by a larger amount of speechifying. All through this, in the blue sky above, planes were battling.

Overnight they were no longer the Internationals, no longer the Brigades, the IBS. They'd turned into "foreign volunteers." Those other foreigners, the Italians and the Germans, were clearly not about to pack their bags and run along.

They were standing in the sun, and someone up front was yapping away, and the plane that was ours, the little Mosca, dived down in a corkscrew and disappeared behind a hill. By now nobody, not even the guy speaking, was listening to a word he was saying. All eyes were on the outcome of the fight in the sky. They were waiting for the sound of the crash as the plane tore into the earth.

No, it was just a manoeuvre. The Mosca zoomed back up in the sky and kept buzzing about after the fascist. A mighty cheer erupted.

That was the farewell at Marçà.

A BRIEF LETTER FROM Ned. He's been asking around about Ross and his mate Tony. No word yet on Ross, but he promises he'll keep on trying. Unfortunately, he has some bad news about Tony. Tony was with those who crossed the Ebro at the very beginning. On the second day of the offensive, he was killed.

If they got Tony it means they won't get Ross. It makes sense, the law of averages: not everybody can be equally unlucky.

I'VE SHORTENED FLUTTERKICK'S NAME to the Kicker.

The Kicker takes my breath away. The Kicker is putting weight on me, I've begun wearing a shawl; I blend in with the rest of the women. I use a safety pin to link the shawl across the front and nobody notices a thing (who am I kidding?). While I'm busy trying to reach Ross, the Kicker's up to its greedy mischief. Pushing into an even better hiding place, demanding larger quarters.

It doesn't show; it just looks as if I'm putting on weight around my waist. Nobody seems to have noticed, not yet. They've plenty of other things to worry about.

I've no idea how we'll live in London, how we'll raise the fare home. In the short run I'll hit up Helen, tell her we have become a committee of two in dire need of a whip-round.

MARÇÀ IS OVER, PACKED up, done. I think maybe Ross had to stay behind, gather up the gear, in preparation for the move up to Ripoll. Isn't that the kind of thing they do in the transport regiment? Some of the lorries would have to take up the last of the equipment.

I should go to Marçà; the trains are running. But I'm beginning to think Ross must have gone to Ripoll instead. Ned is still making inquiries. Ned was in Marçà, and now Ned's up in Ripoll. It makes sense that Ross will be there too. Perhaps he hasn't arrived yet, what with having to pack up at Marçà.

RIPOLL, NED REPORTS, IS a grim, grey place, cold as stone. Bickering breaks out over small things.

I can reach Ripoll. No problem obtaining permission to travel; I can obtain a safe conduct. The trains are packed these days, not with people travelling to Ripoll, but simply going out into the country to look for something to eat. The city has swollen to two-and-a-half times its normal size. Refugees are packed in; they sleep and eat in any available public place, including the waiting room at the train station.

The Kicker is keen to make the trip, game for anything.

Ned is meeting me in Ripoll. I won't be on my own. I won't be one of those women who trail heavily along after every army that has ever existed, belly swollen, fist raised in reproach.

RIPOLL TURNS OUT TO be a town among mountains, heavy with the defeat of withdrawal. The men waiting in Ripoll are cantankerous and hungry. What they'd hoped for, not lost; but gone back, deep inside.

I fit in well enough.

Ned greets me, takes one look, is not fooled. I tell him it's a fine old mess. And the odd thing about admitting to humiliation is that it isn't as bad as you feared. When it's been said, it's even a kind of relief. Problem is, if Ned can figure it out, it must be getting obvious. The last thing I want is for Ross to see before we can talk; I couldn't do that to him. Just like I can't write a hey-guess-what letter; it wouldn't be fair.

Ned has asked around for Ross but no luck. If he isn't here at Ripoll he must still be at Marçà. I know Ned says it's all over at Marçà. But there are mix-ups. That's the one sure thing you can count on.

Ned has one lead that might prove really helpful. There's a team here from the League of Nations. I gather they are supposed to be overseeing the withdrawal of the International Brigades, presumably so they can report back to Signor Mussolini and Herr Hitler. That part is just a sham, as everyone realizes now.

NED HAS SET UP some snares in the river and in the afternoon we walk down together. The sand on the river bottom is whiter than chalk. The sun shines on bare trees. Ned wades into the chilly water. Checks the snares.

"No luck this time."

Ned crouches by the riverbank, carefully drying his toes. I watch him as he walks back to sit beside me. I ask him to tell me what he found out about Tony, and in his economical way, he does. Pounded by artillery fire. In the hills before Gandesa.

Having given me this news, Ned gets up, goes for a short walk by himself.

Ned's kept his long, purposeful stride. Thinner than ever, if that's possible. Wearing a cable-knit jumper with a polo-neck collar. Knitted for him by none other than his beloved Edie, down in Sydney.

I picture Edith at a meeting, trying to remember to knit one, purl six, knit one, while pulling together a nursing team, going through the details like a quartermaster. Edie's team, Ned tells me, is soon due to arrive in Le Perthus, on the France-Catalonia border. It is expected that France will soon be opening its borders to women, children, and the elderly.

No, Edith's not coming with them; she's continuing to organize, back home.

"She says good on yer for the work," Ned reports. Ned isn't the kind to make this up to please or appease; it must be something Edith really said.

Talking to Ned about Edith doesn't disturb me. I no longer particularly resent her, despite the trouble she caused when we first came to Barcelona. And the private side of Edith, the exposed underbelly, is obvious in every row of inexpert cable-stitch in Ned's sweater.

Ned wouldn't have blurted out anything about our Christmas night in Valencia; he's too canny for that.

He produces a bottle of absinthe, a great prize.

"Did it fall off the back of a lorry?"

"Won it in a card game, fair and square. When I heard you'd be coming, I saved it."

The only place where we can drink together without having to share with a mob of others is in this freezing park by the river. I'm in my shawl; he's in his cable knit. There is the deep earthy smell of dead leaves.

"Let's get stuck in," he says.

Ned and I pass the bottle back and forth. You can forget your niceties with a glass and sugar cubes.

"What a pair of rubbies," I say. Rubbies, as in drunks.

Ned says something about Spain, then about Germany and what is happening there. He adds, "They've gone to ground."

I'm unable to listen because I'm distracted by the warmth that is advancing through my body. The Kicker has made sure it's toasty. Trust the Kicker to shove in front, put itself first. But even my fingers are filling up with a steady, marvellous heat, which keeps on marching, up into my brain.

"Did you go to the send-off?" Ned asks.

He means the big one in Barcelona, the city's farewell to the International Brigades. There was also that final muster at Marçà and I gather there's been another farewell here at Ripoll.

"I didn't go, but everyone's talking about it," I reply. "So many from the Brigades were there. People in the crowd threw flowers on the ground so the Brigaders could walk on them. Of course, you heard about the speech. Bet you didn't know you were history."

I dig him in the ribs, feel how thin he's become.

"Not ready for the knackers yet," he says.

"You'd be just about right, I reckon. All skin and bone."

We fall silent, thinking of what we've heard about the farewell speech to the International Brigades by Dolores Ibárruri, La Pasionaria.

Political reasons, reasons of state, the good of that same cause for which you offered your blood with limitless generosity, send some of you back to your countries and some to forced exile. You can go with pride. You are history. You are legend ...

I didn't go to the farewell because I've made a bargain with myself. Until Ross comes there will be no farewells for me.

THE BOOZE MUST BE getting to me but I've not entirely lost my grip. I'm sitting on a freezing bench with Ned, and he knows me. In a country far from home, that's a miracle. We sailed over the ocean together. We came from afar to see if there was anything we could do.

"Brass monkey weather," volunteers Ned.

We didn't demand to be heirs of heaven; we never once asked the impossible. Now we've lost and we know it. Still, there's hope — no more than bread and water but enough to keep you going. Hope. My mother's name; the sound of my voice as it lost itself down a Cliffend mine shaft. Bravado and dogged desire. Hope dies last, they say, but they're wrong about that. When all is quiet, when everyone has left, relieved to have the sad day done, hope gathers herself up and walks.

"Where to next, do you think?" Ned asks. "Do you have plans?"

I shut my eyes. Let my head fall back. Listen to the river. Our lives are rivers on their way to the sea. Run softly, small river, run on to Ross.

Ned gives me a friendly shake.

"It's getting dark," he says.

Part Five

Monday, July 3, 1939

TODAY A LETTER CAME from one of the BC boys. He introduced himself by telling me where he'd been in Spain, when he'd been wounded, and how he got home. He promised he was looking into news of Ross. Once he got the bit between his teeth, he assured me, there was no stopping him. He sent you his love (a nice touch) and advised me to sit tight.

With no possibility of any other option, that's what we're doing.

July 7, 1939

ALEC DECLARES THE DEMOCRACIES will have their war after all —
their sanctimonious non-intervention, their efforts to accommo-
date, have turned to failure. He's starting to make plans. His back is
much stronger now.

Last week Alec came back from London wildly excited. I don't
know if you remember me mentioning Josep Trueta. He's the
Catalan doctor who pioneered blood transfusions — along with
the Canadian Norman Bethune. Trueta had to leave Spain and he's
come to London, where I gather he's already involved in plans for
establishing emergency medical services. Alec can't wait to climb
on board.

Here at home Alec's figured out a way to read the papers while
cradling you on his right thigh, which he habitually jiggers up and
down. You appear to love it. He has a dreadful habit of scattering
bits of discarded newspaper over the floor which he then has difficulty
reaching down to grab. I pick up the papers, pass them to Alec, and

we exchange a mild glance. Alec's forgiven me my demands, forgiven the swirl of banked resentments, forgiven even my guilt.

July 19, 1939

I RECEIVED A LETTER from that woman in London. Tore it open, heart like a trapped animal's.

What a disappointment.

She wrote to tell me the files they kept on the Mac-Paps at Albacete had been destroyed at the end, to prevent them from falling into enemy hands. I'd heard that already, it was a common rumour even when I was still in Spain.

July 23, 1939

I KNOW YOU WILL remember the German, Otto, my so-called husband who was hanging about when you were born. Otto has been up in London for weeks, trying to obtain passage to Mexico. He finally got lucky. Alec, who had a hand in the arrangements, is greatly encouraged by this and all the more intent upon organizing us onto a boat to Australia. A country at war is no place for children, he says. He's right. Where does that leave Laia and her sons? No letters arrive from Girona; Catalonia is dark with defeat.

I really need to stay in this part of the world. I need to go to France, go south to the Spanish border. That's where I should be; that's where I'd have our best chance.

At the border, along roads that continue to unfold in front of them they come: the wounded, the defeated, the refugees. There have been so many already but surely there will be more. As they approach, I will be delving into a box to bring out bread — organized from somewhere, definitely not baked by me. And always my eyes will be reaching into the crowd, scanning faces, searching.

I'll recognize him right away. Just as I did at the Ebro, the afternoon he was brought in.

July 28, 1939

I WAS UP IN London today with you in your pram. I'd bought the pram second-hand, from a woman in the village. The pram is one of those weighty hard-bodied affairs made of wickerwork, painted cream, with big spoked wheels.

We dropped into the office where Helen has been working — as a volunteer, of course — on sending refugee children back to Spain. Helen was immensely upset. These are Basque children mainly; they came over quite early in the war. They are going home to families who have been defeated.

Helen says their cards will be marked and who knows what humiliations and privations lie ahead. It has been Helen's sorry job to make the arrangements with the foster parents.

The office was on the point of closing down. Helen was the last one left; she was clearing the place out. I was listening to Helen's descriptions of the children being sent away.

HELEN WAS HELPING ME out of a taxi, with me refusing to be touched.

"Where are you taking me?" I demanded.

To a flat of a friend of hers, someone I had never heard of. She'd bundled us both into the taxi, with the pram in the boot.

"Why, what are we doing?"

"You passed out," Helen said. "You're in no shape."

The cabbie heaved the pram out and hauled it up the steps and into the building. As soon as we'd reached the hallway, the door to the ground-floor flat opened and a man's voice announced that we couldn't park a pram in the hallway; we had to take it up. Four flights.

Helen began protesting and an argument broke out.

Helen persisted: "We can't take the pram up those stairs; it's too much, too much."

Without a word, the cabbie grabbed the heavy contraption, lifted the whole thing, and carried it by himself, all the way.

If I can do nothing else, let it be the force of my waiting that brings Ross to me. I won't give up; I'll keep at it without end.

Nothing is extinguished in me.

Saturday, August 12, 1939

FRIDAY'S SECOND POST BROUGHT an agitated letter from Father, very anxious about the possibility of my being trapped here when war breaks out. Time is short now, Alec pleads. Anyone can see that the slide into hostilities is imminent.

I have not yet heard but I do believe that a letter will come, very soon, from the Mac-Pap in British Columbia who told me to sit tight. He will be as good as his word.

On Friday afternoon a woman arrived at the house with gas masks. In the widespread expectation that poison gas will be used, everyone in the entire nation is being issued with a gas mask. Alec claims this is a propaganda stunt to prepare people for a state of war.

The gas masks have a bit of charcoal in them which is supposed to stop the poison. The masks are stored in little boxes, which we are to carry with us at all times. This poison gas business may be wildly exaggerated, as Alec claims. The woman even gave me a gas mask for you, a hood contraption I'm supposed to pull over your head and inflate with bellows. I can imagine what you'd make of that.

I got talking with the gas mask woman and over cups of tea she found out I'd been in Spain. Hearing this, she became excited, and exclaimed that her driver, sitting out the car, had been there; he was with the British battalion at Jarama. Insisted on rushing out and fetching him right away. From the moment he walked in two things were immediately clear: she was the posher, which was why she was doing the talking and he was doing the driving, and — of vastly more interest — those two were crazy about one another.

I located three bottles of cider in the back passage, and produced them with a flourish. The summer afternoon sun slanted into the kitchen and we sat in a pool of golden warmth and fellow-feeling.

Alec showed up and as soon as he learned what was going on he brought out his best Scotch and within the hour we were embracing and singing, to the tune of Red River Valley:

There's a valley in Spain called Jarama,
It's a place that we all know so well.
For 'tis there that we wasted our manhood,
And most of our old age as well.

After which we moved on to the dirty verses.

You awoke and cried out, so I hurried upstairs to feed you. When I returned, holding you, the mood had changed completely. Alec must have told them something of our situation, because the concern on the visitors' faces reminded me of those women in France, when I visited the war graves with Marcus, all those years ago. But you redeemed the moment, being for once completely affable about strangers reaching out to you.

By the time they left it was evening. I made scrambled eggs on toast and sat talking with Alec.

He started in about the new puppy he had picked out. With Jitters and Custard both gone, it was time for a new pup, he said, and the black Lab was quite the brightest little chap imaginable. For some reason this news brought me right down; I didn't bother figuring out why.

THAT WAS YESTERDAY. TODAY, in the early afternoon, I gathered you up in a large scarf, which I tie around myself, and we set out to pick elderberries. Helen has plans to make wine.

We went along the dyke through the woods and out to the river path where the berries are. We were gone for hours.

By the river you watched cows wade up to their bellies in grass, oblivious to news of Spain and Germany. The church bells in the village pealed four times. The entire nation is in the grip of a wedding epidemic.

The bell-ringing floated across the summer meadows.

When we returned Alec came out of the morning room and called up the stairs to me. Something in the formality of his voice sent my blood rushing. Maybe the post had brought news! Then I remembered that it was Saturday, there was no afternoon post. I settled you in and hurried back down.

Alec was sitting in his favourite chair. Soon, I thought, he'll have a shining puppy curled in beside him. He'd placed a manila envelope on the small table in front of him.

"I've something for you," he said, pushing the envelope towards me. It wasn't sealed; the flap was just tucked in. Easily opened.

"What's this?" I asked, knowing what it was. He'd gone up to London and paid for the tickets himself. Tilbury to Sydney via Suez.

"There are two *Strath* liners leaving over the next month," he said. "Your pick."

"I can't take these from you. It's too much."

"There's the *Strathaird* and the *Stratheden*. The *Strathaird* is the first to set sail, in three weeks' time."

"Three weeks!"

He'd planned it out, gone to London and made the arrangements. He'd been talking about us to the clerk in the shipping office.

"When did you get these?"

"Yesterday. I arrived home and everyone was in the kitchen having such a good time, I put them away."

He came over to where I was sitting, tried to put his arms around me. "It's time," he said. "I think you know it is."

I pushed him away. He returned to his chair. Sat there, without speaking.

After a while he stood up and said in a quiet voice, "I'll leave these with you, shall I?"

Fifteen

Stratheden, September 27, 1939

CREEPING IN THE DARK with portholes closed and painted black, it seemed to me we sailed in a coffin through the Bay of Biscay, through the Strait of Gibraltar, past the southern shore of defeated Spain, on into another world.

Now far beyond the blackout, we are allowed out on deck at night. This is where I bring you, to settle in a deck chair. I wait until the party-makers have tired themselves out, then we come up here when nobody's about. We do not leave the cabin until well past midnight, after the band has packed up and their music evaporated.

I come to hold you, to look at the boat's wake, and to think. One by one the repeated waves fold out behind us until they smooth away, as if they had never been.

I clasp you to myself.

IN THE SIERRA DE Caballs, no time for a cheap pine coffin. Only rocks to deter the carrion birds. Ross is in the care of Catalans now and I know him to be among friends, even if many are ghosts.

I am leaving, perhaps forever. It is a mighty journey and it seems unlikely I will be back. When you are grown the dictators will surely be vanquished and you will make your own voyage, but by then it will be so unimaginably different and all so long ago.

In the place where Ross should stand, you will have only borrowed memory. Will it sustain you? Will it provide you with the beginning to your own story?

For now, you're fed and drifting off. We're almost there. The boat has set its final course, south-southeast. With Colombo finally behind us, next landfall is Fremantle and the small lights of home.

Notes on Clancy's Spain
— *Dolores Ross*

While the involvement of an Australian woman with a Canadian man was of no consequence whatsoever to the issues of the Spanish Civil War, it remains of intense personal interest to me, as the accident of that brief encounter. My mother's stories focused on love, work, and the pursuit of food and warmth; she made no claim to capture the complexities of the times. For this reason I offer the following notes.

Anarchists: The powerful Anarchist groupings included the National Confederation of Trabajo (CNT), and the Federación Anarquista Ibérica (FAI). At the start of the war they played a major role in the running of Catalonia. A leading figure in the Anarchist movement was Buenaventura Durruti. He was wounded at the Madrid front in November 1936 and died the following day. Clancy alludes to Durriti when she treats wounded Anarchists at Grañén. Ross's friend and mentor Tony Rabich was quoting from Durriti when he said, "We carry a new world here, in our hearts."

International Brigades: An estimated total of 59,380 volunteers from fifty-five countries served in the International Brigades. The XV International Brigade, headquartered in Albacete, included Canadian, British, American, French, Balkan, and Latin American battalions. Within a brigade, battalions were typically organized according to country and named after national figures. The German Thaelmann Battalion in the XII International Brigade was named for a leading German communist who had been imprisoned after the Reichstag fire in February 1933. He would later be executed in Buchenwald in 1944. Of the sixty-six Australians who went to the aid of the Republic, ten were women. The Australians were typically attached to one of the English-speaking battalions, as well as to medical and transport units.

Mackenzie-Papineau Battalion, the Mac-Paps: A Canadian battalion launched in July 1937. (The term, Mac-Paps, was also used collectively to describe Canadian volunteers who served in the International Brigades.) The battalion was named after William Lyon Mackenzie and Louis-Joseph Papineau, leaders of rebellions in Upper and Lower Canada in 1837. The battalion included volunteers from countries other than Canada, mainly the United States. At its inception the Mackenzie-Papineau Battalion was incorporated into the Abraham Lincoln Battalion and later became part of the XV International Brigade. Almost 1700 Mac-Paps went to Spain; more than four hundred were killed. Apart from France, no other country gave a greater proportion of its population as volunteers in Spain than Canada.

May Days (May 3–8) 1937: While Clancy was in the fishing village recovering from jaundice and playing with her friend Laia's children, Barcelona was convulsed by events that were to have far-reaching consequences for the war. Beginning on the 3rd and 4th of May, rival factions began to fight it out in the streets. Some members of the Popular Front government called upon the Spanish Prime Minister Largo Caballero to use troops. But this would be seen as an attack on the autonomy of Catalonia, which had its own parliament, the Generalitat. On May 6th, a number of important Anarchists were assassinated and on May 7th, Assault Guards arrived from Valencia, the seat of the Republican government. Eventually they took over the city. By the end of the struggle over five hundred people had been killed, with many more wounded. The May Days remain a touchstone event in any account of the period. Defenders of the Popular Front see the May Days as a time when the government asserted the control necessary to wage the war. Those who focus on an emerging revolution that began in the 1931 see the May Days as a time when the Popular Front government, backed by Moscow, strangled that revolution.

Non-Intervention Pact: Clancy often made disgusted reference to this pact, which she saw as a core reason for Franco's victory. The democracies of France and England instigated the Non-Intervention Pact, the aim of which was to deny assistance to the Spanish Republic on the grounds that non-intervention would prevent the war from spreading to other countries. Italy and Germany both signed the Non-Intervention Pact. At the same time Italy provided over seventy thousand troops to Franco (many of them conscripts) and contributed extensive matériel. Germany gave Franco arms, over nineteen thousand Luftwaffe, army, and navy personnel, and perfected the large-scale indiscriminate bombing of civilians.

Popular Front: In February 1936 the coalition known as the Popular Front won 263 seats out of the 473 in the Cortes (Spanish parliament) and formed the new government. Among other things, the Popular Front promoted Catalan autonomy, released political prisoners, and introduced agrarian reforms.

Second Spanish Republic: In January 1931 the military dictator Miguel Primo de Rivera was forced to resign, having failed to solve Spain's economic problems. The king, Alfonso XIII, abdicated, and the way was opened for elections, the first in over sixty years. In April 1931 the Second Spanish Republic was proclaimed. Between the years 1933–1936 the Republican government was dominated by the right and centre-right. When the Popular Front won the 1936 elections in February, the composition of the coalition government ranged from centre-right to left.

Spanish Civil War: The plot by right-wing generals to overthrow the Popular Front government culminated in the military uprising of July 17, 1936. Hitler and Mussolini supported the uprising, and by October 1936 Franco had established himself as Generalísimo. Franco and his insurgents called themselves Nationalists. Clancy saw that as a propaganda term and never used it.

- After the first few weeks of the war Franco's insurgents controlled some conservative provinces in the north and south of Spain. They were keen to capture Madrid but the Republicans were determined to defend Madrid at all costs. In November 1936, Franco's troops reached the western and southern suburbs of Madrid and a siege of the capital began.
- Having failed to take Madrid, Franco tried to cut the roads that linked the Republic to Madrid. When Clancy was in Barcelona in December 1936, Franco's insurgents were attempting to cut the Madrid-La Coruña road.
- By March 1937, Clancy was in Grañén in Aragón. Republican energies remained focused on the defence of Madrid. Franco's offensive continued in the Basque country and on April 26, 1937 the German Luftwaffe Condor Legion and the Italian Fascist Aviazione Legionaria bombed Guernica. (Clancy, at Grañén, heard about it on the radio.) Franco's insurgents took control of Bilbao in June, which meant the Republic was cut off from an important industrial base.
- A Republican offensive opened in Aragón in the fall of 1937. Ross, with the Mackenzie-Papineau Battalion, was involved in the unsuc-

cessful action at Fuentes de Ebro that began on October 13, 1937.

- Starting at the end of December 1937 Ross took part in the battle · for Teruel, where he first met Clancy. This battle was a Republican initiative to pre-empt an insurgent offensive in Catalonia and to force Franco to divert his attention from Madrid. The Republicans took Teruel, then lost it again.

- From March 16 to March 18, 1938 there was round-the-clock bombing of Barcelona by Italian aircraft based in Majorca. Clancy's one-time lover and brother-in-law, Alec, was wounded and repatriated to England.

- In the spring of 1938, Franco's forces, well supplied by Italy and Germany, opened an all-out offensive in Aragón. Ross was involved in various battles that sought to counter this offensive. He tells Clancy about his experiences in the fighting around Batea.

- On April 15, 1938 Franco's forces broke through the Republican defences and reached the Mediterranean; Republican Spain was split in two. Caught up in the retreats, Ross was wounded and carried across the Ebro River to the hospital where Clancy was nursing.

- On July 24, 1938, when Clancy and Ross were in the village, the Republicans went back across the Ebro in a last-ditch offensive. Ross's friend Tony Rabich was killed at Gandesa in the first weeks of the fighting; Ross joined the offensive in August. The purpose of the Ebro offensive was not only to relieve pressure on the Madrid defences but also to combat the advance of Franco's forces towards Valencia.

- On September 21, 1938 Juan Negrín, Prime Minister of the Republic, announced to the League of Nations that there would be an immediate and unilateral withdrawal of all international troops from the Republican army. The hope was that this would cause the democracies to put pressure on Hitler and Mussolini to withdraw the German and Italian forces.

- By the end of 1938 the International Brigades were going home

— those who had homes they could go to. With no help from the Canadian government, the Mac-Paps were among the last to leave. They waited at Cassà de la Selva, north of Barcelona, where a League of Nations representative made enquires about Douglas Ross.

- Barcelona fell on January 26, 1939, and by the end of the following month, Catalonia had fallen. Back in England, Clancy listened to the reports on the radio.
- By April 1, 1939, the Spanish Civil War was over. Another war was about to begin.

Bibliography

Spanish Civil War

Each year, the Spanish Civil War generates a massive body of historical work and remains a hugely emotive event far beyond the borders of Spain. Major works in English include:

Burnett Bollotten, *The Spanish Civil War: Revolution and Counter-revolution*. Chapel Hill: The University of North Carolina Press, 1991.

Helen Graham, *The Spanish Republic at War, 1936–1939*. Cambridge: Cambridge University Press, 2002.

Gabriel Jackson, *The Spanish Republic and the Civil War*. Princeton: University of Princeton Press, 1965.

Paul Preston, *A Concise History of the Spanish Civil War*. London: Harper Collins, 1996.

Stanley Payne, *The Spanish Revolution*. New York: Norton and Company, 1970.

Hugh Thomas, *The Spanish Civil War*. London: Eyre and Spottis-
woode; New York: Harper & Row, 1961; Penguin 4th revised
edition, 2003.

Sources

The process of writing a novel is totally different from that of
writing history, although it draws upon historical materials. Sources
of particular importance in developing this work include:

Alvah Bessie, *Men in Battle: A Story of Americans in Spain*. New
York: Charles Scribner's Sons, New York, 1939.

Gerald Brenan, *The Spanish Labyrinth: An Account of the Social and
Political Background of the Spanish Civil War. 1943*. Cambridge:
Cambridge University Press, 1964.

Lloyd Edmonds, *Letters from Spain. Amirah Inglis ed*. Sydney: Allen
and Unwin, 1985.

Ronald Fraser, *Blood of Spain: An Oral History of the Spanish Civil
War. 1979*. New York: Pantheon Books, 1986.

Victor Howard, with Mac Reynolds, *The Mackenzie-Papineau
Battalion: the Canadian Contingent in the Spanish Civil War*.
Ottawa: Carleton, 1986.

Amirah Inglis, *Australians in the Spanish Civil War*. Sydney: Allen
and Unwin, 1987.

Judith Keene, ed., *The Last Mile to Huesca: An Australian Nurse in
the Spanish Civil War*. Sydney: New South Wales University
Press, 1988.

> Note: This is a diary of the Australian volunteer, Agnes Hodg-
> son, who was a nurse in Spain on the Republican side from
> October 1936 to October 1937. While the fictional Clancy Cox
> is not a portrait of Agnes Hodgson, I am immensely indebted
> to her diary, in particular for perspectives on Barcelona and
> nursing experiences in Aragón.

Norman Lewis, *Voices of the Old Sea*. London: Hamish Hamilton,
1984.

Lorna Lindsley, *War is People*. Boston: Houghton Mifflin, 1943.

Mary Low and Juan Breá, *Red Spanish Notebook: The First Six Months of the Revolution and the Civil War*. London: Secker and Warburg, 1937.

Rose Macaulay, *Fabled Shore*. London: Hamish Hamilton, 1950.

Cary Nelson and Jefferson Hendricks, *Madrid 1937: Letters of the Abraham Lincoln Brigade from the Spanish Civil War*. New York and London: Routledge, 1996.

Note: I owe a particular debt to the letters of Dr. Leo Eloesser in the chapter, "The Medical Services."

George Orwell, *Homage to Catalonia, 1938*. London: Beacon Press, 1955.

Elliot Paul, *The Life and Death of a Spanish Town*. New York: Random House, 1937.

Michael Petrou, *Renegades: Canadians in the Spanish Civil War*. Vancouver: UBC Press, 2008.

Hank Rubin, *Spain's Cause Was Mine: A Memoir of an American Medic in the Spanish Civil War*. New York: Barnes and Nobel, 1997.

Vincent Sheean, *Not Peace But a Sword*. New York: Double, Doran and Company, 1939.

Mark Zuehlke, *The Gallant Cause: Canadians in the Spanish Civil War. 1936–1939*. Vancouver: Whitecap Books, 1996.

Websites

La Cucaracha — The Spanish Civil War: http://www.lacucaracha. info/scw/diary/index.htm

Spartacus Educational: www. spartacus.schoolnet.co.uk

Acknowledgements

The lines, "I had written him a letter which I had, for want of better / Knowledge, sent to where I met him down the Lachlan, years ago" are from *Clancy of the Overflow*, by Banjo Paterson, 1889.

The lines, "I saw eternity the other night / Like a great ring of pure and endless light" are from *The World*, by Henry Vaughan, 1650.

The lines, "And then he thinks he knows / The hills where his life rose / And the sea where it goes" are from *The Buried Life* by Matthew Arnold, 1852.

The lines, "As the stars shall be bright when we are dust / Moving in marches upon the heavenly plain," are from *For the Fallen*, by Laurence Binyon, 1914.

Lyrics from "Button Up Your Overcoat" are by B.G. DeSylva and Lew Brown, with music by Ray Henderson, 1928. © Chappell & Co.

I wish to gratefully acknowledge the invaluable editorial guidance of Marc Côté and the steadfast support of my agent, Carolyn Swayze.

Notes

The novel's main characters are works of fiction. The political figures, dates and events of the Spanish Civil War are historical.

Some of the place names are Anglicized in the style of the period.